TERMINAL 9

PATRICIA H. RUSHFORD
HARRISON JAMES

TERMINAL 9

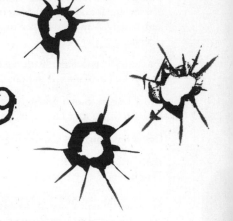

INTEGRITY®
PUBLISHERS
Nashville

Copyright © 2005 Integrity Publishers.

Published by Integrity Publishers, a division of Integrity Media, Inc.,
5250 Virginia Way, Suite 110, Brentwood, TN 37027.

HELPING PEOPLE WORLDWIDE EXPERIENCE *the* MANIFEST PRESENCE
of GOD.

Published in association with the literary agency of Alive Communications,
Inc., 7680 Goddard Street, Suite 200, Colorado Springs, CO 80920.

Cover Design: Brand Navigation, LLC | www.brandnavigation.com
Interior: Inside Out Design & Typesetting

Library of Congress Cataloging-in-Publication Data

Rushford, Patricia H.
Terminal nine / by Patricia H. Rushford and Harrison James.
    p. cm.
Summary: "Book Three of the McAllister Files fiction series. Mac McAllister
with new partner, Dana Bennett, investigate murder of an elderly retired railroad worker"—Provided by publisher.

ISBN 1-59145-212-0

1. McAllister, Mac (Fictitious character)—Fiction. 2. Older people—Crimes
against—Fiction. 3. Retirees—Crimes against—Fiction. 4. Railroads—
Employees—Fiction. 5. Police—Oregon—Fiction. 6. Oregon—Fiction.
I. Title: Terminal 9. II. James, Harrison. III. Title.
PS3568.U7274T47 2005
813'.54—dc22   2004025540

Printed in the United States of America
05 06 07 08 09 DELTA 9 8 7 6 5 4 3 2 1

Dedicated to our families and friends
who unfailingly give support and encouragement
in our writing endeavors

ONE

GOT TO GET HELP. *Call 9-1-1.*

Clay had been feeling poorly all day. He should have called earlier, but being the stubborn old man he was, he thought the pain would pass. It had only grown worse. Never had he experienced such agony. Clay had no idea what had caused the pain or the spikes in his blood sugar despite his regular doses of insulin.

His vision blurred and dimming, eighty-nine-year-old Clay Mullins clutched the back of the kitchen chair and arched his back in an effort to ease the sharp spasms in his side. His breaths came in gasps. Using the chair for a modicum of stability, he scooted it forward on the linoleum floor and shuffled the final steps to the kitchen phone.

Clay gripped the chair more tightly with his left hand while he reached for the cordless phone with his right. His fingers, now numb and paralytic, refused to punch in the numbers he so desperately needed to press. Still he stabbed at them, hoping to depress the three life-saving numbers.

1

Come on. Ring.

What was wrong? His mind raced with possibilities. Was he having a stroke? He could think of no other reason for his fingers to go numb and refuse to cooperate with the dictates of his mind. His diabetes? Clay glanced at his medical kit on the kitchen counter. He had been testing his blood sugar and administering his insulin as he always did. His blood sugar was too high, but . . . no, this was something else.

His legs gave way and crumpled beneath him, propelling him to the unforgiving linoleum floor. The phone fell inches from his face, though it might as well have been miles away with his useless fingers clenched and buried in the palms of his hands.

"Help me!" Clay yelled into the silent phone, hoping his clumsy attempt at dialing had been successful. "This is Clay Mullins. I live in the house by the river at Terminal 9. I think I'm having a stroke." His words sounded garbled and incoherent.

Clay waited for a response, hoping to hear sirens in the background as he used what little strength he had left in his thick arms to drag himself to his knees. The pain in his stomach seemed to worsen by the second, and the numbness in his hands had spread to his wrists and forearms.

Instead of sirens Clay heard only the alarming *beep-beep-beep* from the phone, indicating it had been off the hook too long.

The phone was useless to him now. Even if he could manage to dial, they wouldn't understand him. But there was another way. If he could get to his motorized chair . . .

Clay took a long, shuddering breath, looking at his four-wheeled scooter in the corner of the kitchen. It was still plugged in to recharge its batteries, but there would be plenty of juice to get him to the rail yard. All he had to do was get himself over to the gall darn thing. *C'mon, you old gandy dancer. It's either get to that chair or die on the kitchen floor.*

Old as he was, he had no intention of dying, at least not yet. There were still too many things to accomplish. With a grimace and yelp of pain, Clay lurched forward, nearly passing out from the pain. He lurched again, and again. Finally reaching the chair, he somehow managed to crawl up into the seat. The motorized scooter sat facing the front door, set in forward gear the way he always left it—ready to head out at a moment's notice.

Breathing a prayer of thanks and offering up a plea for help, Clay leaned over the handlebars and snapped the toggle switch to the on position. Not needing throttle assistance to move, the machine lurched forward on idle. With its four rubber tires, sporting aggressive tread, the scooter easily navigated the kitchen floor and the carpeted living room. Using his clenched fist, Clay punched the automated door opener on the wall by the front door.

The scooter, now working on its own accord, seemed impatient as it rammed into the doorframe before the door had fully opened. It bumped over the threshold and rumbled down the handicap ramp extending from Clay's front porch. A harsh east wind tore into his shirt. His breaths turned to clouds of smoke on the chilly March night.

With Clay unable to squeeze the hand brake, the machine picked up speed as it hummed over the wooden ramp onto the packed gravel path. Clay wasn't concerned about the speed though, as he'd taken this same route hundreds of times from his riverfront home near the train yard in St. Helens, Oregon, to Terminal 9. Having worked at the Western Pacific Rail Head at Terminal 9 for more than forty years, he instinctively aimed his vehicle at the twenty-four-hour hub, hoping to find someone there who would call for an ambulance.

Clay heaved his body forward, pressing his forearms against the handlebars to steer the scooter away from the path that led down to the Columbia River and onto the trail leading to the rail yard. The glaring lights and deafening sound of the train brakes guided him more surely than his fading sight. His neck muscles collapsed and his head drooped and bobbed around like that of an unstrung puppet.

A convulsion tore through him. Warm vomit erupted from his stomach and dribbled out of his open mouth, down his chin, and onto his shirt.

Almost there. Clay crossed the footbridge at the first rail crossing that marked the edge of his private acreage and bordered the rail yard property. The right front tire caught in the second rail groove and flipped the scooter on its side, efficiently dumping Clay onto the track.

No. Not now. Please, not now. Tires spun and the chair whirred in protest. Cries for help died in his throat. His tongue felt thick and dry. He saw no one in the hazy dusk, but then he hadn't really expected to. He was lying on a deadhead track—a diversion rail that stored empty boxcars waiting to be placed into service. Clay pulled his knees to his chest as the wicked pain in his abdomen and chest worsened. Two quick blasts on a distant air horn and the vibration in the track told him the deadheads were being moved to the terminal on the very track on which he lay. The yard goat would not see his darkened shadow—and even if he did, he wouldn't be able to stop an engine pushing thirty deadheads.

Soon the old gandy dancer would be crushed beneath the wheels of the train. Ironic, in a way. He'd been born a railroad man—hung around the rail yards all his life. Now he would die here.

The lonely horn from the diesel engine and the vibration on the tracks from the train's rumble would startle most people—terrify them if they lay in its path as Clay did. But the sounds and vibrations only served to comfort him as he ceased his struggle and gave in to the inevitable.

TWO

OREGON STATE POLICE DETECTIVE Antonio "Mac" McAllister had just finished a ten-hour shift and was looking forward to an evening watching basketball in his easy chair with Lucy, his eight-year-old golden retriever. Buried in reports, he'd spent the bulk of Tuesday's shift inside his detective cubicle within the agency's Portland patrol office.

"What do we have here, Lucy?" Mac patted the friendly dog on the forehead and scratched her ears as he thumbed through the mail. "Junk mail, junk mail, and what's this?" He turned the envelope over and sighed. "Junk mail." Mac tossed the pile of advertisements and credit card offers into the recycling bin under his kitchen sink.

Lucy, determined not to let her master break contact, followed him through the small apartment as he flipped on lights and turned the thermostat up to seventy degrees. Although the seasons were changing, March in the Pacific Northwest still offered some cool evenings, and tonight was one of them.

"The Blazers play the Cavs at six, Lucy." Mac glanced at the clock on the mantel as he pulled off his tie and tossed it over the sofa, next to the sports coat he'd shed as he walked in the door. "We've still got fifteen minutes. Should we get some takeout or rough it?"

Mac slipped out of his shoulder holster, wrapping the leather straps over his .40-caliber Glock before setting the rig on top of his refrigerator. He opened the freezer door wide to look for something worth eating. While rifling through the meager contents, he unclipped his badge from his belt and tossed it on the counter. His spare magazine pouch followed, holding an extra fifteen rounds for his handgun.

"Nothing in here," Mac muttered. He really needed to go to the grocery store. He peered inside the refrigerator, knowing it would yield the same results. Besides a door full of condiments, he had nothing but pop and a bag of prepackaged, wilting salad mix inside the crisper drawer.

"Hmm. Think I'll call Leong's and order a little Chinese tonight." Mac pulled the pager off his belt, setting the alarm mode from vibrate to audible before putting it on the counter next to his phone. A magnet on the refrigerator door held a takeout menu for his favorite Asian restaurant, but Mac ignored that as he picked up the phone. He had the restaurant's number on speed dial and always ordered the same thing: hot and sour soup, Kung Pao chicken, fried rice, sweet and sour spare ribs, and broccoli beef. Mac placed his order with the woman who always answered. There was no need to give his address; the delivery person knew exactly where Mac lived.

After hanging up, Mac yawned and rubbed the back of his neck. Using the remote that lay on the coffee table, he clicked on the television set and walked back into the bedroom.

Lucy dutifully followed, her thick tail tapping the hallway wall. The answering machine next to his bed blinked its red eye, and the digital screen indicated he had two messages. He'd been meaning to get a wider notepad to place next to his bed, to document the details of those late-night calls from work. The two-inch square Post-it notes sitting there now barely had enough space to write a phone number, let alone detailed scribbles from a sleepy hand. "Come on, Lucy, let's get a new notepad while I'm thinking about it."

Lucy backed down the hallway as Mac turned on his heels and headed toward the kitchen.

While looking through the kitchen junk drawer by the phone, Mac's department pager went off with the all-too-familiar beep. Mac stopped searching and slammed the drawer closed. "Oh, no. Not now. You know what that means, girl. Work."

The dog wagged her tail, raised her nose in the air, and pushed her head against Mac's hand for a pat. Mac complied as he pulled the digital pager from the black plastic belt clip and read the display. *Call 11-50 at the office for an assignment.*

"Sergeant Evans. Why is he still at the office?"

Lucy tilted her head and looked at Mac as though she wondered the same thing.

"Looks like I'm definitely going back to work."

Mac dialed his office to speak to his supervisor, Detective Sergeant Frank Evans. The old workhorse was always the first one to arrive at the patrol office and the last to leave. Frank ran the small squad of Oregon State Police detectives who were assigned to investigate violent person crimes, primarily death investigations. Mac was one of five detectives assigned to Sergeant Evans. However, one of those officers, Mac's ex-partner and mentor, Kevin Bledsoe, was working modified duty while he battled prostate cancer.

Kevin had taught Mac nearly everything he knew about homicide investigations. Then at the first of the year, Kevin had learned about the cancer and began chemotherapy. Having no intention of taking early retirement, Kevin opted to work various light-duty assignments at the office when he could—primarily administrative backgrounds and evidence.

When the automated attendant answered, Mac punched in Frank's extension. He heaved a huge sigh as he looked over at the basketball game that was just starting. Mac hurried over to the coffee table, picked up the remote, and muted the set as Frank's extension rang.

"Sergeant Evans," the gruff voice answered after five rings.

"Yeah, Sarge, this is Mac. I got a page from dispatch to call you."

"Yeah, Mac, sorry about the delay. I've had this phone screwed in my ear for half an hour. I need you to head out to Columbia County on a twelve-forty-nine. Some old guy got clipped by a train, and the district attorney wants us to take a look at it. It was probably an accident, but there are some loose ends that need to be tied up before we can clear the case. You able to respond?" The sergeant asked the question as a formality, fully expecting an affirmative answer.

Mac looked longingly at the television set and then down at his canine companion. "Sure. I had plans, but I can take off if you need me."

"What's that?" Frank said. "I was putting you on speakerphone and missed what you said."

"Nothing," Mac sighed. "Just wondering where we're staging." He clipped his pager back on his belt.

"That's what I'm looking for. I wrote it down here somewhere."

Mac could picture Frank pacing around his office. He wondered why the sergeant even had a chair.

"Here it is. You need to meet the D.A. down at Terminal 9 in St. Helens. It's between Highway 30 and the river. I've got the address here somewhere."

"That's okay, Sarge. I know the place. It lights up the area like a football stadium at night, so I won't have any trouble. We're going to be on the big clock. Do you want Dana on overtime too?" Mac asked, knowing the sergeant was as tight with agency money as he was his own checkbook.

"Yeah," he said after a long moment. "Better take her along for the experience. Don't go making a fuss on this one, Mac. If nothing's there, hang it up. If it looks like an accident, then call it and get out of there. Let the local P.D. clean this fish. We're only involved because the D.A. wants us to take a look at it."

"Got it. I'll give Dana a call and we'll get going."

"Good. Leave me a voice mail on your progress if you aren't going to be in the office on time tomorrow morning—in case you pull an all-nighter."

"Yes sir." Mac heard a click on the other end, indicating Frank had ended the call. He set down the phone and hunkered down to rub Lucy's head. "C'mon, girl. Back to your kennel." Mac made his way back to the utility room and opened the door. Lucy walked in without complaint and, after rounding and adjusting her thick pad, settled inside the oversized kennel.

Mac hated to keep her in there, but she scratched at the front door when he was away. His neighbor, Carl, had a key to the apartment in case Mac worked overtime and needed someone to let Lucy out. Carl was a doting dog lover, often coming in to let Lucy free just so he could spend time with her. "I'll see you later, girl." Mac shut the door to the room, walked back to the kitchen phone, and dialed Dana's home phone.

He got the machine. "Come on, Dana; it's Mac. If you're there, pick up." She didn't answer.

He frowned. *Wonder where she is. We left work at the same time.*

Dana, Mac's new partner and old friend, lived in the Fairview Apartments on his side of the river in Vancouver, Washington. She should have been home by now. He dialed her pager with 9-1-1 at the end of his number.

Fresh out of patrol and still on probation, Dana had been part-nered with Mac after Kevin went on light duty in February. Although Mac enjoyed working with Dana, he hoped Kevin would be back in the saddle soon. Mac was a fairly new detective to the homicide division too, and he had hoped to spend a few more years working with the veteran, instead of a rookie detective. Not that she didn't have experience. She'd spent the last year on patrol and had studied and worked hard to get into the department. Mac wasn't exactly a newcomer either, having worked for several years on patrol and as a detective in property crimes, as well as the Child Abuse Unit.

Besides, he didn't like the idea of having Dana as his partner in another way. He had been hoping to date her again, but anything other than a working relationship at this point was not a good idea. They had dated for a while in college until they went their separate ways. He'd run into her a few months ago while working on another case, and their friendship had solidified again.

Mac was slipping his shoulder holster back on when the phone rang. He checked his weapon out of habit to ensure it was loaded before stuffing the handgun back in the holster under his left arm. Mac reached over the counter and grabbed the phone.

"This is Mac."

"Mac, hey. Dana here. Got your page."

"We have a death out in St. Helens. It sounds like there might be some odd circumstances, since the D.A. wants us to check it out. Sarge is sending us out to work the scene."

"What happened?"

"Guy got hit by a train. Are you available?"

"Sure. I need to run by the house and grab my gear and my work car. I can be at the office in thirty."

"Want me to pick you up at your place? It's on my way."

"No—uh, the office is fine. I'll see you there."

Mac set the receiver back in the cradle. "Why not your house?" he grumbled to himself as he walked back to the bedroom to exchange his dress shoes for a pair of hiking shoes. He left the coat and tie on the sofa, selecting a rain jacket with a fleece liner from the hall closet. Mac then grabbed his keys off the counter and opened the front door, startling himself and the delivery boy who was standing in the entryway.

"Your order, Mr. Mac." The young Asian held up a bag to eye level.

"Sorry, I almost ran out on you. Got a call to go back to work." Mac pulled a twenty from his wallet and handed it to the teenager. "Keep the change." After taking a deep whiff of the tantalizing food, he hurried back to the kitchen and stuffed the bags into the refrigerator. "Should make a good breakfast."

As he locked the front door and headed for his duty car, an unmarked white Crown Victoria, Mac's frustration at missing dinner and the game melted into anticipation. He wondered what they'd find at the scene and why the district attorney felt compelled to call in the State Police detectives. An old guy, Sarge had said, hit by a train. Mac slid in behind the wheel. He couldn't say why, but something told him this wasn't going to be as simple as Sergeant Frank Evans made it sound.

THREE

Mac PULLED INTO THE BACK LOT of the SE Portland office shortly before 7:00 p.m. The slow security gate opened wide enough for his car, and he parked next to the building's back entrance. Dana's unmarked blue Pontiac Grand Am was already in the office lot with its trunk open. Dana leaned inside to collect her gear.

Mac pulled up alongside and rolled down his window. "Going my way?"

"'Fraid so," Dana answered without looking up. She slipped her blue crime scene windbreaker over a white blouse, sweater vest, and suit jacket that went with her black dress slacks and sturdy black shoes.

"You don't have to sound so happy about it," Mac complained, feeling put off.

She rolled her eyes at him. "Give me a break. You know what I mean."

"I have everything we'll need. Just grab your notebook and let's get a move on." Mac glanced over at the dash clock on the car, then back at his watch to press his point.

"I'm not worried about the gear. This stupid gun is so uncomfortable with slacks." Dana held up her Glock pistol, which was still tucked inside a black leather holster. "They really don't make comfortable plain clothes duty gear for women."

"Sorry." Dana looked great to him, though black and white didn't suit her near as well as some of the other colors he'd seen her in, like that soft pink cashmere sweater she'd worn when they'd had dinner together a couple of months ago. Unfortunately that dinner had been the end of anything romantic and the beginning of their business-only routine.

Mac wasn't really into hearing about women's clothing. And since when did detectives call their guns stupid? Still, he tried to look sympathetic. "I don't think we have time to go shopping for something else right now."

"Come on, Mac. Cut me some slack," she grumped. "I'm looking for my fanny pack so I can give my ribs a break. The thumb brake on this department-issue holster is killing my ribs."

Mac could empathize. The thumb brake sat at the top of the gun sight, four to six inches above the belt line, and dug into the ribcage. "You'll get used to it." Mac thumbed the steering wheel impatiently with his fingers.

"Here it is." Dana waved her black leather fanny pack, then secured her gun inside the large zipper pouch. She closed the trunk and jogged around to the passenger side of Mac's vehicle.

Trying to keep his impatience under wraps, Mac kept his mouth shut while he maneuvered onto the street. "Why didn't you want me to pick you up at your place?" Mac finally asked, trying to sound like he was just making light conversation. "It was on the way." *And we could have saved at least twenty minutes.* He thought it best not to add the last part.

Dana sighed and stared out the windshield. At first Mac thought she wasn't going to answer. "Impressions, Mac. I don't want anyone thinking I got this job for any reason other than that I was qualified and I deserved it."

Mac shook his head. "No one has ever indicated that you didn't earn your way into the detective slot. I certainly don't think that."

"I know." Dana turned in the seat, her dimples deepening with a smile. "At least you better not. Maybe I'm being a little too cautious, but it's different when you're a woman. I can't explain it. I'm trying to fill Kevin's shoes while he's out sick, and that's an uphill battle alone."

"I don't know about that." Mac frowned, choosing his words carefully. "I think . . ."

"I said that wrong." Dana paused. "I could never fill Kevin Bledsoe's shoes. What I meant is that I know I'm getting this chance because he's sick and is working light duty. I hope Kevin kicks his cancer, but I'm not going to waste the opportunity to prove myself. I'm sure not going to put up with any office gossip, even though it would be totally unfounded."

Mac bit into his lower lip. *Unfounded?* She was right about that, but her being right didn't stop him from wishing otherwise.

"That's why I don't want to give anyone *anything* to raise their eyebrows at—like seeing you come or go from my apartment. Can you understand where I'm coming from?"

"Sure, I guess so." He doubted there'd be a problem. Still, Mac respected Dana, and if she felt she needed to distance herself from him for appearance's sake, he could accept that. He just didn't like it. "I feel like there's a double standard, though. No one would give it a second thought if I picked Kevin up."

"Kevin is a man. I'm a woman. There's a difference, in case you haven't noticed."

"No kidding." Mac chuckled.

"And there are double standards—even if there shouldn't be. Women are still scarce in this agency."

DANA HAD ALMOST CALLED MAC BACK to pick her up at her apartment instead of the office, knowing it would be faster and closer for them. But she loved her job too much to risk it. Maybe if it had been anyone but Mac, she wouldn't have given it a thought either.

With Mac, she had to go out of her way to avoid the appearance of anything more than friendship. It would be far too easy to fall back into the kind of relationship she'd had with Mac before. They'd dated back in college, and if she were completely honest with herself, she'd admit her feelings for him were even stronger now than they'd been back then. Sadly, their lives had taken separate paths. She'd been thrilled when they'd met up again some months ago when Mac began his first homicide case as a detective with the Megan Tyson murder.

Maybe someday there would be an opportunity for them, but not now. Not with both of them so new to the detective arena. Not with walls that have eyes and ears and fellow workers who already teased her and Mac about being more than partners.

"There are several female detectives in our outfit," Mac said. "I'll bet they wouldn't worry about whether their male partners picked them up. Take Jan Adams in the arson section. She's top notch; nobody ever gives her any flak."

Dana nodded. "Jan's been in detectives since you and I were in high school, Mac. I bet she had her share of hurdles too—more than I do. Women are finally being accepted into the good old boys' group."

"I don't know. I can't imagine anyone messing with Jan; she's like your grandmother and Dirty Harry combined. I don't know how someone so sweet could be so tough at the same time."

Dana laughed. "I'll ask her for you tomorrow and tell her how much you admire her."

"What?"

"Don't worry, I'll leave the Dirty Harry reference out. Though personally, I think that's the best part."

"You're meeting with Jan? Why?" Mac glanced over at Dana. His eyes held a hint of concern and hurt. He'd been mentoring her and doing a pretty decent job, but she needed a woman's perspective.

"Jan and I are meeting for lunch. I wanted to go over a few things. Sergeant Evans suggested it—mainly so we can get to know each other. If nothing else, maybe she can help me shop for some functional detective clothes that look halfway decent."

"What about me? I'm your partner," Mac asked jokingly. "Why not let me help spend your clothing allowance?"

"You mean the eight hundred dollars the department gives us to buy two years' worth of professional attire?"

"What? Isn't that enough for you?"

"I can spend that much on shoes alone." She lifted her foot and inspected her thick-heeled shoe. "Have you shopped for women's clothes lately?"

"Can't say that I have."

"Mac." Dana turned serious. "We talked about our relationship when I made detective and you said you were okay with being friends and nothing more. I know you haven't asked me out or anything since then, but I'm still sensing this thing from you—I don't know . . ."

"Attraction?"

"Hmm." She ran her hand along the seat belt. Unfortunately, she felt more than an attraction for him.

"It's not something I can turn off. I'm sorry if I'm making you feel uncomfortable."

"I'm sorry too, Mac. For now, we can't . . ."

"Don't worry about it. Just so you know, I am not sitting around waiting for you to change your mind. I'm moving on."

"You are?" That wasn't what Dana wanted to hear. She wished she'd kept her mouth shut. She hated the thought of Mac dating anyone. She even felt jealous when women gave him admiring looks. But she'd made a decision and needed to stick with it. He was moving on? Fine. She could live with that. She needed to start dating as well. Maybe she'd take Jonathan Carter up on his offer. The attorney she'd met two weeks ago had called twice asking her out. Each time she'd made an excuse. If he called again maybe . . .

MAC PICKED UP THE RADIO MIC. "Station twenty from eleven-fifty-four." He'd had enough of the conversation and with the relationship that was going nowhere. Dana's rejection stung, and the more he thought about her determination not to get involved with him, the more upset he became.

Best to move on, he told himself. He'd lied in a way. He wasn't dating anyone yet. Maybe he'd have to change that. There was this cute gal in his apartment complex who had hinted more than once about getting together. And there was Kristen Thorpe. Doc Thorpe did a lot of teasing, but Mac bet she'd take him up on dinner or a movie if he asked. He just wasn't sure he could handle her quirky personality. She was attractive enough if you could get beyond the purple spiked hair and the fact that she worked on corpses and liked her job.

"Eleven-fifty-four," the dispatcher acknowledged Mac's radio number.

"Eleven-fifty-four, I'll be twelve-thirty-eight to channel fifteen." He changed his radio channel from the Portland Metro frequency to channel fifteen, the rural Columbia County channel as he started west on Highway 30. On that channel, he could monitor the play-by-play as the uniformed officers worked the scene. "I have eleven-fifty-eight riding with me to the call if I didn't advise earlier. Any updates?"

"Negative, fifty-four. The only information I have is that Dr. Thorpe is on scene and awaiting your arrival."

"Thanks." Mac signed off without further comment and noticed Dana's questioning look.

"Dr. Thorpe? For being the state's head medical examiner, she sure takes her share of cases."

"She likes to be on the front lines."

"She likes to be with you."

"Don't go there, Dana," Mac warned.

"Why, Mac. You're blushing."

"It's warm in here."

"Sure it is." Dana leaned back into the seat, arms folded. If Mac didn't know better, he'd say she was jealous.

"What if I was dating Kristen?" He glanced over at Dana again. "Would that be so bad?"

"Not at all. I think she has feelings for you."

Mac shook his head and turned his attention back to the radio. There wasn't much chatter at the moment, just a trooper working traffic along the highway. Mac and Dana passed the trooper calling in the stop near Scappoose. Mac slowed to make sure he didn't need any assistance.

The trooper never broke eye contact with the suspect vehicle as he gave a code four, an all-clear signal, by raising four fingers on one hand.

"You miss the uniform yet?" Mac asked wanting to move their conversation to safer ground.

"No way. The pants never fit right—once again, men's clothing. No more shift work and court on your days off. I like this detective job just fine, thank you very much."

"Yeah, me too."

They continued west to the town of St. Helens, then north toward the Columbia River and Terminal 9. As they approached, the lights from the terminal turned the dark March evening into daylight.

Dana squinted. "Those lights should make this case a little easier to work. Hopefully the scene isn't too big."

Mac agreed. "Have you ever worked a train accident?"

"Not personally, but I understand the body can be spread out over a pretty long stretch of track. I have a hunch this won't be pretty."

At the opening to the rail yard, Mac rolled down his window and stopped for a uniformed officer from the city police department. "Detectives McAllister and Bennett from OSP."

"Right. The D.A. said you'd be coming. Just head north toward the river."

"Thanks." Mac drove over at least a dozen tracks, lined with thousands of yards of gravel and crushed asphalt, as he maneuvered through the terminal.

"I hope this is the right way. Those floodlights are blinding me." Mac shaded his eyes with his hand.

"Over there, by that gold and black train engine." Dana pointed to the right.

Mac nodded and steered toward three black and whites, parked alongside a single rail track that seemed to lead directly to the river. He recognized Kristen Thorpe's Dodge pickup among the patrol cars, backed toward the nose portion of the diesel train engine. Doc Thorpe may have been the head medical examiner, but she worked every bit as hard as the deputy medical examiners under her. Maybe harder.

Kristen gave Mac a nod and her somber face broke into a broad smile. Dana looked at her and then Mac. "See, I was right. Kristen has a thing for you."

"Enough. You're beginning to sound like a teenager." Mac gave her a scalding look that said this was neither the time nor the place.

"Come on, Mac, lighten up."

He sighed. "I've said it before and I'll say it again, the woman isn't my type. I like women with . . . normal hair."

"Since when did you get so superficial?"

"I'm not." When he looked back at the woman in question, she had turned her attention to the older man who was dressed in a dark suit with no tie. Mac recognized him as the Columbia County district attorney, Darren Volk.

Mac parked and checked out on the radio with dispatch. Since detectives rarely carried portable radios, he advised that he would be available on his mobile phone if needed.

"You ready for this one, partner?" Mac asked, looking over at Dana. "I've never been to a train accident either, but I can imagine what we're about to see."

All hint of teasing gone now, Dana exhaled, rubbing her hands down her thighs to her knees in a nervous gesture. "Can't be any worse than that sawmill murder. Let's go."

Mac thought about Kevin asking him a similar question when they were just starting out together. He remembered how Kevin would always start out a new investigation with a prayer. Mac actually considered doing the same, but the prayer would be silent and terse. He was nowhere near the man of God that Kevin was—didn't know if he ever would be. Mac wished Kevin was with them now. Not that he didn't like being partnered with Dana; he did. But in a crime scene investigation, Mac couldn't be the kind of mentor to Dana that Kevin had been to him. Kevin seemed to have all the answers, and Mac, though gaining more experience all the time, still felt somewhat insecure.

Kevin had covered a lot of ground with Mac, but you could never encounter every possible situation. *You can't be what you're not, partner.* Mac could almost hear his partner chastising him. *Just do your best.*

He would. Even though this was reported to be an accident, Mac planned to do it "by the numbers," as Kevin would say.

Mac glanced over at Dana, trying not to look as apprehensive as he felt. "First thing we need to do is make note of the time we arrived on scene and of the weather and wind conditions."

"I'm already there, Mac. Got the time." She looked up from her notebook. "Any guess on the temperature?"

Mac opened the car door. "I'd say in the mid-forties."

Dana held her notebook up to the bright lights of the rail yard to write, then reached up and snapped on the red dome light. Police package cars had the dome light disconnected so they would not turn on when the door was opened for safety reasons; consequently, the light had to be turned on manually.

Mac's car was even equipped with a switch that would eliminate his brake lights from illuminating in the event he was sitting blacked out on a surveillance and wanted to go undetected. This switch was unfortunately a little too easy to forget and had contributed to a rear-end crash a while back when Mac forgot to turn on his brake light switch and was hit from behind. Although there were no injuries, the incident cost Mac more than a little embarassment and a letter of reprimand from Sergeant Evans.

Mac pressed the dash-mounted trunk release button and walked to the rear of the car. Dana gathered her gear, snapping her jacket to the top as a gust of east wind blew off the river. Mac removed the clipboard binder from his leather briefcase, checking to make sure his legal pad had plenty of blank pages. He was about to snap the binder shut when he recognized Kevin's handwriting on the top page of the legal pad. He pulled his mag light from the trunk-mounted charger and spotlighted the pad. What he assumed were notes from a prior crime scene turned out to be a personal note to

Mac. He glanced around to make sure Dana wasn't approaching then read it.

> *Hey, partner.*
>
> *I thought I'd slip you a note while I was taking some of my gear from your trunk. I knew it would be only a matter of time before you and Dana got the ticket and you'd read this. Even though I'm not with you on whatever case you're about to tackle, I have every confidence in your ability to get the job done. Just take it slow, make your crime scene boundary bigger than you think you need to, and trust your instincts. If things don't feel right, they probably aren't. You are in my prayers, buddy. I'm proud of you.*
>
> Kevin

Mac swallowed back the lump in his throat as he ripped the page from the notepad and folded it neatly into a size that would fit into his back pocket.

"Hey, Mac, Dana. What are you guys doing over here, making out?"

Mac had been so intent on the note, he hadn't noticed Kristen and the D.A. approaching his car. Startled, he shut the trunk. He raised his shoulders and rubbed his left arm to feign a chill. "Just getting our gear together." He avoided looking at Kristen. "Cold out here tonight."

"You want my coat, Mac?" Kristen joked, pulling the zipper of her hot-pink windbreaker halfway down.

"Not my color. Thanks anyway." Mac smiled and extended his hand. "Always a pleasure to see you, Doc." He quickly diverted his attention to the district attorney. "How you doing, Darren?" Mac shook his hand as well.

"Been better. We've got quite a mess on our hands." Darren pushed his glasses back up on the bridge of his nose with his right index finger.

"Darren, have you met my new partner, Dana Bennett?"

"Don't believe I've had the pleasure. I'm Darren Volk, County Chief Prosecutor." Turning back to Mac, he said, "Thanks for coming out. I'll give you the *Reader's Digest* version and you guys can take it from there."

Dana and Mac both opened their notebooks to take notes.

"About forty yards behind us is a deadhead rail line for the terminal." Darren pointed to the area. "You see that white house to the east, down by the river?"

Mac nodded.

"That's our victim's house. The guy's name is Clayton Mullins, goes by Clay. He's a bit of a local fixture around here. Worked at the terminal for decades before going into mandatory retirement about twenty-five years ago. The poor guy was almost ninety. He lived in that house and owned some fifteen riverfront acres between the terminal and the river. His house is on the county historic registry— it was built in the early 1900s. I've never been in it but understand it's full of railroad memorabilia."

"Did he live alone?" Dana asked.

"Yes." Volk directed his answer toward Dana. "Clay was a widower. His wife died shortly after he retired. I'm told his daughter lives in Tualatin. She's an attorney, and her husband is a doctor up at OHSU. Someone thought he may have had a son also, but that hasn't been confirmed."

"Is this the train that hit him?" Mac cut to the chase, nodding toward the closest engine.

"Yes, that's the one. The train on the deadhead rail between here and his house."

"Deadhead?" Kristen raised a black eyebrow. *"Deadhead* as I know it usually refers to some people I know. Somehow I doubt my definition agrees with yours."

Dana snickered and caught a scolding look from the D.A., whose sense of humor seemed about as rigid as his spine. Darren turned away and Kristen gave Dana a wink. Mac rolled his eyes, finding their behavior rather juvenile.

"A deadhead is an empty train car," Volk explained. "One that has no cargo. Once the cars are unloaded they are stored on one of the four deadhead rail lines like this one, a straight set of track that goes nowhere but can store fifty or so rail cars or engines."

"If the train wasn't going anywhere, how did it manage to hit Mr. Mullins?" Dana asked.

"They were putting these deadheads into service." Volk pointed to the property on the other side of the boxcars. "This eastern rail marks the boundary from the terminal property to our victim's property. He was apparently on his way to the terminal when he was hit."

"Do we have any idea why he was on the tracks?" Mac asked.

"It wasn't at all unusual for Clay to come over to Terminal 9," Darren said. "In fact, the locals tell me he came over to the terminal hub nearly every day with that fancy motorized scooter of his. Old Clay would rub elbows with the boys and tell stories about the good old days. I understand he could be a nuisance."

"So you're thinking maybe someone used a train to get rid of him?"

Darren shrugged. "Not necessarily, but his death raises some questions. Clay was a diabetic, on top of other age-related afflictions. He didn't usually come to the yard at night, and we don't know why he was heading over here. Whatever the reason, he never got to the terminal. The thing is, he knew trains and knew to stay off the track when one was coming. That's why I'd like to have you guys take a look and give an opinion. Your investigation, coupled with the medical examiner's report, should paint a pretty good picture of what happened."

"Sounds like a good plan." Mac's gaze roamed over the tracks to the small house, now bathed in lights.

"I don't want to sound like the specter," Volk added, "but Clay's death has already started a few rumors around the terminal and with some folks in town. Heck, he's only been dead a couple of hours and there is already talk of a murder and cover-up."

"How's that?" Mac frowned, his earlier instincts of foul play growing stronger.

"Old Clay was a bit of an eccentric. His land down by the river was worth a bundle, but he refused to sell it. I heard that some developers had offered top dollar for the riverfront acreage. Clay was a controversial guy—had his share of fans and, I'm sure, a few enemies. Like I said, there was also talk of him overstaying his welcome at the terminal. Apparently, Clay was critical about the management and the way things have been run since his retirement. Nothing you could really put a finger on, but you know how these small towns are. I'd rather have a clean investigation so we can put this thing to rest than be dealing with rumors and speculation. This type of thing can grow legs and take off if you don't get a handle on it early."

"I agree." Mac snapped his folder shut. "Does the local police department want involvement, or do they just want us to handle it?"

"As the chief law enforcement office for the county, I want this to be a State Police investigation. It would go a long way toward rumor control if an outside entity investigated the death."

"I understand, but do the local authorities know that?" Mac nodded toward the two uniformed officers standing alongside the yellow crime-scene tape that surrounded the scene. Mac recognized the gold star on one of the men's collars, which designated him as chief of police.

"Taken care of." Darren pushed his glasses back again. "I won't lie to you—the chief isn't too happy about it. I'll handle the press releases and mention that he was involved in the initial investigation, but I want you guys handling the bulk of the load. Your sergeant said that was okay, so I assume you two are on board as well."

"Yeah. We wouldn't be here if we weren't." Mac frowned, a little perturbed by Darren's high-and-mighty attitude. He had the authority to call the shots, but Mac didn't appreciate anyone throwing his weight around regardless of his level of authority.

"Okay to take a look at the body now?" Mac looked to Kristen for an answer.

"Go ahead," Darren said. Then, as if remembering protocol, he deferred to Kristen. "As long as you're okay with it, Doc."

Mac gave him a cursory smile. The law required medical examiner approval for examination or removal of a body.

"I'm good. You do have my permission, Mac." Kristen winked at him, acknowledging that she hadn't missed the nuance.

Mac strode ahead, feeling all eyes upon him. "Okay, let's see what we're up against."

FOUR

THE POLICE CHIEF MOVED FORWARD as Mac approached the yellow crime-scene tape. Mac's suspicions were confirmed: the heavy-set man was Harry Spalding. They'd met briefly several years ago when Mac had been on patrol.

"You with OSP?" Spalding offered his hand as a greeting, but the tone of his voice and stance negated the polite gesture. The man clearly didn't want OSP involved.

"We are. I'm Detective Mac McAllister out of OSP, Portland." Mac shook the proffered hand, though he didn't especially want to.

"I'm Chief Spalding. We've got things under control here, but as you undoubtedly know by now, Volk wants you folks in on the investigation. I can't imagine why. Old man Mullins's death looks to be nothing more than an accident—but he's the boss, so have at it."

"Look, Chief Spalding," Mac said, wanting to establish a modicum of diplomacy, "I'm not here to make this investigation anything other than what it is. Truth is, I don't want to be here any more than you do. I would have been more than happy to kick back and watch the Trailblazers play the Cavaliers." He shrugged and sighed. "But I got the call, and here I am."

"A Blazer fan, huh?" The chief offered a crooked smile.

Good. Some common ground. "Not really," Mac answered honestly and added a companionable grin. "My favorite team is the one playing against the Lakers."

The chief laughed. "You're my kind of basketball fan, McAllister. Come on inside the crime-scene tape and I'll tell you what we know so far."

Before slipping under the plastic tape, Mac introduced Dana and Kristen, who'd been standing behind him during the exchange. With a scribble motion he signaled Dana to sign the crime scene log before coming inside herself. The log documented anyone who came and went from the area of the body—or body parts, in this case. Once Dana signed the log, she left it in the charge of the second uniformed officer.

"Mullins visited the terminal every day," Spalding said. "I suppose Volk told you that Mullins lived on the other side of the grounds."

"Yes. The D.A. mentioned the land alone was worth a bundle and the house had some historic value."

"Humph. You don't know the half of it. Realtors were lined up at the door for that land. I heard he turned down offers of over a million dollars. Old Mullins refused to sell. He liked living by the river and did a fair amount of fishing. Even more, he liked the direct access to the terminal. He'd come over and yak with the other gandy dancers."

"Gandy dancers?" Mac tried to remember where he'd heard the term.

"Sorry; you didn't grow up around a rail yard, I take it."

"No, unless you count Chicago, but I never hung out around trains."

"*Gandy dancer* is slang for a railroad worker or laborer. It's as familiar to them as the term *cop* is to us."

"Interesting."

"At any rate, Mullins would head out bright and early nearly every morning, come up that trail over there across the tracks, and wheel into Terminal 9. The guys at the terminal would worry about him and call the police if he didn't show, thinking maybe something was wrong with him. Some of our uniforms actually responded to the house on 'welfare checks' if he didn't show up by 8:00. Once his motorized chair had a dead battery and another time he was visiting his daughter in Washington County."

"Did he stay all day? What did he do here?"

"He usually stayed until lunchtime, counting deadheads and timing the loading and unloading of train cars." The chief rubbed the back of his head. "I guess he would report inefficiencies to the management at the terminal before going back home."

"I bet that would get a little old." Mac hunched his shoulders against the wind.

"That's putting it mildly. I heard more than one guy complain about Old Mullins getting on their nerves."

"Can you give me any names?" Mac glanced at Dana and scribbled the information on his pad.

The chief shook his head and rolled his eyes. "I don't see much point to this. Being annoyed with the old coot doesn't translate into killing him with a train. These guys aren't killers—just regular guys whose biggest crime is smoking too much or getting a little loaded down at the local bars."

"Humor me, Chief. I need to do this by the book."

"Humph. This is a small town and you hear a lot of rumors. Some may be true, some not. Talk around here was that the day shift foreman—guy by the name of Dan Mason—didn't much like Mullins telling management how he was mismanaging his shift and that his crew was a bunch of lazy sluggards."

"Is Mason working tonight?"

"No, he works the morning watch." The chief scowled at Mac

and patted his shirt pocket before extracting a package of cigarettes. "I was just using Mason as an example. Mullins got to a lot of the guys. Old Clay wasn't the subtlest or the kindest person in town, if you know what I mean. But like I said, they wouldn't kill him. This was an accident, pure and simple." He pulled out a cigarette and lit it, turning slightly to inhale and blow the smoke off to the side.

"You're probably right," Mac said, wanting to placate the man. From what he'd been hearing, however, he'd noted more than one motive for murder. "Can you tell us what went down? I imagine you've talked to the engineer."

"Right. He's pretty shaken up. We figure Mullins was headed over here on that trail. Must have somehow gotten stuck on the track. Looks like the diesel engine pushed him about thirty yards to the east. Gabby didn't realize he'd hit anything right away. He was connecting to some cars and backed over him again. It's pretty gruesome."

"Okay. We'll have to take a look." He pulled out his latex gloves and shoved his hands into them. Turning to Kristen, he asked, "Any suggestions as to how we should go about it?"

"It won't be easy." She scanned the area. "I recommend walking the path from the house to the first harmful event. It would be even better if we can get inside the house and take a look around." Kristen motioned over her shoulder. "Then we need to walk the tracks and collect whatever evidence we can." She eyed the carnage along the railroad tracks and blew out a long breath. "This is going to take a while."

Pieces of flesh, clumps of hair, and torn clothing had been scattered along the tracks and caught under the engine's axles. The shiny rail tracks, wiped clean by the heavy steel wheels of the engine and cars, were a stark contrast.

"We'll need a warrant to get into the house." Mac snapped the cuff of his jacket around his rubber glove.

"A warrant?" The police chief frowned. "Is that really necessary?

One of my guys did a cursory search of the house to make sure there was no one else home. He didn't see anything suspicious."

"Yes, it's necessary." Mac was losing patience with the guy. As police chief, Spalding should know the procedure better than anyone. "I don't want to get into the house and start rooting around without one. If we happened to find evidence of a crime and didn't have a warrant, it would be suppressed in a heartbeat because we didn't take the time to pump out an affidavit for a warrant. It'll be a no-brainer for a death investigation," Mac added. "I can have it done by tomorrow. Only thing is, I'll need your officers to keep a perimeter on the house through the night. We'll go through it with the crime lab guys in the morning."

"I'm shorthanded as it is, but I suppose I can get a guy out here if you think we need to." The chief obviously didn't see the need.

"I'd appreciate it. Thanks." Turning to his partner, Mac said, "I agree with Kristen, Dana. Let's take the path from the house that leads down to that rail bridge before we start picking up pieces."

"Sure." Dana scanned the tracks with her flashlight.

Mac followed the beam of her flashlight and added his own. Although it was dark in the shadows of the massive boxcars and engines, the floodlights and exhaust from the engines gave the ghostly appearance of a foggy October night rather than springtime. Mac, Dana, and Kristen exited the crime-scene tape and made their way down to Mullins's house.

"Let's walk well away from the main path," Mac suggested. "Once we get on the north side, by the house, we should be able to contrast the tracks of his motorized chair a little easier. This way we won't grind any potential evidence into the hard-packed gravel."

"I'm staying here," the chief told them. "I've got a management representative from the terminal on the way to meet us. He should be here any time."

"Anyone notified the next of kin yet?" Kristen asked.

Mac bit into his lower lip. He should have been the one to ask.

The chief nodded. "I sent an officer to the daughter's house in Tualatin. He checked out about an hour ago, so I assume he made contact. I'll get an update for you on that as soon as I can."

"Thanks. I'll need her information so I can get a disposition on the remains once I complete the post. I'll need for her to provide funeral arrangement information."

"You got it," the chief answered.

The trio walked alongside the raised gravel path to Clay's white-washed house.

"What a cute house." Dana jotted something on her pad. "He kept the place up really well."

"Probably hired someone to help him." Mac noted how neat and tidy the house looked from the outside with a white detached garage and black shutters. "In his condition and being in a wheelchair, I doubt he could have kept the place up by himself."

The single-story home looked to be around fifteen hundred square feet at the most and sported an exceptional view of the Columbia River and of Ridgefield, Washington, on the other side. Once at the house, they began tracing Clay's path to the terminal yard and the eventual site of his death.

Mac, armed with a digital camera, and Dana, with her notepad at the ready, scanned the packed gravel and earth path with their rechargeable flashlights while Kristen walked behind. The medical examiner's primary interest lay at the end of the path, where Clay's remains were spread along the track. Mac wondered how many collection bags she would need to transfer the remains.

Mac could easily trace Clay's route, noting that at times the tracks from his scooter veered away from the well-traveled tracks, getting dangerously close to going off the five-foot-wide path. As they approached the raised rail bridge over the deadhead line, Mac held a hand out to stop the women.

"Hold your light up here please, Dana, so I can get a few shots at this displaced gravel before people walk all over it." Dana stepped back a few yards and widened her flashlight beam so Mac could take the pictures.

"Thanks." He swung the camera lens to the mangled chair that lay clear of the tracks. Dana followed with her flashlight beam before he had a chance to ask. As the light illuminated the motorized vehicle, the shiny metal basket and handlebars reflected the light. The gray rubber tires and flat black frame had been mauled by the impact, evidencing the horrific collision with the train engine. Mac took several photographs of the twisted wreckage. "It's a mess, but I'm surprised at how much of the machine is still intact. It must have been thrown off the track with the first hit."

As they moved onto the track itself, Dana hunkered down. "Take a look at this, guys. Looks like he might have high-centered here on the gravel and caught his wheel on the rail." Dana shined her light for Mac and Kristen. "See how the gravel is churned up here?"

"Good find, Dana," Mac said. "Looks like he got stuck and was trying to power out, but his wheels couldn't get traction in the loose stuff." Mac examined the indentation, snapping two pictures from different angles. He set a small ruler in the gravel trough, then measured the width of the chair's back rubber wheel.

"Looks like the same width. The poor old guy must have gotten stuck, like the chief said."

Dana nodded. "We'll have to get that chair into the crime lab, make sure there isn't something on the machine we aren't able to see. Right?"

"Right," Mac agreed. "It's not going to fit into our vehicles, though. Maybe we can recruit a truck from one of our fish and wildlife troopers. Those guys all drive pickups."

"Maybe Chris is free," Dana grinned.

Mac felt a moment's jealousy. Chris Ferroli had worked with

them on a recent case involving a poaching operation. Did he and Dana have something going? Mac pushed aside the feeling. "I don't see anything else of evidentiary value on the path." He pulled out his phone and requested a wildlife trooper with an available truck, giving the pertinent information to the dispatcher and not mentioning anyone specific. "You two ready for the fun part?" Mac motioned toward the train engine.

"Born ready." Kristen blew out a long breath.

"I'm not." Dana caught Mac's gaze. "But we don't have much choice in the matter, do we?"

FIVE

Mac scanned the length of the rail line before stepping over the tracks and took a couple of deep breaths to prepare himself for the gruesome task of collecting body parts. He'd asked Dana to go to the management office to speak with the terminal manager. Now he was wishing he'd gone instead. The chief, who'd been hanging around near the crime scene perimeter, was now inside the terminal with Dana and the management.

Kristen had gone back to her vehicle for some large black plastic bags, leaving him alone. Mac thought about Kevin, wondering what his experienced ex-partner would do if he were running the investigation. Maybe he'd ask him tomorrow. Kevin would probably offer some sage advice. Mac was pretty good at obtaining information while acting as though he didn't need it. Probably because the guys loved to give advice whether or not anyone wanted it.

What he did know was that he needed to gather all the evidence he could and make certain the crime scene, if it turned out to be that, remained as pristine as possible. From all appearances, the old man's death was an accident. But Mac couldn't shake the feeling that they were only looking at the surface.

"I'm all set," Kristen announced as she approached. "You want to hold the bags for me while I collect?"

"Sure, glad to." Mac extended his gloved hands to take the proffered bags.

"I'll shoot some digitals on scene, but most of them will be at the post," Kristen said. "Most of the remains are dirty. Lots of grease and debris." All of which Kristen and Henry, her assistant, would clean up at autopsy.

Mac and Kristen began walking east on the tracks from the first impact, the area of the chair, and the rail crossing on the trail. Less than twenty feet from the motorized chair Mac and Kristen located most of the victim's upper torso and left arm. The clothing had been torn from the body, which was lying facedown in the gravel beside the shiny rail.

"Looks like we have a clean cut above the pelvic girdle." Kristen snapped several digital photographs then slipped on a heavy set of rubber gloves. She rolled the torso over and Mac held his breath. Both the victim's eyes were partly open in the deadpan stare only seen on a corpse. Mac shuddered in revulsion and momentarily looked away when the large intestine stubbornly stuck to the gravel and lengthened as Kristen continued to turn the torso.

Apparently unaffected, Kristen said, "I'd say his legs fell under the train on the first pass, Mac. The train probably discarded his scooter and sliced through his midsection in the initial collision. That will make my job a lot easier. Most of the remains under the engine and along the rail will be right arm, lower torso, and legs. Let's recover this big piece last. We'll place the smaller collection samples in the body bag with this one."

"You're the boss." Mac had seen his share of mangled bodies, but for some reason he felt more affected by this one than he should have. Maybe because he'd come to know a little about the old guy. He admired the man's perseverance in motoring out to the rail yard on a daily basis. He believed in a job well done. Retirement must have been hard on Clay Mullins.

"Would you grab my toolbox, Mac? I need my thermometer and syringe for fluid collection."

"Sure." Glad for something to do, Mac walked back to where Kristen had set down her box and brought it to her, placing it on the ground within easy reach. She placed several small pieces of tissue and bone inside the smaller bags after photographing them and supplying a number to each evidence item.

Kristen glanced up at him and smiled. "Thanks. Now could you open it and get my thermometer out? My hands are a little messy."

Mac complied. Kristen took the thermometer from him and thrust the tip into the torso near the left clavicle.

"The bladder's been ravaged, so we can't get a urine sample. I'll take blood from the heart before it degrades too much." Mac handed her the long syringe she pointed to and watched as she inserted it between the victim's ribs and into the chest, quickly and efficiently withdrawing a sample. She made note of the temperature of the body, finding the temperature was consistent with the purported time of death and the weather conditions. They then worked their way west on the deadhead line toward the train engine.

Dana arrived just as Kristen and Mac made their way back to the torso.

"Don't step on that side of the tracks," Mac warned.

Dana switched to the south side of the tracks and gave a salute motion with her hand to her forehead, back at Mac. "You guys doing okay?" Dana asked, covering her near mistake.

"Don't worry, kiddo." Kristen snapped Dana's picture. "We saved plenty for you."

"The upper torso was fairly intact," Mac said, bringing Dana up to speed. "We're looking to collect the remains from here back to the train." He nodded toward the terminal. "What did you find out from the management?"

"Not much. They have corporate lawyers on the way, so they were a little hesitant to provide any information. The suits are already gathering upstairs in the main hub. The yard goat operator—the guy who was operating the train that killed Mullins—was in there too. He's pretty broken up, but I was able to talk with him for a few minutes before management made him clam up."

"Humph. They're no doubt more concerned about a lawsuit than about the employee or the victim."

"For sure."

"What the heck is a yard goat operator?" Mac asked, thinking back to the term Dana had used.

"That's what they called him. I didn't know what it meant either, so I asked. Apparently, a yard goat is a small train engine like that one." Dana pointed at the engine that had struck their victim.

"If that's small, I'd hate to see what a normal-sized one would do."

"They use it in the terminals to transfer cars around," Dana went on. "Anyway, the yard goat operator said he gave the highball signal on his air horn."

"Highball?" Mac frowned.

She squinted at the writing in her notebook. "Yep, that's what he said. The highball signal." Dana shook her head. "Honestly, these guys deal in total slang. They're worse than we are. I guess they have a series of signals they give with their air horns that convey movement and direction. The operator gave the signal and was backing a group of empty cars to the east. He apparently didn't see Mr. Mullins until he backed completely over him and was proceeding to the west to enter the main terminal."

"Makes sense." Mac examined the engine and the cars. "He was pushing these cars and wouldn't have seen the victim until he had an unobstructed view."

"That's right. He saw Clay's scooter on the return trip and, in his words, 'freaked out.' Poor guy. He was really upset. Gabby knew Clay and swore up and down that it was an accident. The terminal management shut him up after that, said we could speak to him in a couple of days after he'd coped with the loss."

"After the attorneys get to him, you mean."

Dana shrugged. "That too. Thing is, Mac, I believe him. He struck me as an honest guy. I've got his name and horsepower for a comprehensive interview if we need it."

"Was he the guy the chief was talking about? The one who didn't like Clay hanging around?"

"No, you're thinking about Dan Mason. The yard goat operator's name is Gabby Dean. He mainly works nights. I asked about Mason, though. The manager said he'd be in to work tomorrow morning. He didn't think it was necessary to call him down tonight."

Mac nodded. "He's probably right."

"One more thing, Mac. A couple of the guys looked at each other kind of funny when I mentioned Mason's name. I tried to talk to them, but no dice. I got their names. If we need to, we can question them later."

"Good work, Dana. We'll pay a visit to Mr. Mason tomorrow. We'll need to talk to him for the record, especially since the chief mentioned he had a little heartburn with our victim."

Dana slipped her small notebook into her jacket pocket. "That's another thing I noticed. The chief is a little too friendly with the terminal management, if you ask me. Did you know he's only the acting chief?"

"Really?" Mac held out a bag for Kristen.

"Yep. The actual chief is at the FBI executive management class in Virginia. This Spalding guy is only filling in for the next few weeks."

"Interesting," Mac mumbled. "Wonder why the D.A. didn't mention that? For an acting chief, he sure knows how to throw his weight around. Where is he now?"

"Still up there with the terminal brass; said he'd catch us later."

"Hey guys!" Kristen shouted. "Take a look at this." The flash of her camera lit up the rear axle of the lead boxcar. "That is, if you're done with your break."

Mac ignored the smart remark and walked with Dana to where Kristen was crouched down on one knee, peering under the car. "We're in luck," she said with an odd enthusiasm. "Looks like the rest of the big pieces are under here."

"Amazing what some people get excited about," Mac teased.

"Bring me some more plastic bags, please, Mac. I think we can get the rest into two of those large ones." Kristen handed the camera to Dana and then slipped her heavy rubber gloves back on before dragging the legs out from under the boxcar. "Dana, get some shots of this operation."

"Sure thing."

Kristen grunted. "I can't reach the arm. Mac, can you get to it?"

Mac unfolded one of the plastic body bags and spread it on the gravel to protect his clothes. He grabbed the frame rail with his left hand and stretched out enough to reach the index finger of the severed arm. Once he pulled it into the clear, he let Dana photograph it before sliding it into the bag Kristen held for him.

Several minutes later, satisfied that they had recovered the majority of the smaller remains, they returned to recover the torso.

"Hey, Mac," the D.A. called from outside the crime-scene tape. "Got a minute? I'm about to head home."

"Sure." Turning back to Dana and Kristen, Mac asked, "You two think you can manage without me?"

"Well, sugah," Kristen batted her eyes, drawling like a Southern belle, "I just don't know how we'all are gonna hold up without a man around."

Dana chuckled.

Mac didn't appreciate Kristen's humor one bit. He left before the insults got any worse. Not that he blamed them. Picking body parts off a railroad track could get pretty intense. Mac walked to the periphery of the crime scene and ducked under the tape.

"Anything raising hairs?" Darren Volk asked Mac, but he kept his gaze on the women as they worked on getting the victim's remains into the large rubber body bag.

"Not so far," Mac answered. "Evidence-wise, everything is pointing to an accident, but we'll go ahead and run the gambit. Hey, I heard Chief Spalding was filling in for the real chief of police while he's at the national academy."

"Right. Spalding was the chief until a couple of years ago. The guy was born and raised in St. Helens and wasn't ready to leave the job. The city thought they needed someone on the outside. They hired George Potter to replace him, and Harry is still carrying a grudge. I got used to calling him Chief years ago and it stuck." He frowned. "Why do you ask? Is there a problem?"

"No. No problem. My partner just got the impression he was pretty tight with the management here at the terminal."

"She's right about that." Darren frowned. "That's one of the reasons I wanted OSP to look into the death. Spalding has a lot of connections in this town—which is why he's no longer the chief. I'm sure Potter would agree with my decision."

"I'm glad you called us in. We'll need to get a comprehensive interview with the guy driving the rig that hit our victim. I also want to interview the day shift foreman, this Dan Mason character. I hear he was less than amiable regarding our victim's visits to the yard. I don't know how receptive they'll be to interviews, though. Looks like corporate lawyers are on their way in."

"Stop by my office in the morning. We'll cut some grand jury subpoenas for you to take along. If they refuse to talk, we'll subpoena them in for death inquiry testimony. That is, of course, unless we consider them suspects instead of material witnesses."

"I appreciate that, but they're just persons of interest right now. I'll plan on meeting you at your office at nine, if that works for you."

Darren nodded.

"I also want to get a warrant to search our victim's house for anything relevant to the investigation. I want to know why he was heading out of Dodge at night. That seems to break with his regular routine."

"Sounds good. I'll see you in the a.m." Darren hesitated. "Will you be releasing the scene tonight? The manager is anxious to get things rolling. This thing has put them behind."

"Sorry," Mac said. "There's no way I can release anything at this point. I'll need some officers to lock this area down. It's a crime scene until we prove otherwise."

"Okay, I figured as much. I'll meet with the management and the local police to smooth things over."

"Appreciate it." Mac started to rejoin Kristen and Dana when a trooper from the wildlife division drove into the terminal, pulling up to the yellow crime-scene tape. Mac assisted him in gathering the wheelchair parts and sent him off to the Portland patrol office's evidence compound, where the chair would await transport to the OSP crime lab.

When he finally got back to Kristen and Dana, they had placed Clay's remains on the metal gurney and were loading it into the truck.

"You two ready?" Mac asked.

"No thanks to you." Kristen covered her harsh tone with a half smile.

"I'm sorry. I had to go over a few things with the prosecutor and had to get the wheelchair squared away."

"I was teasing, Mac," Kristen said.

"I knew that." He shook his head. "We'll secure the scene tonight and get a fresh start in the morning. Dana, you and I have a meeting with the D.A. at nine. We'll need to get going on the warrant for the home and gear up for some interviews here at the terminal. We also have to get with Clay's daughter; I'm sure she'll have a lot of questions."

"I'll spend a little time with my new friend here." Kristen patted the bag. "We'll try to get you some answers before noon. You can come in then."

"Great, it's a date." Mac stripped off his gloves and tossed them in the waste receptacle in Kristen's truck.

Kristen leaned toward him and whispered seductively, "Why, Mac. Are you asking me out?"

For once Mac didn't back off. He locked his gaze into hers. "What if I am?"

This time it was Kristen's turn to blush.

SIX

WEDNESDAY MORNING AT 6:15, Mac balanced his large Starbucks coffee on his leather notebook cover as he fumbled with his keys to open the door to the detectives' office. Turning the key and pushing the door open with the same hand, Mac was surprised to find someone was already in the office. The lights were on and the coffeepot was simmering on the hot plate.

"Philly?" Mac called, wondering why the veteran detective hadn't left the door unlocked.

"Yello." Philly popped his head out the door of his private office. Lifting his cup in a salute, he said, "Morning, sunshine. Decide to get to work on time for a change?"

Ignoring the slam, Mac stepped partway into Philly's office. "Sarge here yet?"

"Nope. He has court in Washington County today. Probably won't be in all day."

"Has Kevin been in yet this morning?" Mac peered around the

corner. "I thought he was scheduled back today." His partner had been gone for the better part of a month after having surgery and beginning chemo.

Philly shook his head. "He's not coming in until this afternoon. Another chemo treatment this morning. I told him I'd pick him up and bring him to the office so his missus could get a break."

Mac nodded. "What are you doing here so early?"

Philly shrugged, spilling a few drops from his cup onto the carpet on the way back to his desk. He rubbed his black wingtips over the drop on the carpet, massaging the liquid into the fibers along with the other stains. "Paperwork. What else?"

"You and Russ are up for the next call." Mac folded his arms and leaned against the doorjamb. "Dana and I got one last night to Columbia County."

"Oh yeah? That's good. I've got a date with my barber this morning, just wanted to get some reports dictated before the phones start ringing off the hook."

Mac settled his gaze on Philly's thinning hair. For a guy who seemed to let everything else go, Philly was very conscious of his hair and always had a comb in his pocket. In his early fifties, his heavy frame weighed well over two-fifty. He had a protruding stomach that always seemed to catch crumbs from the mega-portions of food he ate.

Mac had learned early on that, as far as Philly was concerned, appearances could be deceiving. Philly might be a little uncouth, but he was one of the best detectives in the department—right up there with Kevin Bledsoe. Many an offender had been fooled by Philly's sloppy outward appearance, and Philly played it to his advantage.

"What did you and Dana go out on?" Philly asked. His attention seemed more focused on the reports than on his question.

"A retired railroader got hit by a train out at a Western Pacific terminal near St. Helens. It will probably end up being an accident, but there are a few odd things that need to be looked in to."

"Like what?" Philly took a sip from his coffee then leaned back in his squeaky chair, hands behind his head.

Not feeling entirely sure of himself, Mac was glad for the chance to talk to Philly about the case. "The guy was a worker at the rail yard for years and still enjoyed hanging out at the terminal. From what I've heard so far, he had a house and chunk of land next to the terminal that was worth a bundle. I haven't actually confirmed that yet. There was also a guy at the terminal who didn't care much for the old man." Mac shrugged. "Like I said, there are some things I need to look at."

"Need any help?"

"Not at this point. I'll let you know, though. I'm starting with a search warrant for the house. We're meeting the district attorney out at the courthouse this morning. I want to get started on the affidavit here on my laptop and finish it up with the prosecutor. I'll let you know if I run into any roadblocks."

"Sounds good." Philly went back to sipping his coffee and began dictating reports into his mini cassette recorder.

Hearing his phone ring, Mac headed for his desk, which was situated in one of the small cubicles in the detectives' office. He caught a glimpse of the empty chair at Kevin's desk as he walked past his open office door and felt an intense sadness.

"Detective McAllister," Mac said as he hit the speaker button on the phone.

"Oh good, you're there."

"Morning, Dana. What's up?"

"Just wondering if it was okay if you picked me up to go to the courthouse in Columbia County instead of meeting you at the office this morning. I told Jan I wouldn't be able to make lunch. She suggested getting together for coffee in St. John's, so she just picked

me up at the OSP lot. I could make the meet on the way out west if
that's okay with you. I'll be at The Java House on Vaughn."

"Sure," Mac said. "I'll just peck away on the warrant for a while
and meet you there by 8:30."

"Are you sure? I don't want to miss out on anything, but I've been
trying to get some one-on-one time with Jan all week."

"It'll be fine. You should go. Jan has a lot to offer."

"Thanks, Mac. I'll see you out there."

AT A FEW MINUTES TO NINE, Mac and Dana entered the stone
World War II-era courthouse and jogged up the stairs to the
second floor, where the county prosecutor's offices were housed.
Mac pressed the buzzer to the heavy metal door leading into the
office. Almost immediately, the receptionist unlocked the electric
door.

"Hi, Mac," the receptionist greeted the two detectives, smiling at
Dana as they entered the office. "You must be Dana Bennett."

"That's right."

"Darren said you'd be coming. I'm Lila." The women shook
hands.

"Is Darren in?" Mac asked.

"He is. You know where his office is, Mac; go on back."

"Thanks." Mac led the way past her desk and down a long
hallway to the third office on the right. "Knock, knock." Mac
pushed on the already open door.

"C'mon in, Mac. Good morning, Dana." Darren stood up at his
desk and gestured for them to have a seat in the two chairs facing
him. "I've already briefed the grand jury. I need for you to give a
quick testimony before the jury, and we'll cut some subpoenas for
Clay's medical records and personal finance records so you don't
have to write a warrant affidavit."

"Good." Mac appreciated the D.A.'s efficiency. "Is there a judge on the premises today? I have a warrant affidavit prepared for the house." Mac set his briefcase on an empty chair, removed a file folder, and placed the packet on Darren's desk.

"I'll need the autopsy information and probably the lab work before the judge signs off on it, but it's a starting point. I'll review it this afternoon if I get the chance. I have trial all day." Darren glanced at his watch. "If you're ready to give testimony before the grand jury begins hearing other cases, we can get subpoenas for financial companies today and get that medical information over to Dr. Thorpe." Darren motioned toward the employee break room that doubled as a grand jury hearing room one week a month.

"They're ready now?" Mac asked.

"Ready and waiting." Darren grabbed a pad from his desk. "If it's okay with you, I'll hold off on testimony subpoenas for Dan Mason and the others. Let's see what kind of reception they give you at the rail yard today."

In Oregon, grand juries were mainly used as a primary charging forum for issuing felony indictments. Citizen jurors would listen to police testimony and decide to pursue formal felony charges against suspects, some in custody or others considered for warrant status.

The grand jury also had an investigative function, issuing subpoenas to compel testimony or obtain protected records that may assist in investigations into serious crimes or suspicious deaths. These protected records included financial information, medical files, and phone records. After his testimony, Mac requested subpoenas for all these records from the jury, which were granted without hesitation.

Seven citizens from the county of venue were summonsed to serve on jury duty, as opposed to twelve in a criminal trial. In the larger Oregon counties, the jurors could expect to serve on a grand jury for up to four weeks, hearing dozens of cases. In rural Columbia

County however, these jurors would only sit for a week at the longest, rarely hearing cases more severe than felony driving cases or an occasional assault. Evidence presented on a death would surely be the talk of the town once these citizens returned to their homes and jobs.

Mac thanked the jurors and went back to the work station, where he faxed the subpoena to Kristen at the medical examiner's office so she could request the medical records from Clay's primary caregiver before beginning the post. While he did that, Dana requested a crime analyst from their department headquarters in Salem, who would conduct a credit search for Clay to determine where he maintained his bank accounts or other holdings.

"I think that's all we can do here, Dana," Mac said when they'd finished their calls. "Can you think of anything else before we head over to Terminal 9?"

Dana sighed. "Not right now. I think we should interview some of the day shifters to see what they have to say about our victim."

"My thoughts exactly."

"You think Mason will give us a statement?" Dana asked as they headed for Mac's car.

"Only one way to find out."

SEVEN

WHEN MAC AND DANA PULLED INTO TERMINAL 9, through the east entrance, Mac was amazed at how many buildings and train cars were on the sprawling property. Hundreds of boxcars, many stacked two high, lined the miles of tracks within the terminal.

"I didn't realize this place was so big." Dana peered out the passenger side window.

"I was thinking the same thing." Mac leaned forward to get a better look. "Looks like they still have a sentry on the house. There's an officer posted in that marked car."

"Look, Mac." Dana pointed to the deadhead line that had occupied most of their time the previous evening. "The train that hit our guy is gone. Wonder what they did with it? Didn't we ask them to leave the scene intact?"

"We sure did." Mac pulled into the gravel parking lot in front of the main terminal office, setting the emergency brake with a little more force than necessary. "I didn't give the release for the train engine. Did you?"

"No way."

Mac frowned. "It may not be that big of a deal, but I wasn't planning to release that train until the medical examiner got back to us with the autopsy reports. You know, in case we missed something. Besides that, I was thinking it would be a good idea to examine the scene again in daylight."

"I wonder what they did with the engine," Dana mused. "We may be able to get it back."

"This guy might know." Mac gestured to a tall, thin man in coveralls, who'd just exited the building and was talking into a handheld radio.

Mac rolled down the window and waved. "Hey."

The man hesitated, then walked toward the car, all the while barking orders into the handheld radio. "Yeah, what can I do ya for?" The guy didn't seem any too pleased at being sidetracked.

"Can you tell me where to find the terminal manager?" Mac yelled over the noise at the depot.

"Probably at the golf course until this afternoon. You with corporate?"

"Not exactly." Mac opened the car door and stepped out. "How about Dan Mason? Do you know if he's working today?"

"Who's asking?" The man's eyes narrowed.

"Detectives McAllister and Bennett with State Police." Mac showed him his badge. "We're working on a death that occurred at the terminal last night. We're looking to make a few contacts this morning."

The man turned his back on Mac and held the radio up to his mouth, yelling over the background noise, "Charlie, get that line of reefers over to the westbound on deck and stretch the cars before I get over there. We've got a highball in twenty minutes, you got me?"

Mac couldn't hear what the voice said on the other end of the radio, but the man let out a string of profanity before turning back to Mac.

"Sorry." He said the word, but Mac doubted he meant it. "I've got to move some of these cars that were backed up from last night's logjam. You guys are gonna cost me a lot of overtime. Don't appreciate your shutting down the terminal for hours on end with no good reason."

Unbelievable. Mac straightened to his full height and set his hands on his hips. "You don't think the death of a human being is a good reason to slow down some trains?"

The man took a step back as he peered at Mac.

Dana slipped out of the car and took a position of advantage behind Mac.

The man glanced at her, then at Mac, his gaze slipping to the silver badge attached to Mac's belt. "It, well, it just created a lot of work for me." The man's demeanor softened. "I've got no problem holding the line while you investigate the accident, take your pictures and stuff. I just don't know why you held us up all night, then released the cars this morning. Might as well have let them go last night."

"We *didn't* release the scene. But I sure as heck would like to know who did. I'd like to talk to the guy in charge. Either the terminal manager or the day shift foreman. Guy by the name of Dan Mason."

"You won't find the brass around this morning. They're back in Portland with the corporate lawyers discussing their liability on the death last night. I'm Dan Mason. Don't know as I can help you, though. We all got clear instructions not to talk to the media or anyone else poking around. I'm supposed to call corporate if anyone shows up at the terminal."

"I'm sure that wouldn't include us."

"We're not supposed to talk to the cops, either."

"Look, Mr. Mason." Mac decided it was time for a little diplomacy. "We're not looking to cause trouble. We're just doing our job—the same as you. Nothing would make me happier than to wrap this up and get back to my other duties."

Mason seemed to relax a bit. "I'll tell you what I know, but it's not a whole heck of a lot. You probably know by now, there was no love lost between me and old Clay."

"Right. That was one of the reasons my partner and I were looking to talk to you."

Mason's gaze flashed past Mac to Dana, who was now standing at the rear of the car, arms folded.

"This is my partner, Dana Bennett," Mac said. "She was at the scene with me last night."

Dana walked around the car and shook hands with Mason. "Nice to meet you, Mr. Mason."

Mason nodded then turned his attention back to Mac. "I can give you some time later in the day, but that's it. I've got to get some of these deadheads out of here so I can clear the rails. We've got boxcars lined up from here to Ainsworth waiting to enter the terminal."

"I appreciate your willingness to cooperate. Do you have a number we can call to hook up with you later?"

Mason pulled a grimy cell phone from the pocket of his orange safety vest and read the printed number to Mac. "I carry this with me most of the time; you can give it a try. I keep it on vibrate mode so I can get calls out on the yard. I should get a break after three or so; at least, I hope that's the case. I'm due to be off shift about then."

"Thanks." Mac jotted down the number Mason gave him and put his pen and pad in the jacket of his sports coat. "Just one thing before we go. Who released the train that hit Mr. Mullins, and where is it now?"

"There's your answer right over there on who cut it loose."

Mason pointed behind Mac at a uniformed officer standing across the terminal by a marked city police car.

Mac glanced over his shoulder. "Chief Spalding?" Spalding raised his silver coffee cup to Mac and they made eye contact. Mac turned back to Mason without acknowledging the chief.

"Yep. He said we could get it to the steam shop and clean it up. That was about four hours ago. The engine was power washed and put back on line." He glanced at his watch. "She's on her way to Spokane for servicing and repairs at our sister terminal. You can ask the mud hop for an exact location."

"Mud hop?" Mac asked. "And just who would that be—in plain English, if you don't mind?"

"The terminal clerk, Roger Perrault. He hangs out over there in the building with that big antenna on the roof."

"Thanks for your help, Mr. Mason. We'll be in touch."

Dan Mason nodded at Dana as he walked past and immediately started talking into the handheld radio.

"Did you hear that?" Mac asked Dana. "The chief released the scene."

"I heard. Should we say something?"

"You better believe it." Mac huffed and slid in behind the wheel. "I can't believe that guy would go over my head. Hop in, Dana."

"Want me to talk to him?" Dana offered. "While you cool down."

Mac shook his head. "No thanks. I'm mad, but I'm not stupid."

"Didn't say you were . . ." She pulled the door shut.

Mac drove over to where Chief Spalding's car was parked. The wheels slid in the loose gravel when he braked, and he shut the door behind him with more force than necessary.

"Top of the morning." The chief saluted both Mac and Dana as they approached his car.

Spalding was in far too good a mood. Mac had a feeling the older man knew exactly what they'd come to talk about.

"Morning yourself, Chief. Any changes overnight that we should know about?" Mac crossed his arms, legs slightly apart in a gesture meant to intimidate.

"Not a thing. Still have the boys sitting on the house. I went ahead and released the train back to the company so they could get it cleaned up and back into commission."

Mac clenched his fists and felt his jaw tighten. "So I see. I really wish you'd called me first. I wanted the scene held until Doc Thorpe was done with the autopsy."

Chief Spalding took a sip of coffee; his eyes narrowed into dark slits. "I didn't know I needed permission to do things in my own town, Detective. Next thing you know I'll have to call you guys before I use the john."

Mac took a step forward, measuring his next words. *Diplomacy, Mac.* He could almost hear Kevin's sage advice. "I appreciate your situation, Chief, but it's standard procedure not to release a crime scene until there is no possibility of additional evidence collection. I'm sensitive to the needs of the terminal management, but it is my position as the lead investigator to release the scene. It wasn't your call."

"Sorry, but I didn't think this was shaping up to be *Murder on the Orient Express.* This isn't a crime scene. I'm no homicide cop from the big city, but I don't need to be told how to do my job." Spalding opened his car door. "I told the D.A. that bringing you guys in would be nothing but trouble. I'm going to see the D.A. now and have a word with the city commissioners. We don't need OSP involvement in an accidental death. These people are big-time employers and taxpayers for the city. They won't like things being held up much longer, I can tell you that right now."

"I really don't care about that. Right now, I'm working for Clay Mullins." Mac managed to hold his anger in check, but just barely. "I'm pretty sure he and his family would want things done the right way. You go do what you have to do, Chief, while I salvage what's left of this investigation."

Spalding muttered a string of obscenities as he put the car in gear and sped out of the terminal lot. The uniformed officer watching Clay's house looked up as the car spewed gravel onto the metal tracks.

"That went well." Dana slapped Mac on the back in a friendly gesture. "I'd say your political future in this town just went down the drain."

"Lucky for me, I'm not planning to run for mayor." Mac pursed his lips. "I better call Sarge and give him a heads-up. While I'm doing that, why don't you make contact with the dispatch clerk and get a handle on where the engine is now."

"Sure thing." Dana strode across the gravel parking area to the building Mason had pointed out earlier.

Mac called Sergeant Frank Evans at the Portland office, but not without some degree of anxiety. Detectives have found themselves back in a uniform assignment for less.

"Yeah, Mac," Frank said when he finally answered.

"Just wanted to let you know we're getting some political flak over here." Mac told him about the chief releasing the scene and his confrontation with him.

"He was obviously in the wrong. I wouldn't worry too much about Spalding. One of our guys is a good buddy with the actual police chief over there. If need be, he can put in a call to Potter and soothe things over."

"Good. I appreciate your help, Sarge."

"You got it. Just follow the investigation through. You got any feelings about it one way or the other?"

"Evidence-wise, it's too soon to tell; but instinctually, my antenna is up."

"Okay, Mac. Keep me posted."

Mac checked his voice mail while waiting on Dana. then called his neighbor to check on Lucy. She was doing fine, as usual, without him. Carl had her over at his house spoiling her with treats and a brushing. The other call was from Kristen, saying she'd already started the post. "I've ordered the medical records. Thanks for faxing over the subpoenas." After a moment's hesitation, she added, "You standing me up, Mac? We had a date, remember."

Not until noon. Mac smiled as he dialed her office. Kristen was otherwise occupied and couldn't come to the phone. He left a message with the receptionist that they'd be there shortly.

Dana was in the dispatch office for about fifteen minutes before coming back to the car. She got in and closed the door. "Did you get hold of Sarge?"

"Yep, he's taking care of the politics. I think my career is safe for the time being. Checked my voice mail—looks like Kristen is getting the medical records from those subpoenas we faxed out. She's beginning the post and wants to know why we aren't there."

"Did you tell her we haven't gotten around to cloning ourselves yet?"

"No, I said we'd be there soon. What took you so long?"

"I got a few interesting tidbits from the dispatch clerk. He confirmed the train had been cleaned and was on its way to Spokane for maintenance, although I bet it's so they can hide the engine from us. He also confirmed the bit about Mullins tattling to the terminal management about Mason doing a sloppy job. Mason had told him more than once that it made his blood boil to see Mullins out there every day, watching from his chair, counting and watching, counting and watching."

"Interesting. We'll have to ask Mason about that this afternoon when he gets off work."

"That's the part I think you will find really interesting." Dana pulled on her seat belt and snapped it into place. "Mason signed off duty while I was speaking with the dispatch clerk. I heard it over the radio, and the guy I was talking to confirmed it. Looks like Mason is skipping out on us."

EIGHT

Mac and Dana drove back into downtown Portland, hitting a drive-thru at a fast-food restaurant along Highway 30 on the way to the medical examiner's office. Mac had taken his sunglasses on and off a half-dozen times during the forty-five-minute trip. Oregon's weather fluctuated this time of year between sun breaks and rain showers, making it difficult to predict the proper dress for the day, and making driving a royal pain.

Mac pulled into the lot and put the Crown Victoria in park. The extra pair of handcuffs that hung on the shift knob clanked as they slid down.

Dana zipped her light jacket up to her neck and brushed the hair that had escaped her chignon behind her ears. Mac envisioned Dana with her hair tumbling down around her shoulders, the way it had been during their last date—check that—the dinner they'd had together. He sighed. *You have to stop thinking about her that way*, he told himself. *She's off-limits. Period.*

"I hear the medical examiner division is getting a new office down in the Clackamas area," Dana said. "They'll be sharing it with the crime lab."

"Where did you hear that?" Mac examined the faded red brick on the old single-story building while he popped the trunk.

"Jan told me this morning. Don't know where the funding is coming from—especially with all the budget cuts."

"I've given up understanding the political ins and outs of all this stuff. Seems like they can find the money when they want it. I'm not complaining, though. With both their offices in Clackamas, it would be one-stop shopping for us. We could attend the autopsy and run the evidence across the hall instead of driving it all the way downtown."

Dana nodded, accepting the digital camera bag from Mac as he hoisted it out of the trunk. "That would be nice."

Mac grabbed his leather briefcase, slipping in a few small evidence bags and evidence forms before snapping it shut.

Dana walked just ahead of Mac as they approached the employee entrance to the morgue and punched in the digital code to the back door. The door opened, forcing them to step back to make room for a mortician.

"Coming through," the man pushing the gurney yelled as he balanced the human cargo with one hand and pushed with the other. The man expertly slid the body and gurney into the back of the hearse and checked his clipboard before leaving the parking lot, probably double-checking the directions for the delivery.

Once the man had cleared the entry, Mac gestured for Dana to go ahead.

"Busy place," Dana observed.

"That's for sure." The state medical examiner produced a steady clientele for local funeral directors, who picked up the bodies after the autopsies were completed.

Mac had been in on a number of autopsies now. He remembered his first time, when he and Kevin had attended the Megan Tyson autopsy. That had been a rough one. Not only was Mac a novice detective, but he'd never witnessed an autopsy. The corpse had been about two weeks old and the stench unbearable. Kristen had kindly supplied him with smelling salts. Her teasing and focusing on collecting evidence had saved him a lot of embarrassment.

Only suspicious or unnatural deaths went through the Oregon State Police Medical Examiner's Office. Everything from accidents, to murders, to deaths during surgery was brought here for examination to determine the cause and manner of death.

It still amazed him that Dr. Kristen Thorpe was Oregon's head medical examiner. She managed six other pathologists in addition to several medical assistants and support staff.

Kristen didn't look the part of a medical doctor with her knit tops, jeans, and spiked hair. Mac smiled, remembering their first encounter. He hadn't been able to take his eyes off her. She'd noticed and accused him of flirting with her. He'd gone from being skeptical to having nothing but respect for Kristen. She was one of the few state doctors, let alone a head medical examiner, to make field visits with the detectives. That job was usually left to the deputy medical examiners. Kristen liked to "stay in the game," as she put it.

"Enter, my pretties." A shrill voice came from the office at the end of the hall.

Mac and Dana started down the hall when Kristen poked her head out. Mac rolled his eyes and shook his head. Kristen was about Mac's age, youthful in looks but mature in wisdom and experience, and a kid when it came to goofing off. Henry, her well-past-retirement-age medical assistant, called Kristen an old soul.

"What, don't you like my wicked witch voice?" Kristen stood with her hands on her hips and tried to look insulted.

"Hardly." Mac released a reluctant smile.

"I thought it sounded just like her," Dana teased. "You don't look the part, though. You need some of that green makeup and a bigger nose."

"What? More makeup? I'm calling my mother so you can tell her that. She won't believe it, after all those years of telling me to use less." Kristen's eyes sparkled and Mac got caught in their magic. She noticed and gave him one of her infamous winks.

Embarrassed, he pulled his gaze away. "Did you get to Mullins this morning?" Mac asked.

"What, no bribery? You want to get right to the hard questions? Where's my latte?" Kristen's mouth shifted into a pout.

"You should have asked." Dana lifted her cup. "I can share."

"Thanks." She waved a hand at them. "I don't need one. I was just giving you a hard time. You'll be happy to know that I completed the requested task. Please step into my parlor."

"What's all this character acting stuff?" Mac asked as he ducked into Kristen's office.

"I'm taking acting classes down at PSU. Do you think I'll be discovered?"

"I wouldn't quit my day job if I were you." Mac tried to regain some semblance of composure as he settled into one of the chairs by Kristen's cluttered desk. Not wanting to look at the outrageous M.E., Mac studied the picture of the little boy on her desk. "That your kid?"

Kristen beamed. "Sure is. Can you believe he's in preschool? Smartest four-year-old you'll ever meet. He's already reading and listening to jazz music."

"Takes after his mother." Dana looked over at the picture of the dark-haired boy.

"Except his mother hates jazz. I'm more into hard rock."

"What's his name?" Mac asked.

"Andrew." Kristen admired the photo a moment longer, wiping a thin layer of dust off the frame before placing it back on her desk.

Kristen turned all business then and removed a file from her top left drawer, pulling several loose papers from the manila folder. "Here's the fax I received from our victim's doctor." Kristen handed them over to Dana. "Our guy had several age-related illnesses, including diabetes. He took regular doses of insulin and had it pretty well under control. He was taking medications for high blood pressure and levostatin to lower his cholesterol, which according to the doctor was around 150. His arteries looked okay—some sclerosis, but for a guy his age, he was in pretty good shape."

Kristen looked from one to the other. "I found evidence of needle injections on his upper thighs and on his arms. The preliminary lab work indicates that there were no intoxicants or depressants in the blood, only elevated blood sugar. The state of his blood sugar wasn't high enough to send him into a coma, but it could have disoriented him."

"Which might explain his going out at night," Dana mused.

"If that's the case, we could be looking at an accidental death." Mac shifted his gaze to Kristen's, and for once she didn't seem to notice. "Maybe he was out of insulin and was trying to get some help, like we were thinking last night. How are you going to call this one?"

"I'm not making a ruling yet, Mac. I want to stew on it for a while." Kristen nibbled on the end of her pen.

"Why is that?" Dana asked, taking the file from Mac when he offered it to her.

"Call it a hunch, but I'd like to do a more thorough workup. I can only test for the basics here at the morgue. The blood work will go to the crime lab for analysis. There was no urine sample; the bladder was shredded during the crash with the train. I dissected and weighed almost every major organ though. The brain and heart were in exceptionally good shape for a man of his age. The heart was slightly enlarged, which may indicate some heart disease, but nothing that I would classify as a cause of death. The lungs and liver dissections held nothing remarkable, so he must have stayed away from cigarettes and booze."

"But your instincts are up?" Mac ran a hand through his hair.

"Yeah, they are. I really want to know what got this old guy out of the house that night. I want to know why he couldn't get across those tracks. Might be as simple as the blood sugar, but I need more."

"Good. I do too. When do you expect the blood work from the lab?"

"I sent it out with Henry about an hour ago. I'd expect it back sometime tomorrow, the day after that at the latest."

"Could you call and get a rush on it? Dana and I had a couple of odd experiences at the train terminal today."

"Such as?"

"We had a guy skip out on us," Dana said.

"What guy? That pudgy cop with the comb-over?"

Dana chuckled. "You saw that too?"

Mac cleared his throat. "No, it wasn't Spalding. We had an employee from the terminal who was less than excited to see our victim come rolling into the terminal every day to critique his work."

Turning to Dana he added, "Tell her what you found out."

"I went in to talk to this . . . what did he call it, a hop scotch guy?"

"A mud hop." Mac laughed. "Slang for a dispatcher at the terminal," he said to Kristen.

"I knew what you meant, Dana—hop scotch, mud hop, same thing in my book." Kristen gave Dana her full attention.

"Thank you." Dana told Kristen about the incident in detail then asked, "Is that bizarre behavior or what?"

"Yeah, I'd say so." Kristen frowned. "And highly suspicious. What are you going to do with the guy?"

"He did say he'd talk to us at three so we'll go back then. I'll get really suspicious if he's still AWOL this evening. Who knows what Mason's up to? The thing is, I'm not sure whether to be concerned at this point or not. Mason takes off. The police chief releases the scene . . ."

"What scene?"

"Not the house," Mac assured her. "The railroad car that hit Mullins."

"That jerk!" Kristen pounded her fist on her desk in frustration. "I hope you gave him a piece of your mind."

Mac assured her that he had. "Chief Spalding wants us to close this thing today, but with this Mason guy lurking in the shadows and this bit about the property value, I just don't feel comfortable calling it an accident."

"Hmm. I bet property down by the river doesn't come cheap," Kristen said. "Have you checked out the price of condos on the river by Government Island and Jantzen Beach? Those places are going in the seven figures for thousand-square-foot condos."

"That's nothing for a doctor's salary though," Mac said. "Right?"

"Some doctors. I work for the state, the same as you, *Detective.* I clip my coupons with the best of them. You don't know debt until you've seen medical school tuition. That's why I have to work in this joint, because I can't afford the malpractice insurance."

"Ha," Mac countered. "Who do you think you're kidding? You'd do this job for free. I know you better than that."

Hands on hips, she looked up at the ceiling. "You're probably right. But I have my reasons. This was actually my chosen field."

"You think you'll ever go into private practice?" Dana asked, looking at Kristen's framed certificates on the wall. Her education and merit awards were impressive, to say the least.

"Nah. In case you haven't noticed, I don't exactly have the best bedside manner. Here, my patients could care less. I prefer to deal with my current clientele—they complain less. I may teach someday though."

Dana smiled at the statement and then looked again at the

picture of Kristen's grinning son. "Is Andrew's dad a doctor too?" She paused. "I mean, if it's okay for me to ask."

Mac focused on the floor. On one hand he wished his partner hadn't brought up the subject; on the other, Kristen's marital status interested him.

"It's okay, Dana. I'm cool with it." Kristen glanced at Mac then back to Dana. "Brian—my ex—is long gone. Wasn't ready for fatherhood, I guess. He lives in England now, still trying to find himself. It's just Andrew and me." She chuckled. "I'm free and interviewing for a mate. Know any cute guys?" Kristen tossed a wadded up piece of paper at Mac.

"Dr. Thorpe?" A young intern interrupted the awkward moment, saving Mac from having to answer. The guy's gaze touched on Dana as he leaned over to hand Kristen a note.

"Thank you, Paul." Kristen gave the paper a cursory look, then sat back in her chair and grinned at the two detectives.

"What?" Mac straightened.

"Your job just got a little more interesting. A lawyer named Addison Shaw just called, representing our victim's estate. He needs a copy of the death certificate so he can transfer the deed on Clay's property. Humph. You'd think he could at least wait until the dust settled."

"What are you going to do?" Mac stood up. "I can't say for sure there's no foul play involved here."

"Same here," Kristen said. "I'll hold up on the certificate for now and give you a call when I get my test results back."

"Do you mind if Dana and I grab a few photos and take some samples for our evidence kit?"

"Knock yourself out; he's back in the cooler. I'm going for coffee."

Mac followed the two women out of the office. It really wasn't that uncommon for lawyers or insurance agents to come calling;

even the same day as a death, but Mac felt an odd excitement churning in his stomach. As soon as they were finished here, he'd make a call to Shaw. If nothing else, it would be interesting to get Shaw's take on things.

NINE

Mac followed Dana down the hall to the large walk-in freezer where they would gather their evidence. The old man's remains, which had been cleaned by Henry and Kristen during the autopsy, lay in a rubber-coated body bag with only the head exposed.

Today Clay Mullins's expression was placid, eyes closed in a peaceful slumber. Peaceful, that is, until Mac unzipped the bag down below the neckline. Then he was reminded all too clearly of the carnage resulting from the collision with the train.

Dana photographed the remains while Mac placed hair samples in small manila envelopes. He then swabbed the inside of Clay's mouth with a cotton evidence swab to collect a saliva cell sample from the gums, which, coupled with the hair, would serve as their DNA standard for the victim after the body was disposed of.

Although there seemed to be no present need for DNA comparison, Mac preferred to err on the side of caution. His former partner tended to collect all possible evidence while they had the chance.

You don't want to find out that you need DNA after the body has been buried or cremated, Kevin would say.

"That should do it," Mac said. "Anything else we should get samples of before we cut him loose?"

"Should we get some nail clippings?" Dana asked. "Like Kevin had you do on that sawmill victim out in Estacada?"

"Good call. Kevin would skin me if I released this guy to the funeral home without taking some fingernails." Mac tried to hide his embarrassment as he clipped the old man's nails, placing the trimmings in a small envelope.

Evidence found under fingernails often proved to be the nail in the coffin for suspects. Victims of violent attacks often fought back, scratching their attackers. The cells left under the nails provided the DNA and the evidence needed to put the bad guys away. And Mac had forgotten to do it, proving he wasn't anywhere near qualified to be working with a new detective.

"That should do it." Dana sighed and stepped away from the gurney. "I can't think of anything else."

"All right." Mac pulled off his gloves and tossed them in a nearby trash can. "Let's head back to the office and check in with Sergeant Evans. Kevin is supposed to be back in the office this afternoon, and I'd like to see him."

"Great." Dana grabbed the jacket she'd hung on a hook near the door. "Maybe he'll be able to offer some advice."

"He'll be glad to see you. And I can guarantee he'll have all kinds of questions for you. I'm sorry you got stuck with me for a trainer; you really got shortchanged by not having Kevin as a mentor. He's the best."

The dimples in Dana's cheeks deepened in a wide smile. She pushed against Mac's shoulder as they walked out of the freezer.

"Don't sell yourself short, Detective McAllister. I think I'm making out okay."

They walked back to Mac's car and tossed the camera and Mac's evidence briefcase back in the trunk. Kristen sped into the parking lot in her personal car—a two-door silver Volvo—and whipped into her assigned parking spot. In a fluid movement she exited the truck and locked it with her remote. She lifted her right hand in a wave before jogging into the office, all without spilling a drop of her steaming coffee.

Dana watched her until the door closed. "Kristen surprises me sometimes."

"You can say that again."

"She impressed me as being a really good mom."

Mac shrugged. "I wouldn't know."

"You can tell. Didn't you notice that look in her eyes when she talked about Andrew?"

"Um—sure." Mac hadn't. Maybe because he'd had a hard time making eye contact.

Returning to their office in southeast Portland, Mac punched the gate code into the keypad to enter the back lot, then pulled through the gate when it finally opened enough for him to slip the car through. "Is it my imagination or is this gate getting slower?"

"Same as it's always been," Dana said. "I think you're just getting more impatient."

Mac grunted in response, not especially wanting to hear about his shortcomings. He parked, and the two of them went in through the office's south entry.

Mac veered toward the men's room. "I have to use the john. See you in the office."

While washing his hands, Mac noticed a large man with a wide girth standing at the mirror and rubbing a hand over his bald head.

A thick finger on his right hand sported a familiar horseshoe-shaped silver ring. Mac's jaw dropped as he realized who it was.

"You got a problem?" He turned to face Mac.

"Philly?"

"Do you think this hairstyle—or lack of it—makes me look fat?" Philly eyed himself in the mirror again, his lines and wrinkles more pronounced than ever.

"What? Why? Your hair. I didn't even recognize you from behind."

"What were you doing looking at my rear?" Philly's face split in a wide smile. He turned back to look in the mirror once again. "Look how white my scalp is. It hasn't seen the light of day since I was in basic training. Think I should use some of that tanning stuff?"

Mac stifled a laugh. "How should I know? I've never been bald." Mac examined Philly's bleached-white scalp, which sported a couple of scars and number of tiny red dots, the latter undoubtedly caused by the electric shaver's close trim. Still unable to believe Philly's new 'do, Mac reached out to touch the top of the detective's shiny scalp.

Philly ducked. "Hey, hey, hey. Don't touch the merchandise, pal. You can look, but don't touch."

"What's this all about, Phil? Did you do that Crop a Cop fundraiser for the children's hospital?"

"Nah. It's a charity case all right, but not as good a cause as the one for those kids. I shaved off my locks for that rotten old partner of yours."

"You shaved your head for Kevin?" Mac pulled a paper towel from the dispenser. Then understanding finally sank in. "Oh, I get it. The chemo. I'm impressed, Philly. That was a nice thing to do."

"You think? I did it this afternoon. Now I wonder if I should have. Russ and I have to go down to Coffee Creek Correctional in Wilsonville. They got a stiff down there we need to take a look at."

"So?"

"I look like a Q-ball. Those female cons aren't going to say a word to me now that I've lost my hair. That's what gave me my charm."

"I think you'll fare okay. Some women find bald men sexy." Mac tossed the paper towel in the garbage can.

"You got a point, kid."

"Is Kevin here?" Mac asked.

"Yeah, he's in his office." Philly eyed himself in the mirror again.

"Has he seen it yet?"

"What? Oh, yeah." He sighed. "I picked him up from the clinic today."

"Right. I remember. I'm going in to talk to Kev. See ya." Mac hurried out of the bathroom and into the detective's office.

Dana was in with Sergeant Evans, probably briefing him on their case. Kevin's door was open so Mac stepped inside, giving the doorframe a couple of knocks. "Hey, Kev. Got a minute?"

Kevin had been staring at his computer screen, his muscular frame bent over his desk as he sat too close to the monitor. His bald head looked smoother than Philly's.

"Mac. Good to see you, buddy. Come on in and sit down." Except for the hair loss, Kevin didn't look much different than before he'd started the chemo. He'd lost some weight, and his face seemed thinner and pale.

"How are you feeling?" Mac sat down in the chair opposite Kevin's desk.

"Been better. They got some great medications these days. The chemo's rough, but the doc gave me some stuff that controls the nausea. I'm weak and some days I can hardly get out of bed, but I'll lick this thing. You wait and see."

"I have no doubt," Mac said, not feeling nearly as positive as Kevin sounded. He admired his partner's attitude. Though he was working light duty, primarily case management and evidence disposition for Sergeant Evans, Kevin still wore a jacket and tie whenever he came in—just as he had done for more than two decades.

Mac smiled. "Don't tell him I said so, but you still look a darn sight better than Philly does."

Kevin chuckled and leaned back in his chair. "That was quite the gesture, wasn't it? He looks kinda goofy, but I'll tell you, Mac, he sure pulled on these old heartstrings when he picked me up after my treatment today."

Mac nodded and felt his throat tighten. He needed to change the subject. "Philly said he and Russ are heading down to Coffee Creek prison on a death. What's that all about?"

"Female inmate at the prison hanged herself. Looks like a suicide, but you know how those things go. She had some things in her cell that she shouldn't have had access to, like the wire hanger she used to do herself in."

"Did she have a cellmate, or was she in solitary?"

"Don't know; just heard Russ get the ticket from Sergeant Evans when Philly and I walked in the door. I wasn't feeling that great, so I didn't stand in on the details. I'm sure they'll be happy to share."

Mac picked a piece of lint from his slacks, wanting to leave, but not wanting to.

"How are you and Dana getting along on that Columbia County death?" Kevin asked. "Any red flags?"

"Several actually, and we really haven't gotten a lot of answers as yet."

"How so?" Kevin sat forward and put on his glasses as if he had to visualize Mac's explanation to render an opinion. Mac missed that look. He missed being with his partner as they were just getting preliminary details on a new case.

Kevin listened intently while Mac outlined what he and Dana had learned so far. "Where are you going from here?"

"To be honest, I'm not sure." Mac already felt like they were being pulled in too many directions.

"If you don't mind my making a suggestion, Mac, I'm thinking you need to search the house as soon as possible, and talk to the daughter. That's how I'd proceed. I agree with you though—it's too soon to close the book on it."

"I'll call the daughter now and set up an appointment. She lives in Tualatin. The D.A. says she's a lawyer and her husband is a doctor up at OHSU."

"Lawyer, huh?" Kevin raised an eyebrow, his face breaking into that familiar grin.

"Yeah, but I'll try not to hold that against her." Mac smiled back and stood. "Much as I'd like to sit here and shoot the breeze, I gotta get back to work."

"Wish I were out there with you guys." Kevin took his glasses off and set them on the desk. "You'll be happy to know I'm there in spirit though. Praying for you."

I'm praying for you too. Mac couldn't bring himself to say the words and rolled his eyes instead. "Don't know why you bother. I'm a hopeless case."

"I know, but God isn't giving up, so I can't either."

Mac swallowed back the lump in his throat. He wanted his partner back. He wanted Kevin working on this case with him. "See ya." Mac waved and stepped out of the office.

"Watch it, kingfish." Russ put out a hand to keep Mac from running him down.

"Sorry." Mac mumbled the apology. "I was thinking about something."

"You okay?" Russ glanced into Kevin's office then back to Mac. Russ Meyers had been partnered with Philly since well before Mac joined the team. Russ had known Kevin longer than Mac, and he shared the same respect for the man. Kevin's illness had hit them all pretty hard.

"Yeah, doing great." Mac glanced back at his former partner's office. He wasn't ready to talk about his feelings, and judging from the look on Russ's face, Russ wasn't either.

"You girls going to dance out in the hall all day, or can we get going now?" Philly's wisecrack dissolved the awkward moment.

"Let's go, baldy. I'm ready," Russ told his partner. "You're the one who's been in the bathroom primping all morning." Russ poked Mac with his elbow and winked. Russell Meyers was only about five years older than Mac, but he'd been a detective for four years. He had been Philly's partner since he made detective, after proving himself in the patrol division and department SWAT team.

Sergeant Evans stepped out of his office and handed Philly a yellow Post-it with a name and number written on it. "Your contact at the prison will be Captain Warner. Give me an update when you get down there. I need to know if this is going to tie you up all week. I may have to put a detective team from Salem on standby if all four of you are working active deaths."

"Salem?" Philly shook his head. "Those guys from the puzzle palace couldn't investigate their way out of a paper bag."

Sergeant Frank Evans folded his arms and looked as if he were about to embark on a stern lecture. Instead he lifted his hands in the air, probably realizing that no amount of talk could change Philly. Frank shook his head and went back into his office, slamming the door behind him.

"Poor guy," Philly said.

"What do you mean, 'poor guy'?" Russ frowned. "You're the one who's driving him nuts."

"Naw." Philly pursed his lips. "He isn't mad at me. He's frustrated at the staffing situation in the detective office. That's why he's been so gruff lately."

That was probably true. Less than two years ago Sergeant Evans had supervised four separate teams of experienced homicide investigators. Now, thanks to budget cuts that left retirement and transfers unfilled, he was down to two. The "back room," as detectives called their office, was located in the primarily uniformed office and was down nearly a dozen positions in person crimes and dope investigators.

"To make things worse," Philly went on, "old Sarge is doing two jobs. Brass gave him a second detective section, so he's having to supervise the sex abuse detectives as well as the five of us."

Mac hadn't heard about that. "No wonder his feathers are ruffled. 'Poor guy' is right." Mac glanced at the door. "Good thing Sarge has Kevin around to pick up some of the slack."

"You guys having a party and didn't invite me?" Dana walked up to them, a cup of coffee in her hand.

"No time to party now." Russ raised his eyebrows and grinned at her. "But you'll be the first to know if and when we do."

"Be still my heart," Dana teased. "Mac, we need to talk."

"Oooh . . ." Russ glanced back at them. "Sounds serious."

Dana ignored the innuendo, her gaze shooting to Philly's bald head.

"Don't ask. It was a moment of weakness," Philly mumbled.

"Looks good, Phil. Some girls dig bald guys." Dana took a sip of her coffee.

"Sorry, Dana, but I'm a married man. I'll have to ask you to keep our relationship purely professional." Philly made a note on the grease board indicating that he and Russ were checking out.

Russ let loose with a gut-splitting guffaw.

"I said *some* girls like bald guys, Philly. Not this girl." Dana's cheeks flushed as she laughed along with Russ.

Not to be outdone, especially by a rookie, Philly patted her shoulder. "You're only human, Dana. Now just hush. You'll only make it worse." He and Russ left before she could get in another dig.

"Arrgh." Dana tipped her head back. "How do you put up with him?"

"He may be a clown, but he's one of the best detectives around."

"So I hear." She headed toward Mac's cubicle. "Like I was saying—we need to talk."

"I noticed you in with Sarge earlier."

"Yeah. He says we need to hustle on this, Mac. He's not too excited to have us working on the Mullins case any longer than we have to."

"You told him about our findings?"

"Yep. He wants us to follow up, but he says not to let it keep dragging on just because we don't feel right about it."

"In other words, he wants hard evidence yesterday."

"That's about it. I got the old budget-cut lecture and had to hear about his caseload and how he's doing the work of three men."

"Three? I knew he was running homicide and sex abuse . . ."

"Yeah, well, now the powers that be have forced Frank into supervising a three-person arson investigative section in addition to a half-dozen narcotics cops that were assigned all over the city to state and federal task forces. The narcs are only temporary while their sergeant is on vacation for a couple of weeks, but c'mon, how much can one guy do?"

"That's brutal." Mac's chair squeaked as he eased into it. "No wonder he's been so short-tempered lately."

"Tell me about it." She leaned against his desk and examined a nail. "I understand where he's coming from, but bottom line is we need to get moving."

"Right. First thing I'd like to do is talk to the daughter."

"I thought you might." Dana flashed him a sly grin. "Which is why I called her while you were talking to Kevin."

"When did you get so efficient?" He shouldn't have been annoyed, but he was. "You talked to her?"

"Yep, Kelly Mullins-Cassidy is at home and has consented to an interview. I told her we'd be right over." She moved away from his desk. "That's okay, isn't it?"

"It's fine. More than fine. Thanks."

Dana nodded. "Something odd though."

"What's that?"

"She wanted to know if she should call her lawyer before talking to us."

Mac shrugged. "Not so odd when you consider that she's an attorney."

"I suppose, but it almost makes me wonder if she's hiding something. When I asked if she was Clay Mullins's daughter, she thought I was a real-estate agent. With her father's death she stands to inherit his property. I'm thinking we'll need to take a really close look at her."

Mac shrugged. "I think you're absolutely right. Let's do it."

TEN

"Do you know where you're going?" Mac slid into the driver's side of his Crown Victoria.

"Of course." Dana settled into the passenger seat and pulled a folder out of her briefcase. "I looked up the address online and got directions."

My, aren't we efficient. Mac kept the comment to himself. He was being unreasonable, feeling something akin to jealousy and resentment just because she was doing her job. *And maybe doing it better than you are.* "Good, then you won't mind navigating." Despite his annoyance, he managed to keep his tone light.

Kevin had always praised Mac for acting on his own. Dana didn't need much direction—she seemed to know when something needed doing and did it. And that was a good thing. Mac merged onto southbound I-205 from Foster Road in southeast Portland while Dana studied the printout.

"Looks like they live in that new Copper Mountain development.

We should take I-5 north to Nyberg exit and head up toward Sherwood."

"Nice area."

"Are we still going to hit Mullins's house with a warrant today?" Dana asked.

"Hopefully. We need to make it out to Columbia County by the end of business hours. All we need is a call from Kristen to wrap up our warrant. We need to get out there by six at the latest if we want to catch a judge." He adjusted the visor and slipped on his sunglasses to minimize the glare. The patches of blue were getting larger as the day went on. "I was just thinking, maybe we should call Mason—see if he's surfaced yet." He glanced at his watch. One-thirty. Time was getting away from them.

Dana nodded and pulled her cell phone out of the pocket of her black wool jacket. A colorful scarf that she'd tied around her neck made the black pantsuit and white blouse less severe. Mac wondered if it had been Jan's influence. "That scarf looks good on you. Were you wearing it this morning?"

"Thank you." She tossed him a smile. "No, I'd brought it with me to work but didn't put it on. I wasn't sure if our dress code allowed it. Jan assured me it did, so I decided to wear it this afternoon."

Mac nodded.

Before making the call, Dana pulled out a notepad then closed the briefcase and set it on the floor behind her seat. After flipping back several pages, she paused and punched in Mason's number. Moments later she glanced at Mac. "Voice mail." After the beep, she said, "Mr. Mason, this is Detective Bennett with the Oregon State Police. Just wanted to remind you of our appointment this afternoon at three."

She sighed and dropped her cell back into her pocket. "Think he'll be there?"

"I wouldn't hold my breath." Mac rubbed the back of his neck, trying to ease an especially tense and painful muscle.

Fifteen minutes later, they pulled up in front of a three-story home that was built into a treed hillside in an upscale neighborhood. Mac recognized it as one of the homes that had been in the Street of Elegant Homes a few years before. The first and only time he'd gone. The homes had been elegant all right, but extravagant and way over his budget. This and other homes like it went for around three-quarters of a million or more. "If you don't mind, I'll take the lead on the interview," Mac said.

"Sure."

Kelly Cassidy greeted them at the door wearing a fashionable version of pale pink sweats. Mac couldn't identify the material, but it looked like she'd paid a chunk of change for it. "Mrs. Cassidy?"

"Kelly." Her gaze drifted from Mac to Dana. "You must be Detective Bennett."

"Right." Dana extended her hand. "This is my partner, Detective McAllister."

She stepped back allowing them access to the spacious entry. To their right was a large waterfall area. Mac remembered the feature from his tour. Water rushed over the rocks inside, forming a pool, then escaped through a short pipe in the wall and continued its journey outside. "This is amazing." Dana's eyes sparkled as her gaze followed the course of the water.

Kelly smiled like a parent indulging a wonder-filled child. "Thank you. We enjoy it. The house was built over a waterfall. The water actually runs from a cascade behind the house and . . . well, let me show you."

She led them on a short tour through the entry and into an open kitchen and great room. "The stream runs along here under this acrylic flooring." She pointed to a strip of clear floor that connected seamlessly to the natural-looking tile.

"I've never seen anything like it." Dana seemed to have forgotten their mission. "You even have fish swimming in there."

"The architect created some artistic curves, but otherwise it's a natural spring." She spoke in a dull tone—as if she'd repeated it numerous times, which she probably had.

"Wow. It's beautiful."

Mac cleared his throat. "Um—we should probably get on with our interview, Dana. No sense in taking up too much of Kelly's time."

"Oh, right. I'm sorry. It's just that you have so many beautiful things." Dana's gaze flitted to a bronze statue of a mermaid and a porpoise swimming, spiraling down. "That's a Jerry Joslin bronze, isn't it?" Dana sighed. "I would love to have one of his pieces. Someday, maybe." Her smile faded. "I'm sorry, Kelly. Mac is right. We shouldn't be gouging into your time with my curiosity."

"I'm used to it." In a graceful motion she waved her hand toward the sofa, loveseat, and chair to the left away from the kitchen. "Have a seat. Can I get you anything? Tea, coffee, water, a soda?"

"Water would be great," Dana said as she made her way to the sofa.

"Coffee for me." Mac's stomach was growling. He realized he'd had nothing substantial to eat since lunch.

When she'd served them and they were all seated, Mac began. "First of all, Kelly, we'd like to express our sorrow at the loss of your father."

She pinched her lips together. "Thank you. I'm still in shock, really. I can't imagine him not being in that old house of his, tooling around in his scooter. It was top of the line. We bought it for him a couple of years ago when his legs got so bad." She clenched her hands on her lap and closed her eyes for a moment. When she opened them there were tears. "They told me he was hit by a train. I can't imagine how that could have happened. And being out in the evening? He just didn't do that. He had a routine and never wavered from it. He'd have dinner at six, eating it on a tray in front of the television set watching the news. Then he'd do the dishes and settle in to watch the evening shows. At nine sharp, he'd get ready for bed . . ." Her words drifted off.

"Do you have any idea why he might have gone out?" Mac asked.

"No. The police officer said he might have been sick and trying to go for help, but that doesn't make sense. He had a phone. I guess it was an accident, but . . ." Her gaze met Mac's. "If it was an accident, why are you here? You people don't come in unless there are questions. Do you think someone killed him? I wondered why the medical examiner is withholding the release of the death certificate. It's starting to make a little more sense with your visit."

"The delay in the release of the death certificate is routine," Mac said. "I can assure you of that. Without extensive testing, the medical examiner won't be able to certify the cause of death."

Kelly arched her eyebrows. "Plus, you want to hold off for a while and see who makes requests on the certificate so you can determine who might benefit from his death?"

Mac gave no reply.

"I'm sorry. I didn't mean to make you feel uncomfortable."

Unfazed, Mac continued. "Do you know of anyone who might benefit from your father's death?"

She sighed. "Unfortunately, yes. My father was worth a lot of money—probably in the millions. As his daughter, I would inherit something, I suppose. Though we really don't need the money. Dad probably left something to my brother, but he's been estranged from the family for years."

"Do you have any idea where we might find your brother?"

She wrapped her hands around one knee and looked at a spot on the rug. "Jacob isn't good about keeping in touch. Unfortunately, he's been in and out of trouble since he was a teenager. Not serious stuff. I think the worst was a drunk driving charge a few years ago."

Mac jotted the information down. "If he's in the system, we may be able to track him."

"He and Dad had their differences, but Jacob isn't a killer. I can't imagine him ever hurting Dad."

"Can you think of anyone who might?"

Kelly paused for a moment. "Well, there's a real-estate developer who's been trying to buy the land. Dad refused to sell, and the developer actually came here and tried to talk me into having Dad declared incompetent so we could sell the land to her. She offered to pay us a premium."

Dana raised her eyebrows but didn't comment.

"And what was your reaction?" Mac asked.

"We were appalled. Ray and I threatened to file a complaint against her, and we basically kicked her out. I couldn't believe it. Makes me wonder how far people will go to get what they want."

"Can you give me her name?"

"Gladly." She went into the kitchen and pulled open a drawer. After rummaging around, she produced a card. "Here you go. Reagan McCloud."

"You kept her card? I'm surprised you didn't toss it." Mac slipped it into his jacket pocket.

Kelly looked at Mac a moment before finally saying, "I don't know—maybe I was thinking I'd better hang on to it in case there was a problem."

He nodded and glanced at Dana, who seemed a world away.

"Not everyone liked my father, Detective. He was always good to me, but he and my brother were like two pit bulls, always fighting. Of course, Jacob could be a handful. He was born rebellious. Not that he'd do anything to hurt Dad. Like I said before, Jacob would never hurt anyone. You've probably already heard about the guys down at the terminal. Dad was always going on about how the new guys weren't doing the job right—especially Dan Mason. I'm surprised the guy is still working there."

"We're planning to talk with Mr. Mason later today."

"Good." She rubbed her hands together as if they were cold. "You should talk to Rita too. She is—she was Dad's housekeeper. I wonder if anyone has told her about Dad."

"Housekeeper? Does she work every day?" Mac hoped the police were still maintaining the integrity of the house.

"Um—twice a week, I think."

"Do you have Rita's last name?"

She rubbed her forehead. "It was Hispanic, um—Gonzales, I think. Rita is a very nice lady. She's been working for Dad for ten years now."

"All right. Thanks. Shouldn't be too hard to locate her."

Kelly glanced at her watch. "I really should be getting back to work."

"Before you go, we'd like to get your consent to search your father's house. We're hoping that will help shed some light on what happened to him."

"Of course." She hesitated. "Well, on second thought, I think I'll hold up on that."

"We can get a warrant," Mac told her.

"I know. It's just that . . . I don't want to be too hasty. I need a chance to think."

"I understand."

"Was there anything else?" she asked.

"Not really," Mac said. "At this point we're just doing a preliminary investigation and waiting on the autopsy report."

"Oh, right." Kelly frowned. "I should call and make arrangements with the funeral home. I'm not thinking clearly."

"Have you been in touch with your father's lawyer?"

"You mean Addison Shaw?" She sneered. "Humph. That guy is a joke. A few years ago, I offered to take care of Dad's legal affairs, but Dad wasn't comfortable with that. He felt his legal affairs should be separate from family. He's right, I suppose, but the guy he hired is a shyster if I've ever seen one."

"In what way?" Mac asked.

"Oh, nothing specific. He just reminds me of a snake." She bit her lip. "I shouldn't be saying that. The poor man is probably just trying to make a living. I'm most likely being paranoid. But you know how it is—some people you trust, and some you just don't. I only met him once, so it's not really fair of me to be so negative."

"We'll talk with him as well." He turned to Dana. "Can you think of anything else?"

"Not right now. We may be calling you later though." Dana stood when Mac did.

"I'm not going anywhere," Kelly assured the detectives. "If you'll hold on a minute, I'll give you my card. It has my office and cell phone, as well as my home number."

Kelly went into another room and came out with a card for each of them. "Let me know if there is anything I can do. I'm glad you're looking into Dad's death. He was an old man and it could have been an accident, but . . ."

"There are enough circumstances to make us take a closer look," Mac finished.

"Exactly."

Dana paused on the way out. "There is one thing, Kelly. We may want to interview your husband as well."

"Ray?" She seemed genuinely surprised. "I'm sure he wouldn't mind. Though he's extremely busy." She frowned. "If you're thinking Ray had anything to do with my father's death, you can forget it. For one thing, he has back-to-back medical conferences out of town. He's been in Philadelphia this past week and just got home last night."

"When is the best time to call him?"

"There really isn't a good time. I'd suggest you call his cell and leave a message." She slipped back inside and came out with a number written on the back of his professional card. *Raymond Cassidy, M.D. Internal Medicine, Oregon Health Sciences University.* "I'll let him know you want to talk to him."

"Thanks." Mac slipped the card in his pocket. "Appreciate your cooperation."

"WHAT'S YOUR TAKE ON HER?" Dana asked Mac as they headed back to the office.

Mac shrugged. "She seemed down to earth, nice for a lawyer."

"A little too nice, if you ask me." Dana chewed on the inside of her cheek. "She's hiding something, Mac."

"And you know this because . . ."

"Intuition." Dana tossed him a knowing grin. "Plain old intuition. That and the fact that she didn't want to okay us searching her father's house."

"I'm sure Sergeant Evans will be thrilled to hear about your *feelings* on the matter."

"Well, I just hope that if this is more than an accident, we come up with something soon."

Mac agreed. He hoped the hard, fast evidence would show up before they were forced to drop the case.

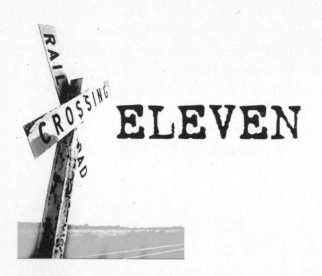

ELEVEN

WE NEED TO GET HOLD OF JACOB MULLINS and see what he's been up to the past few days." Mac's pager vibrated and he pulled it off his belt. Checking the digital readout, he said, "It's the medical examiner's office. Would you mind calling so I don't run us off the road?"

"Sure." Dana pulled her phone from her purse and punched in the number to Kristen's office. While Mac mumbled about the potholes in the road, Dana pulled a notepad and pen from her briefcase. He could drive and talk just fine, regardless of the road conditions. He just didn't want to talk to Kristen.

"This is Detective Bennett with OSP. May I speak with Dr. Thorpe? I'm calling about the Mullins case."

"Hey, Dana," Kristen answered moments later. "Thanks for getting back to me so soon."

"Just call us rough and ready." Dana glanced at Mac, who seemed a little too intent on maneuvering the car. "What's up?"

"Nothing much, just some preliminary lab results on Mr. Mullins's toxicology screen. No unlawful drugs on board, just some prescription meds. We expected those from his doctor's fax."

"So you're ruling his death accidental?" Dana chewed her lower lip, disappointed that her intuition might not be correct.

"Not yet. The initial blood work indicates some liver damage. I won't know the extent of that without more tests. There's something else bothering me too."

"Oh yeah?"

Dana held a hand up at Mac's questioning look, indicating she'd tell him later.

"I'm concerned about the tissue around the injection sites for his insulin shots. The flesh around some of the needle marks have decayed to a degree that's accelerated far beyond what I'd expect for postmortem decay."

"No kidding. What would cause something like that?"

"I'm not sure. I'm not overly concerned about it yet, but I want to run a few more tests before I give old Clay a clean bill of health."

Dana chuckled at the phrase. "I'll let Mac know."

"You do that." She hesitated. "Dana, I was wondering . . . are you and Mac—you know, dating or anything?"

"No." Dana's tone came off sharper than she intended. "Why do you ask?" The question irritated her. Part of her wanted Mac to find someone, but part of her liked him too much to give him up completely. Which was totally selfish. She'd made a decision to keep her relationship with Mac strictly business, and she would stick to it. She had no business being jealous.

"I've been thinking about asking him out. Do you think he'd go?"

Dana shrugged. "Maybe. The best way to find out is to ask."

"Humph. You're no help at all."

Dana could almost see Kristen pouting, and the picture put her in a teasing mode. The conversation seemed out of character for the unflappable Dr. Thorpe. "Want me to ask him for you?"

"Actually, that would be great. Would you?"

"Sure, hang on a minute." Dana covered the mouthpiece and glanced over at Mac. "Kristen wants to know if you'll have dinner with her tonight."

"What?" Gravel crunched under the tires as Mac drifted off the road. He pulled the steering wheel to the left, moving deftly back onto the asphalt.

Dana smiled, enjoying his discomfort. Speaking into the phone again, she said, "He'll be happy to."

Mac gave her a look that could melt the ice off a glacier.

"Really? Wow. Great. I honestly didn't think it would be that easy."

Dana wished she could take back her flippant response. What if Mac broke the date? She didn't want Kristen to get hurt. She'd just have to make certain Mac went. "Don't worry about it."

"Right." Kristen cleared her throat. "Look, I need to get back to work. Tell Mac to be at my house at seven or so. If he'll call before he comes, I'll give him directions."

"Will do. Keep us posted on Mr. Mullins."

Mac's lips had tightened, as had his grip on the steering wheel.

Dana blew out a long breath. "Come on, Mac," she said, hoping to soothe things over. "I know you've been wanting to go out with Kristen. I just hurried things along a little. You're supposed to be at her house at seven. She said for you to call before you come and she'll give you directions."

"I don't need a dating service," he growled.

"I'm sorry. I just got caught up in the moment."

"I should make you call her back and cancel."

"But you won't. Come on, partner." Dana's rosy cheeks dimpled.

"You like her and you know it. You don't want to hurt her feelings any more than I do."

Mac shook his head. "Okay, I'll go, but don't set me up with anyone else. It's definitely not in your job description, and I definitely don't want it to be."

"Duly noted." Dana glanced at her notes, barely hiding her amusement.

"Did Doc Thorpe have anything earth-shattering to say about Mullins?" Mac asked, wanting to bridge the uncomfortable space. He wasn't sure how he felt about seeing Kristen outside of work. In a way the prospect appealed to him. Trouble was, the woman intimidated him. She was not only eccentric, but she was smart—actually, brilliant, according to Kevin. Mac dismissed his discomfort and focused on Dana's report.

Dana went over Kristen's concerns. "She's not ready to give us a cause of death. Says she wants to run a few more tests at the crime lab before she gives the guy a clean bill of health."

Mac raised a brow at the comment.

"Her words, not mine." Dana grinned.

"Good. That buys us more time. I really want to get into that house. Especially with what we've learned about Clay."

"Too bad we couldn't get consent from Clay's daughter to search the house. Wouldn't that have saved us some time?"

"Not necessarily. Legally, the house isn't hers. And we have no idea whether or not Mullins left the house to her. We still have a sibling out there who's undoubtedly going to start making claims, and there may be others hiding in the bushes. There may also be property at the home that doesn't belong to Mullins or his family— the maid, for instance, may have items there."

"Great. There's nothing like a lot of loose threads. How about I work on the missing son while we're driving? I'll call the Salem office and see if we can't get a phone number and address."

"Go for it." Now that the road had evened out, Mac took out his phone and dialed the D.A.'s office in St. Helens. "Anything new going on out there I should know about?"

"Not a thing," Volk responded. "I'm still working on finding a judge to sign the warrant, but there's only one judge in today and he's got a full caseload this afternoon. I should be able to talk to him around four."

"Maybe we'll have something from the medical examiner's office by then."

A search warrant affidavit generally took about as much time as typing a couple of chapters in a book. Every fact had to be accurate or the warrant would be worthless even when signed. The affidavit must include the type of incident being investigated, a full description of the house—down to the color, numbers on the door and legal owners, what the searchers expect to find in the house, and the medical examiner's cause of death. In most death investigations, this process takes ten hours to a full day while the scene is held.

Mac spent the next few minutes grumbling about their complex legal system. Seemed like detectives and uniforms alike were always having to jump through legal hoops and wait for the proper paperwork before they could do anything. Unfortunately, if they didn't have all their ducks in a row, the case could get thrown out of court.

"Got it." Dana broke through Mac's reverie.

"What?" It took him a second to figure out what she was talking about. "Oh, you mean Jacob's info."

"He's working at an insurance brokerage firm over in the Lloyd Center area. Lives in an apartment off southeast 182nd in Gresham. Want to head over there?"

"He's in the opposite direction, and we still need to go back out to St. Helens." He glanced at his watch: two-thirty. He really wanted to eat, but they needed to get out to St. Helens if they expected to meet up with Mason by three o'clock.

"Give Jacob a call and set up a meet time. Say tomorrow morning unless you think he's going to go sideways on us. I want to leave plenty of time to talk to Mason and take a look at Clay's house."

"Tomorrow it is."

Mac tossed her a forgiving grin. Somewhere between the Copper Mountain housing development and the bridge, he'd softened a bit and was actually looking forward to getting to know the quirky medical examiner better.

"Yes, I'm calling for Jacob Mullins." Dana cupped the phone. "He's there," she whispered.

"Hello, Jacob?" She poised her pen and flipped to a fresh page on her notepad. "Mr. Mullins, this is Detective Dana Bennett with the State Police. My partner and I are assigned to investigate your father's death."

Mac could hear the male voice on the other end of the line but couldn't make out what he was saying.

"Yes, sir, I understand that. But we just learned how to get hold of you. To be honest, Mr. Mullins, we are not quite ready to release the death certificate. The case is still under investigation."

Dana rolled her eyes at Mac. "Yes, sir. We're working on that right now, but we can't let you into the house or release the death certificate until we have completed the investigation. We plan to search your father's home later today and conduct some interviews. We'd like to include you in the interview process."

The other voice went on for some time, and from the loudness of it, Mac figured Jacob Mullins wasn't thrilled with the request.

"I understand." Dana's soothing voice seemed to have no effect on the man. "And to answer your question, we need to ensure that your father's death was accidental. When someone dies under unusual circumstances, an autopsy must be performed." She hesitated again. "I'm sorry you feel that way, but you're not really in a position to keep us out of your father's home. And the medical examiner calls the shots on the autopsy. We're in the process of getting a search warrant . . . Hello? Mr. Mullins, are you there?"

Dana snapped her phone shut and frowned. "That creep hung up on me. Can you believe it?"

"Maybe we should have made a cold call to his home. I'd like to have studied him."

"Yeah, but I didn't think he'd be so uncooperative."

"So, what did he have to say?" Mac thrummed his fingers on the steering wheel.

"He was mad about the autopsy. He wanted to know why we had to search the house. He asked if his sister had been in the house and said he wanted to go through it before we did. He threatened to sic his lawyer on us and hung up."

"Interesting. Wonder if there's something in the place he doesn't want us to see."

She nodded. "Could be. He might just be a control freak—you know, the kind who wants a say in everything."

"Why don't you phone his horsepower into dispatch and see what they can turn up on his criminal history?"

"I did that when I called in to get his address and phone number. He had a few traffic tickets and that DUII his sister told us about, but nothing that ever landed him in handcuffs. Not according to the FBI data, anyway. Sounds like he's pretty clean."

"I wonder what his story is."

"Who knows? Maybe he's just upset about his dad. It's tough to lose a parent—even if you didn't get along with him."

"If you say so." Mac ignored the gnawing in his own gut—passing it off as hunger pangs. His father didn't deserve a second thought or even a first. Jamie McAllister had been a poor excuse for a cop and an even poorer excuse for a father.

Mac shoved the annoying thoughts away. "It's after two-thirty. Why don't you try Mason again?"

"Good idea." Dana tried Mason's cell phone again, getting the same voice mail she got earlier. She left Mason another message, this time leaving her pager number and the phone number to her dispatch center.

They drove the rest of the way to St. Helens in relative silence. Dana's cell rang as they approached the small town.

"What can I do for you, Kevin?" she answered. "Do you need our expert assistance, or are you just checking up on us?"

Kevin laughed. "Neither. I just wanted to know how the investigation was going."

Dana filled him in on what they had so far. "We're concerned about Clay's son—the guy has an attitude and could cause some trouble for us."

"Want me to have one of the troops bring him in for a little questioning?"

"Not yet. We don't have anything on him except bad manners— last I heard, that wasn't a crime."

"Too true."

"Did you want to talk to Mac?"

"Yeah. Put him on." Dana handed off the phone.

"Hey, partner," Mac greeted. "What's up?"

"How's Dana doing, Mac? Are you two getting along okay?"

"Sure. She's doing great, in fact."

"I feel bad that I can't spend more time with her. Not that I don't trust you to do a great job, but . . ."

"I know. I'm the new kid on the block too. Don't worry—if we hit any snags, we'll give you a call."

"I know. Wanted to remind you that I'm here for you. For both of you. So are Philly and Frank."

"I appreciate the reassurance. We'll keep you and Sarge posted."

Mac folded the phone and handed it back to Dana.

Dana caught his gaze. "Did I do something wrong?"

"No. Why would you think that?"

"You were obviously discussing me."

Mac tossed her a crooked grin. "Kevin just told me I'd better treat you right or he'd break my arm."

"Right." Dana's dimples deepened. "I'm serious."

"You're doing fine, Dana. Kevin would be the first one to tell you if you weren't. For that matter, so would I."

Once at the terminal, they waited until three-thirty before giving up on Mason. While they waited, Dana tried two more times to call, but Mason didn't answer.

"He's not going to show," Mac finally said.

"Want to go looking for him?"

"Not right now. We need to get cracking on the warrant affidavit." Mac whipped the car around and headed for the courthouse.

"YOU COMING IN?" Mac asked as he pulled into a parking space near the door.

"Go ahead," Dana said. "I'll stay here and sort through my notes."

Mac jogged up the steps and made his way to the D.A.'s office on the third floor.

"Hey, Mac," Darren greeted. "I was just going to call you. I'm almost ready to apply for the warrant so you can search the house. Judge Saunders should be clear in another hour. He's okay with our affidavit; we just need the description of the house for the actual warrant. Once we get that, we'll present it to the judge."

"Sounds good." An hour would give them plenty of time to gather the information they needed and grab a bite to eat. "Any heat from the terminal or the community?"

"No more than I'd expect. So far they haven't threatened to blackball me."

"We appreciate your cooperation. We'll head over and get a description and grab a bite. Be back in less than an hour."

Mac jogged down the stairs and to the car. He eased into the driver's seat, adjusting his Glock and holster before snapping on his seatbelt. "This thing is killing me." Mac arched his back and rubbed a sore spot, rocking his holster forward.

"Try wearing it with hips," Dana teased. "Do we have the warrant?"

"Not quite." He explained their final mission.

"Good. I was afraid something would go wrong. Between Clay's kids and the railroad and the police chief, we could be looking at a lot of roadblocks."

"Well, let's not celebrate until we get it signed. Don't get me wrong," Mac mused. "Darren is a good guy and I doubt he'd compromise an investigation. Unfortunately, D.A.s are still elected officials. He has to be feeling the pressure from the biggest businesses in the community. We know the railroad officials have already gotten to the police chief."

"Let's hope Darren and the judge don't cave."

"Let's get something to eat before we head over to the house. I'm starved." Mac pulled into the drive-thru lane. "Want anything?"

"Yeah. A Diet Coke and some chicken strips, with honey mustard sauce."

Mac spoke their orders into the microphone on the outdoor menu. "And give me one of those blackberry shakes," he added as an afterthought.

"That'll be twelve-fifty," the disinterested voice announced. "Pull up to the window."

Mac handed the server a twenty. A few seconds later, the server appeared at the window again and Mac took the change as well as the bags she handed him. He looked in the bags and handed them both to Dana before driving on to a small park where he pulled in so they could enjoy the view while they ate.

As if they'd been working together for years instead of months, Dana placed their drinks in the holders, pulled out Mac's hamburger, and wrapped a napkin around it. She settled the fries into a space in the console then fixed her own.

They ate without talking and when they'd finished, Mac wiped his greasy hands on a napkin. He checked the digital clock on the dash and took a long sip of the thick shake. "It's already starting to get dark. We'd better get going."

They discarded their trash in one of the garbage cans in the park's entrance, then drove the short distance to Terminal 9, stopping to wave at the lone police officer in his black-and-white cruiser who was sitting security on Clay's house. The officer, probably a reserve, looked up from his newspaper and nodded as Dana displayed the five-point badge that hung from a chain around her neck.

The officer nodded. "Hey, if you guys don't mind, I think I'll go into the terminal for a break while you're here."

"Sure," Mac said. "But we won't be long."

"Be back in five."

"Since when did you start wearing your badge on a chain?" Mac asked when the officer left.

Dana tucked her badge back inside her shirt. "Jan loaned it to me. It takes a little getting used to. Does okay as long as I put the weight of the badge in a pocket and don't let it hang on my neck. I just ran out of room on my belt with the pager, extra magazine, and cuff case."

Mac smiled. Dana's waist was pretty small. "Well, I wouldn't worry about the space for too long. A few months in detectives and that waistline will be plenty wide for everything."

"Mac!" Her eyebrows shot up.

"Just telling it like it is. I started out in the back room with a thirty-two-inch waist on my slacks. Now it's up to a thirty-four."

She groaned. "I have no intention of letting my waistline expand. But I know what you mean. I have never eaten out so often in my life. I need to get on a regular diet again, start brown-bagging it. I was able to go home for lunch on patrol; now I never get over to the Vancouver side unless we have a witness interview or something. Seems like downtown takes all my time nowadays."

"Tell me about it." Mac slammed the gearshift into park, and the extra pair of handcuffs slid down the shift knob to the steering column with a clank.

"Hey, I've been meaning to ask you, where'd you get that old set of Smith & Wesson handcuffs with the heavy-duty links? They look ancient." Dana flipped the swinging cuffs with her left index finger.

"Those are Kevin's bracelets. He hated carrying cuffs." Mac offered a wan smile. "Kevin said that's why he kept me around, in case there was any handcuffing to be done."

Dana smiled. "Hmm. I bet if those things could talk, they could tell a story or two."

"Yeah, I'm sure they've seen their share of action. Can you imagine all the murderers and rapists those have been on over the past two decades?"

Dana tipped her head back. "I heard a story once about Kevin being kidnapped by a suspect once—back in the late '70s . . ."

"I know the one you mean. Kevin wasn't kidnapped; that was Frank."

"Sarge?"

"He was a corporal back then, when we still had that rank, and Kevin ended up rescuing him. Sarge was working a homicide and this woman was suspected of killing patients in a nursing home. She took a liking to Sarge and starting mailing him love letters during the investigation."

"Our Frank Evans? Are you kidding me?"

Mac chuckled. "Remember, this was over twenty-five years ago. Sarge was walking out of the office when this gal's husband nabs him at gunpoint and forces him to drive out to the Mt. Hood National Forest in his detective car while he's sitting in the backseat with a gun in Frank's ear. This guy thinks Frank is having an affair with his wife and plans to take him into the woods to shoot him. Once they got out of town, the guy forced Frank into the trunk. Fortunately, the guy got cold feet and drove back to town. Kevin sees this stranger driving Frank's car and pulls traffic on him right out on 92nd Avenue. After taking the guy down, he lets Sarge out of the trunk and they hook the guy up. Strange thing is, they never ended up charging the wife with anything."

"You're kidding me. That sounds like a made-for-television cop show or something."

"No kidding." Mac shook his head. "Kevin's not one to exaggerate, so you can bet it's a true story. That's why we have those emergency pull cords in our trunks now so we can pop them open from the inside. They started installing them in our police cars way before it was the industry standard. All thanks to Sergeant Evans and his two-hour ride in the trunk of a Dodge Diplomat."

"Wow, hopefully I'll never have a similar story to tell."

"You and me both," Mac said. "You want to grab your tape recorder so we can dictate the description of the house? I'll grab the flashlight. I hate these short days. Can you believe it? Five o'clock and it's already getting dark."

"You got it." Dana stepped out of the car and grabbed a tape recorder from her duty bag in the backseat. Mac took his flashlight from the charger and slipped his portable radio into his jacket pocket.

They walked to the front of the house, which faced the wide Columbia River. The lights coming from the terminal made a shimmering path on the water. They could see the lights on the other side. "What a view," Mac said. "No wonder Clay didn't want to sell."

"Test: one, two, three," Dana said into the tape recorder, then played the message back to ensure she had good batteries. "Want me to go ahead with it, Mac?"

"Sure, let's do a description of the front of the house and work our way to the—" Mac stopped cold as he caught sight of a silver metal disk coming straight at him. It sliced into his shoulder, sending him to the ground. Struggling to sit up, he tried to fix his flashlight beam in the direction from which the disk had come. A dark figure descended on him like some kind of alien being.

Mac held his right arm up at the last minute, protecting his face from the business end of a boot. The assailant stomped on his right hip and left leg before running toward the river.

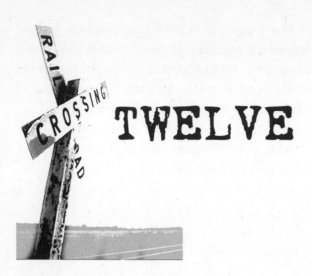

TWELVE

"Y<small>OU OKAY, MAC?</small>" Dana hunkered down beside him.

"Fine." Mac grunted. "Let's get him."

Dana tore off after the shadowy figure, still faintly visible in the dimming light. "Police officer! Stop!"

Ignoring the pain, Mac struggled to his feet and ran after his partner. As he ran, he pulled the portable radio from his jacket. The antenna snagged on his pocket.

"Police! You'd better stop!" Dana yelled as she bolted down the riverbank in pursuit.

Mac sprinted after Dana, but she continued to outdistance him. Mac felt like a first-class klutz, juggling the radio with his flashlight beam bouncing up and down. Mac indexed his Glock as he pumped his elbows and knees trying to gain on them. "Eleven-fifty-four, foot pursuit," he panted into the radio. Then, releasing the mike, he barked out orders. "Stick him, Dana. Stick him." Dispatch answered on the portable. "Fifty-four in foot pursuit downriver from Terminal 9, St. Helens," he said between breaths.

Some fifty feet away, Dana approached his attacker. She snapped open her expandable police baton, its shiny metal shaft and heavy round tip reflecting in Mac's flashlight beam. Dana swung and the steel nightstick connected with her target's upper right thigh.

Grabbing his crotch, the suspect hit the dirt with a scream.

"Get on the ground!" Dana yelled.

Mac winced. *Poor guy.*

"I'm down, I'm down," the suspect howled as Mac caught up to the pair. Dana stood over him like Superwoman, her nightstick cocked and ready to deliver another blow.

"On your belly." Not waiting for the suspect to comply, Mac pulled the cuffs from his belt before pushing him prone to the ground and placing a sharp knee firmly into his lower back. Mac cuffed the suspect's right wrist before pulling his left hand down and snapping the other cuff cradle into place.

Dana picked up the flashlight Mac had dropped on the sandy beach, still keeping her weapon at the ready on her right shoulder.

"Roll him over, Mac." Dana blew her hair off her forehead. "I want to get a look at this guy."

Their collar muttered something that was totally unsuitable for mixed company.

Mac yanked the suspect to his knees. "You want another trip to the batter's box?"

"N-no sir," the shaky voice replied.

"Then you do as you're told." Mac helped him stand up for a pat-down.

Dana shined the light in the guy's face as Mac took a step back, pulling the suspect's jacket down off his shoulders. "He's just a kid."

"I'm twenty." The kid gritted his teeth. "I want an ambulance, and I want my lawyer."

Mac leaned forward, placing his hands on his knees, still trying to catch his breath. "You got a name, kid?"

"I don't have to say anything without a lawyer. I suggest you get on it, pig." He stared at Mac in defiance, his blue eyes full of hatred. "I want these cuffs loosened up too."

"Hey, Mac. Take a look at this." Dana pointed to a small brown leather case that looked like a travel bag or shaving kit. "He dropped the bag when I hit him."

"You steal that from the Mullins's place?" Mac asked.

"I'm not telling you nothin'."

Mac picked up the radio he'd dropped in the sand. "Looks like our death investigation just got a little more interesting, wouldn't you say, Detective Bennett?"

"I'd say so." Dana lowered her metal baton, snapped it closed, and placed it back inside her leather belt case.

"Nice stick." Mac whispered to Dana as he brushed past her.

"Thanks. On top of assault on a public safety officer, we can add burglary and attempted escape third-degree." Dana raised her voice for the suspect's benefit.

"Yeah." Mac crossed his arms. "I'm glad you're not a juvie, pal. I'd hate for you to get by with a slap on the wrist. See, I don't take kindly to guys who try to clobber me with a deadly weapon."

"What deadly weapon?" The kid spat sand out of his mouth. "That was a garbage can lid."

"Looked pretty deadly to me." Sirens sliced into the growing fog. Mac waited for some dead air and held his portable up as high as he could, so he would get good reception, then called a code four into dispatch. "Eleven-fifty-four, we have one detained and we're all clear."

The dispatcher acknowledged, then repeated the message to responding troopers. The sirens instantly cut off, though one of the cars was close enough for Mac to hear the engine's four-barrel carburetor open up. Even though they'd caught their assailant, these guys were still coming to their aid.

Still high on adrenaline from the hard run, Mac again gave a 12-94, or the OSP code saying he and Dana were all right. He told the responding trooper where to meet them with their custody.

Dana picked up the brown leather case, sliding a stick under the handle so as not to smudge any fingerprints or destroy evidence.

The St. Helens officer from the house approached. The guy had been running and was barely able to talk. "I got here as soon as I could," he puffed. "I don't have your frequency on my primary channel, just picked up your troopers on scan. You guys okay?"

"Yeah, we're fine now," Dana answered. "You know this skinny burglar? He tried to brain my partner."

The officer shined his light in the kid's face. "Yeah, I know him. Tyler Cohen. We are all too familiar with him around here."

"Says he's twenty. Is that right?" Mac asked, taking Tyler's arm to propel him forward. "Looks younger to me."

"Naw, I'd say more like seventeen. Kid's been in and out of juvie since he was fourteen. Started with minor in possession of booze and smoking, worked his way up through petty theft, and now is up to burglary and stealing cars. All to pay for his meth addiction."

Mac dusted Tyler off and pulled his camo jacket up on his shoulders before moving behind him. "Any idea how he managed to get into the house you were supposed to be watching?" Mac didn't bother to hide his annoyance.

"Sorry about that. He must have come up from the riverside." He frowned at Tyler. "Hard to keep an eye on both sides of the house at once."

"Maybe we need a second officer out here."

"Good luck. The chief isn't about to release another officer for this gig."

Annoyed, Mac grabbed the kid's arm to pull him forward.

"Hey, take it easy!" Tyler winced when Mac steered him. "These cuffs are too tight. I'll tell my lawyer you were harassing me."

"Do I look worried, Tyler?" Mac loosened the cuffs a bit. "You don't mind if I call you Tyler, do you?"

"I don't care what you call me." Tyler trudged up the hill ahead of him.

"Well, Tyler, you can call me Mac. I'm a detective with the Oregon State Police. And this nice lady with the homerun swing is Detective Dana Bennett. I'll tell you what, Tyler. My partner and I are homicide investigators for the state. I don't care what you are involved with as long as you're not a murderer. You understand?"

"Murder?" He glanced from Mac to Dana. "I didn't kill anybody."

"That so? Tell you what. I can call a lawyer and a doctor—if that's what you want. I doubt you need a doctor. It looks like you are standing okay, probably just some bruises. And as for the lawyer—well, I doubt an attorney will be able to get you out of the charges we'll be bringing against you. Now Tyler, we might be willing to work with you and maybe let you off the hook so long as we get the right answers."

"Keep talking," Tyler said, his voice softening.

"We'd like to know what you were doing here. If you aren't directly involved in my investigation, then I may forget about the garbage can lid and the fact that you ran from an officer in an attempt to escape."

"Like I said, I got scared and ran. I didn't do anything wrong."

"This is Oregon, Tyler. Once an officer tells you to stop, you are under arrest. But you kept running. That's attempted escape. Bummer, isn't it? I definitely heard my partner yell for you to stop."

The kid bobbed his head in acknowledgment. "So what do you want to know?"

"I want the truth. Are you willing to talk to me?"

"I don't know. Ask your questions."

"Not here. I'll get one of the troopers to take you in their police car and we'll talk once everyone settles down. Cool with you?"

"Guess it has to be," Tyler answered.

Mac led the teenager back to the house and passed him off to a uniformed trooper. "Don't ask him any questions since we haven't read him his Miranda rights yet." Mac didn't want to read the kid his rights until he calmed down. "Take notes if Tyler makes any statements to you though."

"You got it." The trooper helped Tyler into the backseat of his car and shut the door.

Once he'd gone, Mac asked the officer on watch to beef up his security methods. With a promise to keep a closer watch on the house, the local officer went back to his vehicle.

Dana placed the leather bag that Tyler had dropped in the backseat of the car. They would not open the case until they determined ownership. Mac hoped they wouldn't need a separate warrant to examine the contents.

The two detectives then went back to their original task, taking notes on the outside of the home for their warrant. Mac called Darren to let him know they'd been held up but would get there as soon as they could. "Sorry about this, but we really need to get this kid's statement."

"Not to worry," Darren said, agreeing to wait for them. "I'll grab a bite to eat and get caught up on some paperwork."

Mac and Dana met up with Tyler back at the county courthouse where they used an interview room in the sheriff's office, which occupied the ground floor of the building. When they came in, the trooper greeted Mac and Dana, then excused himself from the interview room. Tyler was seated behind a small table, now handcuffed in the front.

"You guys care if I smoke?" Tyler asked.

"Yes, we do," Mac said, but gave no further explanation. He took a chair on the other side of the table. Dana set the leather bag Tyler had dropped on the table then leaned against the wall near the door.

Tyler sat back in his chair, the chains from the handcuffs scraping across the table as he moved.

"What do you guys want?" He looked scared, which would hopefully work to their advantage.

"Let me explain a couple of things to you." Mac opened the briefcase he'd brought in and pulled out a legal pad. "First of all, I'm sure you'll have a lot of questions. I don't feel comfortable answering your questions without advising you of your rights."

Tyler frowned. "What do you mean?"

"You're not charged at this time, but you are definitely not free to leave. That means you are in custody as far as the law reads. If you're in custody, that means we have to read you your rights. Got that?"

"Yeah, I guess so."

"Good." Taking a play right out of his former partner's play-book—surprise the rookie detective with a lead in a key interview to see how he reacts—Mac turned to his partner. "Detective Bennett, go ahead with the rights and consequences," Mac said.

Dana handled the transition like a pro. Mac thought he recognized a curl on her lips that indicated she was actually amused by his move. "Thank you, Detective McAllister." Dana pulled a laminated card from the breast pocket on her jacket. "Mr. Cohen, you have the right to remain silent. Anything you say can and will be used against you in a court of law. If you cannot afford to hire a lawyer, one will be appointed to represent you without cost. Do you understand these rights of which I have advised you?"

"Yeah, I've heard them a time or two."

Dana was experiencing a new kind of adrenaline rush, different than the kind you get from fights or chases. Mac was taking notes, relieving her of the responsibility so she could establish rapport with the kid. Things had started clicking between her and Mac on this case, and for once Dana felt like they were becoming a real team and not just two people assigned to work together.

Dana moved to a chair at Tyler's left and cleared her throat, trying to remember Mac's style for making suspects feel comfortable. His was good, shifting from smooth and kind to serious and even menacing. She had a few tricks up her sleeve as well.

"Do you need anything, Tyler? Water or coffee?" Dana smiled and lightly touched the young man's hand when she asked the question.

"Um . . . No, no thanks. I'm cool." Tyler's wary gaze followed her. His shoulder slumped and softened a little.

"I'm sorry you can't smoke in here," she said. "The building's rules, not ours."

His Adam's apple rose up and down when he swallowed. "I can handle it."

"Good." Dana tipped her head to one side. "Do you have any questions for me? I know you've been arrested a time or two, but I bet you've never been involved in a death investigation before."

His head snapped up. "What death investigation?"

"Clay Mullins. The man whose house you were in when we showed up."

"Oh, him. I heard the old dude got whacked by a train. The guys at the pool hall were talking about it."

"Did you know Clay Mullins?"

"Everyone knew about him. I didn't know the guy personally."

"Hmm." Dana pursed her lips and frowned. "Okay. Help me understand what you were doing at his house."

"I heard he had a lot of cool things in his house—stuff that might be worth a lot of money. I figured nobody would miss a few things, and he sure didn't need the stuff any more."

"Where'd you hear that?"

"One of my buds. His mom worked for the old guy. You know, cleaned the place up and bought his groceries and stuff. I needed a little cash and thought I could help myself to some of the things in the house."

"So you broke in and then we came along and spoiled the party?" She smiled at him. "Tell me, how did you manage to get by the police officer?"

She said it in a way that made Mac sit up straighter. Had he been the bad guy, he'd have confessed to anything just to please her.

Tyler chewed on his bottom lip for a moment, probably weighing his words.

"Go ahead, Tyler. You're doing fine."

"I—uh—I came in along the river like he said. Did some fishing and skipped some rocks. I could see the cop pretty clear from where I was. He sat there most of the time, reading and drinking coffee. Every once in a while he'd get out and walk around. I'm not sure he ever did see me. When it started getting dark I went in on the river-side."

"How did you get into the house?"

"The door was unlocked. I just walked in."

Dana looked him in the eye. "And it was already getting dark. Must have been hard to see what you were doing."

"Not really. The lights from the terminal were shining in through the windows. Light enough."

"How convenient. What did you find in the house?"

"Humph." Tyler moved forward, resting his arms more fully on the table. "Nothing worth stealing, that's for sure. Just a bunch of junk—some old signs and pictures and stuff lying around."

"What about the bag you took?"

He shrugged. "It was sitting on the counter in the kitchen. There were some bottles and pills and a bunch of needles. I figured I could sell the stuff."

"Or use it yourself?" Dana asked.

"Yeah, I know I got a problem. Me and my girlfriend are quitting after the first of the month, going cold turkey."

"Yeah, right," Mac mumbled.

"Go on, Tyler," Dana prodded.

"I was in the back bedroom when you guys pulled in. I got as far as the porch when you came around the corner."

"So you knew we were cops?" Mac asked.

If the guy had been a turtle his head would have disappeared into his shell. "Yeah, I knew," he admitted. "I'm sorry, man. I just freaked out and tried to get out of there. I didn't want to hurt anyone, just confuse you so I could get away."

"Is this the bag you took from Mr. Mullins's house?" Dana inched the bag toward him.

"Yeah. That's it."

Dana shifted her gaze from Tyler to the bag, then over to Mac with a take-it-from-here look.

"Let me get this straight," Mac said. "This bag isn't yours."

"No sir, it's not mine."

"So you would have no problem with us looking in the bag?" Mac asked.

Tyler shrugged. "No."

"Are you willing to give a taped statement, Tyler?" Mac reached for the bag and placed it under his chair without opening it.

"Sure, if that's what you want."

"I don't have any additional questions. Detective Bennett, why don't you put him on tape and we'll go from there." Mac pulled a mini cassette recorder from his briefcase and handed it to Dana.

Dana recorded a test message then set the recorder on the table, again advising Tyler of his rights and going through his statement. Once he gave the account, both detectives locked him into his story with some follow-up questions.

"Tell you what, Mr. Cohen." Mac snapped off the tape recorder and removed the mini cassette tape. "If your story checks out and we find that you had nothing to do with the old man's death, I'll forget about that garbage can incident." Mac pulled a pocketknife from his pocket and punched the plastic tabs from the cassette, to ensure it wasn't used for recording again. "That sound like a deal to you?"

"Sure. Like I said, I never meant to hurt anybody."

"We'll book you on the burglary and resisting arrest, and for now we'll put a hold on the assault of a police officer and attempted escape charges. Sound like a winner?"

"I guess."

Dana asked the uniformed trooper waiting outside the interview room to step back in. Mac instructed the trooper to take Tyler downstairs to the county jail and book him. "Get him an appearance date and release him." Since Tyler was a juvenile, the jail wouldn't hold him.

"Good job, partner," Mac said to Dana when Tyler and the trooper were out of earshot.

"Thanks, I guess." Dana let out a sigh.

"I know I put you on the spot. Kevin did the same thing to me on several of the cases I ran with him. Hope you don't mind. I just wanted you to know I trust you."

"Thanks, Mac, but I could have throttled you at the time. How about trusting me with a heads-up next time?"

"Sorry, just passing along the tradition." Mac grinned and held up a hand, which Dana high-fived.

"What do you want to do with the bag Tyler stole?" Dana asked.

"Let's get it introduced into the warrant. We'd better get upstairs and punch this into our affidavit so we can get a judge's signature."

"Doesn't it need to be dusted for prints?"

"No, not now that the kid has admitted to taking it. The crime lab doesn't like to process evidence we don't need."

Dana looked at her watch. "It's seven o'clock already."

"I hope Darren is still here. I'll get the warrant going; you need to call Sergeant Evans and tell him about your use of force."

"Right." She frowned and seemed unsure of herself. "Do you think I did the right thing? I hit him pretty hard."

"You brought him down—he's alive to tell about it. By the way, slugger," Mac winked, "remind me never to mess with you."

Dana's dimples deepened into a sly smile as she batted her eyelashes at him. "Why, Mac," she said in a sweet Southern drawl, "whatever do you mean?"

THIRTEEN

Mac JOGGED UP THE STAIRS to the District Attorney's office while Dana took the bag to the car and called Frank. He buzzed on the door to the D.A.'s office, but when no one answered, he paged Darren on his cell phone.

Darren called him back a few minutes later. "Hey Mac, I'm across the street having some dinner. I'll be right up."

"Mind giving me the access code so I can finish my warrant affidavit?"

"Not at all." Darren gave him the code. Mac let himself in and went to work on Darren's computer.

He typed in the description of the home and the autopsy results, labeling the request to search the home as a suspicious death investigation since he was nowhere near ready to call the death accidental or medical. At the same time, they certainly had no real evidence of a murder—just a feeling that was growing stronger by the minute. Mac also added the mysterious bag they'd retrieved from Tyler to the affidavit.

The plan had been to search the home for evidence of Clay's reason for leaving, more so than the cause of death. As Spalding had indicated, just after Clay's death, a responding uniformed officer would have done a cursory search of the house to make sure there was no one else home. That kind of search fell under a public safety provision that allowed for warrantless searches for community care-taking measures. Once the police were sure there were no additional citizens in the home, they had to leave. That search had been done long before Mac and Dana were called in.

Before the break-in, Mac had planned to go in and have a cursory look at the place today. Now they'd have to bring in a CSI tech, and that meant they'd probably be waiting until morning—assuming a tech was available then. With all the budget cuts, the Oregon State forensic lab had been hit hard.

Besides, the break-in had eaten up a lot of their time. Better to start fresh in the morning rather than work through the night and risk sloppy work by two very tired detectives. He had no doubt that Kevin would agree. On top of that, he doubted Frank would sign off on more overtime.

Once again Mac grumbled about the necessity of the warrant. He really wanted to get inside Clay's house, but he could lose the evidence in a suppression hearing if he tried to skirt around the paperwork. Unfortunately, without a warrant, they would need consent from all parties, and that hadn't happened. Clay's daughter refused to give consent until she looked into the matter, and Jacob refused to even talk to them. If they did find something in the house indicating foul play, Mac would have to look seriously at the denied consents from both parties.

Mac hit the print key a bit harder than necessary. Paperwork frustrated him to no end. But he intended to do it right.

"Hey, Mac." Darren poked his head inside the office. "How's that warrant coming?"

Mac looked up from the monitor. "All done. I'm printing it out now." He scooted his chair back and stood.

"Did you get your burglar squared away?"

"Yeah."

Volk nodded. "I'm glad you and Dana are okay. We've been dealing with the Cohen family for some time. I'm afraid the fruit didn't fall far from the tree with Tyler. I'm just thankful he didn't have a gun. Do you think he had anything to do with Mullins's death?"

Mac shrugged. "Not at this point. He copped to the burglary. We think he was just looking for an easy score to feed his addictions. But if we find evidence of foul play where Mullins is concerned, I'm certainly not ruling him out. It's possible the kid wanted the old man out of the way and put him on the tracks so his death would look like an accident."

Darren nodded. "Possible, but unlikely. Tyler's not too bright."

"He could have had a partner." Mac sighed and shook his head. "Listen to me. Already making a homicide out of this."

"I've got Circuit Judge Perkins standing by at home for the warrant. He said we could do a telephonic job if you wanted to call him. You can use my phone recorder if you like; it's all ready to go."

"Thanks." Mac grabbed the affidavit off the printer. "You have the number for Perkins?" Even though he now planned to search the house the following morning, Mac wanted everything in place so they could hit it bright and early.

"On my phone, on that yellow sticky note."

Mac dialed the number, getting Judge Perkins on the second ring. "Yes sir, this is Detective McAllister, OSP. I'm applying for a search warrant."

"Right. Darren said you'd be calling. I was sorry to hear about Clay's death," Judge Perkins said. "He was a fixture around here. The community has lost a good man."

"So I understand. I appreciate your help, sir. Darren said you'd agreed to do this over the phone. I have a recorder ready when you are."

"That's fine. Go ahead."

Mac activated the cassette recorder and began reading the affidavit out loud.

Warrant applications made over the phone in Oregon must be recorded so the judge is protected from liability in the event the affiant provides inaccurate information. Usually the judge has the affidavit to read, keeping the original once the warrant is signed. Judge Perkins listened intently on the other end, then agreed to sign the warrant. "Just fax me the paperwork; I'll fax back a signed copy and we're in business. You can bring me the original affidavit tomorrow morning."

"Thanks."

"Glad to do it. When are you planning to serve the warrant?"

"We were hoping to go through the house tonight, but I've decided to wait until tomorrow morning—that is, if I can hook up with a CSI technician. With the burglary tonight we'll have to treat it as a crime scene." Tyler's burglary had complicated matters and they now had a contamination problem. They would have to eliminate and separate his actions or damage from that of a possible murderer.

"Sounds like a wise move. Let me know if you need anything else."

"Will do." After obtaining his warrant, Mac called the Portland office of the State Police forensics lab, requesting a CSI technician to accompany him and Dana in the morning. He gave directions and set a time of 9:00 a.m. After updating Sergeant Evans he met up with Dana in the car.

"You ready to call it a night?" Mac loosened his tie and slid behind the wheel.

"You didn't get the warrant?"

"I did, but there's no point in going over there now. I called for a lab tech. We'll hit it first thing in the morning."

"Good." She glanced at her watch. "The evening isn't completely shot. By the way, did you call Kristen?"

Mac winced. "I totally forgot."

"Better let her know what's going on."

Mac hesitated. He had to call but he sure didn't want to. He'd much rather face a gunslinger than a woman scorned.

"She'll understand." Dana sounded as though she knew what he was thinking. "Come on, Mac. Kristen isn't Linda. Besides, how often is she called out on a job?"

"Probably at least as often as we are." Once they started driving, Mac pulled out his cell and checked for messages. Kristen's number showed up and he dialed it, feeling a little like he was going into battle.

"Mac." Kristen greeted in a cheerful voice. "I heard about your little adventure. Are you and Dana okay?"

"We're fine. Doesn't look like I'm going to make dinner though."

"Have you eaten?"

"Not since four-thirty, but it's nearly nine."

"And that's a problem because . . . ?"

"I don't want you to go to any trouble on my account."

"Trouble? Fat chance. I just got home myself. I was going to suggest you stop at Chen's for takeout. Get whatever you want and bring me their number three special."

"Where's Chen's?"

"On Alder, just off Broadway." She gave him directions to the restaurant and then directions to her house, which was in an older but trendy neighborhood in southwest Portland.

"You're sure?"

"I'm sure, Mac. You're not getting out of our date that easily." She laughed, but Mac had a feeling she was serious.

"Okay. I'll be there in about forty-five minutes."

"Hurry. I'm starved."

MAC COULDN'T KEEP THE SMILE OFF HIS FACE when he hung up and turned to Dana. He wasn't sure why the prospect of having Chinese takeout with Kristen pleased him. He only knew it did.

"I take it she wasn't upset." Dana kept her eyes focused on the rain dotting the windshield. If Mac hadn't known better, he'd have thought she was angry with him. But that didn't make sense. She was the one who set the crazy thing up.

"Nope. She understood."

Several minutes passed with only the rhythmic *swish-swish* of the windshield wipers. Finally, Mac asked, "Are you okay? Are you mad that I'm having dinner with Kristen?"

"Of course not. Why would I be?" Dana was still staring straight ahead, not looking at Mac.

Mac maneuvered the car onto Highway 30 toward Portland. Women could be so exasperating. "Would you like to join us? I'm sure Kristen wouldn't mind, and I sure wouldn't."

She heaved a frustrated sigh. "Honestly, Mac. Do you really think I'd do that?" She leveled an annoyed look on him and turned to look out the side window, clearly putting an end to their conversation.

A few minutes later, she turned back and apologized. "Okay, I am upset that you're seeing Kristen. Are you satisfied?"

Mac was a bit startled, not only by Dana breaking her long silence but by her admission that she was jealous. Was it possible that she still had a romantic interest in him? "If you feel that way, then why did you set us up?"

"We've been over this before. I really don't think it's a good idea for us to be together. But that doesn't mean I can turn off my feelings."

She folded her arms and shivered. A tear glistened on her cheek and she brushed it away.

Mac's heart leaped at the possibility that Dana might finally agree to date him. "Maybe you should reconsider. I'm only going out with Kristen because—"

"I know. I set it up. And no, you should go. I'm—I'm just coming off the adrenaline rush. It's hitting me a little late, but . . . Wow. I didn't think taking that guy out would shake me up like this."

Mac reached over and patted her arm. "You did good, partner. In fact, if it hadn't been for you, Tyler would have gotten away." Mac hadn't really taken time to think about it before; maybe he hadn't wanted to. He didn't much like the idea that a female cop could not only outrun him but subdue the bad guy without his help. "Where did you learn to run like that anyway?"

"I ran track in high school and college, remember?"

"Now that you mention it, yeah." He grinned at her. "Guess I won't feel so bad about not being able to catch up with you."

She knuckled him in the shoulder. "Next time I'll wait for you."

"Right." Mac frowned. "Just one thing. I'd just as soon you not broadcast your conquest around the guys—especially Philly and Russ. When they hear I got beat by a girl, they'll never let me live it down."

Dana laughed out loud. "Thanks, Mac. You've just given me the ultimate weapon. I'll keep my mouth shut—for a price."

"What's that?" Mac feigned a worried look. Or maybe the look was for real. His stomach was in knots and Mac couldn't contribute it all to hunger.

"I'm not sure." She rubbed her chin. "I'll have to think about it."

MAC DROPPED DANA OFF at the OSP parking lot and followed the directions Kristen had given him to Chen's. The restaurant was small and smelled fantastic. He placed his order and, while he waited, called Kristen to let her know he was on his way. He had the food and was on the road again in less than five minutes.

Mac took SW 14th and followed it to the end, then made a left into an established neighborhood, wishing all the while his stomach would settle down. It had been giving him fits since he left St. Helens. He was hungry, but that only accounted for a small amount of his discomfort. His date with Kristen had him flustered and fighting butterflies.

On top of that, the incident with Dana still worried him. He didn't really care if she told the guys how she'd outrun him. He was more concerned about his condition. He should have been there for her. What if the guy had had a gun? Dana could have been hurt and where was he? He had to do something about his diet and his workout schedule. He'd told Dana about packing on the pounds and realized the pounds he'd put on had caused him to lose his edge.

Mac pulled up in front of an older Cape Cod home. Kristen opened the door before he could knock. Her pink-red-purple hair stood up in spikes as usual. She was wearing some kind of lip gloss. Her gaze traveled from his face to his hands. She grabbed the food and left him at the door.

He stood there a moment before stepping inside.

"Come in and close the door, Mac. I can't afford to heat the outdoors."

He obliged, stepping in far enough to close the door behind him. He wasn't sure what he'd expected for décor and was pleasantly surprised at how normal Kristen's home looked. He'd expected Gothic stuff or leftover Halloween decorations, but it was small, warm, and cozy. The fireplace was real—not gas. A vase of flowers and some candles decorated the mantel. The place smelled homey—like she'd baked a spicy apple pie.

Kristen had gone into the kitchen, which was situated to his left.

The room he was in went from an entry to a living room and dining area. The table was already set for two, and a candle arrangement and wine glasses indicated a level of intimacy Mac was less than ready for. Straight ahead was a hallway with a bathroom and probably two or three bedrooms.

Standing in the second doorway was a small boy with curly hair. He held a scraggly looking blanket in one hand and a teddy bear in the other. Andrew watched Mac warily for several seconds before stepping into the hallway and inching toward him. Once he'd made the decision, he ran, then stopped abruptly in front of him and held out a skinny arm. "You must be Mac."

Mac hunkered down to the boy's level and shook his hand. "I am. What's your name?"

"I'm Andrew. Mama said I could wait for you to get here, then I have to go to bed."

"Aren't you going to eat with us?" Mac asked, thinking the kid could run interference.

"He already ate." Kristen came into the room with two serving bowls, which she set on the table. "Andrew had dinner at my mother's. Mom takes him when I have to work late." She sighed. "Which is way too often."

Kristen came toward them, her face filled with adoration as she stooped down and picked up the child.

Andrew slipped his slender arms around his mother's neck. "Can Mac read me a bedtime story and say prayers with me? Please?"

Kristen laughed. Turning to Mac, she asked, "Do you mind?"

"Uh—no." What else could he say? He followed them down the hall and into a room decorated in shades of blue. Andrew had a toy car collection that could rival Toys 'R' Us. One wall was covered with large framed posters of NASCAR drivers. The kid was definitely spoiled.

Kristen kissed Andrew and said a childhood prayer, then handed

Mac a book and left to finish getting dinner on the table. Mac sat on an old-style Quaker rocking chair with Andrew curled in his lap. He read all of five pages before the boy fell asleep.

Not certain what to do next, Mac set the book on the floor and glanced toward the open door, hoping Kristen would come in and put the child to bed. When she didn't, he held Andrew close and tried not to wake him as he stood. Mac placed him on the bed, then tucked the covers around him. He'd never had much experience with children and had no idea why the sight of the sleeping child brought a lump to his throat and a catch in his heart. He gave into the urge to kiss the boy's forehead.

He straightened and felt a movement at his side as Kristen slipped an arm through his. "There's something special about a sleeping child, don't you think?"

"Yeah, I guess there is." Mac's heart pounded as he turned toward Andrew's mother. Here, in her little boy's room, Kristen seemed softer, warmer, more . . . he stopped his thoughts before they took him to a place he had no intention of going. "Um—I don't know about you, but I'm ready for some of that chow mein."

Kristen stretched up and kissed his cheek. "Thanks for putting him to bed."

"Right." He swallowed hard. "No problem."

Kristen took his hand and led him to the table, where they ate and talked about work. Mac relaxed as Kristen told him about the shooting victim who had come in at closing time. The conversation stayed on a safe level, with neither of them drifting into a deeper, more intimate place. To be honest, the scene with Kristen in the kid's room had terrified him. He didn't want to get that close to her or feel something so deep. It was way too soon. While Kristen was an interesting dinner companion, Mac couldn't see himself getting involved.

They talked shop until eleven. "I need to get going," Mac told her. "Dana and I are heading out to St. Helens to search Mullins's house in the morning."

"Good. Let me know if you find anything. I may have my lab results by then."

They stood in the doorway for a moment, Mac wondering if he should kiss her good-night. "Thanks for dinner," he managed.

"Thank you for bringing it." Kristen tipped her head down. "I liked having you here, Mac. I so seldom . . ." She made eye contact and grinned. "We'll have to do this again."

"Right." Mac stepped outside and Kristen closed the door, leaving him alone.

What's going on with you? Mac asked himself on the way home. *She's not your type and . . . what you felt in that little boy's room was simply a normal reaction to a sleeping child.*

A lot of guys his age were married with families. Women talked about their biological clock ticking. Maybe guys had one of those too. Maybe it was time for him to find someone—settle down and have kids.

Only a couple months ago, he thought he'd found the right woman. Linda Morris was so beautiful and had seemed perfect for him. But Linda couldn't accept his being a cop. Couldn't handle his hours. He'd thought for a while he and Dana would make a go of it, but she had been very clear that it just wasn't going to happen—at least not while they were working together.

He definitely felt something for Kristen. But she had a strange hairdo and a tattoo on her shoulder and who knew what else? Mac pulled into his driveway, determined not to think about women at all. He had a job to do and had to be up early in the morning to do it. He'd told Dana to meet him at the office at seven, which meant he had to get up at six. Morning would come far too early.

MAC HAD NO TROUBLE FALLING ASLEEP. It was the waking up that bothered him.

His eyes refused to focus as he stared at the numbers on the alarm clock. The all-too-familiar audible tone on his pager chimed away on his bedside table. *Two-twenty-one. This can't be good.* Mac yawned and turned on his bedside lamp, then grabbed the pager. "Please let this be a low battery alarm," he groaned as he pressed the green button that would light up the digital display.

Call me at dispatch ASAP re: Columbia County—Tammy

Mac knew Tammy only by voice. She was a night dispatch supervisor at the OSP dispatch center in Salem. Tammy had delivered dozens of wake-up calls to him during the past couple of years, all of them to deliver bad news.

Mac picked up his cordless phone and sat up in bed, pulling his scratch pad and pen from the bedside to take notes. He scratched out details from a previous call to make room for tonight's information.

"State Police Dispatch, state the nature of your call," the male voice answered.

"This is eleven-fifty-four, McAllister. I'm responding to a call from the supervisor."

"Mac?" Tammy came on a moment later. "You awake?"

"I am now." Mac rubbed the top of Lucy's head. She had walked into his bedroom after seeing the light on and laid her head on his bare thigh. "What's up?"

"I received a call about fifteen minutes ago from Columbia County Rural Fire Department. That house we were security posting, the one that belonged to the train victim case you are working by Terminal 9?"

"Yeah, Clay Mullins's place. You said the fire department called?" Mac's heart plummeted.

"It's up in flames, Mac. Thought you'd want to know."

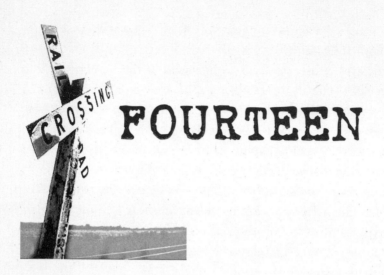

FOURTEEN

"IT'S ON FIRE? Tell me I didn't hear you right." Mac switched the phone to his left hand and hurried to his closet.

"Sorry, but from what I understand the entire structure is engulfed."

"Great. That's just great."

"You want me to get anyone else going on it?"

"Yeah, page Sergeant Evans please and let him know I'm heading out there. I'm requesting an arson detective also, so if you'll ask Sarge to call my cell phone I'd appreciate it. I'll turn it on now."

"Consider it done. Is that it?" Tammy had already typed in the request. Like most dispatchers, she could type at warp speed.

Mac switched on the overhead light and grabbed a pair of jeans. "One more thing. Page Detective Dana Bennett and let her know we need to respond out there. I'll swing by her house to save us some time."

"I've already called her. Our new system shows the assigned

personnel alphabetically, and the dispatcher saw her name first. In fact, we just heard her on the radio air. She's already en route to the fire."

Mac tried to contain his irritation that Dana always seemed to be one step ahead of him. "No problem," he said to the dispatcher. "I'm just happy I didn't read about it in tomorrow's paper. Make that today's paper. I'm on my way, thanks."

Mac dressed in a hurry, choosing jeans and a sweatshirt rather than a sports coat and slacks. He locked Lucy in her kennel and told her he would call the neighbor to pick her up in a few hours. Mac grabbed his gun and holster from the top of the refrigerator then snapped up a ball cap from the hall closet before running out the door.

He slipped on the icy sidewalk, surprised at how cold it had gotten in the last few hours. His duty car was sitting at the curb, and he had to scrape the windows clean before jumping in the car. Mac slammed his rechargeable flashlight into the charger after starting the engine. He probably wouldn't get a chance to get too close to the scene until it was rendered safe by the fire department, but he wanted to be ready.

After pulling out of the parking lot, Mac notified dispatch he was en route to Columbia County. Dana told him she was west at St. Johns when she heard him on the radio.

A good fifteen minutes ahead of me. What's she trying to prove? Mac acknowledged her radio traffic, trying not to sound miffed. He was being petty and he knew it. Dana was just following protocol. "I'm coming through Longview to shave off some travel time. I'll meet you at the scene."

"Anything special I need to be doing, Mac?"

"Yeah. Start getting names of responding fire personnel as soon as you get there. And while you're at it, find out what happened to the officer who was supposed to be guarding the house."

"Will do. Drive careful."

Once he reached Highway 14, he hit his siren and lights. It was freeway clear to Longview and he aimed to get there in record time.

Kevin never liked it when Mac drove to the north coast or even eastern Oregon by way of Washington State highways. Mac wasn't sure why. They were often less crowded and quicker than the Oregon routes. Kevin always argued they were being paid by the citizens of Oregon and should be looking out for their highways while traveling around the state.

Mac smiled, thinking of the friendly banter he had shared on the topic with his former partner. Mac's cell phone brought him up short and he realized he had experienced one of those rather scary moments—driving on autopilot and daydreaming.

Leaving on his flashing lights, Mac flipped off the siren so he could hear. "Detective McAllister."

"Mac, this is Sergeant Evans. Heard about your little problem out in Columbia County."

"Yeah, Sarge. Sorry to wake you, but I needed to get going and wanted to make sure you knew Dana and I were out and about."

"Generally, the process I operate under is that I approve call-outs and you get the call from me." Mac winced at the comment until he heard Frank's chuckle and realized that the sergeant was just kidding.

"Sorry about that. I can go back home if you want to go out instead, Sarge."

"No thanks, hot shot. You need anything from me?"

"You already know about the search warrant we were going to serve. I'll let the lab know they can stand down for now, but I would like to have an arson detective meet us out at the scene."

"There's not much they can do tonight. Not until things cool down and our hose-dragging brothers get their evidence-wrecking axes and boots out of the scene."

"Yeah, you're right. Would you mind getting one out there in the morning?"

"Sure, I've got some follow-up in the morning at the prison with Philly and Russ but I'll get someone out to you. Ray and Stan are already on a fire out in Canby so I'll send Jan your way around 6:00 a.m. Let me know if it'll be longer."

"You got it, Sarge. Jan will be great. Besides, I like her dog. Her lab reminds me of Lucy."

"Except that her lab is worth about fifty grand. I can't believe the price we pay for these accelerate dogs. You'd think every dog could smell gasoline."

Mac grinned at Frank's comment. "They probably can, just not tell you about it like Polo does."

"Humph. You or Dana give me a call at sunup and give me an update, one way or another." Mac maneuvered into the far right lane as I -205 merged with I-5 just north of Vancouver, then hit the siren again.

"Sounds good, Sarge. Thanks." Mac clicked off his phone.

Mac thought about Frank's retirement and wondered what that would mean for the department. Especially with Kevin being sick. Kevin had talked with him about the possibility of promotion. Mac wanted to promote someday, but probably not for a while. He liked being a detective and found the idea of being a respected journeyman detective like Kevin intriguing.

Although Frank could be tough, he knew his business and Mac couldn't help but wonder who their next boss would be. Even though the sergeants weren't considered the "brass," the first-line supervisors could make all the difference to the morale in a specific workgroup. Troopers and detectives rarely had contact with captains and majors from headquarters in Salem, so the sergeants and lieutenants pretty much set the tone for the office. Mac dismissed his concerns about the department. Whoever they got would work out. They pretty much had to.

Off to the southwest, across the Columbia River, Mac could see the glow of the fire. He made it into Longview and crossed the

Rainier Bridge in record time, arriving at Terminal 9 shortly after 3:00 a.m. Two media vans were already at the scene with cameras rolling.

Dana, who was leaning against her car and wearing a T-shirt and jeans, waved at Mac as he drove into the lot. She was standing over one hundred yards from the fire, which was still putting out some serious heat.

Mac pulled off his sweatshirt before joining Dana at her car. "Can you believe this?"

"Incredible. This case gets stranger by the minute."

"Did you get any kind of report from the fire captain?" Mac asked.

"They have both engine companies on the fire. The call came in around 1:30 a.m. through 9-1-1. The house was fully engulfed when they arrived. The unattached garage, over there on the right, was far enough away so they were able to save most of it."

"Do they have any idea on the cause?" Mac asked.

"Nothing yet. We won't know until they get it put out. They've been dumping water on it since I got here. It's settling down now. They have a fire boat coming up from the Portland Fire Bureau to throw water on it from the riverside."

"Jan and Polo will be here a little later," Mac said. "I want her to take a look around without the firemen in the event we're looking at an arson." Mac blew out a long breath. "So what's the story on our so-called guard?"

"Apparently a call came into 9-1-1 around 1:30 reporting a gunman on the west side of town. The chief put every available officer on it, including our guy."

Mac shook his head. "Guess I can't fault him for that. Did anything come of it?"

"Apparently not. By the time they got to the site, the guy was gone and the house was in flames."

"Gone, huh? Wonder if he ever existed." Mac shook his head. "Could this case get any more complicated?"

"Let's hope not." Dana turned back to look at the fire. "Seems like we're getting blocked at every turn."

An hour later the fire had been reduced to a smoldering mass. Fire personnel would continue to look for hot spots in what remained of the structure for some time before giving the investigators the go-ahead.

Jan and her arson dog, Polo, arrived shortly after sunup. She pulled up to the crime-scene tape in her Chevy all-wheel-drive van, stepped out with her coffee thermos in hand, and stretched. Her hair was pulled back in a neat ponytail under her blue baseball cap. She was wearing jeans and a sweatshirt with brown slip-on shoes. Comfortable traveling clothes, Mac supposed. She'd soon be suiting up in her fire turnout—the thick, suspendered brown pants and jacket.

"Hey Jan," Dana greeted.

"Morning, Dana, Mac. What do you have for Polo and me?"

"This is the house Clay Mullins lived in," Mac answered. "The man who was hit by the train a couple of days ago. We had a warrant signed to search his place this morning, but as you can see, we never got the chance."

"And this is the place you thought might be worth a fortune?" Jan's eyes narrowed. "Mighty strange there'd be a fire only hours before a search."

"We're thinking the same thing."

"All right, before we go tramping around there I want to run Polo over what's left of the structure to look for accelerates." Jan opened up the side door to her van and unlocked a kennel. Polo, the three-year-old black lab, jumped from the vehicle and sat at Jan's feet while she secured a beacon strobe to his collar. She then placed fire-resistant booties over his feet to prevent damage from the heat.

Once her partner was properly dressed, Jan placed her fire turnouts on, along with her fire helmet and respirator.

Jan and Polo walked toward the structure and met with investigators from the fire department before going toward the house. Using a long leash, the arson detective lead Polo around the outside of the foundation. The dog sniffed and pawed at the water-soaked rubble. Polo's shiny black coat rippled as the eager dog worked through the charred remains of wood, glass, and metal.

"Hey, Dana," Jan yelled. "Bring me some of those metal cans from the back of the van, please."

"Sure thing." Dana went into the back of Jan's van, digging through piles of picks, axes, and evidence-collection equipment. She grabbed two stainless steel containers that looked like empty gallon paint cans.

"These the ones you want?" Dana held them up. At Jan's nod, she and Mac met up with Jan at the yellow crime-scene tape.

"You two can come on in now. Polo hit on a possible site and I want to secure it before we move on."

Dana turned to Mac. "Should I be keeping a log at this point?"

"No. It's still a fire scene. We won't need our log until the fire captain releases the scene." Mac sighed. Firefighters were a detective's worst nightmare to try and work around. They were all over the scene, making a huge mess and stomping out almost every piece of physical evidence.

Jan took one of the metal cans as she passed Polo's leash to Mac. She then pulled a small metal shovel from her leather tool belt and began scraping a singed two-by-six that would have been part of the home's frame.

"Isn't that the entrance Cohen said he used to get in?" Mac asked.

"Yeah, I think you're right," Dana answered, keeping her gaze focused on Jan.

Jan popped the lid off her metal can, placed the black wood scrapings inside the can, and sealed it. "Now the other one." Dana handed her the second can and Jan repeated the process, this time setting some black melted plastic in the metal container before sealing the lid.

"What do you think?" Dana asked.

"Judging by Polo's reaction, I'm thinking gasoline. Did you see how he hit on this spot? I mean, he didn't hesitate for a second. The crime lab will have to confirm it though."

Jan and the fire crew dug around for the best part of an hour before coming back to where Mac and Dana were waiting.

"We all agree that the place Polo sniffed out is the origin of the fire. There may be secondary incendiary origins that we haven't located from within the residence. It's too early to tell until I get some lab results. But the fire took off from this point and burned hot. There are some directional clues that indicate it started in this area and worked to the other side of the structure. This old paint and timbers were ripe for a fire. We can't rule out accidental yet, but my gut is telling me someone set this one."

Dana knelt down to pet Polo. "Good dog."

Mac looked out over the remains of the house. "What are the odds? We finally get our search warrant, and the place goes up in smoke."

"They're never easy. That's what makes this job so interesting." Jan scratched her chin with her wrist to avoid touching her face with her blackened gloves.

Mac smiled at the action. Jan had half a dozen black smudges already on her face. He was glad she had been assigned to help with this case. According to the guys, Jan had been around the back room almost as long as Kevin and Philly. She'd worked person crimes like sex abuse, murder, and assault for years before the agency began their arson units about ten years ago.

"Time to look at the garage. I want to take Polo around the structure before the scent dissipates."

Mac handed over the leash to Jan. "Here you go. I think he likes you better anyway."

"Polo likes anyone who'll feed him. C'mon, boy, time to earn your keep." The two hurried off to resume the investigation.

"Shoot, that reminds me," Mac searched for his phone inside his jacket pocket. "I need to get my neighbor to let Lucy out. I bet she's hating me about now." Mac dialed his neighbor, relieved to find out Lucy was already in his care and had enjoyed a long morning walk.

"You're lucky to have a neighbor who'll take care of Lucy like that. Carl sounds like a gem." Dana sighed. "Is he married?"

Mac shook his head. Carl was great with dogs, but he wasn't sure where he stood with women. "No. Maybe I can introduce you one of these days."

"Don't sound so eager."

Maybe I don't want to share. Mac shrugged and kept the comment to himself, forcing his gaze back to the arson detective. Jan searched around the garage while the fire department investigators continued to examine the main structure. Several minutes later, she brought Polo back. "No hits by Polo around the garage. I'm going to put him away."

Polo wagged his tail and looked up at Jan as if asking for a handout. "You want a treat?" Looking up at Mac and Dana she asked, "You know how these guys eat, don't you?"

"What, you mean their food type?" Dana asked.

"No, I mean how they eat. These arson dogs are fed only when they make a hit on some type of fire starter. Basically, they sing for their supper. Several times a day I have to drop little traces of gas or kerosene around the office or at home and let Polo find it before I give him a few bites of food. No find, no food."

"Poor Polo," Dana patted him on the head. "I'll bring you a big cheeseburger the next time I see you."

"Don't even think about it." Jan led Polo back toward the van.

"I was just kidding," Dana called after her.

"I wasn't." Jan looked back and smiled, softening her answer.

One of the firefighters searching through the rubble caught Mac's attention as he motioned for the fire captain to come over to his location. The firefighter lifted up a charred sheet of plywood. After taking a look, the captain signaled for Mac and Dana to join him.

"We got us a problem." The fire captain glanced up at the media people and frowned.

"What's up?" Mac looked in the direction of the cameras and leaned forward to better hear the captain. "One of my people just found a body over there under that piece of plywood."

"You've got to be kidding." Mac raked a hand through his hair and glanced over at Dana.

She stared at the plywood. "Whoa. This is getting too weird."

"It gets worse. The body is in pretty good shape. Appears to be an adult male." The captain lowered his voice. "There's a gun in his waistband. Hate to be the bearer of bad news, but we don't do guns. This one's got OSP written all over it."

FIFTEEN

Unbelievable." Mac shook his head. "I'll call Sergeant Evans and get the medical examiner out here ASAP."

Dana handed her crime scene log to the fire captain. "I think I have all the names of your fire personnel. Captain, would you mind looking over this list to make sure I haven't left anyone out?"

While she took care of the paperwork, Mac jogged back to the car and called Sergeant Evans, filling him in on the latest details.

"Thanks for the call, Mac. I'm on my way. Philly and Russ are cleared on the prison detail, so I'll have them respond to the scene as well. They should be there in about an hour."

Mac hung up, feeling relieved. Philly, Russ, and the sergeant would be welcome additions. The so-called simple death investigation was turning into a three-ring circus.

His next call to the medical examiner's officer brought Kristen rushing to the scene. He wasn't surprised that she insisted on responding personally—especially since she'd taken such a keen interest in Clay Mullins.

She arrived in forty minutes, and Mac helped her get her gear out of the car.

"So you found the burn victim in Clay's house, huh?" Kristen hoisted her bag onto her shoulder and let Mac deal with the stretcher and body bag.

"Right. The body isn't in too bad of shape. The fire crew's been all over the place, taking care to soak or chop up the entire scene, so our chance of trace evidence is slim to none. We haven't gone over the body yet, no idea on any biographical information. Thought we should wait on you."

"All right." Kristen snapped the cuff on her purple glove. "Let's move."

He and Dana gloved up and stood by as Kristen did her usual on-scene examination. With the firemen and their water hoses contaminating the scene, they wouldn't bother to wear booties to protect the scene from footprints.

Dr. Thorpe confirmed the gender. The victim had been partially shielded from the intense heat by an old piece of ceiling that had fallen on top of him. The section of ceiling, still coated with asbestos building insulation, provided a good barrier.

The victim was lying prone, faceup. His face was burnt beyond recognition, along with his lower arms and hands. The lower torso was still in good shape, considering what it had been through, with the jeans and denim jacket still intact along with a pair of Nike tennis shoes. "Well, well." Kristen hunkered down and pointed to the man's open jacket and the gun tucked into his belt.

Mac secured the weapon, a small .22 rim fire pistol. The semi-automatic Taurus pistol had a half-full magazine with one in the pipe, indicating it may have recently been fired. The .22s were too small to test for bullet examination. "Let's bag this and get it over to the lab right away," he suggested. "If we're lucky we'll get some good prints." It didn't take an autopsy to know the victim's hands were too far gone to render any kind of ID or gunshot residue.

Dana held open a paper evidence bag, and Mac dropped in the gun and magazine.

"How soon can you get to this guy?" Mac asked Kristen.

Kristen rolled her eyes. "What is it with you detectives? Always in a rush. I'll jimmy my schedule a little—fit him in as soon as I can get him to the morgue. In fact, why don't you two come with me to collect any additional evidence we find during the post?"

"Sounds good to me, but I'd better check with Sarge."

"I saw him drive in a few minutes ago," Dana said.

Kristen nodded. "Let's get this guy bagged and into my van. The sooner I can get him there, the sooner I can get started."

"You got it."

Once they'd gotten the body into the back of the van, Mac asked Dana to get his car while he checked in with Evans.

"I have my car here too, Mac," she reminded him.

His eyes felt gritty. "Would you mind leaving it here for a while?"

"Not at all." Dana caught his keys and jogged to their vehicles. "We can pick it up later or have Philly or Russ drive it back."

Mac found his boss talking to the arson detective.

"From what I can see so far," Mac overheard Jan tell Frank, "it looks like we're dealing with an arson."

"Any idea on the guy inside?" Sarge's gaze followed Kristen as she pulled out of the lot and onto the main road.

"Your guess is as good as mine. For all we know the victim inside started the fire and got caught in his own mess. Or maybe the arsonist didn't know anyone was inside. Or maybe he did know."

Sarge nodded, leaning down to give Polo a good rub between the ears.

"We have something interesting to add to the mix." Mac held up the gun, offering the evidence bag to Frank. "There are rounds missing from the magazine, so it may have been fired. Wish I knew who he was and what he was up to. Might be another opportunist helping himself to Mr. Mullins's treasures."

Frank peered at the gun and frowned. "I'll have a uniform take this in to the lab right away. We don't have any casings yet, I assume. Maybe the mag wasn't topped off."

Mac shrugged. "Your guess is as good as mine. If it's okay with you, Sarge, Dana and I will head to the morgue. Kristen's doing the post right away."

"Good thinking. Philly and Russ should be here any minute."

Dana drove up and stopped, then waved to Jan and the sergeant. Mac climbed in and lowered the window.

Frank leaned down, hands on the frame. "We'll stay here and work the crime scene with Jan." His gaze shifting to Dana, he said, "You guys doing okay? You're both looking a little bedraggled."

"I'm good," Dana answered. "Got used to long hours on patrol." Her animated smile put some muscle behind her words.

"Good, 'cause you're probably not going to get much rest for a while." Frank seemed genuinely concerned for the detectives.

"Hey Sarge, would you mind having Russ drive my car back to the office, so I can head to the post with Mac?"

Frank extended his hand to take Dana's key, his eyes wary. He was probably wondering, along with Mac, how honest she was about her ability to perform under stress after pulling an all-nighter. Frank patted the hood and turned toward Jan. "Since this is your bailiwick, you're giving the orders. Where do we go from here?"

Confident that Jan and the others would methodically process the rubble for evidence of arson and/or murder, Mac leaned back into the seat. Hopefully Kristen could put some identification on the remains and give them an idea on the cause of death.

Mac was definitely fighting heavy eyelids—his adrenaline rush having worn off. They were about eight hours into their workday and, as Sarge had said, it was far from over. Mac had no intention of falling asleep, but the next thing he knew he and Dana were sitting in the parking lot at the morgue.

Dana jabbed his upper arm. "Hey, Sleeping Beauty. We're at the castle."

"What?" His mouth felt dry and sticky.

She chuckled. "I thought about calling you Prince Charming, but the way you were serenading me with snores, I changed my mind."

"Humph." Mac yawned. "Sorry I fell asleep. I didn't mean to." He stretched and yawned.

"Don't worry about it. Next time, you drive and I'll snore."

It was just after eleven, and Dana had made good time. Kristen was just pulling in. Kristen honked the horn on her pickup as she backed into the covered bay. Henry, her longtime assistant, opened the heavy steel door and kicked a wood wedge underneath to keep it open.

"Special delivery, Henry!" Kristen yelled out the open window. "We have a burn victim."

Henry held up his hands to guide her back to the door, making a fist with his right hand when he wanted her to stop.

"Let's get him ready for post ASAP. I want to take some temperature readings before he has a chance to cook any longer."

"Sure thing, Doc." After dropping the legs down from the rolling gurney, Henry pulled the body from the back of her truck.

"Didn't you check the temp at the scene?" Dana asked.

"I did, but with the fire factoring in, we have to do it again. Meat keeps cooking after you take it out of the oven, you know."

Dana grimaced at the analogy.

"Anyway, I need a post temp too."

"Whatever you say." Dana bit into her lower lip. "I honestly don't know how you do this day after day."

"Sometimes I don't either." Kristen paused next to Dana. "The job isn't pretty, Dana. It never is. But it matters. That's what keeps me going. That, and finding answers to help you people catch the bad guys." Her gaze shifted to Mac as if looking for affirmation.

Henry glided the charred victim into the tight hallway then took a hard left into the autopsy room with an ease that only comes from experience. He mopped the condensation from the top of the bag, unzipped it, and then heaved the body onto the stainless steel table.

"Sorry about slipping this one into the schedule, Henry. It's going to mean a longer day for you." Kristen put on her heavy rubber apron and gloves.

"No problem, Doc. It'll reflect on my bill though," Henry joked as he continued mopping up water.

"What's all that water from, the fire hoses?" Dana slipped on her own latex gloves.

"Condensation from the heat of the body," Kristen answered. "No different than when you wrap a piece of hot meat with plastic wrap. That's why we want to post him right away, so all that moisture doesn't freeze in the cooler."

"And I thought it was to appease us." Mac glanced over at the body, now lying facedown on the table. Since the door had protected the victim from some of the flames, parts of his jeans and denim jacket looked almost normal. The question would be whether the victim had been dead before the fire started or if he'd been overcome by smoke inhalation.

"Hope we don't have to go the DNA route to identify this guy." Mac began photographing the body. "Of course we do have the gun, so we might get some prints there."

"And if we really get lucky," Dana added, "it'll be registered."

"Speaking of lucky." He pointed out the outline of a wallet in the victim's back pocket and then clicked off a few more photos. "I've got enough pictures, Kristen, if you want to pull that wallet out now."

"Hang on a sec." Dana grabbed a manila evidence envelope and labeled the outside *Left rear pants pocket contents*. She set it on the metal evidence collection table that was situated along the room's east wall.

They held a collective breath as Kristen pulled a black leather wallet from the victim's pocket and set it on the exam table. "It's all yours, guys."

Mac photographed the wallet then asked Dana to open it.

"Here goes." Dana opened the wallet and began laying the contents on the steel table for examination. The first item to emerge was an Oregon identification card with green print, often used by adults with suspended driver's licenses who required valid state identification. Dana set it on the table for Mac to see.

The three of them stared at the card. Mac was the first to break the silence. "Well, that's interesting."

"Do we know a Jacob Mullins?" Kristen asked. "If not, we do now."

"He's Clay's son," Dana said. "We just found out about him yesterday. We talked to him via phone. He wasn't too cooperative."

"Hmm. This guy is probably Jacob, but we need proof. We aren't going to make a physical identification. No fingerprints either." Kristen grimaced. "Let's roll him over, Henry, and see what kind of dental work he has. I may have to take some bone marrow for DNA comparison from that upper thigh."

When Henry and Kristen rolled the body over, the stench of burnt flesh permeated the room. Mac stepped back for a moment.

Kristen peered inside the mouth while Henry held a flashlight up to where the man's lips had once been. "Can't see inside. The muscles along the mandible are constricted." She stood on her toes and placed her palms on the victim's chin and forehead. With a quick thrust on both points of contact, she pulled open the mouth.

Dana winced at the sickening crack. "Yikes. That hurt."

"Felt that one, did you?" Kristen offered Dana a sympathetic smile. "If it's any consolation, it hurt you worse than it did him." She examined the teeth. "We're in luck; this guy's mouth kept some dentist in sports cars. He's got fillings, crowns, and at least one partial bridge. I'll get on the horn to find his dentist after the post and see what I can come up with in my insurance database. Any idea where he lived?"

Dana turned her attention back to the ID card. "His ID has him living in Gresham, which matches the info I got earlier. She pulled out the rest of the contents in the wallet. There's an outdated Oregon Trail card in his wallet too."

"That means he'll be in the system." People who needed state-assisted medical care carried Oregon Trail cards. Mac puzzled over the find. "He had a job—how old is the card?"

"Coverage ended six months ago. Maybe he recently started working."

"This is good," Kristen said. "The card will make it fairly easy to track him down. That is, if the wallet is actually his. To be certain, I'll locate some records and get our forensic dental expert on his mouth before we release the body. We'll assume he's Jacob Mullins at this point; looks like the right height and weight."

Dana pulled out the remaining contents of the wallet while Mac photographed each item. After documenting a small amount of cash and various membership cards, Dana came upon a singed business card for Addison Shaw, Attorney at Law.

"Wasn't Shaw Clay's attorney?" Dana asked. "The one handling his estate?"

"I'm sure that's the name Clay's daughter gave us," Mac said. "I remember because she mentioned how much she didn't care for him."

"He called me too," Kristen said. "Yesterday. Remember? He wanted the death certificate."

"Guy's been busy. We'd better pay Mr. Shaw a visit soon."

"Right." Dana continued bagging the evidence. "How about we

grab something to eat when we're done here and then head back to St. Helens."

Kristen continued the autopsy while Mac and Dana finished examining the contents of Jacob's pockets, which in addition to the wallet revealed some spare change, a set of keys, a single key, and a small pocket knife. Mac held the single key up to examine it. "Looks like a house key. Wonder why it wasn't attached to the other keys in his pocket?"

"Maybe the key went to Clay's house," Dana suggested.

"It's as good a guess as any, but where did he get it?"

"And how did he get past the guard?" Dana asked. "Maybe he's the one who made the fake call."

"Good a guess as any. Somebody's head is going to roll on this one." Mac shook his head. "Unfortunately, a small town like St. Helens probably used reserve officers or volunteers. And we know how much weight Spalding was giving the case."

Kristen removed the internal organs. After photographing and weighing them, she began to dissect the lungs.

"Uh-oh."

"What?" Mac asked, turning toward her.

"These lungs are pink as a baby's behind, kids, both in the upper and lower lobes. Our guy didn't die from smoke inhalation."

Dana came to stand beside Mac. "Which means he was dead before the fire started, right?"

"Looks that way. Let me take a look at the esophagus." Kristen made a long vertical incision down the throat to get to the inner esophagus. After a few minutes, she said, "There's a small amount of discoloration here, but I don't see any hemorrhaging along the throat or any burst damage to these tiny air chambers in the lungs, things I would expect to see if he was breathing superheated air." She frowned. "Odd, I haven't seen any outward trauma to the body, though." Glancing up at Henry she said, "Let's get into his head and take a look around."

Mac stood back, knowing what was coming next.

Henry peeled the scalp back for Kristen to examine before removing the top of the cranium with a bone saw, properly referred to as craniotomy in the autopsy reports.

"Don't see much damage on the outside; these natural fissures are slightly separated on the anterior portion. On the posterior," Kristen lifted the head up from the plastic supporting block, "the paired cranial nerves don't appear to have anything remarkable going on. They reach the skull periphery and appear to be unbroken."

"Could you dumb that down for me, Doc?" Mac asked.

Kristen grinned at him. "Sorry. There is no obvious damage to the outside of the cranium, but there is an abnormal tissue mass on the back of his head. Go ahead and open him up, Henry."

Henry pulled up the circular bone saw and cut a round cap off the top of the victim's skull, then efficiently removed the brain from the skull cavity.

Dana sucked in a sharp breath.

Mac pulled off his glove and picked up a pack of smelling salts from Kristen's stash on the counter, cracked it, and placed it under Dana's nose. "You okay?"

She took a good whiff and stopped weaving. "I think so."

"Maybe you should sit down." Mac offered her an arm to lean on.

"No. I'm okay. I'm usually pretty good with this kind of stuff." She straightened and took another whiff of the smelling salts.

"We definitely have some trauma here," Kristen said as she examined the back portion of the brain. "This corresponds with that unusual tissue mold in the back of the skull." She studied the interior of the skull, shining Henry's penlight around the cavity. "Looks like Jacob, if that's who our victim is, took a whack on the head. There's an oblique wound across the back of his skull. Could be from the falling timbers in the fire, but our guy was dead before the fire burned to the stage where we'd have falling timbers. I can tell you that this wound would be enough to kill him. That's about as close as I can get you. Nothing else is jumping out at me. I'll be doing some toxicology screens and blood tests, but for now, we can go with blunt force trauma to the back of the head."

"Any guess on the murder weapon?" Mac asked.

"Something heavy with a long, flat edge. You don't crack a skull like this without something substantial; the break covers at least three inches on the skull. That's why we didn't see the fracture from the outside. It actually reset back into place after the initial blow. The trauma to the brain itself indicates the severity of the blow."

"Looks like we got us a murder gig, then," Mac said. "Even if we find that Clay wasn't actually murdered, his son was."

Dana pursed her lips. "Right. You want to tell Kelly about her brother? This will be rough for her. Losing her father and brother within a couple of days."

"Yeah, unless she did them both in." Mac had already begun thinking of suspects, and Kelly Mullins-Cassidy was definitely on the list.

"Because she's the only heir left?"

"Right," Mac admitted. "I can't help but wonder if her refusal to sign a consent for us to search the house was because she had some unfinished business there. Let's hold off on the notification until Kristen gets confirmation on his identification through his dental records."

"Good idea," Kristen said. "I should have those for you by the end of the day if I can get his records sent to me right away. The dentist who looks at these things is in town, so if our victim is Jacob Mullins, it won't take him long."

"Thanks. Dana and I need to start tracking down a few people. Addison Shaw is on the list of people to interview. I want to know why Jacob was carrying his father's lawyer's card. I also want to find the developers who were looking to buy the land."

"Sounds like you two have your work cut out for you." Kristen looked up and caught Mac's gaze. "Good luck."

SIXTEEN

Mac paged sergeant evans as he and Dana headed into a fast-food joint. Frank phoned him back moments later. "Yeah, Mac. I'm here at the crime lab. It's time for a briefing—we need to get all these bits and pieces of the investigation into something we can put our hands around. Can you two make it back to the office at, say, 1300 hours?"

"That's doable. We're grabbing lunch right now—we were on our way to talk to Clay Mullins's attorney, but we can put that on hold. The fire victim had the attorney's card in his wallet."

"Interesting. You'll definitely want to follow up, but I'd like you all here for a briefing ASAP. I have some new developments from the scene and from the lab, and I'd just as soon we lay everything on the table at once."

"We'll be there." They had exactly fifteen minutes to get their food and inhale it. He closed his phone, pocketed it, and scooted into the plastic seat across the table from Dana. Their food came as he told her about the briefing.

"I wonder what's up." Dana took a long sip of her raspberry smoothie. "Did he give you anything?"

Mac shook his head, his mouth too full of hamburger to speak. They didn't talk much during the meal—didn't have time, really. They seldom did. Mac couldn't count the number of times he would gulp down the junk food he'd ordered, wash it down with a cola or a milkshake, and be on his way again. Or the number of times he'd ordered to go and eaten in the car.

As Dana pointed out, on-the-go meals didn't have to be unhealthy. She was eating a chicken Caesar salad. He should have ordered salad, but old habits died hard. Maybe next time.

He thought again about how Dana had outrun him by about forty yards down along the river. Of course, he had been flat out on the ground when the chase started, giving her a good head start, but he should have caught up. A year ago, he would have.

Rubbing a hand across his not-so-flat stomach, he made a commitment to get those extra pounds off. He'd up his visits to the gym—maybe work out daily instead of sporadically like he had been doing.

DANA SPEARED THE LAST FEW PIECES OF LETTUCE with her plastic fork and stuffed them into her mouth. She was beginning to think having Mac as a partner was a bad idea. While she'd had moments when things seemed right between them, he often seemed distant and upset. She had a hunch a lot of the antagonism came out of his bruised ego. "Mac." She wiped her mouth with her napkin. "We need to talk."

"Huh?" He had a sort of dazed look about him.

"I said we need to talk—and not about the case." She crumpled her napkin. "Would you like to see about getting someone else as a partner?"

His surprise seemed genuine. "Why would I do that?"

She shrugged. "Well, for starters, you seem to be upset with me most of the time. I mean . . . it's like you're mad at me for something. If this is about my not wanting to date you—I just wonder if we'd be better off not working together."

Mac glanced at his watch, grateful for an excuse to change the subject. "We better get moving. Can we finish this conversation in the car?"

"Sure."

They got up from the table and took their trays to the garbage bin. Mac didn't want to talk at all. Why couldn't she just leave it alone? The food he'd just inhaled churned around in his stomach, and for a few minutes he wondered if it was going to stay down. He didn't like dealing with problems—especially relationship problems. How could he have been stupid enough to think that he and Dana could be more than friends? She was more committed to her job than he was to his. And now she wanted another partner?

Once they were situated in the car and heading for the office, Dana pressed Mac for an answer. "So, do you want to request another partner?"

"Do you?" *Throw the ball back in her court. Stall for time.* He hadn't even considered asking for another partner. For one thing it wouldn't look good on his record. Might seem like he didn't get along with her. But then it wouldn't look good for him if she requested a change either.

"No, it's just . . ."

Mac pressed his lips together. "I don't want another partner. You're a good cop, and I trust you."

"But?"

He shook his head and smiled. "I'm sorry if I indicated that you weren't doing a good job. Thing is, you're just a little too good at times and I feel—intimidated."

"You hate it when I get ahead of you or when I take the initiative. You're upset that I single-handedly caught the kid at Mullins's place."

"That was a good catch, Dana. Like I said, you're top-notch."

"And it scares the heck out of you."

"It doesn't scare me." Mac stared out the windshield, wishing he could think of something wise and wonderful to say. She was right. He was scared, which, when he thought about it, was totally ridiculous.

Dana folded her arms and flashed him a knowing look. "I'm not going to dummy down so I don't hurt your feelings, Mac. I'll never throw a game so some guy can come out feeling like a jock."

"It's not a competition. I expect you to do your job and I'll do mine." Mac believed that. He just wished he could put his feelings aside.

"Okay. Maybe I read you wrong."

Mac sighed. "You didn't. My feelings have been getting in the way of my common sense lately."

"I'm not out to compete with you, Mac. I just want to be the best detective I can be. I won't be as good as Kevin, and I know you miss him. That has to factor in."

Mac pulled into the parking space at the OSP office. "You're right in a way. I feel like a fraud next to him. And to be honest, this case has me spinning in circles. I don't know which end is up."

"Me too." Her dimples deepened as she gave him one of her great smiles. "We'll figure it out. We're young, but we're smart. We may not be as experienced as Kevin and Philly, but we can pick their brains whenever we need their seasoned advice. One thing I've learned being around these guys—it's okay to admit when you don't know something. They don't hold it against you."

He set the brake and pulled the key out of the ignition. "I hope you're right."

"I am. Just have more faith in yourself. Loosen up."

Dana had wisdom beyond her years and a positive attitude that put his to shame.

"I'm glad we talked, Mac. I feel so much better."

"So do I, partner." And he did in a way, but it still irked him that she was so darn smart and fast.

IT SURPRISED MAC TO SEE KEVIN in the briefing room, though it probably shouldn't have. Even with the cancer, he'd want to stay on top of things. The large meeting center in the detective office was set up with a large television and VCR combination at the head of the room next to a wooden podium, facing sixteen chairs that sat alongside four long tables. The detectives often used the room to prepare cases for trial or to gather resources before a search warrant. This time they would assemble to make assignments on their case and bring one another up to speed on what they'd each learned in the past few hours.

"How you feeling, old buddy?" Mac patted Kevin on the shoulder as he sat next to him.

"Better than I look, believe it or not." Kevin rubbed his hand over his bald head.

I sure hope so. Looks like you could use a little sun. Mac kept the retort to himself, not sure if he should be joking around.

Dana settled into the row behind Mac and Kevin. She slipped her hair band around her wrist and shook her mass of golden hair free. She then pulled it together into a ponytail, wrapped it around a couple of times, and secured it again.

Mac frowned at the direction his thoughts were taking and looked away before she or someone else caught him staring at her.

Jan walked in then, followed by Russ and Philly. She sat behind Mac and Kevin, next to Dana, and greeted Kevin with a squeeze of the shoulder as she sat down. Jan and Kevin had been friends for years. The concern in her eyes mirrored the way Mac felt.

"Hey, cue ball." Philly rubbed Kevin's head before heading for the back row with his partner. "Lookin' good for a desk jockey."

Kevin chuckled and turned around. "Looking good yourself, scar head. If it wasn't for all those nicks on that noggin of yours, I'd say you should stay with that look."

"Humph. Unlike you daisies, I've been in a few tussles in my life. Besides, chicks dig scars. Right, Jan?" Philly held out his arms to welcome a compliment. "You don't find rugged good looks like this every day, you know. I'm thinking about a modeling career."

Jan smiled and shook her head, all too familiar with Philly's odd sense of humor. "If I were single, I'd be begging to go out with you, Philly. That's assuming you were between wives. What are you up to now, four . . . five?"

Mac and the others chortled. Jan was one of the few people who could put Philly in his place.

"I married my first wife twice; you know that doesn't count." Philly folded his arms, resting them on his more than ample stomach. The sight strengthened Mac's resolve to get back into his fitness program.

"Let's get started." Sergeant Evans entered the room, his coffee spilling over the edge of his cup. "Toss me those paper towels, would you, Russ?"

"Sure, Boss Hogg." Russ tossed the box of towels to the front of the room.

They'd been using the towels to replace the long-lost grease board eraser for as long as Mac had been there. Frank used one of them to wipe the bottom of his cup. "Thanks." He set his cup on a clean paper towel. "Okay, people. Listen up. I'll start with an update from the lab on the gun found on the burn victim and some interesting news I learned while I was down there."

Mac straightened, as did the others, showing respect for the sergeant as he moved behind the podium. Sergeant Evans was old school State Police and former military. He believed in leading from the front and always stood at the podium when he did his speaking.

"For those who don't know already, Mac and Dana were dispatched to a probable accidental death of an elderly gentleman, a Mr. Clay Mullins, who was hit by a train a couple of nights ago. It was his house that burned down this morning. Said house was supposedly under watch by the local P.D. for warrant application. We received the call around 2:00 a.m. The dwelling was fully engulfed, further complicating the case Mac and Dana were working. The old guy was apparently worth a bundle in real-estate assets among other things. Jump in here, Mac or Dana, if you have anything to add."

Mac stood up and turned around to face the other detectives. "Thanks, Sarge. We started the death investigation at the request of the D.A. in St. Helens. Like Sarge said, we have an older gentleman who was struck by a train while traveling a packed gravel path from his home to the rail yard, where he'd worked for years and still visited daily. His assumed wealth and some of the circumstances surrounding his death are puzzling. We have more people of interest than Bayer has aspirin. There's a railroad employee who has no love lost for the old guy." Mac shrugged. "The guy stiffed us on an interview, by the way. In addition, we have real-estate types looking to buy the land, one of which suggested to Clay's daughter that she have the old man declared incompetent. Also, we have a local kid we caught burglarizing the place just hours before it was torched. There's an estranged son who turns up out of the woodwork to lay claim to his old man's estate then turns up dead in the home, and there's Clay Mullins's attorney, whose name seems to be popping up all over the place."

Mac went on to tell them about the second victim. "Dana and I just came from the medical examiner's office. Dr. Thorpe says he took a blow to the head, which apparently killed him before the fire had a chance."

"Is the identification confirmed?" Kevin asked.

"A tentative positive right now. Doc Thorpe expects to have the confirmation this evening. He had picture I.D. in his wallet. His sister—Clay Mullins's daughter—lives on the south side, but we haven't made next of kin yet. We'll wait for the positive tag from the M.E."

"Any space aliens or Elvis sightings?" Philly leaned back.

Russ snuffled.

"Sorry, Phil—that's your department," Mac quipped. Then getting back to business, he said, "We understand from Mullins's daughter that there is a maid, but we haven't been able to hook up with her as yet. She apparently has a son with ties to the guy who burglarized the home the night before the fire—a local druggie by the name of Tyler Cohen. We caught him coming out of the house while we were getting a description for the warrant affidavit." He glanced at his partner. "Fortunately, Dana apprehended him."

"How come *she* caught him, Mac? What were you doing?" Russ grinned, seizing the opportunity to embarrass Mac. He knew perfectly well what had happened.

Dana flashed Russ a dark look. "Mac was the suspect's primary target in the attempted assault. Believe me, he had his hands full with a flying garbage can lid."

"That and the fact that Dana runs like greased lightning," Mac added. "She's pretty handy with her stick too." Mac was surprised at the real sense of pride he felt in his partner.

Kevin gave him a knowing wink. "You got anything else on this guy?"

Mac cleared his throat and continued. "Yeah. Cohen admitted to hearing about the old man's death and thought it might be a good opportunity to steal a few things for drug money. At any rate, the case keeps getting muddier." Turning to Dana he asked, "Did I cover everything?"

"I think so. We have a very long list of people to interview. Hopefully those people will give us a clearer picture of what we're dealing with. We still don't have the physical evidence of wrongdoing on the Clay Mullins case, but it's looking more suspicious all the time."

Sergeant Evans thanked them. "As Mac and Dana indicated, this supposed death investigation has grown legs. As you know, we found a firearm on the victim in the fire. I had the gun dropped off at the lab. Jacob Mullins purchased and registered the gun two weeks ago. Wain Carver took a quick look at it and agreed that it had been fired recently based on the powder residue in the barrel and the missing cartridges from the magazine. He's going to give it the once-over and take a test fire for the IBIS database, see if it's been used on a past crime. It's hard to get a bullet out of those .22's in good shape, but if anyone can do it, Carver can."

Frank pulled a photograph from a pile of paperwork and displayed it to the group, which was an enlarged snapshot of a latent fingerprint. "Now, the guy who stiffed you and Dana on the interview?"

"Dan Mason," Mac acknowledged.

"This print belongs to your Mr. Mason. Our I.D. Bureau lifted it off the chrome handlebars on Mr. Mullins's scooter before it was logged into evidence. Dan Mason has an extensive criminal history for assault fourth degree and fraud, mainly bad checks and identity theft. Looks like the two assault arrests are D.V. related, both dismissed—although it was enough to get his prints on file."

"Domestic violence, huh?" Jan sneered. "Dismissed because the punk intimidated his wife not to testify, I'll bet."

Mac sat at attention, adrenaline charging his tired bones. So the guy had a record. Why was he not surprised?

"I'll get a workup on him, Sarge," Kevin offered. "See what I can find out on the computer." He'd been taking copious notes. "This Mason guy would be my next stop if I were you." He directed the comment to both Mac and Dana.

"Just what I was thinking," Frank agreed. "I want you and Dana on this guy until you find him. Bring him in on a material witness hold if he won't cooperate."

"You got it, Sarge." Mac could hardly wait to get on it. No wonder Dan Mason hadn't made the interview. He could see the guy getting mad enough to beat up Clay Mullins, then put the old guy under the train to hide his crime. The train would hide any damage he might have done.

"Philly and Russ, I want you two on the kid Dana and Mac corralled last night. Find out where he went after he was released. Question him on the arson, murder deal. The sheriff's office should have a good address for him. And see what you can turn up on Mullins's maid. Do you guys have a name?"

Mac consulted his notes, but before he could flip back to the page where he'd written it down, Dana had it. "Rita Gonzales."

"Check and check," Philly answered.

"Jan, I need the cause and origin confirmed on this fire ASAP. You want to update the group on the fire and contents of the house?"

"Sure, Sarge." Jan stood up to brief them. "Most of the house and the contents are a total loss, though there may be some recoverable stuff in the basement. I recovered what I think will be accelerates from the entry on the riverside, but it will be a while before the lab confirms my suspicions. With the discovery of the body and Polo's hit on the evidence we seized, I went ahead and wrote a two-page search addendum to Mac's affidavit and received a telephonic warrant in case we recovered something that wasn't listed in the initial warrant."

"What kinds of things did he have in the house?" Dana asked.

"Old railroad documents, artifacts, all of it related to railroads. The place was a museum."

"So it's all lost?" Dana seemed genuinely concerned.

"Not all," Jan said. "Fortunately, the concrete construction of the basement, along with the asbestos in the sub floor, protected some of it. The fire department arrived in time to saturate the flooring. It's charred and burned through in places, but a good portion of the floor remained fairly intact. Some of the items can be cleaned up. Luckily the detached garage had more of the same that was undamaged."

Turning to Frank, she added, "I'm waiting on the lab so I can help out if you need me, at least until the next call comes in."

"Why don't you help Kevin with a little background work? We still need info on Jacob Mullins."

"I have a couple of things to add." Mac opened his notebook. "Jacob, assuming he's the victim we found in the fire, had a business card for a local attorney by the name of Addison Shaw. Shaw happens to represent his father's estate, so that may be why he had the guy's card. We have a grand jury subpoena for Clay Mullins's medical and financial records, although we haven't served it on any accounts or bank resources as yet. We mainly got the subpoena so the M.E. could get hold of the medical end."

"I've ordered up an Equifax from headquarters and am in the process of seeing what kind of debts or accounts Mr. Mullins held," Kevin offered.

"You okay with all that, Kev?" Frank asked. "You're signed up for quite a bit of work." He winced and rubbed the back of his neck. "Sorry, Kev. I probably shouldn't have asked in front of everyone."

Kevin smiled good-naturedly. "No problem. I'm fine. I'll let you know if it becomes too much."

"I'll get that workup on both father and son by tomorrow." Kevin glanced at Mac then turned around to look at Dana. "With Jan helping, we should have it whipped in no time. You guys think of anything else, just let me know."

"Guess that fire pretty much messes up our finding anything that tells us why Mullins left his house the night he was killed," Russ mused.

"Actually, Russ, we do have one item." Mac thought about the small black bag. "We have a medical bag we're certain belonged to Mullins. It had his insulin and syringes in it. We recovered it from Mr. Cohen. The kid thought he was ripping off the old man's stash of drugs and hoped there'd be something saleable in it or something that would get him high. We have it in temporary evidence right now and we haven't had time to go over it thoroughly."

"I'll have the evidence technician run it to the lab in the morning to test the vials and dust for prints." Frank added, "Anything else?"

No one responded. Probably because they all had assignments and weren't looking to get more.

"Okay, one more thing. Nobody works past eight tonight. We can pick this up in the morning unless something significant turns up. You've all had a long day already. You won't do anyone any good if you're too tired to think or you stack up a car."

"I second that." Mac punctuated the comment with a yawn. "Hey, partner." Mac eyed Dana. "Let's go get Mason. It'll do me good to see that scumbag behind bars."

"You got it. I knew there was something amiss with that guy the minute I saw him."

SEVENTEEN

Do you want to call out there first or try to catch Mason at work?" Mac thrummed his fingers on the steering wheel while he waited at the take-out window of the espresso cart. He'd been working more than twelve hours, and he needed a caffeine jolt badly.

"I vote we surprise him," Dana said. "A call will just alert him and he'll take off again."

"Assuming he went back to work. With his record, he might have decided to split for good. Especially if he had anything to do with Clay's death."

"Hmm. True. I guess we'll soon find out." Dana reached for the iced latte Mac handed her: a twenty-ounce almond soy latte with four shots.

Mac had ordered a four-shot latte as well—going for the raspberry concoction. He handed the gal a ten-dollar bill and told her to keep the change, which wasn't much.

The drink, with whipped cream on top, wasn't going to do his waistline any good and he grumbled about it.

Dana laughed. "Try going without the cream."

He grinned. "That's the best part."

"Are you serious about losing weight, Mac?"

"Yeah, why?"

"I have an idea. Why don't we put a photo of Philly on the dash? He's a great reminder of why you don't want to let yourself go."

Mac grimaced. "Thanks, but the last thing I want to do is look at Philly's mug all day. Besides, he'd just tease you about having a thing for him."

"Yikes." She took a sip of her coffee and set it in the holder. "I hadn't thought of that."

"Don't worry about it. I'm revamping my workouts and my eating habits as soon as we put this case to bed. Maybe I'll go on that low-carb diet. I figure I only need to lose ten—maybe fifteen pounds."

"Diets don't work. You need to go for the lifestyle change. I have a great plan if you want to see it."

"Thanks, but I'll handle it."

"Okay." She said it as though she fully expected him to fail. Humph—he'd show her. Within a month he'd be back in top physical form.

Forty-five minutes later they pulled into the Terminal 9 parking lot and headed for the office.

They introduced themselves and showed their badges to the receptionist and asked to talk to Mason.

"Dan Mason." The clerk checked the duty roster. "He was scheduled to work today but called in sick."

"Sick, huh?" Dana tossed Mac a disbelieving look. "We need to talk with him about Clay Mullins's death."

The clerk wrinkled her nose in disgust. "Wasn't that awful? Dan has been taking it pretty hard. We all have. Poor old Clay." She frowned. "Then to have his house burn down. You guys are OSP detectives?"

"That's right," Mac answered.

"But it was an accident, wasn't it?"

"We don't know whether the death was accidental or not at this point. That's what we're trying to determine."

"Oh, wow."

Mac leaned against the counter, making eye contact. "You could help us out by giving us Mason's home address. Like my partner said, we need to talk to . . ."

She shook her head before Mac could finish the sentence. "I can't give out that kind of information. Company policy."

"Can I help you with something?" The guy they had talked with the morning after the wreck came up behind the secretary. He'd apparently overheard their conversation.

Mac explained the situation. "We need to talk with Mr. Mason, and it would be a big help if you could give us his address."

His lips turned up in a half smile. "I'll be happy to give you Mason's address and personnel file, detectives. Just as soon as you show me a subpoena."

Mac straightened. "We were hoping to catch him here. He was supposed to meet us yesterday afternoon."

"I'm sure he has his reasons. I can't help you with that."

Mac clenched his jaw but managed to keep his uncomplimentary comments to himself. It ticked him off royally when people refused to cooperate. But then he wasn't exactly expecting an open door.

"We might be able to set you up with our attorneys," the man offered.

"Forget it." Mac stalked out of the office with Dana close behind.

"What now?" Dana folded herself into the passenger seat.

"Call information—see if they can give you an address and phone number. I'll call Kevin. He should be able to locate an address through the power bill records."

Mason wasn't listed in the book, and the address Kevin had on him at this point was an old one putting him in Eugene. "I'll keep looking," Kevin had told them. About the only thing they had come up with was the vehicle description and license number of the car registered with the Department of Motor Vehicles, listing only a post office box for the address.

At seven-thirty, Mac and Dana gave up. The interview with Mason would have to wait until the following day—if they were able to secure an interview at all. Mac had a feeling the guy was long gone. On the way out of town, he put a call in to the Patrol division, asking them to keep an eye out for Mason's vehicle. "If you find him, bring him in for questioning and give me a heads-up."

"Wonder how Philly and Russ are doing with Tyler." Dana sighed. "I hope they had better luck with him than we did with Mason."

"One way to find out," Mac said. "Let's give them a call. See if they need help."

Dana grinned. "Like they'd admit it. I can't believe Russ would make a big deal out of my taking that kid down."

"I think Russ is threatened by you. I'll bet if you'd been with him out there, you'd have outrun him by even more than you did me and he knows it."

"You think?" Dana laughed.

Mac put in a call to dispatch asking to be connected with Philly.

"Yo," Philly answered right away.

"How's Operation Tyler Cohen coming? Dana and I are about to head back to Portland and wondered if you needed some help."

"In your dreams, glamour boy."

"So you found him?"

"Not yet, but we will." Philly grumbled. "How'd you guys do?"

"Nothing yet." Mac told him about their snag with Terminal 9.

"All we got so far is a list of places Tyler likes to hang out. Video arcade, the pool hall, and the state park—so far we got nothing. No one's seen him—or if they have, they aren't telling us about it. Word is the kid and his druggie friends like to hang out along the rail line. They spend the day shooting up and breaking their empty beer bottles. We're heading in too. Figure we'll be able to track him down easier in the daylight."

"Good idea. We could all use some rest."

He hung up and turned to Dana. "I hate giving up on Mason. The longer we wait to catch this guy, the more miles he can put between us."

"Do you really think Mason skipped town?"

Mac shrugged. "Maybe the lawyers got to him and told him to steer clear of us."

"We'll find him in the morning." Dana yawned. "Right now I'm too tired to care."

Once Mac dropped Dana off, he called Kristen. He wasn't sure why. His call could have waited until morning. And probably should have.

"Hey, Mac." She sounded tired.

"I'm sorry for the late call. I was just on my way home and . . ."

"And you wanted to swing by and see me, right?"

He smiled at the hopeful tone in her voice. "What I wanted," he said, "was to know if you made a positive ID on the guy we pulled out of the fire."

"Have you had dinner?"

"No."

"Come over and have dinner with me, and I'll fill you in." The invitation sounded appealing. He had nothing edible in his refrigerator and would have to pick something up. On the other hand, he wasn't sure he wanted to pursue a relationship with Kristen.

"Come on, Mac. It's not like I'm asking for a commitment. Just a little company while I eat. I have some roast beef and potatoes in the crockpot. Andrew's asleep and I'm sitting here alone in front of the fireplace feeling sorry for myself."

"All right." Mac told himself it was the roast beef and potatoes that did it. Not the catch in her voice or the fact that he didn't much like being alone either. Of course he had Lucy, but that was different. "I'm on my way. Should be there in ten."

"Perfect."

Kristen opened the door before he had a chance to knock. "Hey." Her hair looked stranger than usual—like she'd slept on it. She touched her head. "Whoops. I must look wild. I laid down with Andrew and fell asleep."

Mac smiled. "Actually it looks pretty much like it always does."

She punched his shoulder. "Gee, thanks." Kristen stepped back, allowing him entry. The fireplace and living room looked inviting, and the distinct scent of meat and seasonings took him back a few years to when he'd lived with his grandmother McAllister. Her kitchen always smelled like heaven. He slipped off his rain jacket and draped it on the end of the couch. "Smells great."

"Thanks. I enjoy cooking—when I get the chance." Kristen gestured toward the table. "Dinner's ready to go. Have a seat." She'd set it for two, much like she'd done the previous evening when he'd brought takeout.

Mac felt a little like he was walking into a trap, but the bait was too good to pass up. He tossed off the feeling, willing himself to relax and enjoy the moment and the food.

The food was everything he'd hoped for and more. Perfectly seasoned roast—melt-in-your-mouth tender. Kristen had mashed the potatoes with butter and garlic and cream. As sides she'd served baby peas and a tossed salad.

"You were going to eat this kind of meal alone?" Max dabbed his mouth with the cloth napkin and took a drink of the sparkling cider she'd poured earlier.

She cocked her head. "Yeah. My mother served every meal with a certain amount of pizzazz. I don't always get the chance with my schedule being what it is, but I try to carry on the tradition. At home I always felt special, you know. Like we were all royalty to her. Company never got better treatment than we did."

Mac grinned. "This meal was fit for a king, that's for sure."

Kristen rolled her eyes. "Well, your highness, you are about to turn into a scullery maid. Time to help with the dishes."

"Another tradition?"

"Yep." She got up, gathered some dishes, and headed for the kitchen. Mac pitched in, not minding the task at all. His grandmother had expected him to help her as well—not that Kristen was anything at all like his grandmother. When he'd finished clearing the table, he leaned against the counter of the small kitchen and watched Kristen rinse the dishes and place them into the dishwasher. He fought off the urge to go up behind her and wrap his arms around her, drawing her back against him and kissing . . .

Whoa. Mac folded his arms, effectively closing out the thought. Where had that come from? He moved out of the kitchen and into the living room. This was bad—too domestic. Too tempting. Kristen was too eccentric for his tastes. Not his type at all.

So what are you doing here? he asked himself. *Why did you call her, and why did you accept her invitation?*

Mac settled on the sofa and watched the fire, then leaned his head back for just a moment.

"Hey, sleepyhead." Kristen's voice penetrated the thick fog infiltrating his brain. "Wake up, Mac."

He jerked his head up, eyes flying open. "What . . .?"

"Relax." She touched his arm. "You fell asleep. I thought about letting you spend the night, but I'd rather not have to explain your presence to Andrew in the morning."

Mac closed his eyes for a moment to get his bearings. "Right. We wouldn't want that," he murmured.

"No, we wouldn't." Kristen's gaze caught his for a long, heart-stopping moment.

Mac couldn't say who'd made the next move, but his arms went around her and her lips were only a heartbeat away. He kissed her then—a sweet, lingering kiss that roped his stomach in a thousand knots. She leaned into him, and he panicked.

"I'm sorry."

Kristen grinned. "For kissing me or for stopping?"

"Both." He remembered to breathe. "We shouldn't . . ."

"Why?"

"I . . . uh . . ."

Kristen sat up. "Forget I asked, Mac. It's okay. I thought maybe you felt something too."

I do. Mac couldn't put voice to the thought. Kristen had a strange effect on him for sure, but he wasn't ready to get involved. He'd put sadness in her eyes and hated himself for doing that. But the last thing he wanted was to lead her on. He still cared too much about Dana. Mac rubbed his forehead. Why did women have to be so complicated?

"I made a positive ID on the corpse you found in the fire." Kristen got up and walked closer to the fire.

EIGHTEEN

GET SOME SLEEP LAST NIGHT?" Kevin asked as Mac dragged into the office at seven-thirty, still in the process of looping his tie around his neck.

"A little. I'd love to have slept in though." Mac didn't mention that an hour of his sleeping had been done on Kristen's sofa, or that he hadn't gotten home until almost midnight.

"I know the feeling." Kevin turned back toward his own office. "Once you get a cup of coffee, let's meet in the briefing room—say in about fifteen minutes. Dana and Jan ran out to get scones or something; they'll be right back."

Mac peered into the briefing room, surprised to see Philly and Russ already inside and jawing about yesterday's events.

Don't these people ever sleep in? Mac finished with his tie and then bought a cup of coffee from the carafe in the break room. He didn't exactly buy it. They had a donations cup to keep them supplied. Taking a sip of the bitter stuff, Mac wished he'd taken an extra few minutes to pick up some Starbucks on the way in. He met Dana and Jan on his way back to the briefing room. They were both laughing.

"My, aren't we chipper this morning?" Mac growled. He stepped aside so they could enter the room first.

"It was hard getting up," Dana said, "but I feel a lot better after hitting the gym."

"You've gotta be kidding." Mac paused the coffee midway to his mouth.

Dana laughed. "I wish I weren't. I should have gone to the gym. Truth is, I rolled out of bed after hitting the snooze alarm a half-dozen times." She sat down next to Mac and waved a small paper bag in front of him. "Here, grumpy, I brought you something. I didn't know if you'd picked up breakfast or not."

He opened the bag and sniffed appreciatively at the icing-covered pumpkin scone. "Mmm, my favorite. Thanks, Dana." Mac pulled off a huge chunk and stuffed it in his mouth.

"I figured you could use a little pick-me-up."

Mac washed down the bite with a swig of coffee. "You guessed right. I was thinking I might pour the coffee on my head this morning and let it soak in through my pores. I didn't sleep all that well last night."

Fortunately, Dana didn't ask why. "Me too. It takes a while to make up for an all-nighter. I never got used to it, even on patrol. Working graveyard then going to court all day—not my idea of a good time. All you feel like doing on your days off is sleep."

"Hey, what's this?" Philly brushed remnants of a powdered donut from the front of his shirt. "You buy a scone for Mac and not me?"

"Like you really need another treat, Phil. What are you up to this morning, five?"

"Four, but who's counting. Besides it takes a lot to fill my tank."

Dana grinned at him. "Just saving you from yourself, big guy."

Mac wolfed down another huge bite of scone and washed it

down with coffee as Kevin and Sergeant Evans walked in. "Glad to see you were all able to make it," Frank said.

Kevin lowered himself into the chair beside Jan. "You still in on this one with us?"

"As much as I can. Unfortunately, with the dedicated funding position I'm in, I can't become too involved. The State Fire Board is paying most of my position now, and Polo was purchased by the feds so I have to dedicate most of my job to arson investigation rather than homicide. I'd be glad to help with the background work; I just can't get involved in anything that would tie me up in court."

"Understood," Kevin said. "If you can give us an idea of how and where that fire got started, we'd be much obliged."

"And if you could tell us who started it," Mac said, "you'd really make our day."

She laughed. "If I can prove a fire setter, you'll be the first to know."

Sergeant Evans set his notes on the table and took his usual place beside the podium. He took a long sip of coffee before speaking. "Okay, let's get started here." He then took one more sip from his cup before setting it down. "Mac and Dana, let's start with you on the update."

Mac gave Dana a nod. Finishing the scone was his most important objective at the moment, and since he couldn't talk with his mouth full, he'd let Dana give the report. She didn't seem to mind.

Dana stood. "We struck out in our attempts to locate Dan Mason last night. He didn't show up for work—clerk says he called in sick. The powers that be at Terminal 9 refused to give us a current address, and we couldn't locate him through the phone book. We're hoping Kevin was able to come up with an address. Mac put out a call to our patrols with a description of his vehicle and plates. We'll head out there again this morning. If and when we find Mason, I'd like to hook him up to a polygraph. Of course, the way things are going, I doubt he'll cooperate. We're thinking the lawyers for Terminal 9 might have a hand in all this as well."

"I'm curious as to why Mason's prints were on Clay Mullins's chair," Frank said. "We need to get a statement from him one way or the other. Find out where the guy was the night Clay was killed and during the time of the fire."

"Right." Mac wiped his mouth with his hand. "We'll get him one way or another—unless he's left the area. Considering his priors, that's a possibility." Mac hesitated. He needed to let the others know about the positive ID. "One more thing. I called Dr. Thorpe on my way home last night. She told me we had a positive ID on the corpse found in the fire. It is definitely Jacob Mullins. That means we'll be paying another visit to Clay's daughter."

"Right." Sergeant Evans glanced down at his papers. "I got the fax just before I went home last night. Figured you two would want to take care of it."

"Thanks. We need to talk to the husband too." Mac glanced at his watch. He doubted they'd catch either of them at home this morning, but it wouldn't hurt to try.

"Okay, Philly and Russ, what do you have?" Frank asked.

Russ stood and told the group about their efforts to find Tyler Cohen, which had been unsuccessful so far. "We'll head back out to Columbia County again today. Plan on spending some time in the transient camps along the rail line also. Thought we'd check around for potential witnesses to the arson incident. As far as the maid goes, we know where she lives and have an appointment to talk with her today."

"Sounds good. Kevin and Jan, were you able to come up with anything?"

Jan stood first. "I'm still waiting on the arson evidence from the lab. Sorry it's taking so long, but . . ." She spread out her hands. "You guys know how it is. In the meantime, I'll keep working with Kevin on the background checks. I think Kevin received some news back from the credit inquiry, didn't you, Kev?"

"Sure did. Looks like Clay Mullins had a bank account at the U.S. Bank in St. Helens. He didn't have any credit cards or make any house or car payments. The only bills he had electronically removed from his account were for his insurance payments to State Farm, and his post office box and a safety deposit box at the bank."

"Good." Mac mused. "It'll be interesting to see whose name is listed as a beneficiary on his insurance policy."

"I'll see if I can get that information. In the meantime, I'll work with the D.A. to get a grand jury subpoena over to the bank, see what Mr. Mullins kept in the box. I'll page Mac and Dana as soon as we get the go-ahead to pick it up."

"Great. Thanks, Kevin," Mac said. "If we have time today, I'd like us to hit up the real-estate agent who's been pestering Clay's daughter on the land." He glanced at his notes. "Reagan McCloud. I'd also like to touch base with the lawyer who represents Clay's estate."

Frank nodded. "I'll make sure that insulin kit gets down to the lab for processing too. I'll have them check for prints on the bottles and examine and weigh the contents of his prescriptions. Maybe that will shed some light on Clay's medical condition." He frowned. "I know we're tapped for resources, but we have homicide teams ready to go from some of our southern field offices or McMinnville if needed."

"When pigs fly." Philly snorted. "They couldn't even find their way through their own towns. No way are we going to let another OSP office work our tickets."

Frank shook his head, a smile evident in the tip of his mouth— a telltale sign he personally agreed but would never admit it professionally. "Get out of here, and you all be careful."

The detectives filed out of the room, and minutes later Mac and Dana were in the Crown Victoria, heading toward Copper Mountain, which was about half an hour away.

"You want to do the interview?" Mac asked as they pulled up to the curb.

"Sure."

Mac was surprised when Kelly opened the door. This time she was wearing a mint green pantsuit and what was probably a silk blouse the color of rich cream. She had accented the outfit with a string of pearls. "Did we catch you at a bad time?" Mac asked.

"I was just leaving for work." She stepped back to let them in. "I thought I'd be seeing you two again. I suppose you're here to tell me about the fire. I'm surprised it's taken you so long. I read about it in the paper."

"Actually it's more complicated than that," Dana said. "Do you mind if we all sit down?"

"Sure. Come on in." She led them to the great room. "Can I get you anything?"

"No thanks." Mac glanced around. "Is your husband here?"

"I'm afraid not. He's out of town for a medical convention—Atlanta."

"How long has he been gone?" Dana asked. She didn't seem as intrigued with the house as she had on their first visit.

"He left yesterday. Since he's a guest speaker, he couldn't very well cancel." Kelly perched on the arm of the sofa.

"When will he be back?"

"Hopefully the day after tomorrow. He hated leaving right now and said he'd try to come home early. What's this all about?"

"There's no easy way to tell you this, Mrs. Cassidy." Dana gentled her tone. "We found a body in the fire at your father's place."

"A body?" She clasped a hand over her mouth and after a moment she said, "I don't understand."

"The medical examiner has positively identified the victim as your brother."

"Jacob? Jacob was at the house?" Kelly sprang to her feet and began pacing. "What happened?"

"We believe he was murdered. It's possible the fire was started to cover up his death."

"I can't believe this. Why would he go out there?"

"We were hoping you might help us figure that out." Dana shifted so that she could track Kelly's movements. "Did you talk to Jacob after your father died?"

"Yes. He called me. He was so worried about not getting his share. Can you believe that? Not one word about feeling sad about Dad's death. He must have gone out to look at Dad's things." She sighed and sat down on the arm of the chair again. "I guess it doesn't matter now, does it? It's so sad. Dad loved his collection of railroad artifacts and memorabilia. Now it's all gone."

"Kelly, I hate to ask, but we need to have the information in our files. Would you mind telling us where you were on Wednesday night?"

"You think I killed my brother and . . . and started that fire?"

"Not at all," Dana smoothed. "Like I said, we need to ask. And we need a statement from you for our records."

"I was at the office until seven, then went to a political fundraiser. You can ask the mayor. I sat next to her through dinner and spent most of the evening chatting with her. I got home around one and fell into bed."

Dana nodded. "Thank you. I really appreciate your cooperation."

"There's no reason not to cooperate." She shook her head. "I just can't believe Jacob is dead. Who would want to kill him?"

"We're hoping to find that out." Dana tipped her head to one side. "Did he have any enemies that you know of? Did he say anything at all . . . ?"

"No, nothing." She stood up again. "As for enemies, I wouldn't know. Like I told you the other day, we didn't have contact with him."

"When he called, did he give you any indication something might be wrong?"

"Only that he was afraid of being left out of Dad's will. I told him he didn't have anything to worry about. I felt certain Dad would be fair. He wasn't very nice. If he treated others like he treated his family, I imagine he had a lot of enemies."

"Did he know about all the railroad artifacts?"

"Of course. Dad spent his entire life collecting. We never really thought anything of it, but I would imagine some of his collection was worth a lot of money."

"Any idea how much?" Dana asked.

"Not really. I just know that antiquities are a big business. I was planning to hire someone to catalog Dad's things and put a price on them. I guess that's not necessary now."

"Actually, some of his stuff survived," Mac told her. "He had a lot of items in the garage and our arson detective said that some of the things in the basement might be salvageable."

She nodded. "Then I suppose I should go ahead with the assessment." She stared at the carpet. "Maybe you can tell me when you are finished with the house."

"We'll do that," Dana assured her. "I'm so sorry for your loss."

Kelly glanced over at her, then at Mac. "I feel badly that I didn't give you consent to search. Maybe if I had . . ."

"Please don't blame yourself," Dana said. "Your approval wouldn't have gotten us in there any sooner."

She nodded. "Thanks for coming by."

"If you think of anything your brother might have said . . ."

"I'll call. I have your cards from before." She frowned. "Have you talked to Addison Shaw yet? I've left a dozen messages for him to call me, but he hasn't."

"We're hoping to hook up with him today."

"Good, if you do, tell him I'd like to talk with him. I have a hunch my father paid dearly for his services."

"What do you mean?" Mac stopped in the doorway.

"Shaw had Dad's bill forwarded to me. Can you believe it? My father has been dead three days and I get a bill? The man has no scruples whatsoever."

"Could we see the bill?"

"Sure. It's at my office, but I'll fax you a copy."

"That will be great," Dana said as the door closed.

"Did you get the feeling she wanted to get rid of us?" Dana glanced back at the house.

"Maybe she was just anxious to get to work."

"Maybe," Dana said.

"Your intuition kicking up again?"

"Uh-huh."

"Mine too. I guess Kelly came by the morgue yesterday. Kristen said she was pretty cool and collected for someone who's just lost a father."

"Kristen said that?"

"Yeah, when I talked to her last night. Remember, I said I'd called."

A Cheshire grin spread across her face. "You went over to see her after you dropped me off, didn't you?"

Mac could feel the heat climbing up his neck and into his cheeks.

"You did! Why, Antonio McAllister."

Darn flush always gave him away. His grandmothers could always tell when he was lying. "I called to see if she'd made a positive ID and she asked me if I'd eaten."

"Ah. So it's true. The way to a man's heart *is* through his stomach."

"Cut it out." He really didn't want Dana to tease him about Kristen. He'd much rather she be upset.

"Was it good?"

"What, dinner?"

"Of course, dinner. What did you think I meant . . ." Her mouth dropped open. "Oh, Mac, you didn't."

"What I do or don't do off duty is none of your business." He slid into the passenger side seat and pulled up the seat belt, snapping it in place.

Still grinning, she closed her mouth and started the car. "You are absolutely correct. It's none of my business." She tucked a few wayward strands of hair back into her chignon. "So Kristen was suspicious of Kelly?"

"Not suspicious, really. She just told us to be careful."

"Hmm." Dana flipped down the visor to make sure her hair was tidy and professional.

"And just so you know. Dinner was exceptional."

NINETEEN

MAC AND DANA drove to St. Helens and Terminal 9. Hopefully, they'd catch Dan Mason at work. They arrived shortly before 9:30 a.m., making contact at the dispatch center, rather than in the administrative offices. The same terminal clerk, or mud hop, they'd talked to after Clay Mullins's death was standing at a small microwave in the office heating up a breakfast burrito.

"Roger Perrault, isn't it?" Dana asked. Mac was surprised she remembered.

"You guys back again?" The man squinted at them, probably more from poor vision than from suspicion. "After I read the paper last night, I figured you would be. You here to see Mason?"

"Actually, we are." Dana answered in a friendly tone. "Could you tell us where he is right now?"

"Would if I could, folks, but Mason called in sick." He clicked his tongue. "Second day in a row. I talked to him around four this morning; he said the faucet was running from both ends, if you know what I mean."

"Yes, I do." Dana put on a sympathetic smile and took a step closer. "Say, Roger, could you tell us where he lives or where he hangs?"

Mac stood back, enjoying the view. She was deliberately invading the guy's personal space and getting close enough for him to smell the light, sophisticated scent she wore.

"Yeah." He nodded. "I guess I could. I mean it's no secret around here. Mason's got himself a little gambling problem. Likes the bottle too. Most of the time when he ain't working or sleeping, you'll find him down in Scappoose at Gussie's Tavern." Roger looked down at his shoes. "Don't suppose you'll find him there today though—not with him being as sick as he is."

"I'm sure you're right about that. Where does he live?"

"Same place I do. In those apartments north of town—Shady Oaks. They're about thirty years old. A little run-down, but the price is right. I don't need nothin' fancy."

"Thanks," Dana told him. "You just saved my partner and me a lot of legwork. I owe you one."

"What do you say I buy you a drink when you get off work?"

Dana smiled. "Ah, Roger. You know a professional woman never mixes business with pleasure. I'm afraid I'll have to decline." She shook his hand. "But thanks for the offer."

"Anytime." He grinned back, charmed right out of his steel-toed boots.

Dana handed Roger her business card. "By the way, if you happen to see Mason before we do, give me a call."

"I'll do that."

Once out of earshot, Mac said, "Why do I get the feeling I wouldn't have had the same effect on that guy?"

She chuckled. "Because you wouldn't have."

"I don't ever want to hear you complain about how men have the edge in this business."

Dana raised an eyebrow. "You don't think I should have used my womanly charms on the man?"

"Hey, who am I to argue with success?" Mac climbed into the car. "Let's go see if Mr. Mason is home. Though I doubt he will be. I'll bet you anything your friend back there gave him a call the minute we left."

"Are you skeptical or what? You must be one of those glass-half-empty guys."

"Nope. Just being realistic."

MAC WAS RIGHT. Mason wasn't home. The manager hadn't seen him around, but that didn't mean much. When they asked to see his apartment renter's file, they were hit with harsh resistance. "You know I can't do that without a warrant," the older woman had said.

Mac tried to appeal to her sympathies. "Mr. Mason reported in sick. Aren't you concerned about him? I think you should at least have a look."

"The man's car is gone. Sick or not, there's no way you're getting into his file, and I'm not telling you his unit number."

"Can you give us a call if he shows up? We really need to talk with him."

She took the cards but made no promises.

They struck out at Gussie's as well. No one had seen Mason for the last couple of days.

Back in the car, Mac called Frank. "I could be wrong, but it looks like Dan Mason has skipped town. No one has seen him. He's called in sick two days in a row."

"All right. You alerted our patrol guys, right?"

"Right. And the sheriff's office. Maybe someone will spot him. In the meantime, since we're in town, I'd like to pay a visit to the legal eagle handling Clay's estate."

"Good thinking. Let me know what you turn up."

"What do you think?" Dana asked when Mac pocketed his phone. "Shall we give Addison Shaw a call or pay him a visit?"

"Let's cold-tap him and see how he responds."

Dana drove into St. Helens old town and parked near the bookstore and the shops. "If we have a few minutes after we talk to Shaw, I'd like to do a little shopping. That gift shop over there looks interesting, and I need to get a birthday card for a friend."

"I'm okay with that. I'll get coffee while you shop."

They checked the address and walked into the law offices of Addison Shaw & Associates. Being in the downtown area, he was within walking distance of the courthouse and not far from the river. A bell hanging from the doorknob jangled as Mac and Dana walked in.

"Lilly, is that you?" a man's voice called from the back room.

"Nope," Mac answered.

A tall, thin man in his late fifties stepped into the reception area, his sleeves rolled up on his neatly pressed dress shirt. "Sorry, I thought you were my office assistant. We had a toilet back up this morning and she went to the hardware store to buy a plunger."

"Sorry to hear that," Mac said.

"It's not what you're thinking though. We share a line with the restaurant next door. When their grease trap backs up, we get sludge that starts coming up from the sink. Usually a few good pumps on the plunger frees it up, but I took it home for another project and forgot to bring it back."

"I see." Mac was not the least bit interested in the man's plumbing problems. "I'm Detective McAllister and this is Detective Bennett with the State Police. We're investigating Clay Mullins's death."

"Yes, of course. I expected you sooner, actually. But then you've been tied up with all the goings-on at the house, haven't you?"

"Right." Mac nodded. "The case seems to have taken on a life of its own."

He extended a hand. "I'm Addison Shaw. But then you already know that."

Mac shook the proffered hand, as did Dana.

"Come on into my office, such as it is. I'm in the process of moving into a new place, so excuse the boxes."

"You're moving?"

"Mmm. Been in practice for twenty years at this location. There's a new office opening up next to the courthouse. The price was right, so I decided to move."

"Congratulations. Your practice must be pretty lucrative."

"I make a living. In a small town like this folks aren't exactly breaking down the doors. But we manage."

I'll bet. Mac caught himself assessing the guy based on Kelly Cassidy's opinion, which wasn't at all fair. He needed to have an open mind. "We would have been over sooner, Mr. Shaw, but as you said, we've been busy. You've heard the news about Jacob Mullins?"

"Jacob? What news would that be?"

Mac had hoped to trip the guy up. There's no way Shaw would know that Jacob had been in that fire unless he'd been there. Apparently he hadn't been, or he was a good actor. Frank would only just now be releasing the information to the media. All the press had at this point was that an unidentified body was found at the house. "The body found in the fire was Jacob Mullins."

"No!" He rubbed his chin. "That's terrible."

"Did you know Jacob?" Mac asked.

"Yes. Yes, I did." Shaw pulled his shirt-sleeves back down and buttoned the cuffs. "Watched those kids grow up, actually. Clay and I went back a long ways. I haven't seen Jacob for years, though." He eased into the executive chair behind his desk, indicating that Dana and Mac take the cushioned chairs across from him. "Any idea why Jacob happened to be at the house or how the fire started?"

"We aren't at liberty to discuss that right now, primarily because the matter is still under investigation." Mac sat down and waited for Dana. "Do you have time to answer a few questions, Mr. Shaw?"

"Sure. Be happy to if I can." Shaw set some papers aside. "What can I do to help you folks out?"

"We'd like to ask you about your relationship with Clay Mullins, as well as anything you might know about his son. We found your business card in Jacob's wallet during the autopsy."

"Really? You're sure Jacob had my card in his pocket?"

Mac nodded.

"Hmm. I have no idea why—unless he got it from the house. I suppose that's possible. Clay probably had a few of my cards lying around since I usually put one in with my correspondence." Shaw placed his folded hands on the large oak desk. The desk was an antique—aged, but still beautiful.

"Let's start with Clay." Mac pulled a pad and pen out of his briefcase. Dana had already started taking notes.

"Not much to tell. I've represented his estate for the past two years. Of course, we were friends long before that. He came to me, wanting to establish his will and testament when his health began to fail. I drafted the document, which was signed and notarized shortly after he employed my services. I can't show you the will, but I can tell you that he left nearly everything to his grown children. They were his only living family."

"Nearly everything?"

"Well, he left a small amount to his housekeeper and some to a charitable organization."

"The housekeeper. Are we talking a substantial amount?"

"I really can't say, but if you're suggesting she might want to do away with him, that's ludicrous. Rita Gonzales is a saintly woman."

"What about her family? I hear she has a son who isn't entirely spotless."

He sighed. "So true, but murder? I don't think so. At any rate, Clay's death was an accident, wasn't it?"

"We're checking into that," Mac said, watching the attorney's eyes and face. So far the man seemed competent and aboveboard. Mac could see no indication that he was lying.

"Hmm." Shaw rubbed his chin. "Do you think there's a connection between Clay's death and the fire?"

"It's possible."

"Then, money wouldn't have been the motive."

"I don't follow you, Mr. Shaw."

He smiled. "Well, I was just thinking. If Clay was killed so someone could inherit his money, why burn down the house? The fire diminished his estate significantly, you know. His house was full of antiques and railroad memorabilia—things that could never be replaced by the insurance company. I just can't imagine anyone getting rid of those assets."

"How much money are we talking about?" Mac asked.

"Oh, hundreds of thousands, maybe half a million."

Mac jotted the figure down. Shaw had a point. Anyone likely to inherit would have wanted the house intact. So exactly what were they looking at here? "Had you talked with Kelly or Jacob prior to Clay's death?"

"Not prior to. But I did talk with Kelly the day after the accident to let her know about the will. As for Jacob. . ." Addison pursed his lips. "I was in the process of trying to locate him. Actually, I'm surprised he turned up at all. And so quickly—it's almost as if . . ." He paused, as if realizing the implications of what he was about to say.

"As if . . ." Mac repeated.

"Well, you do the math. Jacob hasn't been around for years and then turns up shortly after Clay dies. Seems pretty strange to me. But maybe not. He may have read about his father's death in the papers."

"How about the daughter?" Mac interrupted. He didn't much like Shaw's attempts to play detective. "Did she keep in contact with Clay?"

"Oh, yes. She came out once or twice a month. Kelly made sure he was cared for. She was in contact, but they weren't all that close, if you know what I mean. It was Kelly's idea to hire Rita. Clay balked at first, but after a while he came to depend on her."

"Do you have any idea what Rita did for him?"

He shrugged. "Cleaned the house mostly. Made sure he took his medications and got to his doctor appointments and checked his blood pressure. I think she probably went shopping for him as well."

"You said you talked to Kelly after Clay's death."

"Yes. I called her to let her know I was executor of the estate and told her I wanted to arrange a meeting with her and Jacob. She's an attorney too, you know. She wasn't too happy to hear about my involvement, but Clay wanted an impartial attorney handling his affairs."

"Was that Clay's decision?"

"Of course. A man should never place his finances in the hands of a family member if he wishes for the estate to be divided according to his will. Getting an independent attorney is the prudent thing to do. Besides, she's an environmental attorney with little or no experience in these matters."

"So Clay left everything to his children?"

"Essentially, yes. Like I said, a portion went to Rita and some to charity."

"Can you give me an idea of how much money we're talking about here?"

"A fair amount, actually. Some cash and antiquities. Most of Clay's assets were tied up in real estate. The house was on the list of prospective historical sites for the state, and you are aware of what riverfront property goes for these days—even if it is near a noisy rail yard."

"You mentioned insurance. Were you aware of what kind of insurance Clay might have had and who might be the beneficiary?"

Shaw shook his head. "I know he had insurance, but to be honest, I haven't had a chance to look into it. Even if I had, I couldn't tell you. Confidentiality, you know."

"How about your fees?" Mac ventured. "How much were you paid for your services?"

He raised an eyebrow and smiled. "I'm afraid I'm not at liberty to say, Detective McAllister. I don't work for free, but I can assure you, my fees are fair and in line with what other attorneys are making."

"I understand. I'm just inquiring. Any chance we can get a look at that will?"

"I'm afraid not. Only Clay's daughter can show it to you at this point. I'll be forwarding a revised copy of the will to her this afternoon, once I add the addendum regarding Jacob's death."

Mac shook his head. "Mr. Shaw, it wouldn't hurt you to be a little more cooperative where the will is concerned. We can get a subpoena, but as you know all that takes time."

"I'm not sure I like your attitude, Detective." Shaw took a condescending tone. "I certainly have the right to protect my client's privacy. They taught you that in the academy, I hope."

The bell on the door jingled as a woman entered the office. "I've got the plunger, Addison," she said as she entered his private office. "Oh, I'm sorry. I didn't mean to interrupt."

"No problem. We were just leaving." Mac stood up. "We'll be in contact, so don't leave town."

"Or what?" Shaw got to his feet.

"Or I'll lock you up in the county jail as a material witness. They taught you that in law school, didn't they?" Mac turned and left the office, with Dana following behind.

"WHAT HAPPENED IN THERE, Mac?" Dana asked once they were back in the car. "We were having a nice conversation and all of a sudden you're at each other's throats. Can we really lock up Shaw as a material witness if he tries to leave town?"

"Probably not." Mac shrugged his shoulders. "He just got under my skin with the will issue." He flashed Dana a grin. "Not a good idea really—to make threats we can't back up."

"He didn't look too sure about it though, so I think you achieved your goal of having the last word. I can see why Clay's daughter, Kelly, didn't care for the man.

"So what's your take on him?" Mac asked. "Think he's telling the truth about not talking to Jacob?"

"It's a tough call. He oozes self-importance, but he acted like he had no idea who the body found in the fire was."

"You noticed that too? Could have been genuine." Mac pulled on his seat belt.

"Could have been a ruse. One thing for sure—I'm keeping Addison Shaw on my list of people of interest."

Mac's cell phone rang. "Mac here."

"You two still in St. Helens?" Frank asked.

"We just finished our interview with Shaw and were heading back. Did you have something for us?

"Sure do. Glad I caught you. Got a call from one of our guys in St. Helens. He spotted Mason's car at Gussie's Tavern. Wants to know if he should make an arrest."

Mac gave Dana a thumbs-up. "Tell him to keep an eye on the vehicle—let us know if Mason bolts. We'll go by and talk to him. Thanks."

TWENTY

Mac and Dana arrived at Gussie's Tavern shortly after 11:30. They parked in the back near the tavern entrance, near the OSP vehicle. Mac gave the officer a high sign. After thanking him and asking him to hang around in case Mason tried anything, they headed for the entrance.

The dining room faced the highway. The back of the restaurant was walled off from the tavern's array of pull tabs and video poker games. Mac squinted as he stepped inside. Once his eyes adjusted to the dim light, he took a good look around. One man sat at the bar playing keno and smoking cigarettes.

Two older men were sitting at one of the small tables nursing a lunch-hour pint of ale. None of the men looked anything like Dan Mason. The officer who'd called in the lead sauntered in and hitched himself up on a barstool, then ordered a coffee.

Dana motioned over to the small room off the main bar to the area where the video poker machines were maintained. Oregon law required the machines be out of view from the regular patrons, which was a feeble attempt to discourage gambling and thus reduce the number of addicts. Even though they couldn't see the machines, Mac and Dana could hear the noisy chirps and bleeps coming from the other room. Mac nodded at Dana and the two of them walked into the next room, with Mac following a few steps behind.

Dan Mason was seated on a tall stool playing video poker. The long ash from his cigarette evidenced the trance he was in. With his gaze focused on the screen, he didn't seem to notice Dana's approach.

"She paying out much today?" Dana asked.

"Made about forty bucks or so . . ." Mason stopped midsentence as he turned and caught sight of Dana. Mac folded his arms, feet slightly apart. With his build and height, the stance could look threatening, which is exactly what he wanted.

"You look pretty good for someone needing a sick day." Mac uncrossed his arms and rested his hands on his hip, nearer his gun.

Mason's gaze darted around the room. His only escape was through Dana and Mac. Apparently he decided not to risk it.

"Am I under arrest?" Mason flipped the ash from his cigarette butt to the floor before taking a long pull. Mac had seen the motion all too often. Criminals often took a long pull from a cigarette when they expected an arrest. They weren't allowed to smoke in jail. Maybe Mason thought he already knew the answer to his question. He'd be wrong, of course. They had nothing to hold him on as yet. The fingerprint on Clay's wheelchair wasn't enough to charge him.

"Why would you ask that, Mr. Mason?" Dana responded. "We were just wondering why you didn't keep your appointment."

"Things came up, I lost track of time." Mason pulled his cash-out ticket from the video poker machine. "What now?"

"We'd like to talk to you. Would you mind coming with us over to the Scappoose Police Department so we can have our conversation in a more comfortable environment?"

"And if I say no?"

"That's your right, Mr. Mason," Dana answered.

Mac moved alongside her. "But then we'd have to draw our own conclusions as to why your fingerprints were found on Clay Mullins's scooter, which he was riding when he was killed. We'd also have to explain to the district attorney why you skipped out on an interview. We'll probably have to go back to the train terminal and do some asking around. If we do that we'll have to tell your supervisors that we just spoke to you at the bar . . ."

Dana smiled. "And you just called in sick for your shift."

"I see your position." Mason smashed his cigarette in the ashtray by the machine. "Looks like I don't have much of a choice."

"You always have a choice as to whether or not to do the right thing," Mac said. "You can spend a half hour with us and tell the truth, or you can make us run all over town wasting time for both of us. We don't want to cause you any heartache if you don't have it coming. You heard about the fire at Clay's place I assume?"

"Who hasn't? I had nothing to do with that. I was home with my wife all night, after we spent the evening here. I was sitting right here on this stool."

"See there?" Dana smiled. "That's the type of information we need. What do you say we drive over to the P.D. for some privacy? You'll be back over here cleaning up on your machine in no time."

"So I don't have to go out of here in handcuffs?"

"Nope. Just take a little ride with us. We have no plans to arrest you today, Mr. Mason." Dana added, "Unless you give us just cause."

Mason agreed to an interview and moments later climbed into the passenger seat of the unmarked car. Mac opted to sit in the back—better to sit behind the man if he tried to do something. On the way to the Scappoose Police Department, they had to wait for a westbound train to pass. As Mason scanned the train's cars, his features gentled. Mac wondered what he was thinking. He seemed to like trains; that was a given.

Once the train passed, they crossed the track to the small police building, located in back of the city skateboard park.

They checked in with a supervisor at the police department, and were provided access to a private interview room in the city council chamber within the building. Mac left the door to the room open, pointing out the exit to Mason before they sat down. It was important they document this in their report in the event Mason claimed he was not given the freedom to leave. The legal standard in Oregon that points to a custody situation would require reading a suspect his rights and providing a lawyer upon request. They weren't at that point with Mason.

The three of them sat at one end of a long table in the middle of the floor.

"You need anything to drink before we get started?" Mac asked.

"No thanks. I just want to answer your questions and get out of here."

"Great." Mac scooted up to the table. "I want to make it clear you are not under arrest and can leave anytime you want. We appreciate your cooperation, but if at any point you want to walk out of here or ask us to drive you back to Gussie's, all you have to do is say the word. You clear with that?"

"Yeah, I understand. I have nothing to hide."

"Good. First of all, why don't you tell us why you didn't keep your appointment? For the record this time."

"I just got busy, you know. I never felt that comfortable talking to the cops. Every time I've met a cop they put a set of handcuffs on me. You guys never listen to my side of the story."

"So every time you've been arrested it was the police officer's fault." Dana looked none too happy with the man's response. "You never had it coming?"

"I . . ."

"I've seen your arrest record, Mr. Mason, and I don't think all of those arrests were as a result of trumped-up charges."

"Most of them were dismissed." Mason took a defensive tone. "I hope you noticed that."

"Humph. Is that because your wife wouldn't prosecute you on domestic violence charges after the cops made mandatory arrests for you slapping her around?" Dana leaned forward in her chair.

Mason glanced over at Mac. "You know men don't always start the fights with their old ladies. Mine likes to drink, and she gets a little crazy sometimes. It takes all the strength I got to keep her from trashing our place and me. Like I said, the cops show up and see a chair turned over and a few scratches on the woman, and I get to go to jail. Like I said, you guys never listen."

"We're not here to argue with you," Mac assured him, "but I have to know in my gut that you're being honest with us at the end of this meeting."

"I understand. I just didn't want you guys to make me out to be a wife beater. I've got some problems, but I'm not a violent guy."

"What kind of problems would you say you have?" Mac asked.

Mason shrugged his shoulders. "I've been told I have a gambling problem and I might drink too much. I've thought about calling that number on the machines that the state offers to help out with poker, but I don't think it's anything I can't handle myself. It helps me relieve a little stress, that's all."

"Anything else we need to be aware of?"

"That's it, man. Maybe I've got more of a problem than I think. You know, a few bad checks and the like. To be honest, that's why I missed our appointment the other day. I was a little stressed from the whole thing—talking to the cops again just wasn't on my wish list, you know. I went to the tavern and started playing, the hours and the drinks just started to add up. I ended up losing a few bucks and got into it with the old lady again. I knew I was blowing you guys off but . . . anyway, I didn't do anything wrong so I figured you guys would just go away."

"I can live with that." Mac tapped his pen against his hand. "Tell us about your interaction with Clay Mullins. How do you explain your fingerprints being on his chair?"

"Like I told you, Mullins was a big pain in the neck, but I wouldn't kill the old buzzard. Sure he would show up every day and count deadheads along the rail line and give his report to management." Mason held up fingers in the quote sign when he said the word *report*. "Mullins was a legend at the terminal, and I actually respected the guy. He held a similar position to my own, back before we had shifts. In his day he was actually responsible for the work three of us do now. I don't know how he did it."

"How did that make you feel, having your work criticized?" Mac asked.

"How do you think? I had great production numbers, but I just happen to work the morning shift—that's when the old geezer would come over. The swing and graveyard shift guys didn't have to put up with him because Mullins was home by then. The old guy was always getting in the way in addition to making my life miserable by giving these reports to management. I've got bills you know. I didn't need this guy running flak for me with the brass."

"What do you mean by 'getting in the way'—you mean for a promotion or what?"

"I mean physically in the way, he was like having a kid on the terminal property. I don't know why management tolerated him. He was always getting stuck with that scooter of his."

"The scooter we recovered the night he was killed?"

"Yeah. He would high center that thing all the time. I bet I jerked him back on the footpath a dozen times when he got in a jam."

Convenient excuse for the fingerprint on the handlebars, Mac thought. "Why do you think management tolerated Mullins on the terminal grounds? Wasn't he a liability for the company?"

"Thank you, someone finally agrees with me. There was a rumor going around that the old coot was leaving some or all of his estate to the terminal. I thought that was bunk—I mean who leaves property to the railroad? But that's the only reason I could think of for the brass letting the old-timer hang around. He wanted the terminal to build a railroad museum and fill it up with his collection. I suppose all that got lost in the fire. Too bad. I heard he had some cool stuff."

"Speaking of the fire," Mac said, "can you give us the names of people who can put you at the bar—confirm your alibi the night of the fire?"

"You bet. My wife and the bartender."

Mac jotted down a few notes. "That's about all I have right now. Detective Bennett?" Mac turned the interview over to Dana.

"Just a few things, Mr. Mason. Did you know either of Clay's children?"

Mason shook his head. "I never met his family. Heard he had a daughter living in Portland. She came to see him sometimes."

"He also had a son, named Jacob Mullins."

"Never heard that. Anyhow, I didn't know either of them. Alls I can say is that I saw a fancy white BMW outside the old guy's house once in a while. That was about the only time he didn't come over to the terminal. We'd know his daughter was visiting. The only other car I ever saw on a regular basis was the maid, but she drove a Ford Escort."

"Sounds like you paid attention to what went on at his place."

"Not really. Guess I would notice when he didn't show up. We all got a little worried on those days. You couldn't help but look out for the old guy. My own father died about ten years ago. I guess I did respect Mullins even if I couldn't stand the sight of him. Everyone kinda looked out for old Clay; nobody here would have wanted anything bad to happen to him. Nobody hated him enough to kill him, if that's what you're thinking."

"Would you be willing to take a polygraph examination to verify the things you told us today?" Dana asked.

"If it would help get me uninvolved in this thing, sure. What do I do?"

"We'll drive you back over to the tavern and make some calls on the way. I'm pretty sure we can get someone to come out here to do the test in the next day or two."

"Bring it on."

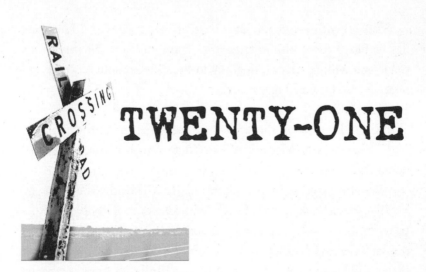

TWENTY-ONE

Aᴄᴛᴇʀ ᴅʀᴏᴘᴘɪɴɢ ᴍᴀꜱᴏɴ ᴏꜰꜰ at Gussie's Tavern, Dana drove over to the gift shop. While she was there, Mac went into the café across the street and ordered a roast beef sandwich and coffee. A few minutes later, he brought it outside and sat down at the small round table. The chairs weren't the most comfortable things—those ornate metal jobs with round seats.

The day had surprised them with warmth and sunshine. Too nice to waste sitting inside. While he ate, he ran through the case—or cases—in his mind, occasionally checking his notes. It was a weird one for sure. He'd thought they had something going with Mason, but if the guy was telling the truth, he would soon be out of the loop as a suspect.

When Mac finished eating, he picked up his garbage and took it to the trash can beside the door. He then returned to his chair and placed a call to Kevin.

"Hey, partner. Do you have anything new for us?" Mac watched Dana emerge from the shop, bag in hand.

"Talked with Jacob Mullins's boss," Kevin told him. "The same day he heard about his father, he took some time off. No one seems to know anything about him going to St. Helens though. We're still digging—so far nothing unusual."

"Let us know."

"Right. By the way, the subpoena's ready for you at the bank."

"That was fast." Mac pulled a pad out of his briefcase and jotted down the details.

"We aim to please." Kevin chuckled. "It'll be ready when you are. You'll want to hook up with Clay's housekeeper too. Philly and Russ talked to her briefly. You knew her son and Cohen are friends. She thinks Tyler is a bad influence. Wants Philly to lock him up and throw away the key. At any rate, Russ and Philly are more interested in finding Tyler at this point, and she had a lead for them to follow. They don't think she had anything to do with the fire or Clay's death. Seems like a nice lady. Not taking her boss's death too well, I guess. Philly said she got pretty emotional so they figured the full interview could wait." Kevin gave Mac the housekeeper's address and phone number.

"So they don't have Tyler yet?" Mac asked while he wrote.

"Nope, but it sounds like they're closing in."

"Good." Mac hesitated. "We sure miss you being out here with us, Kev."

Kevin sighed. Mac visualized him with both elbows on his desk, running a hand over his bald head. "I wish I could be out there too, partner. But that isn't going to happen for a while. My doc tells me I'll be able to return to work full time once the chemo sessions are done and I get some strength back. I don't know, though. Seems like I keep getting weaker. Guess that's to be expected."

Mac didn't know how to answer. "I'm betting you'll be back in no time. I doubt there's anything that can keep an old workhorse like you down for long."

"I hope you're right. Say, did you get a chance to interview Clay's attorney?"

Mac gave him the details. Kevin listened intently then said, "Sounds like you two are doing great without me."

"I don't know, partner. We're floundering here."

"It'll all come together. Piece by piece." Kevin really believed that. "Just look at the cases we've worked. Those first few days are the hardest. Once we gather all the evidence we'll figure it out."

Mac smiled at the optimism. Dana would appreciate that.

"How's Dana doing?" Kevin asked.

"Great." Mac raised a hand to greet the subject of their conversation as she placed a bag next to the empty chair across from Mac. "She just walked up—want to talk to her?"

"That's okay, just tell her I said hi."

"Kevin says hi," Mac told her.

"Hi back." She waved and went inside to order.

"Oh, one more thing, Mac. Melissa Thomas will set up for a poly tomorrow on Mason and Rita. She can stay longer if you want anyone else in there. Hey, buddy, I gotta go; I'm getting another call. I'll let you know when I get anything else."

"What's happening?" Dana slipped onto the chair and dropped a teabag into a pot of hot water.

Mac closed his phone and took a sip of his coffee before answering. "We got a subpoena for the safe-deposit box. I'm thinking we should hit the bank, then drop over to see Clay's housekeeper. Philly and Russ talked to her briefly and got a lead on Tyler Cohen."

"Philly and Russ found the kid?" Dana asked.

"Not yet, but they will. Philly's like a bloodhound."

"Did they interview Rita?" She swirled the bag and put the lid back on the hot water.

"Briefly."

"Good. I'm glad for the opportunity to talk with her."

"From what Kevin says, Rita is pretty shaken up about Mullins's death and the fire."

"I imagine. She lost her boss and her job. Did they have anything to say about the interview?"

"Just that they didn't think she had anything to do with the fire. She'll be taking a poly. By the way, Kev's arranged to have Melissa Thomas come out tomorrow to run the polygraphs on Mason and Rita—Cohen if we can find him. I'd try to set up Addison, but I doubt he'll bite."

"Doesn't hurt to ask." Dana leaned back as the gal behind the counter brought her a green tortilla wrapped around something.

"Here's your fish taco," the woman said. "Let me know how you like it."

Mac watched the woman walk back inside. "A fish taco? I didn't see that on the menu."

Dana examined it and nodded. "I know. I asked if they could put it together for me. Looks wonderful."

Mac shrugged. "Hmm. About Addison. It's your call. Anyway, Rita did have some information on Tyler. The kid hangs out with her son sometimes. Guess she isn't too happy about that. Told Philly and Russ that she hopes they get the guy and put him away for good. He's a bad influence."

"I'll bet." She poured the tea into her cup. "I'm glad we'll have a chance to talk to her."

"Me too." Mac grimaced at the pea-green tea in his partner's cup. "What is that stuff?"

"Green tea. I'm really trying to take care of myself, so I've started to have at least one cup a day—for the antioxidants. It's good for you."

"If you say so." As much as Mac wanted to start eating healthier, he wasn't sure he wanted to follow Dana's lead. "Green tea and green tortillas, yuck."

"It's actually quite good." Dana paused to take a bite. "Do we have anything on Jacob yet?"

"Kevin is still trying to dig up more background on him. He took a couple of days off work—for his dad's funeral and such."

"Bet he had no idea he'd be going to his own."

"So far no one seems to know anything about his visit to St. Helens. I find it odd that no one knew he was there."

"Yeah, especially since he had a key to the place. Maybe someone isn't being completely honest with us."

"Like his sister?" Mac asked.

"Or Addison Shaw. We did find Shaw's card in Jacob's pocket."

Mac waited while Dana finished off her fish taco, discarded her trash, and complimented the gal who'd made it for her. "All set?" she asked.

"I'm ready."

Mac opened the driver side door and started to get in. Dana had pulled the seat forward, making the fit a little too tight. "Um—I thought I'd drive, if you don't mind."

"Not at all."

Mac hit the lever, sending the seat back into its farthest position.

Dana pulled out her notebook and scanned the pages. "Did Kevin say whether Russ and Philly asked Rita specifically about Jacob?"

"I don't think so." Mac backed into the street. "Best thing to do is call them. No sense duplicating things."

"Mmm. Sure would be nice to get some idea about who might have wanted him dead."

"Just speculating again," Mac said, "but the sister comes to mind. With her father and brother dead, she ends up with the entire estate."

"Follow the money, huh?"

"Darn right. Then again, maybe Jacob found something incriminating and had to be eliminated."

"My head is swimming, Mac. Even with writing everything down I feel like we're being bombarded on all sides."

"I know what you mean. I'm not even sure which case we're working on. We're still trying to figure out what happened to Clay and all of a sudden we have a break-in, a fire, and a murder victim."

"Not to mention the acting chief of police releasing the train car and sending our security officer on a bogus call the night Clay's place was torched. I'm still steamed about that."

Mac agreed. "Yeah, but I doubt the guy has anything to do with our case. He's playing politics with the big guys at the terminal. You know, it's 'you pat my back, and I'll pat yours.'"

Mac pulled up in front of the U.S. bank. "Kevin says the district attorney has already issued subpoenas for Clay's safe-deposit box in St. Helens and his post office box. Darren was supposed to have faxed the subpoena to the bank manager, who's promised to release the property as soon as we get there."

"Great." Dana opened the car door. "Let's go in and take a look."

Mac stopped at the door. "Care to make a wager? I'll bet the manager won't know what we're talking about."

Dana chuckled. "What kind of wager?"

"Coffee for a week."

"Make it a month."

"Okay."

"You're on, Mr. Negativity. I'll bet everything is in order."

They pushed through the heavy glass doors and walked over to the only human in sight: a redhead wearing a colorful, gauzy tent dress. The woman looked ethnic and beautiful.

She stood when Mac approached. "I'm Ginger Stern, the branch manager. Are you from the district attorney's office?"

"Actually we are with the State Police. I'm Detective McAllister, and this is Detective Bennett."

"Right." The heavyset woman offered her hand to Mac, then to

Dana. "Please have a seat. She motioned toward the two chairs in front of her desk.

Mac made no move to sit. He glanced at Dana, who was by now giving him a "ha-ha-I-win" look. "We were told the required subpoena was faxed over so we could view and seize the effects of the late Clayton Mullins."

"Yes, I received the fax," Ginger said. "I apologize for the legal loopholes, but it is bank policy to protect the privacy of our clients. Now, did you say *seize*? I was told you would only be reviewing the contents."

"That may be the case, but we won't know until we take a look. Don't worry; I'll supply an itemized receipt for any items we remove from the box. The contents will eventually be turned over to Mr. Mullins's only living heir, a daughter who lives in Washington County."

"That will be fine. I must admit I've never had this kind of request before. We don't get much excitement in the banking business." Giving them an amicable smile, she led Dana and Mac through a locked door into a large security room. Pulling two keys from her pocket, Ginger unlocked the safe-deposit box gate door and pulled the large metal box from the sleeve. "Do you want a private viewing room?"

"No thanks," Dana answered. "The table will be fine."

Ginger placed the large metal box on the small table in the middle of the room and placed the keys back in her pocket. "I'll leave you two to your business. Just let me know when you're done or if you need anything."

"Great, thank you so much." As soon as the door closed, Dana punched the air with one fist then the other as she danced in a circle. "I won, I won! Coffee for a month. Does my heart good, Mac."

"Humph, you don't have to be so happy about it." Mac opened the steel lid to the safe-deposit box and pulled out the contents, the bulk of which were old black-and-white photographs and some letters.

"They must be of his wife and kids." Dana flipped through the photos. "They were a pretty handsome couple in their day."

Mac glanced at a wedding photo bearing the date 1943.

"Oh, I bet this was her wedding band." Dana held up a slim gold band that was well worn on one side.

"Take a look at this," Dana said, peering into a thick envelope bearing the logo and address for Addison Shaw, Attorney at Law. "Looks like a copy of Clay's will."

"Is it an original or just a copy?"

She pulled out the document and flipped through the pages. "A copy. Look, there are no signatures on the lines at the end where he and Addison Shaw have spots to sign. It's not notarized either."

"Read it over. Where does it have all his assets going? Does everything go to the kids like Shaw told us?"

"Yeah. Kelly and Jacob get most of it—well, now it's just Kelly. Rita gets fifty thousand dollars."

"That's not small change. People have killed for less."

"Looks like Kelly inherits everything else. Didn't Shaw say something about a charity?" Dana frowned. "Oh, here it is. Five thousand dollars to his church."

Dana pulled out a thick envelope with an insurance company logo on it. "Looks like his insurance contract." Perusing it, Mac said, "Nothing surprising here. Kelly is the beneficiary."

"Here's something else." Mac drew papers out of a larger manila envelope. "Looks like a letter and some blueprints."

Dana leaned in closer and read aloud. *"To whom it may concern. Enclosed are plans for the new railroad museum and interpretive center. I, Clay Mullins, require the terms be met prior to title and deed transfer of my lands and holdings to the City of St. Helens, Terminal 9, and the Columbia County Historical Society . . ."*

"Terms, what terms?" Mac flipped to the next page.

"Mason was right. Looks like Clay had plans for all that railroad stuff of his," Dana murmured. "What a shame. He died before he could build the museum, and now with his home gone and so much of his memorabilia lost it will probably never happen."

"According to this document, Clay was planning to spend the bulk of his fortune."

Dana scanned the two documents again. "If he had lived to implement this, Kelly and Jacob wouldn't have gotten squat."

Mac whistled. "I think we just found a motive for murder."

"What's the date of the papers where he talks about the museum?" Dana asked.

Mac shook his head. "No date. Looks like he might not have finished it."

"Hmm." Dana's eyes narrowed. "I wonder if Addison Shaw knows anything about this."

"If he's responsible for the estate, how could he not know? Clay must have told him about these plans."

"Maybe he did know," Dana said. "That doesn't implicate him."

"True. And if he knew, he's sure not about to tell us. We'll have to get a warrant to search his office for a revised will. In the meantime, we'd better document all this. Did you bring in an evidence form?"

"Got one right here." Dana pulled the form from her leather binder and set about itemizing the list of documents and personal effects. Once they'd finished, Dana gave Ginger a copy of the evidence sheet, so she could make a duplicate copy.

"Did you find anything interesting?" Ginger asked. "I suppose it's none of my business, really. It's just that I'm going to miss the old guy. He'd come riding into town on that scooter of his about once a week, and almost always he'd stop by the bank to make a deposit or withdrawal or to check on his box."

"That often?" Dana said.

"He was lonely, you know. Missed his wife something awful. At least now they're together in heaven. I think he used the box as an excuse to visit too." She smiled. "Clay was quite a character, you know."

"How so?" Mac asked.

"Oh, he was such a tease, kept asking me when we were going to run away together." The woman's round shoulders rose and fell with a sigh. "Of course we never would, but it was fun making plans." Her eyes filled with tears. "We're going to miss him."

Mac nodded. "Thanks for all your help, Ms. Stern."

"Oh, please. Call me Ginger."

"Ginger." Mac shook her hand. "We'll be in touch."

"Oh, Detectives," she called after them. "I meant to tell you something. I don't know if this has any bearing on your case, but— well, it's about Clay's son."

Mac stopped in his tracks. "You have information about Jacob?"

"Well, like I said, it's probably nothing, but Jacob was in here the day after the accident wanting to get into his father's safe-deposit box. I told him there was no way we could do that unless he had paperwork giving him access—like a will or something. He wasn't too happy."

"Did he say what he wanted or why?"

"I got the feeling he was looking for something. I heard him mumbling something about it maybe being at the house."

"Anything else?" Dana asked.

"No, nothing. I'm sorry. He left and the next thing I heard, the house had burned down." She frowned. "You don't suppose he started that fire, do you?"

"Hard to say, ma'am." Mac didn't tell her that Jacob had been murdered or that it had been his body in the fire. While they'd given the media an ID, they hadn't released the specifics on his death. "But thanks for the information. We'll definitely get back to you."

TWENTY-TWO

THE TWO DETECTIVES STARTED FOR THE D.A.'S OFFICE, and phoned Sergeant Evans to bring him up to speed on their recent developments.

"Interesting," Frank said. "We may have enough to obtain a search warrant to go over Shaw's files and computers. I'll talk to Volk while you two hustle over and interview Rita Gonzales. Find out if Jacob had any contact with his father prior to their deaths. Meet me at the DA's office when you're done."

"Will do."

"We'll do what?" Dana asked.

"Meet Sarge at the D.A.'s office after we interview the housekeeper."

"Why is he coming?" Dana asked. "We're handling things okay, aren't we?"

"You mean there's something you don't know?" Mac chuckled.

Dana frowned. "That's a backhanded compliment if I've ever heard one."

"Sorry. I couldn't resist. Seems like you're always on top of things. Anyway, department policy requires that a supervisor be present when officers are serving a search warrant."

"I knew that." Her lower lip jutted out in a pout. "I just forgot."

"Sarge will squeeze the warrant out of Volk—hopefully we have enough for one. In the meantime he wants us to talk to Rita Gonzales."

RITA LIVED IN A NICELY KEPT OLDER HOME on the west side, settled among several acres of rolling hills. Dana had called en route, and Rita quickly answered the doorbell and invited them in. She'd obviously been crying and made no apologies. Speaking with an Hispanic accent, she began talking about her boss in glowing terms. "I cannot believe Mr. Mullins is dead. Such a good man. He always give me more than he owes. Tells me all housekeepers should get tips." She smiled. "He was a generous man to everybody—to the paper boy and to the mail carrier."

"Mrs. Gonzales, did you ever meet Clay's son?" Mac asked.

She frowned and shook her head. "No. Only the daughter. Kelly was so kind to him. Came once every week or two. She'd bring his medication and things he needed from Costco or some of the other big stores in town. No son. His son never came. Not while I was there."

"You're sure?" Her answer fit with what Kelly had said.

"Oh, yes. There were pictures in his house of a young man, and when I first began working for him, I asked who it was. Mr. Mullins grew very sad and told me his son went away and never came back."

"Did Clay ever talk to you about his will?" Mac met her gaze, and she looked away.

"No . . ." She slowly moved her head from side to side.

"You don't seem certain."

"Mr. Mullins would say things sometimes."

"Like what?"

"'Someday, Rita,' he tell me, 'someday this will be a museum. And all this land will be a park.'"

"Did he mention how that would happen?"

"No. I didn't know how that would happen. Maybe you should talk to Mr. Shaw. He was Mr. Mullins's lawyer, and they talked sometimes."

"Did you ever hear Clay tell Shaw about his plans?"

"No. Mr. Shaw never came when I was there."

"When was the last time you were at the house?"

"Three days before Mr. Mullins died. I came in two times a week and sometimes a little more if he needed me there."

"How was his health that day?"

"Good. He went over to the rail yard after I got there. He often did because he didn't like the noisy vacuum."

"Mr. Mullins was a diabetic," Mac said. "Did he have any problems with taking his insulin?"

"No problems. He took care of himself very well. Always, like clockwork, he check his blood sugar and take his medicine."

"Did you know you were mentioned in Clay's will?"

She nodded. "He told me one time he was going to leave me some money, but I said no. I have enough. My husband and I both work. We do okay. See, we have this nice house."

Mac nodded, affirming that it was indeed a lovely home. "Did your son know about the possibility of your getting an inheritance?"

"No." She pinched her lips together. "I never told anyone. My son would not have hurt Mr. Mullins. He's a good boy. He just goes around with the wrong people sometimes."

After a few more questions, Mac was pretty well in agreement with Philly and Russ that Rita had nothing to do with Clay's death or the burglary or fire. Still, he asked her to take a polygraph, to which she readily agreed. Mac didn't have the same assurance about her son, however, and planned to keep him on the list.

After the interview, they headed over to the D.A.'s office, where Darren Volk and Sergeant Evans were still discussing the warrant.

"I don't know that there are grounds for a search warrant," Darren said. "I can't believe that Addison Shaw would be involved in anything underhanded. Addison was once a senior prosecutor in this office. I met him when I first started working here. Addison was my mentor."

"I'm sorry, Darren," Frank pressed, "but according to Shaw, Clay's kids are the primary beneficiaries of the estate. What Mac and Dana found in the safe-deposit box indicates that Clay wanted the bulk of his estate to be used in creating a railroad museum."

"The housekeeper verified that," Mac said. "Told us it was Clay's dream to see his place turned into a museum and a park."

"Shaw may be out of the loop on that," Frank said to Volk, "but you have to admit things are looking fishy. We also have opportunity and intent for a murder. Maybe one of Mullins's kids decided to murder their father before the new will could be implemented. We need to know if Shaw had any information at all about Clay's plans. And we need to know if Clay had another will. If he did, Shaw is likely to have a copy or at least some notes on it."

"All right, I'll agree. Though I have to tell you, I have a lot of respect for Addison. I just can't believe he'd be involved in any of this."

Reluctantly, Darren assisted the detectives with drafting the search warrant affidavit for Addison Shaw's office, adding the disparity between the will and the papers found in Clay's safe-deposit box.

The Circuit Court judge for Columbia County reviewed the affidavit and finally authorized the search of Shaw's legal office for files associated with Clay and or members of his family.

The judge warned the detectives not to review or seize any documents associated with any other clients, as this was highly protected information. He also declined to allow a search of Shaw's personal residence, although he allowed a search of his person and the seizure of computers at the law office if required.

Philly and Russ met up with Mac, Dana, and Sergeant Evans at the district attorney's law library for a quick warrant briefing. They had just talked with one of the real-estate agents who had hoped to talk Mullins into selling. "Reagan McCloud. She's a real piece of work," Russ said.

"Yeah, real sweet. Russ here was drooling all over her."

"I was not drooling. I was being polite—something you could take a few lessons in. She's a nice lady—assertive. Knows what she wants and isn't afraid to go after it."

"Pushy," Philly corrected.

Russ gave him a sidelong look. "She's a top agent in her company and got there by digging up sweet deals like Clay's. She claims to have investment offers in the seven figures. There's a large investment group from Portland wanting to buy, and there's an offer from Terminal 9 wanting the property for commercial use."

"With land worth that much, there's a potential for more than wheeling and dealing," Mac said.

"She admitted to going over the line talking to Clay's daughter like she did," Russ indicated.

"We won't want to write the woman off," Philly added, "but she was over in Lincoln City meeting with a contractor while all the stuff with Mullins was going on. She left a week ago and didn't come back until last night. The contractor confirms that she was there. We don't know about the investors, though."

"Check them out when you can," Frank told them. "We'll want alibis for the night Clay was killed as well as for the night the fire was set and Jacob Mullins was murdered."

Frank hadn't heard back from the crime lab on the contents of the bag containing Clay's medicines but thought they should be calling anytime. Tyler Cohen was still at large, but Philly and Russ were negotiating something with Tyler's mother. The polygraph detective, Melissa Thomas, would be coming out to Columbia County the following morning to offer the tests to Rita Gonzales and Dan Mason.

When they had completed the briefing, the four detectives and their sergeant walked the short distance to Addison Shaw's office. Dana and Mac went in alone while the other three waited outside for their cue to come in.

"May I help you?" the receptionist asked.

"Lilly, isn't it?" Mac asked.

"Yes, it is."

"Lilly, we're here to see Mr. Shaw." Mac craned his neck to peer into the office and caught a glimpse of the attorney's shoulder.

"Mr. Shaw can't see you right now. You might call after . . ." The assistant stopped midsentence when Mac held up his hand. "Oh, I think Mr. Shaw will see us. He really has no choice. Have the others come in please, Dana," Mac said. "We may need their assistance."

Dana signaled for the others to join them.

Mac was starting to walk into the office when Shaw came out.

The attorney straightened his tie and smiled. "Detective McAllister, I apologize. I'd asked not to be disturbed so I could catch up on some paperwork. I'd have come right out if I'd known it was you. What can I do for Oregon's finest?"

"I'd like to talk to you about some papers we found in Clayton Mullins's safe-deposit box that didn't match up with the will you told my partner and me about."

"I don't know what you're talking about. And I certainly don't like your accusing tone. Are you suggesting I did something wrong?"

"I don't know—you tell us."

"I don't have to tell you anything. And I don't have to stand here and be insulted." His face turned a dark ruddy color as he pointed toward the door. "I'd like you and your little friends to leave now."

"He's calling you 'little,'" Russ said in a stage whisper to Philly.

"Really?" Philly replied out of the corner of his mouth. "Amazing, isn't it? I've been on that diet for three hours now. The fat must be melting off." Enjoying the moment a little too much, Philly stepped up next to Mac, moving into position in case Shaw put up a fight.

Mac stood firm, legs slightly separated. He doubted Shaw would try anything, but you never knew. Sometimes it was the least likely people who tried to pull a stunt out of desperation. "We'd like to ask your cooperation in a search of your person and your law office for evidence of an altered will and any evidence related to the suspicious death of Clay Mullins and the murder of Jacob Mullins."

"That's out of the question, detectives, and unless you have a search warrant I must insist you leave now."

Mac pulled the warrant out of his inner jacket pocket. "I do indeed, Mr. Shaw." Mac held up the warrant, supplying a copy to the bewildered attorney.

Philly, definitely in his element, wore a wide grin. He seemed to take great satisfaction in serving a warrant on a lawyer. "You are entitled to stay on the premises, though you may not interfere or conduct any business. As you can see, a search of your person is commanded in the warrant."

"This is ludicrous. I demand the opportunity to speak to the judge." Shaw stormed back into his office and attempted to slam the door.

Philly pressed against the door, pushing it and Shaw out of the way. Shaw ran to his phone, but Philly grabbed it away and set it back in the cradle.

"I want to speak to your supervisor immediately."

"Knock yourself out, partner." Philly pointed to Sergeant Evans, who was now standing in the doorway. Frank folded his arms and leaned against the wall. "I'd suggest you cooperate, Mr. Shaw. The warrant is legal, and I'm afraid you have no choice but to comply."

"You hear that, Mr. Shaw?" Philly taunted him. "First, you can empty the contents of your pockets and place your wallet on the desk. Don't make me feel like you're holding back either, or I'll be forced to conduct a more intrusive search—if you know what I mean."

"I'm reporting you and your hooligans." Shaw all but spat the words at Frank. Then, looking back at Philly, he backed down.

Smart move, Mac thought. Tangling with Philly would be a little like taking on a grizzly. Mac almost felt sorry for Shaw. Philly was being a little more aggressive than necessary, though his methods were working.

Shaw finally complied by emptying his pockets on the table. At the same time, he went through a litany of threatening insults, of lost jobs, and lawsuits.

They found nothing of value on Shaw's person, and his items were returned to him. "Why don't you come outside and talk with me now, Mr. Shaw?" Sergeant Evans said in a friendly tone. "I understand your frustrations and would be happy to explain our intentions to you."

"Finally, someone with some common decency." Shaw hurried out of his office, making a wide berth around Philly.

While Frank soothed Shaw's ruffled feathers, Dana videotaped the office before the detectives started searching. Philly, Mac, and Dana conducted the actual search, while Russ acted as the evidence officer, collecting the evidence that the other officers found and documenting it on the evidence form after bagging and tagging each piece.

They seized two office computers, the one in Shaw's office as well as the one used by his office assistant.

Mac could hear Frank talking to Shaw in the reception area. "I'm sorry for the inconvenience, Mr. Shaw. Your office equipment will be taken to our office and will be examined for evidence by a forensic computer expert, who will supply you a copy of the hard drive by tomorrow morning so you can continue to conduct your business."

"Is this really necessary, Detective?" Shaw seemed to have mellowed a bit. "I can assure you, I have done nothing wrong."

"Perhaps not, but as you and I both know, you'll stand a much better chance in court if you don't argue with us about the validity of a search warrant at the time of service. The time to press your point is in front of a judge."

"I agree," Shaw said. "And make no mistake, I will be protesting and talking to your supervisors about your bullying tactics."

"You do that, Mr. Shaw. My lieutenant can be reached at the same number on the business card I gave you." Frank didn't seem the least bit worried.

The detectives examined several files, seizing only those documents associated with Clay Mullins. Mac couldn't really blame the attorney for being upset—especially if they were wrong and Shaw didn't know about Clay's desire to donate his money to creating a railroad museum.

Mac stepped into the lobby, aiming his stern gaze at Shaw and his office assistant. "Do you have any other documents or records associated with Clay or Jacob Mullins on the premises?"

"Not unless there's something in the safe." The assistant cast a furtive look at her boss.

Shaw's warning gesture came too late.

"What safe?" Philly asked.

The assistant glanced at Shaw and gripped the back of her swivel chair. She'd probably lose her job, but she apparently balanced her options and made her choice. "It's behind the green law books. The books are a false front. It's a combination safe, and only Mr. Shaw has the combination."

She turned to Shaw. "I'm sorry, Addison."

Shaw glared at her, his jaw working overtime.

Mac stepped into the office and examined the shelves in question, then pulled the false front of hardbound books from the shelf. "It's a clever way to disguise it; I'll give him that."

Sergeant Evans turned to the lawyer. "The combination please, Mr. Shaw."

Shaw hesitated. Frank added, "You can unlock your safe if you'd like to preserve the integrity of its security, although I must insist you open it."

Shaw's narrow shoulders slumped as he made his way to the safe. Mac stepped back to give him room. Standing in front of it to obstruct their view, Shaw punched in a series of numbers then tugged on the handle to release the lock and stepped away.

Philly moved in first and with a gloved hand swung the door open. "Well, well, what do we have here?" He pulled two large stacks of cash from the safe. "Looks like about ten grand to me." Philly held the bills to his ear and flipped through a bundle.

"More like fifteen," Shaw replied. "I want a receipt for every bill. It's all reported income."

"That so." Philly handed the cash to Mac. "What do I look like, an IRS agent? We aren't interested in your money, Shaw." Philly reached into the safe again, looking through the documents briefly and placing them back in the safe if he deemed them unrelated to the case.

"What's this?" Philly asked, pulling two keys from a white envelope.

Shaw sucked in his cheeks but didn't comment.

Mac studied the larger one. "Looks like a house key to me." In fact, it looked a lot like the key they'd found on Jacob Mullins. Of course it would be impossible to tell unless they put them side by side, which they would eventually do. "The other one looks like a key to a safe-deposit box."

Lifting the small round label attached to the smaller key, Mac read, "Mullins."

"Do you have keys to all of your client's houses and safe-deposit boxes?" Mac asked.

"Of course not. But there's certainly nothing illegal about it. If you must know, Clay wanted me to have it in the event anything happened to him."

"So they *are* Clay's keys. And something did happen, didn't it?" Mac pressed.

"I don't know what you're insinuating, but all of this is ludicrous. I'm his estate manager, for crying out loud. I have done nothing wrong."

"That's what we're trying to determine, Mr. Shaw," Frank said in an appeasing tone. "But considering the nature of this case, I'm sure you'll understand that we have to investigate everyone involved."

"Is there anything you'd like to tell us?" Mac asked.

"Yes, as a matter of fact." His nostrils flared. "Regarding your roughshod takeover of my office, you'll hear from me in court. With regard to Clay Mullins, I am simply carrying out my client's instructions, which were carefully laid out in his will."

"Which will?"

"The only one I have."

"We'll see about that," Mac said.

The detectives took the two computers, plus all of the documents obviously connected with Clay and Mullins. Before leaving, Russ provided Shaw with a copy of Form 65, the OSP evidence receipt, and a copy of the warrant, as required under Oregon law. Sergeant Evans would transport the potential evidence back to the Portland office to secure the items in temporary evidence. "It's getting late," Frank said before taking off. "Why don't you guys call it a day and pick things up in the morning."

"Will do, boss." Mac fingered the small safe-deposit key he'd kept out for comparison. "But I'd like to see if this key we found in Shaw's safe fits Clay's safe-deposit box."

"All right. Just make sure you tag and bag it when you're done."

Mac and Dana stopped back by the U.S. bank on their way back to Portland and requested access to the now-empty safe-deposit box. Dana tried the key they'd found in Shaw's safe in the lock. It was a perfect fit. The bank records indicated that they had assigned three keys to Clay Mullins's box: two independent to the bank's master key and one additional branch key. Apparently Clay had two keys assigned to outside access points, although there were no names assigned other than his.

"It seems odd that Clay would entrust his keys to Addison Shaw," Dana said.

"Maybe not. Mullins was in his late eighties. Maybe he wanted the attorney to have quick and easy access in the event of his death."

"Maybe," Dana concurred. "I'm confused, though. If Shaw had a key to the box, why didn't he remove the papers concerning the railroad museum? If we hadn't found those papers, we might not have gotten a search warrant."

"Maybe he didn't know it was there." Mac yawned. "At any rate, I'm taking Frank's advice to head home."

After dropping off Dana at her car in the compound where Russ had left it the day before, Mac parked and went into the office to log in the safe-deposit key. From there he headed straight home, collected Lucy, and after eating a Mexican TV dinner, fell into bed.

TWENTY-THREE

Mac FOUND DANA AT HER DESK when he arrived the next morning and set the extra cup of coffee he'd bought for her next to the empty one.

"Thanks." Her acknowledgement told him she wasn't in the mood for conversation any more than he was. She took a sip from the fresh cup and went back to her computer.

"You're welcome." Mac headed over to his own desk. Barely after seven in the morning and she was already working on her second sixteen-ounce cup of coffee. *How long has she been here?* Mac wondered.

"Where's mine?" Kevin called from his office as Mac walked by.

"If I'd known you'd be in this early, I'd have picked one up for you." He lifted the cup. "I could go across the street . . ."

"Naw. The missus is limiting me to one cup a day. I'm thinking about giving it up altogether."

"That's got to be tough." Mac stepped into the office. "How you doing?"

"Not bad, feeling pretty good actually." Kevin sat back in his chair and grinned. "Went for a walk with Jean this morning. It wasn't a run, but the fresh morning air got me going."

"You hear about our new developments yesterday?"

"Sure did. Frank brought me up to speed when he brought your evidence in. All the stuff is in temporary evidence; I'll get to copying the documents this morning while you two are out and about."

"Thanks. Any luck on a polygraph for Mason and Rita?"

"All set up. Melissa Thomas is heading out to Columbia County later this morning to administer the tests. Sergeant Hanson from our Scappoose office is going to give her a hand with Mason in case he gives her any trouble."

"Great, thanks for setting that up." Mac's pager went off. He looked at the number after pulling the pager from the plastic holder. "Crime lab. Wonder why they're calling so early?"

"They called here yesterday afternoon. Allison Sprague was looking for you or Dana. She said she wanted to run some results by you; I told her you were in the field and gave her your pager."

Allison Sprague was one of the few sworn forensics supervisors within the agency who held the rank of Criminalist. Most of the forensic scientists hired in the past fifteen years were non-sworn, a cost-savings measure primarily to prevent paying the expensive pension costs the state afforded to police officers.

"I'll call her in a bit. I need to get those computers over to Carl Jensen so he can start digging through the hard drives for evidence on our case. We need to get a copy made so I can return the hardware to Addison Shaw."

"I'll take care of that. You know how fast those computer guys work. I bet he can copy the hard drive this morning and have it examined in a day or two for documents. You can't hide much from Carl, not even the deleted documents."

"Thanks, Kevin. I really appreciate it." Mac lifted his cup in a salute and headed for his cubicle. "Still wish you were out in the field with us, though."

"Not me—I'm getting a full night's sleep," Kevin yelled after him.

Mac knew better but didn't respond. He called the lab and spoke with Allison.

"Hi, Mac. I got some results on the examination I did on Clay's diabetes drug kit. I think it might be best if you came over here. It's a bit complicated to explain over the phone."

"Sure. But it may take me a while with all the traffic. It was already backed up on the Glen Jackson Bridge on my way in this morning." Even on weekends, getting from the east side of the Willamette River to the west side could be murder.

"I'll be waiting."

Mac and Dana started for the Portland forensics lab of the State Police, located in the Justice Center downtown. The building housed the county jail prisoners on the first four floors, then a few floors occupied by the Portland Police Bureau precinct, and finally the forensics lab on the twelfth floor. They arrived at the lab by 8:30, badging their way through the front-door security to the elevators.

"I'm coming here way too often if the security is starting to recognize me and doesn't need picture identification," Dana muttered as the elevator doors shut.

"Some people are more memorable than others." Mac winked at her. "I'm sure you made an impression on the guy your first time through."

"Oh, shut up." Dana slapped Mac on the arm with her notebook.

"Ow." Mac feigned insult as well as injury. "Sheesh, see if I ever pay you a compliment. You don't need to go ballistic."

She rolled her eyes and faced forward. "I didn't go ballistic."

Changing the subject Dana asked, "Why didn't Allison just tell you what she found over the phone?"

Mac shrugged. "She said it was complicated. She's got me curious, that's for sure."

The elevator opened and they took the hallway to the left, walking past the doors that led to the various specialty units within the lab until they arrived at the main reception area. Mac told the receptionist at the front desk they were there to see Allison.

"Hi you two." Allison came out before the receptionist had a chance to page her over the intercom. "C'mon back."

The receptionist buzzed Mac and Dana through the security door, and they followed Allison to her office.

"Dana, I haven't seen you since . . ." Allison hesitated.

"Since I was shot." Dana finished the sentence.

"Sorry, it occurred to me just in time to stick my foot in my mouth."

"That's okay. I'm fine with it now. I must admit those were not some of my best photos, though. You didn't get my good side."

Mac was confused. "Photos?"

"While I was in the ER," Dana answered, "Allison photographed me in the buff after the shooting to document my injuries."

"Fortunately it wasn't a bullet hole." Allison leaned against her desk.

"For sure. That magnum round would have killed me if I hadn't been wearing the vest."

"If I remember right, you were bruised from your waist to your neck. That must have hurt for quite a while." Allison grimaced.

"Yeah, the next day I remember thinking that getting killed might have been better. My shock plate dispersed the trauma but made for major bruising." Dana winced. "I was sore all the way through my ribs and back, and I couldn't take a deep breath without hurting." Glancing at Mac she added, "Of course, I don't know if that was from the gunshot or Superman here jumping on me to see if I was dead."

"I didn't jump on you," Mac protested. "I was just making sure you were alive."

"Or not. I'm kidding." Turning to Allison she said, "Anyway, thanks for asking. I'm doing great now."

"That's good to hear." Allison gestured to the chairs. "Have a seat. I have some interesting news for you." Mac and Dana sat down in the two chairs across from Allison's desk as she flipped through some files. "I called for you yesterday with some questions. I was getting some confusing results on my initial lab tests, but I was able to work through it without you. Heard you were swamped."

"You might say that," Mac agreed.

"Anyway, after some preliminary testing, I had some questions regarding Mr. Mullins's medical history and insulin dosages, but none of that mattered when I'd completed the final analysis. I called Kevin this morning to give him the news, but he wanted me to tell you and Dana first."

"What?" Mac was surprised Kevin didn't let Allison give him the information.

"He said it was your case and you'd been working hard on it, so you should hear it first."

"Okay. What tests are we talking about?" Mac asked. "His insulin?"

"Yes. More specifically, the contents of his insulin vials. The problem we have here is that much of the liquid in that little glass vile was not insulin; it was ricin."

"Ricin?" Mac choked on the response.

"Exactly. The liquid in the container was insulin infused with ricin."

"Didn't I hear something about ricin being found in a letter to a senator recently?" Dana asked.

"Right. It made national news." Allison handed Dana a folder.

"That stuff is lethal," Mac commented. "The first I ever heard about it was in college. A KGB agent killed a politician with it years ago."

Dana straightened. "I remember that. A big cloak-and-dagger

deal. The guy was stabbed with a cane or something, and they found poison in the tip."

Allison nodded. "It was an umbrella actually, and it happened in the late seventies. The victim was a Bulgarian named Georgi Markov. He was in London when another pedestrian with an umbrella stuck him in the thigh. A few days later Markov died from the wound. They soon discovered the killer had used ricin. You'll see all that in your folder, along with a full rundown on the stuff."

"What is it anyway?" Dana asked. "Some type of chemical?"

"Yes and no." Allison leaned against her desk. "Ricin is produced from castor bean mash. The castor bean plant is primarily used to produce castor oil—you know, the awful stuff every mother had in the medicine cabinet years ago."

Mac nodded. "My grandmother used to tell me it was good for me. I thought she was trying to poison me. Apparently, I wasn't far from wrong."

Dana chuckled. "Well you're still here. I've heard of castor oil but never had to eat it. Sounds like I didn't miss much."

"Castor oil is not the problem. But the same process that makes castor oil produces a waste mash that can be refined into ricin. Ricin can be made into a mist or powder that can be inhaled or eaten in foods. It can also come in the liquid form that would require injection. That's what we have here."

"So we have the liquid form of ricin in our victim's insulin bottle." Mac blew out a long breath. "Now comes the million-dollar question. Was there enough ricin in that bottle to kill Clay?"

"It only takes about five hundred micrograms of pure ricin to kill an adult if injected, less than a pinprick would be enough. An actual injection of a substantial amount, like a hypodermic injection, would be lethal."

"How does it kill you? With a heart attack or something?" Dana asked.

"That's possible, but you might expect total organ failure in as soon as thirty-six hours. The injection of ricin would have no immediate effect. Rather, it slowly destroys cells by attacking their ribosomes."

"Ribosomes?" Mac was wishing he'd paid more attention in his anatomy and physiology courses.

Allison gave Mac a patient smile, like a teacher with an eager student. "Ribosomes are the protein-producing mechanisms of our cells. The ricin enters the bloodstream and starts to slowly destroy the mechanism, causing failure to the lungs, liver, and kidneys. A heart attack could certainly be a by-product of the organ failure."

"How about being delusional and losing motor function prior to death?" Mac glanced at Dana.

"You mean like trying to call 9-1-1 and being unable to speak, so you ride for help on your motorized scooter?" Dana added.

"Yes. You could expect that," Allison said. "The medical examiner will probably have more info for you there. I left a message for Kristen but was told she had three autopsies to do this morning and she was not to be disturbed until she got them finished. Those guys are way behind."

"I'm not surprised. We've had our share of murders around here lately." Mac stood up. He could understand Allison's excitement. He was feeling rather elated himself. Clay Mullins had been murdered, and now they had the murder weapon. "We'll head over there right now. What do you need from the body? We're still holding it in case something like this came up."

"Great. I need samples of the flesh around the injection sites. The tests at the medical examiner's office on the blood work probably wouldn't have caught the toxins associated with ricin. We can run some tests here, but I'll want to coordinate with the Center for Disease Control for confirmation on the test for ricin. That will likely be an overnight job."

"Do you need more blood?" Mac asked.

"Nope. What Kristen sent should do it."

"You'll have those samples within the hour. In fact, we'll hand-deliver them." Mac sensed the same elation in Dana. "Are you going to be around for a while, Allison?"

"Yep. I'm not going anywhere. This is moving up on my priority list. I've never worked a ricin case before, so I had to do quite a bit of research on the subject. I was so curious about the results, I came in early. I really want to do some more homework on the topic, but I'll need those samples for blood and cellular examination."

"You've got it. We'll call Kristen on the way over and have her get our guy back on the table, let her know there's some more work to be done."

"I have a hunch she'll be thrilled. Kristen loves this kind of stuff. Tell her I'll fax my findings to her."

TWENTY-FOUR

Mac and dana could hardly wait for the elevator doors to open on the first floor of the Justice Center, and they practically ran to their car.

Dana made the call to the medical examiner's office while Mac drove. "Henry, hi. This is Detective Bennett. I need to speak to Kristen."

After a moment's hesitation, Dana said, "Somehow I knew she would be. Okay, here's the scoop. We need you to pull Clay Mullins out of the cooler for collection of some flesh samples."

Dana held the phone away from her ear. Even over the car and street sounds, Mac could hear Henry's deep voice. "We're full up at the moment, and I'll have to clear it with Kristen. Shouldn't be a problem though. She's almost finished with number three."

"Thanks, Henry."

Closing the phone, she turned to Mac with a satisfied grin. "Kristen's almost ready to go."

"Something just occurred to me," Mac said. "If the ricin took several days to kill Clay, then we're looking at a totally different scenario with regard to alibi."

"You're right. That vial could have been put in his bag a week before." Dana frowned. "Even longer if he had another bottle to finish. I wonder how he gets his meds?" She pulled out a pad and jotted down some thoughts. "Didn't Shaw say something about Kelly bringing Clay his medications? Rita mentioned that too. She said he took care of his meds himself, but she would have had access."

"Right. Kristen will have Clay's medical records. Hopefully we can determine where the prescriptions were filled."

"This is exciting, Mac. We find out who had access to Clay's medication, and we narrow the search for our killer."

"Hopefully. We still have a pretty long list of suspects to work through." Mac caught sight of a pedestrian out of the corner of his eye and braked hard. "Sorry about that," he said to Dana. "Sometimes I get to talking and thinking and go on autopilot. I need to pay more attention when I drive."

"It's easy to do. We have to multitask most of the time." She grinned. "I'll keep my mouth shut, at least until we get out of this traffic."

Crossing the Burnside Bridge over the Willamette River, Mac thought about the conversation between Dana and Allison regarding the officer-involved shooting he and Dana had been involved in a couple of months ago. The last time they'd talked, Dana was still seeing a counselor. Hardly a night went by when Mac didn't relive the nightmare. Time had frozen for him in that terri-fying moment. The bullet leaving the gun and slamming into Dana's chest—him unable to get to her—his gun useless. He suspected that Dana's nightmares were even worse than his. Now that he thought about it, Dana seemed a little more distant these days. Maybe that was part of what had come between them. Could be she needed some time to heal—needed her space. *Heck, a couple inches higher and that round would have been right in her throat.* Mac glanced over at Dana thanking God that she was still alive—still on the force.

"You still having those dreams, Mac?" Dana interrupted his thoughts. "You know—about the shooting?"

The question didn't surprise him. Often, when they'd get quiet, Mac's mind would drift back. Plus, Dana had an uncanny ability to read his thoughts. "You mean the one where you get shot or the one where I squeeze the trigger and the bullet rolls out of the barrel and into the mud?"

"Yeah, those."

"Sometimes. I'm just glad they're dreams. I sure wouldn't want to relive the real thing."

"I know what you mean. I had weird dreams before the shooting, but now sometimes I see myself lying in a pool of blood. I see everything going on around me, but I can't move. And you know the thing that really bothers me?"

"What?"

"I never got a round off at the guy. He didn't know me, didn't know if I was a mother or someone's wife. He did this totally personal, horrible thing, and I never got a chance to confront him."

Mac cleared his throat. "It wasn't the resolution any of us wanted. Sometimes I wish I had gotten hit instead of you."

Dana placed a hand on Mac's arm. "Don't say that. Don't even think it. This stuff happens. We knew that when we signed on. The memories will fade before too long. Not that we'll ever forget, but we'll move on—are moving on."

Mac adjusted his seat back a notch, stretching his legs.

"Does talking about it upset you?" Dana asked.

"No. Well—it feels awkward, but we should be able to talk about it."

"I know you didn't want me going in there that day."

"I should have made you stay with the cars and wait for SWAT," Mac said.

"No. You did the right thing. I'm a cop and I want to be treated like one. No favors or special treatment just because I'm a woman." Dana pulled her hand away. "I'll never forget what you said while I was lying there in the mud trying to get my breath. And the look on your face."

What I said? Mac couldn't remember. All he remembered was desperately wanting her to stay away from the action—to be safe from potential harm. Being scared to death that she'd been seriously injured. "We detectives are supposed to look out for each other."

"I know. And I like to think you'd have had the same reaction if it had been Kevin or Philly."

"Well, maybe not quite."

"Oh. I didn't mean to make you uncomfortable, Mac. I was just thinking out loud. I'm sorry."

"Hey, it's okay. We really need to talk about it." At least that's what he'd been told. "We probably should have had this conversation sooner. I didn't know you were still having problems with what went on that day—you know, beyond the obvious."

"It's not your fault we haven't talked about it. I just haven't wanted to. I think I'm ready, but we'd better pick this up another time. We've got a case to put together." Dana shoved playfully at his right shoulder. "Besides, I don't want you all misty-eyed when we go in to meet with Kristen. I'm not sure she goes for the sensitive type."

Mac grinned, glad to leave the psychological baggage behind. "Knock it off. We had dinner. Nothing ever came of it."

"Twice, Mac. You've had dinner with her twice."

He might have argued with her if they weren't pulling into the back lot of the medical examiner's office. Mac took a couple of deep breaths to get a handle on things. Sometimes having women in your life could knock the wind right out of you. Especially women like Dana and Kristen.

Mac and Dana entered through the business entrance to find Henry pushing a steel gurney across the hall to the examination room.

"Hey Henry, thanks for setting this guy back up for us." Dana slid the strap of her briefcase off her shoulder, letting it drop onto a chair.

"No problem. I asked the doc, and she said to bring him in. She's just now finishing up on table one, so I imagine she'll want him on two." Henry nodded toward the autopsy room as he pushed the gurney with both hands. His gait was slow and Mac wondered just how old Henry was now. Not that it mattered. He was one of the best assistants in the M.E.'s office and would hopefully be around for a long time to come.

"C'mon down," Kristen called. "You're the next contestants on *The Price Is Right.*"

"She's so weird," Dana whispered, leaning into Mac as she did.

"Not as much as you'd think," he whispered back. "Most of it is an act. She's just trying to cope."

"Defending her, are we? For a minute there, I forgot she was your girlfriend." Dana got in one last shot before walking into the room so Mac wouldn't have a chance to reply.

Girlfriend? Hardly. Mac's attention turned toward Kristen and to the body on the autopsy table. The girl couldn't have been much more than fifteen or sixteen. "What's her story, Doc?" Mac asked.

"Sophomore at Madison High, track star, former member of student council." Kristen blew out a long breath, the burden of her job evident on her face. "Now she's another statistic. Drug overdose. See these blisters around her lips?"

Mac had seen it all too often when he'd been on the narcotics beat, but Dana stepped forward for a closer look. "Yeah, what's that all about?"

"Free-basing cocaine, and smoking crack too, I'll bet. The burns on her lips are from the glass pipe. The kid was so high she couldn't feel her own flesh burning."

Dana bit her lower lip. "That's so sad. Does she have family?"

"Uh-huh. They're on their way now to recover the body. I'm just about done; going to take a few close-ups for the deputy medical examiner training."

"Which is?" Dana's gaze followed Kristen's movements.

"I put on a show for the county medical examiners." Kristen nodded at Henry, giving him the go-ahead to sew up the victim.

Mac's heart caught as his gaze captured the victim's pretty face.

"This was a tough one," Kristen said. "Poor baby will never see graduation, never marry or bear a child. When will these kids learn that death doesn't play favorites? That they aren't immune?"

She pulled off her gloves and turned toward Mac and Dana. "So, detectives, what's going on? Henry tells me you need more samples for the crime lab."

Mac nodded, pulling his thoughts back to the present. "Right. Looks like we got us another murder." He went on to tell her about Allison's findings. "Ricin in his insulin vial. Can you believe it?"

"Actually I can." Kristen's eyes lit up. "That was one of the possibilities I considered when I found the necrosis around the injection site. I just didn't dream I'd be right."

"It's ironic, you know." Mac pulled a pair of latex gloves from the box on the wall. "If that kid hadn't burglarized Clay's house and taken the kit, we'd never have found it, and it would have been lost in the fire. The kid should be doing time, but I'm ready to give him a medal."

Dana gloved up as well. "Kevin would probably say it was a God thing. The Almighty didn't want whoever killed Clay to get away with it."

"Personally, I think God has a hand in everything, but still, I'd like to think we'd have found ricin when we did the final analysis." Kristen walked over to Clay's body, which was still on the gurney. She studied the closed body bag for a moment.

"Did you want him on the exam table, Doc?" Henry asked.

"What?" Kristen looked up to catch his curious gaze. "Oh, sorry, Henry. No, just leave him here on the rollaway." Kristen unzipped the body bag. Mac pulled his Vicks inhaler out of his pocket and took a few whiffs. He reminded himself to breathe through his mouth.

"So, Kristen, you know about ricin then?" Dana used her inhaler as well, blinking back the tears from the onslaught of strong scents.

"Sure, since this whole terrorist focus I've had to bone up on my poisons and toxins. Especially those that can be made into an ionized powder and that present a danger of widespread inhalation."

"You said you might have been able to tell it was ricin without the vial?" Mac steeled himself as he peered at Clay's remains, an all-too-clear reminder of what Clay Mullins had suffered.

"I think so." Kristen gestured toward one of Clay's arms. "Remember when I told you I noted some unusual bruising and advanced decay on the flesh around the injection sites?"

"Yeah." Mac nodded. "Those are the sites we need to get samples from for Allison."

Kristen stepped to the side so they could better examine the sites as she pointed them out. "Here we go, this area right here above the elbow. If ricin is injected, it will kill the flesh around the injection site as well as the lymph nodes."

"Mac and I were talking on the way over about when Clay might have been poisoned. Looks like someone tampered with his insulin. How hard will it be to figure out when he got the first injection?"

Kristen placed the arm back in the bag. "We'll look at the number of injections like this one and then at his schedule. As I recall, he took his insulin twice a day. I should be able to tell you when he started using it, but that's not going to tell us when the bottle was tampered with. He could have had a month's supply of insulin or more on hand."

Kristen examined the second arm. "You may be looking at a day or day and a half of taking the ricin before Clay died. One thing for sure is that he would have been in a great deal of pain before his death. I'd expect liver and kidney failure, then additional complications like trouble breathing and severe intestinal bleeding and stomach pain. He would eventually suffocate or succumb to some type of organ failure or cardiac arrest."

"Allison said pretty much the same thing at the lab." Dana pulled her camera from her bag to snap some additional photos of the injection site.

"I'll get those samples for you." Kristen turned to Henry, who was already reaching for a scalpel and some small glass jars. He set the items on a tray and went back to his sewing. Kristen cut a deep sample around the injection site on the arm, taking great care to produce a sample of the epidermis and the underlying tissue for a comprehensive examination. "Allison still has enough blood, correct?"

"Yeah, she's good with what you sent over," Dana answered. "She just wanted a concentrated sample of the injection sites."

Kristen dropped the flesh sample in one of the glass jars, handing it over to Mac to tighten the lid and label it. "This may be overkill, but let's get a sample from each of the necrotic areas. We may be able to determine when he injected each site by the amount of damage done. Either way, we'll have more than one sample."

Kristen found four necrotic sites in all, which according to Clay's records would have had him starting the injections in the morning on the day prior to his death.

Mac labeled each of the samples: one from each arm and from each thigh.

"There is one thing, and this is a guesstimate at best. There may have been more sites, but I really doubt it. He gave himself two injections of insulin for two days. We'll have to check with Allison on the concentration. I'm thinking your killer expected him to die right away. They didn't realize just how dearly Clay would hang on to life. Clay was a big man too, so that would make a difference."

"What I can't get over," Dana said, "is that none of us would likely be investigating his death if he hadn't gone for help."

"True enough." Kristen zipped up the bag. "If Clay had died in his house—at his age and with his medical problems, the body would probably never have come to me."

"Maybe God did want to make sure the murder didn't go undetected." Dana gave Mac a tight smile.

"You've been around Kevin too long." Mac placed the jars in a sack. He wouldn't admit it, but he missed those asides with Kevin and the mini-Bible studies. Maybe he'd have to take Kevin up on his offer to go to church with him. He wondered how Kristen felt about church. Hopefully she wasn't a fanatic like his ex-fiancé Linda turned out to be. Not that he had time to think about all that now.

"Thanks for your help, Kristen," Mac said. "I appreciate you getting to this so quickly. We'll get these right over to the lab."

"You're welcome." Kristen waved. "Besides, I like you owing me."

TWENTY-FIVE

MAC AND DANA rushed the flesh samples back to the Portland crime lab so Allison could begin her tests. She promised to work as long as it took, but warned them that the definitive results would not be available until morning. The initial blood work indicated they were indeed looking at toxic levels of ricin in Clay's blood. The actual flesh around the injection site would provide investigators with conclusive evidence as to how Clay was killed. The only problem now would be to determine who had killed Clay and Jacob Mullins. Were they looking at one bad guy or two—or more?

While at the lab, Mac received a page from Philly, who was out in Columbia County with Russ. Mac called him back.

"Sitting on the phone, were you?" Philly didn't wait for an answer. "We got an arrest warrant for Tyler Cohen since he didn't show up for his arraignment on that burglary charge. Russ and me got a little caper planned. Do you and Dana want in on it?"

"What's going down?"

"I got a lead from the kid's mother. Says he hangs out at the pool hall most weekends and in the afternoon after school. Not that the kid goes to school. Principal says he's skipped most of the school year. At any rate, he showed up at his parents' place last night to score some clean clothes and cash. Mommy fed him and did his laundry and after thinking things over, decided to call the police. Says she's hoping to get her son off the street before he lands in any more trouble. She's afraid his drug abuse is getting out of control, and she'd rather have him incarcerated and getting help with his addiction than out on the street getting bombed."

"That's a tough call for a parent."

"Well, at this point she thinks we just want to question him on the original burglary. I didn't tell her we were also wanting to question him on the arson/murder thing."

"Okay. We want in on the bust and the questioning," Mac told him. "We'll meet you in the parking lot at the St. Helens P.D. in about forty."

On their way to rendezvous with Russ and Philly, Kevin called with news about Mason's polygraph. "He passed."

"So one down," Mac mused. Even though Mason had passed the polygraph examination, they wouldn't completely eliminate him as a suspect—at least not at this point. Now that they knew Clay had been killed with the ricin, Mason's alibi was worthless.

"The other breaking news is that Jan officially declared the fire an arson."

"We knew that already."

"Yes, but we needed the test results. The lab tests confirmed the evidence at the scene and the hits by the arson dog. We are looking at gasoline as the accelerant and the origin being at the back door like Jan suspected."

"Anything new on the evidence we lifted from Shaw's office?" Mac asked.

"There isn't much of evidentiary value in the paper files. I'm making copies so the originals can be returned."

Mac told Kevin about Allison's findings and said that they were headed out to meet the other detectives in hopes of rounding up Tyler Cohen.

"Looks like things are breaking up," Kevin said. "Good luck and be careful. I'm praying for all of you."

"Thanks, Kevin. We may need it."

Mac and Dana caught the dynamic duo in the middle of lunch. Russ tilted his head back, dropping the contents of a large carton of fries into his mouth.

"Don't want to get your hands greasy, Russ?" Mac joked as he pulled alongside their car in the parking lot.

Russ looked like an opossum caught in the headlights, probably trying to figure out what rule of etiquette he may have broken. "It was the last couple of fries," he explained. "I was just finishing up."

"I can't do anything with him." Philly shook his head, taking a handful of fries himself.

"What happened to your low-carb diet, Philly?" Dana teased.

"I'm still on it. See? I didn't super-size the order. Smaller portions cuts way back on my carb intake. Besides, I'm not eating the bun on my hamburger. Just the insides."

"Gimme a break." Russ shook his head. "You must have eaten a dozen donuts this week. If you call that a diet, you're nuts."

"I wouldn't talk. Looks like you could use a little help in the diet department too, partner." Philly pinched Russ's left love handle. Russ nearly climbed out the window to get away. "Any other comments from the peanut gallery?" Philly guffawed.

"Yeah, I want a new partner." Russ actually looked offended.

"Nobody else would work with you, Russ. Now pipe down." Philly gave Mac a "what-can-I-do-with-him?" look.

"So, what's the scoop on Cohen?" Dana asked. "Are we going to wait for him inside or sit surveillance on the place?"

"Neither. The mother has my cell number. She wanted to make sure the kid was okay, talk to him a little. You know—hug, kiss, bedtime story stuff. She's going to ask him to turn himself in. If he doesn't agree, she'll call me and we'll swoop in."

"You don't want to get in a little closer?"

"Naw." Philly picked at a tooth with a fingernail. "Too risky with this joint. The pool hall is more of an arcade and teen hangout. Anyone older than twenty will look out of place, and I don't want to spook him. Russ and I have been stomping around every railroad transient camp and swimming hole in the county looking for this joker; I don't want to waste any more time. Once Mama calls we can get a description of Tyler's duds and the direction he's taking. He doesn't have wheels at this point, so he'll most likely be walking. We should be able to pick him up without too many problems, assuming he doesn't get any funny ideas and he's not packing."

"I'm confused," Dana said. "Is Tyler at the arcade or at home? Where's his mom meeting him?"

"Tyler was at home, but he left. His mom expects him to come to the arcade. She's in there waiting for him and will try to get him to turn himself in. She'll call me if it doesn't work."

"You can trust her?"

"I think she's on the up and up. If not we'll go to plan B."

"Does Sergeant Evans know what we're up to?" Mac imagined Kevin would pass along the news but wanted to verify that Philly had contacted him.

"Yeah, he's up to speed. By the way, your guy Mason passed his polygraph."

"Right. Kevin paged me on the way out here. Also, Jan ruled the fire at the house was definitely arson. You heard about the ricin, didn't you?"

Philly nodded and rubbed the stubble on his chin. "This caper just keeps getting better and better. I have to admit, though, ricin's a first for me. I've worked plenty of poisonings, but never that stuff. Russ and I were talking about it before you pulled up. My money's on the lawyer."

"Which one?" Mac asked. "The daughter or Addison Shaw?"

"Shaw." Philly pressed his lips together. "He's dirty. I just don't know how dirty."

"You always think the lawyers are dirty," Russ commented.

"Have I ever been wrong?" Philly raised an eyebrow.

Russ chuckled. "You have a point." Looking in Mac's direction, he asked, "Any word on the stuff we hauled out of Shaw's place?"

"Nothing yet. We're hoping to hear something back on the computer files today."

The detectives sat in the parking lot for nearly an hour making predictions and speculations before Philly's cell phone rang. All four of them sat up in their seats, suddenly alert and all business. Russ even straightened his tie.

Philly hit the green button on his hands-free cell phone, so they could all hear the caller.

"Detective Johnson."

"Yes, Detective. This is Tina Cohen," the woman answered, her voice cautious and shaky. "I met with my son and he . . . he didn't want to turn himself in. He said he might think about it, but he had some business to take care of first. He's afraid of having to do jail time. I tried to tell him it wouldn't be long and he needed to straighten up, but . . ."

"I'm sorry, Mrs. Cohen." Philly sounded genuinely empathetic. "Can you tell me what your son is wearing?"

"Um—jeans and a black sweatshirt with a camouflage jacket. He also has on a yellow Pittsburgh Steelers cap."

"Did he have any weapons on him or did he mention any?" Philly started the car.

"I don't think so. He carries a pocketknife, but no guns or anything. He's skin and bones right now, so I think I'd see anything in his pockets or on his hip."

"Which way was he walking when he left the pool hall?"

"Toward Highway 30. I can still see him. He's almost to the tracks."

"Great. Thanks, Mrs. Cohen. We'll exercise due caution and take him in now. I'll be in contact with you. And Mrs. Cohen?"

"Yes."

"You're doing the right thing."

"I hope so."

Philly ended the call. "He's walking toward the tracks. I assume you two know what he looks like."

"Yeah," Dana replied. "Sounds like he's wearing the same clothes as the night we apprehended him."

"Okay, let's do this." Philly pulled out and headed toward the highway.

Mac spotted Cohen ambling along the highway, head down and hands in his pockets. Philly pulled up past Tyler and parked the car on the shoulder. Mac and Dana came in behind him, skidding to a stop on the asphalt before exiting their car.

"Hold it right there, buddy," Philly yelled to him. "State Police, get down on your knees."

Cohen looked past Philly and Russ, then to his right, looking for an escape route. Philly recognized the ten-mile stare, giving him a second warning. "Get down on the ground. Don't make me put hands on you, son."

Cohen took two steps backward, then spun around. Seeing Mac and Dana, he stopped cold.

Mac and Dana fanned out to block his path. Tyler hesitated briefly to weigh his options, then he put his hands in the air and dropped to his knees.

"Down on your belly," Dana yelled, keeping her right hand on her expandable baton. "Now bring your hands out, palms up. And look away from me!"

"I'm not going anywhere," Cohen yelled back. "Don't let her hit me with that thing!"

Philly winked at Dana as he approached Cohen. "So you've met Detective Bennett before?" He handcuffed Tyler and helped him to his feet. "You're under arrest on authority of a Fail to Appear bench warrant issued by Columbia County. Do you understand that?"

"Yeah, I understand. Just keep her away from me."

"Her? As in this lovely young female detective?" Philly asked, trying to look serious.

"Why did you think I stopped? I knew I could smoke you two. But not her."

"What do you mean?" Philly growled. "I would have had you in ten steps."

Cohen looked Philly up and down. "Yeah, I'll bet."

"Any more comments?" Philly cinched the cuffs a little tighter, maybe a little too tight, before double-locking them. "You have the right to remain silent. Anything you say can and will be used against you in a court of law." Philly finished the Miranda rights as he walked Tyler to the police car. "You understand these rights, Carl Lewis?"

"Who's Carl Lewis?"

"You know, the Olympic sprinter who won all the gold medals in the eighties."

"I must have missed that one. I didn't watch too much television when I was learning to crawl," Cohen sneered.

"He was one of the fastest guys in the world."

Philly opted to let Mac and Dana handle Cohen's interview while he and Russ headed back over to search Cohen's place while the boy's parents were still cooperating.

"Okay, Tyler. Looks like you'll be coming with us," Mac said.

"We're going to run you over to the district attorney's office and have ourselves a little chat before we go by the jail." Dana's tone was warm and friendly. "Are you okay with that?"

"As long as you keep that stick away from me."

Dana smiled. "Sure. Just don't try any funny stuff."

"Yeah, okay."

"Here, let me loosen those cuffs for you." Dana adjusted the cuffs before guiding Tyler into the backseat of the car.

"Thanks, I appreciate that. I like you a lot better when you're not hitting me."

"Thank you, Tyler." Dana's dimples deepened. "How about we start all over. You know there's more to that story. I seem to remember a garbage can lid and a foot chase through the dark after one of us was caught committing a felony."

Mac and Dana transported Tyler back to the same interview room they'd used the first time they'd arrested him. They offered him a soda and moved his cuffs to the front so he'd be more comfortable. After the formalities, Mac began to question Cohen about his whereabouts during the past few days and went over some of the same questions that were covered during the first interview, specifically the insulin kit he had stolen from the house. Cohen's story remained consistent on the burglary. He admitted to being a user. "I was just doing pot at first and then my buddies scored some heroin. We got a steady supply and, man, I tried to quit a couple of times, but . . . it ain't that simple."

"No it isn't." Mac felt sorry for the kid. "You admit to being at the Mullins's place the night of March fifth."

"Yeah." Tyler stared at a spot on the floor. "I already said I took the bag. That's all I did."

"What about later that night after you were released? Did you go back to the house and set fire to it?"

He frowned. "No, man. Why would I do that?"

Mac shrugged. "Why did you break in? Why do you do drugs?"

"I didn't torch the place," Tyler insisted.

Mac leaned back and folded his arms. "Did you know Jacob Mullins?"

"Never heard of him."

"His body was found in the house after the fire."

Tyler's eyes widened. "I don't know nothin' about that. I didn't start the fire. I wasn't even there."

Mac almost believed him, but the kid was hiding something. His line of questioning wasn't producing, so he turned to Dana. "Do you have any questions for Tyler?"

She nodded. "Do you want help for your addiction?"

"Maybe. My mom set up an appointment at a clinic in Portland a couple of weeks ago, but I didn't go. Maybe I will this time."

"They can treat you at the Oregon Youth Authority facilities too, you know." Dana set her pen down and folded her hands.

"You saying that's where I'm gonna end up?" Tyler almost looked worried.

"Might be a good thing if you did, Tyler. Maybe getting arrested today will turn out to be the best thing that ever happened to you. I've seen a lot of kids wind up in the morgue because of drugs. We saw one today."

"The O.Y.A. ain't worth spit. I don't want to go to no boot camp. I can take care of myself. What kind of time am I looking at for the burglary?"

"Depends on your priors. You could easily stay in custody until you're twenty-one."

"Twenty-one? No way." He started bouncing his knee and tapping his foot on the floor. "I can't do that kind of time. It ain't fair." He took a long drink of soda, his brows knitted in a frown.

"I hear you guys sometimes make deals," he finally said.

"That's up to the D.A.," Dana told him.

"Yeah, well, what if I can tell you who torched the old guy's house?"

Dana raised her eyebrows. "What do you think, Mac? Can we cut a deal?"

Mac came away from the wall. "Maybe, but if you had anything to do with the fire . . ."

"I didn't," Tyler interrupted. "I already told you. But what if I can help you guys catch the dude that did?"

"Then we'd be very interested in what you have to say." Mac pulled out a chair and sat down next to Tyler.

"I got to know right now if you can drop the charges. I mean, it was just a worthless old bag that I stole, and I answered your questions the last time. And I'm going to need help getting out of town."

"Why out of town?" Dana asked.

"Cause, if this guy finds out I smoked him, I'm dead meat."

"We don't have the authority to make those deals," Mac told him. "We have to consult the D.A."

"Then consult him or do whatever you have to do before I change my mind."

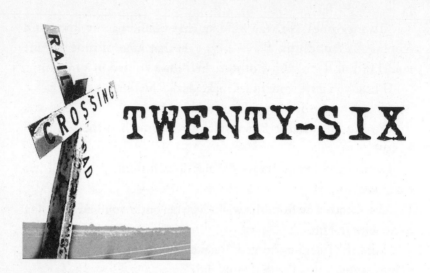

TWENTY-SIX

Mac left Dana with their juvenile delinquent and jogged up the stairs to find Darren Volk, hoping he was close by so they could make some kind of deal once he heard Tyler's story. He found Darren in the law library, studying from one of the large *Oregon Revised Statute* books.

"Darren," Mac puffed. "We may have a break in the Jacob Mullins murder."

"Really?" Darren slapped the heavy book shut and pulled off his glasses. "What is it?"

"We picked up Tyler Cohen today, the burglar who hit Clay's house before it burned. More importantly, the burglar who inadvertently saved our ricin sample for analysis."

"What did he say about the arson fire? Do you think he set it?"

"I don't think so. He's clammed up and won't say a word unless you're present. He said he can help us with the case but wants to cut a deal on the burglary charges."

"I'm not prepared to do that. The kid has had every opportunity, but didn't even bother to make an appearance in court. He's not getting off."

"I think he's telling the truth," Mac insisted. "I have a feeling he knows something. He strikes me as being scared but not necessarily afraid of us. I think you should come down. Talk to him yourself."

"He's here now?" Darren stood up and adjusted his tie.

"Downstairs in the interview room."

Darren sighed and plucked his briefcase off his desk. "All right. I'll go hear what he has to say, but just for the record, I don't like doing business this way."

Darren hurried down the stairs with Mac, pausing briefly before going inside. The D.A. seemed reluctant, and Mac thought it might be that as D.A., Darren had little experience with the rough interview process. He usually got the bad guys when the detectives were finished processing them, and when they were ready to face prosecution. Darren straightened his shoulders and stepped into the room.

"Tyler," Mac said, "this is Darren Volk, the Columbia County District Attorney. He's the one with the authority to talk deals when it comes to your burglary charge."

"Yes, we've met. Hello again, Tyler." Darren took a seat next to Dana, set his briefcase on the table, and pulled out a pad.

"Hey," Cohen greeted. "So what do I do now? I'm not just taking your word for anything."

Mac glanced at his partner and slid into the only other empty seat across from Tyler.

Dana pulled the pad she'd been writing on toward her and noted that the D.A. was talking to Cohen.

"What kind of information do you think you have for us?" Volk asked.

246 Patricia H. Rushford and Harrison James

"I can tell you who blazed that old dude's house by the terminal. He probably killed the guy inside too."

"Assuming you have some information, and assuming I'm willing to help you, what exactly are you wanting me to do for you?"

"I want the burglary charges dropped, a cash reward, and some transportation out of state. Preferably I'd like my own wheels, and my driver's license suspension lifted."

Darren scooted back in his chair and Mac thought he might leave. "Your first request is an outside chance; the rest are laughable and beyond my authority. Even if I wanted to get you as far out of this county as possible, there's no way."

"Suit yourself, dude. Good luck solving your case. According to the news on television, you got nothing so far."

Mac stood up and walked over on Cohen's side of the table, eclipsing the single light in the small room. "Do you believe everything you see on television, Tyler?"

"Enough to know you guys got nothing and need my help."

Mac laughed, irritated by the kid's tough-guy attitude. "We don't tell the media everything." In a way Tyler was right. They had nothing with regard to the fire. He leaned on the table, closing in on the teenager. "You think we need your help, kid?" He made eye contact, and Tyler shifted his gaze to the table. "I think you need our help a whole lot more than we need yours, especially after I tell the media how you cooperated with us on our investigation. We'll let the press know that you fingered certain people to cut yourself a sweet deal."

"You can't do that." Cohen leaned away from Mac. "That's not true."

"Is that right?" Mac moved even closer. "I didn't know there was a rule about hosing drug-dealing burglars. Might not be a bad idea for us to put the word out and let the consequences play out."

"What consequences?"

Mac straightened and paced across the small office and back. "Let's see. For starters, the district attorney here will send you to the big boy prison, not the minimum-security boot camp you scoffed at earlier. Somehow, I don't think country club sentences are in order for you, Mr. Cohen." Mac stopped behind Tyler's chair. Tyler stared straight ahead. "How do you think you'll get along in the joint? The guys in there eat your kind for breakfast. Of course you wouldn't fare so well on the outside either, would you?"

Mac eyed the D.A. "Maybe that's what we should do, Mr. Volk. Let this character go and save the taxpayers' money." Turning back to Tyler he said, "The guy you refuse to name has killed already— what makes you think he won't take you out too? I know the answers to all those questions. That's why I'm so sure you need us more than we need you. You might want to think about that." Mac went around to the other side of the table and leaned against the wall, hoping his little tirade had had the desired effect.

Tyler clasped his hands, nervously brushing one thumb against the other. "How about the burglary charge? Can you at least help me out with that if I tell you who set the fire? And you gotta promise not to let the guy hurt me."

"That I may be willing to do," Darren answered. "Providing your information serves the greater good for the citizens of this county." Stern-faced, he added, "I want to be clear on this, Tyler. If and when I determine this is valuable information I'll talk a deal with you. You have my word on that. But if you wait and drag this thing out, or if you lie to us and your negligence causes another person to be hurt or killed, then I'll tack your hide to the wall. You have my word on that too."

Tyler frowned. Mac figured he was still trying to digest Volk's avowal. "Okay. I'll tell you what I know."

"Wise decision," Mac said as he sat back down.

Dana placed her briefcase on the table. Opening it, she pulled out a tape recorder. After briefing Tyler on the taping and getting his approval, Mac told him to start talking. "So, Tyler," Mac went on. "Tell us why you didn't make your court appearance."

"Yeah, well . . . I was planning on making my court appearance so I could get a court-appointed attorney." He glanced at Dana. "No offense, but I was thinking about suing you guys for hitting me with that nightstick. You didn't have to hit me so hard. I still got bruises."

Dana rolled her eyes. "Give me a break, Tyler."

"Uh—I figured it probably wouldn't work, but . . ."

"Very unlikely, but go on." Darren folded his arms. "Could you get back to the subject please?"

"Where do you want me to start?"

"At the beginning," Mac answered. "Start with what you did and where you went after you were released on your own recognizance from the jail, after your booking."

He frowned and leaned toward the tape recorder. "Okay. I've been doping pretty hard on the ecstasy and weed lately, then I started hitting some serious stuff like coke and black tar. I was pretty hard up for cash, so I needed to work some up. My lady and me were hoping to clean up and kick this dope life. I was looking to make one or two good scores and get out of town.

"So I figured, you know, lightning never strikes twice. I went back to the old dude's place and was gonna hit it again, thinking there's no way the cops would be there two nights in a row. I heard there were some slick antiques and a coin collection stashed away in the house.

"I was caught once so I figure, what are the odds of the cops being at the place a second time? I made sure they wouldn't be there by calling 9-1-1 and reporting a man with a gun on the west side of town, you know, so the cops would head out that way and leave the way clear for me to hit the house."

Smart move, Mac thought. With a small contingency of officers, a call like that would definitely take priority. He remembered thinking at the time of the fire that the call had been a little too convenient. "What time was that?" Mac asked.

"Around midnight. Maybe a little after."

A little early, Mac noticed. If the call was bogus, why hadn't the officer gone back to his watch right away? He made note to ask.

"We can verify that, Darren," Dana said. "Tyler's account matches that of the officer I talked to at the fire scene. Plus, we can have Columbia County Communications check their tapes." Turning to Tyler, she said, "Go on."

Tyler took a deep breath and continued rubbing his right thumb against his left. His right knee still pumped up and down. "I stayed down by the tracks for a few minutes to make sure there was nobody else around."

"Were you there alone?" Mac asked.

He shot Mac an odd look. "I'm not saying."

"You don't have a choice if you're looking to deal. We need the truth," Volk said.

"Okay, but you gotta leave her out of this."

"Her?" Dana leaned forward.

"My lady was lookin' out for me. Only she never did anything wrong."

"What's her name?" Mac demanded.

"Mandy. Amanda's her real name. Amanda Searles. She's sixteen, been living with me in my camp down by the river at the old railroad bridge."

"Go ahead with your story. We'll talk about your girlfriend later," Mac said.

"Mandy and me were sitting down by the water. I was about to make my move on the house when this set of headlights pulls in. They're like twenty yards from us, and these two guys . . ."

"What kind of car?" Mac asked.

"A silver Lexus."

"Did you recognize the car?"

"Yeah, I seen it around town. So the driver gets out and I recog- nize him right away. He's the old guy's lawyer."

"Addison Shaw?" Darren asked, breaking interview protocol by throwing out a name too soon.

"Yeah, but I didn't know his name then. I seen that car and the guy lots of times in town. Thinks he's a real big shot. Real jerk if you ask me, always telling us to get our skateboards off the sidewalk when we go by his place. Anyway, he gets out of the car with this other dude."

"Can you describe the second man?" Mac had a hunch where this was going, but he wanted to get everything on tape. And he didn't want to say anything that might seem like he was coaching the kid.

"He was skinny and had black hair and ah . . . he was wearing jeans with a Levi jacket. Mandy and me watched them go in the house. They stayed there for probably ten minutes and then that Shaw guy comes out by himself. He goes to the trunk of his car and hauls out this big plastic container and starts dumping gas all over the back of the house."

"Just what part of the house would that be?" Mac asked hoping to corroborate the kid's story with Jan's report.

"The riverside, guess that would be east. Close to where I was hiding when you guys busted me that night."

"Where you accessed the house?" Mac asked.

"Right. Then Shaw goes back to his car and opens his trunk and lights up a flare—you know, one of those things that you put out at car crashes and stuff. After he sparks it up at his trunk he tosses the thing at the house and the place goes right up. Shaw jumped in his car and split after that. Mandy and me stuck around until we started hearing the sirens and took off back to our camp."

"Why didn't you tell anyone about this before, especially after learning that police found a victim inside the house?" Darren asked. Tyler had certainly piqued his interest.

"And say what, man?" he whined. Putting his hand to his ear, he made the pretend call. "'Hello, police, yeah, I'm the dude that made that fake-guy-with-a-gun call so I could loot a dead guy's house. Yeah, I'd like to report a crime'?"

"I see your point." Darren drew a square on his legal pad. "Did Amanda see the same thing, and would she be willing to testify?"

"She saw it all; you'd have to ask her about testifying. She'd want to help me out, so I think she'd do it."

"Is there anything else you'd like to tell us?" Mac asked. He had a feeling Tyler still wasn't being completely honest with them. "This would be a good time to put everything out on the table. If we find out later that you weren't being straight with us, we can call the whole deal off."

Tyler's shoulders rose and fell in an exaggerated sigh. "Okay, there's one more thing. Guess I might as well tell you. With Shaw in jail, it won't work anyway."

"Tell us about it." It didn't take a psychic to see through this kid. Mac would have bet anything Tyler had plans to blackmail Addison Shaw.

"There's another reason why I couldn't call the cops." Tyler fidgeted in his chair. "I didn't follow through with it, so technically you can't take me down for it."

"We'll decide that," Mac said.

"Okay. I was trying to get money from Shaw."

"Go on."

"After seeing what we saw, I figured I could make a big score by asking for some hush money. I got his number off the door of his office and called him the next day. Told him what I saw and that I wanted a hundred grand to stay away from the police. He said he wanted to meet with me in private and didn't want to talk on the phone."

"Then what?" Mac wondered if the money in Shaw's safe was meant to be the first installment. A look at Dana told him she was thinking the same thing.

"Yesterday, when I was going down to meet with him, I came around the corner and guess who I see? You guys standing in his office. The place was swarming with cops so I figured I missed my chance."

"He told you to meet at his office?"

"No, but I'd called him half a dozen times trying to set up a meet. He never answered, so I figured I'd stop by and see what the deal was. I didn't have a callback number, you know, 'cause I was using pay phones. You know most of those things don't accept incoming calls now?"

Mac shook his head in disgust. "I guess I'm having a hard time with your callous attitude, Tyler. You know Shaw killed a man and set fire to Clay Mullins's house, yet you act as if it was no big deal. All you can think about is padding your pockets?"

"I didn't know the guy who got killed. He wasn't a friend or anything. I was just gonna mind my own business and get out of town with Mandy. Besides, when me and Mandy first saw him, we figured he was just a fire bug. I thought the other guy was helping him out and figured he'd gone out the front."

"But you saw only Shaw get into his car?"

"Yeah, but that didn't mean the guy was still in there."

"Did you consider reporting the fire or going in to rescue the second man?"

Tyler wrinkled his face. "Why, man? The house was old and the owner was dead. Like I said, I didn't know for sure the other dude was in there. I don't get into other people's business."

"Unless it suits your purpose." Mac dragged a hand down his face, sickened by Tyler's indifference. If it were up to him, he'd lock the kid up and throw away the key. Cohen was a menace, and Mac had no doubt he'd get into trouble again. Still, he had to make the best of the situation. "How would you feel about making a call for us?"

"A call?" He looked at each of them, curiosity settling into his blue eyes.

"We'd like you to call Mr. Shaw and ask for the money. We'll be recording the conversation." Mac looked to Dana to produce the special earpiece that would allow them to record Addison's response.

Without speaking, Dana pulled the device out of her briefcase showing she had brought it along.

"You mean like set up a sting?" Tyler asked.

"Sort of."

"Do you want me to meet him and get the money?" He seemed excited about the prospect.

"No. I just want you to make the call. This will help us gather the evidence we'll need." It would also verify Shaw's involvement. Mac didn't trust Tyler any more than he trusted Shaw.

"I don't know about that. What if he comes after me and Mandy?"

"You do this for us," Darren said, "and if, a very big *if,* your information pans out, I'll deal away the burglary charge and get you and Mandy into protective custody until we make an arrest. If we don't have enough to make an arrest or I find out you've been lying, there's no deal." Darren scribbled something on his pad.

"Will you put us up in a hotel?"

"The County Jail Motel." The D.A. smiled. "Best I can offer on my budget. But you'll be safe."

Tyler grimaced, apparently not too happy with the plan. "Okay. What do you want me to do?"

"Cool your heels at the jail for a few minutes," Mac said. "I'll have some dinner sent over."

"But . . ."

"Patience, Tyler. We have some work to do prior to your making the call. I'll hook up with you in about an hour. First, though, tell me where we can find Amanda."

Seemingly resigned now, Tyler sighed. "She'll be inside an old canvas tent down by the Columbia River at an old rail bridge, upriver from Clay's place."

"Thanks. We appreciate your cooperating with us." Mac used the phone in the room to call for a deputy to escort Cohen to a holding cell. Mac and Dana were on their way out when Darren stopped them. "This Amanda Searles." He hesitated. "I know her parents. She ran away about two weeks ago. Surprised all of us. This kid pulled down straight A's and was on the debate team. Nice girl. I wondered what happened—now I know. She got hooked up with young Tyler here. There's no way we can let Amanda go off with him. I'm going to call her parents."

Mac and Dana agreed.

On the way to find Amanda, Mac phoned Sergeant Evans to bring him up to speed.

"Thanks for the call, Mac. I knew Shaw wasn't on the up and up. I'm on my way to assist. I'm arranging for a SWAT team. If what the kid says is true, and Shaw is a killer, he could be dangerous."

Mac hung up and told Dana the news.

"He's sending a SWAT team? Is that really necessary?"

"With the information we have now, Shaw could be looking at murder. Our protocol is pretty clear—when we're looking at a murder suspect on a hot pop, we want the SWAT team backing us up. They'll do their stuff and hand the case back over to us. With a car involved and the open space of the arrest location, the team should help us avoid a standoff or vehicle pursuit. They don't want court or interviews, so they just do their business and go home."

Her forehead wrinkled. "Must have missed that in the stuff Frank gave me to read. Guess I'll have to hit the books again."

"Don't worry about it." Mac wanted to take the edge off her embarrassment. "You're not expected to know everything your first month, Miss Perfectionist. By month two, though . . ."

She chuckled. "I get your point."

It took them all of twenty minutes to find the tent. When they first showed up, Dana announced herself and asked the girl to come out. "We just want to talk to you, Mandy. Tyler told us where to find you."

"That creep," she groused. "He told me I'd be safe here."

"You are safe, Mandy. And you'll be even safer coming with us."

Mandy emerged, tears in her hazel eyes. The girl wore grunge-style clothes, an oversized shirt covering a once-white tank top. Over that she had a camouflage jacket that looked like it had been used as a rag. Her medium-length brown hair looked like a rat's nest, and she was badly in need of a bath. "You got Tyler?" She sniffled.

"Yes, we do." Dana took hold of her arm and led her to the car.

"Are you arresting me? I didn't do anything. Do I need a lawyer?"

"Running away from home is illegal, Mandy, but we're not arresting you. We just need to ask you some questions." Dana helped her into the backseat of the car and climbed in on the other side. While Mac drove, Dana talked to the frightened girl, eventually getting her to open up. She corroborated Tyler's intent to burglarize the home for a second time when they saw two men enter the home, with only one exiting and starting the fire. She also confirmed that Tyler was planning to extort money from Addison Shaw. "I wanted to report the fire, but Tyler said someone else would and that we needed to get as far away as possible." Tears dribbled down her cheek and she brushed them away. "I didn't know someone had died in the fire until Tyler told me."

They transported her to the county jail, where her parents and an attorney were waiting. Mandy, crying harder now, stepped into her mother's open arms. Hopefully, the teenager had had enough of living on the streets. Maybe her experience had softened her and she'd go through rehab. They could only hope.

"Do I have to go to jail?" she asked, holding tightly to her mother's hand.

"Probably not," Darren assured her. "But you may be implicated on conspiracy to commit burglary, seeing as you were with Tyler and planned to burglarize Mullins's house. For now, though, I'm going to send you home with your parents. If you stay clean and cooperate, you won't have to do time."

Mandy nodded. "I won't run away. It was awful out there. I was so scared."

Mr. and Mrs. Searles thanked them and then left after getting a date for Amanda to appear before the grand jury to present her sworn testimony in the effort to formally indict Shaw.

Mac and Dana began working up an addendum to their original search warrant affidavit, authorizing them to search Shaw's home and car, which they'd finish once they had the car in their possession. Thanks to Tyler and Mandy, they would come to the judge tomorrow armed with the firsthand account of first-degree arson in addition to circumstantial evidence related to the murder of Jacob Mullins.

Mac called Kevin and learned that their forensic computer expert had located an embedded file in Shaw's desktop computer that provided further evidence.

"Let me guess," Mac said. "He found the second will that leaves the money to the city for a museum and park."

"Yep. It corresponds with the papers you and Dana found in the safe-deposit box. And get this: Shaw deleted the document three days before Clay's death. This thing has premeditated written all over it. I was just about to call you and let you know the news."

The deleted file would be handy in proving that Addison Shaw knew about the second will and had not been honest with the detectives. "I'm thinking old Addison was working a deal with Clay's son, maybe the daughter as well. It's entirely possible that Jacob and/or Kelly paid Addison a substantial amount to alter the will and kill their father."

"Good guess, Mac," Kevin said, "but we're a long way from proving anything."

"Right, so let's hope this evening's sting will put the icing on the cake."

Kevin sighed. "Man, I wish I were there to work the sting with you guys. I'll miss all the excitement."

"I wish you were too, partner, but I know you'll be here in spirit."

"I'm heading home now," Kevin told him, "but I'd appreciate a call with all the details."

"Will do." Mac hung up, satisfied that everything was falling into place. They now had the means, opportunity, and intent to circumstantially prove that Addison Shaw had killed Jacob Mullins.

TWENTY-
SEVEN

Shortly after 8:00 p.m., a deputy escorted Tyler Cohen back to the interview room, where Mac and Dana were waiting. Darren Volk, Sergeant Evans, Russ, and Philly were in the sheriff's office, awaiting news from Dana and Mac on the phone call Tyler would soon make to Addison Shaw.

"We still good to go, Tyler?" Mac asked as the deputy released the boy into their custody.

"I guess," he mumbled. Tyler seemed subdued, no doubt upset that his plans had been abruptly cancelled by his arrest. He'd be even more upset when he discovered his "lady" would no longer be accompanying him out of town. At least Mac hoped that would be the case.

"You remember the number?" Mac asked.

Tyler dug a ragged piece of paper out of his pocket. "I got it here. I wrote down his office number and his home number."

"Good. I doubt he'll be at the office, so call his home." Mac motioned for him to sit next to the phone. "Have a seat."

Tyler eased into the chair, eying both detectives warily. Dana handed him a small black earpiece that was connected to a long black cord. She plugged the other end into an elaborate recording device that was equipped with a small speaker.

"Have you ever done this before?" Dana asked.

"Nope."

"That little device I gave you is the earpiece. Go ahead and slip it in. This is a mini recording device that will record your voice as well as anything you hear. In this case, hopefully, we'll get Addison Shaw."

"Won't the number from this phone show up on his caller ID?"

"Not on this phone; it has a special line that will read 'private number' if he has caller ID. All you have to do is talk like you normally would. Detective McAllister will listen in with this full size set of headphones." Dana motioned to the pair Mac picked up. "In addition to recording the call, Mac can follow the conversation and will write down any questions we want answered. All you have to do is confront Shaw with what you told us and ask for the money. Once he agrees, set up a meet at your squatter's camp down by the river. Tonight if possible."

"What if he won't meet me or stiffs me on some of the money?"

"If he won't meet you or plays dumb, don't push him," Mac answered. "If he wants to bargain on the money, let him come down a bit. I'll give you a thumbs-up if the deal he proposes is okay. Are you ready to go?"

"Yeah, let's do this." Tyler took a deep breath and blew it out before reaching for the phone.

Mac picked up the receiver and started the tape. "Tyler, before you dial, give me the date and time, and the number you're dialing."

Cohen gave the requested information and Mac played back the recording. "Okay, everything's working fine. Go ahead and dial the number." Mac put on the headphones and listened intently, his pen poised above a pad.

Tyler's hands trembled as he dialed the number. Shaw answered after three rings.

"Mr. Shaw?" Tyler glanced up at Mac, who nodded to go ahead.

"Yes?" Shaw seemed hesitant.

"This is Tyler Cohen. Remember me?"

"Um, yes, Mr. Cohen. I thought I had lost track of you. Where have you been?" The response sounded stiff and formal. Mac suspected someone, maybe Shaw's wife, was in the room.

"That's not important. You got my money?"

"I'd rather not talk about this tonight. Can we meet in person? Perhaps sometime tomorrow?"

"Answer my question—you got the cash?" Cohen was getting agitated, and Mac signaled for him to calm down.

"I have it, just not all of it. I'd like to meet and work out some of the details."

"What details?" Cohen huffed. "There's nothing to work out. I saw you torch that place and so did Mandy. And I saw on TV what the cops found in the house. I don't think I asked for enough."

"I'll be happy to handle the investments for you. At any rate, I'd rather not discuss this over the phone."

"How much?"

"Fifteen thousand. That's all I can do right now."

Mac nodded to keep going.

"Okay. Meet me tonight, at my camp by the railroad bridge." Tyler gave him directions.

"Will you be alone?" Shaw asked.

"Yeah. I'll be alone, but don't go getting any ideas. Anything happens to me, and my girlfriend will go straight to the cops." Mac smiled. The kid was really getting into it.

"I'm sure that won't be necessary. What time?" Shaw asked, anger evident in his clipped tone.

Mac scratched *11* on his notepad and held it up so Tyler could see.

"Eleven. And come alone."

"Eleven it is."

Mac terminated the call and turned off the tape recorder. "Good job, Tyler. I couldn't have done it better myself."

"You did great, Tyler," Dana said. Turning to Mac she asked, "Did you get much on the phone?"

"Well, he didn't come clean, but he didn't deny the accusation either. And he's agreeing to pay Tyler off. I think that's enough to get him for arson and the murder of Jacob Mullins, even if he doesn't show up for the meet."

"I just hope he shows up with cash and doesn't try to kill me." Tyler had relaxed a little.

"You don't have to worry about that, my friend." Mac gripped his shoulder. "We'll take it from here." He shook Tyler's hand when the youth stood. "Appreciate your help."

"Sure." The kid smiled. "No problem." Maybe there was hope for him yet.

TWO HOURS LATER, the officers were in place, waiting for Addison Shaw to show.

"You doing okay?" Dana asked Mac over the portable radio. From her vantage point on the rail bridge, she could see his silhouette on the tent wall.

"Smells kind of moldy in here," Mac told her, "but really quite comfy with these sleeping bags. Just hope I don't end up with some kind of lice infestation."

Dana cringed. "I hope not either. I have to share a car with you on the way home."

"Any sign of Shaw yet? It's getting down to crunch time."

Dana gazed through her night-vision binoculars into the darkness before answering. The dusty road that led down to the railroad bridge was dark and vacant. No sign of Shaw or his car. "Nothing yet,

Mac. We're ready for him, though." Dana looked back into her night-vision binoculars at the two sets of sniper-spotter groups from their department SWAT team. Sergeant Evans was seated with her at the east end of the bridge, with Russ and Philly on the west. The SWAT members were stationed in the middle of the bridge for an elevated vantage with two .308 sniper rifles. They also had a tactical team under the bridge with their automatic MP-5 submachine guns, in case Shaw came armed with more than a briefcase full of cash.

"I wish I'd have thought to go to the bathroom before I crawled into this thing," Mac said into the radio.

"Go ahead; who's watching?" Dana joked.

"Funny," Mac whispered back.

Mac had been waiting in the stuffy tent for well over an hour, and his nerves were beginning to get the best of him. He'd kept the propane lantern running in the tent so his silhouette was visible from the outside. His scruffy jacket and cap made him look like a transient. It was almost eleven-thirty. Maybe Shaw wasn't going to show up after all. He was about to ask Dana if she could see anything when his radio crackled.

"Set of headlights coming down the road, Mac, hang tight," Dana said in a throaty whisper. "Looks like Shaw's Lexus. He's about a hundred yards out."

The headlights grazed the tent shortly after Dana's transmission and he heard the car's tires crunch on the gravel road before he heard the engine. The car came to a stop.

Mac held his breath when the irritating beep sounded, indicating the car door had opened and the lights were still on.

"Cohen?" Shaw called out speaking just above a whisper.

Mac lifted his Glock .40 from his holster and pulled back the flap of the tent before emerging. "Hello, Mr. Shaw," Mac greeted. "Are you looking for someone?" He held his pistol at his right leg, ready to use it if necessary.

Shaw squinted in the darkness. "Cohen? Is that you?"

"Step into the headlights, Mr. Shaw," Mac told him.

"Who are you? What's going on?" The attorney stepped back from his open door, pulling a silver revolver from his waistband. His gaze flitted from Mac's shadowy form to the tent. He appeared to be contemplating his next move when six red dots appeared on his throat and chest—the end of the line for a series of laser sites on the SWAT member's rifles and submachine guns.

"What the . . . ?"

"State Police!" The SWAT commander yelled from atop the rail bridge. "Step away from the car and drop the gun! Drop it now or you're dead where you stand!" The officer yelled a final warning as the ground team officers held steady on their target.

"You got him?" the SWAT commander asked the sniper.

"I've got him, Lieutenant. Just give me the green light."

"Do as they say, Addison," Mac yelled as he backed toward the bridge, his own firearm aimed at Shaw's chest. "It doesn't have to end this way!"

Shaw panicked and tossed his briefcase into the passenger seat of the car. Before he could get his car in reverse, a SWAT officer with an MP-5 fired a burst into the right front tire of the Lexus and a second into the left, instantly blowing both tires. The sniper on the bridge fired three rapid rounds into the car's engine through the hood with his high-powered rifle. The Lexus sputtered and died.

"Hands, show me your hands!" one of the SWAT troopers yelled from ground level as the tactical team approached the car behind a ballistic shield.

Shaw looked down at his revolver, apparently discarding the initial thought of running. "I give up." He placed his hands out the open window of the Lexus. "I didn't know you were police! I thought I was being robbed!"

I'll bet. "Step out of the car." With adrenaline pumping through his veins, Mac spoke with more force than he probably needed to. "Hit the ground, facedown."

Shaw stepped out. Dropping his revolver, he went to his knees then lay flat on his stomach, placing his hands behind his back like a pro.

"Good move, Shaw," Mac told him.

"Move and you will be shot," the ground trooper yelled. A second trooper from the tactical team quickly handcuffed Shaw and secured his firearm. He then walked back to Mac and handed him the gun. "He's all yours, Mac. Good luck."

"What, you're not sticking around?" Mac teased. As was their usual order of business, the SWAT team handed over the scene to detectives once the threat was secured.

"Naw, I've got to work a graveyard shift tonight still. This was just an appetizer."

"I've got the feeling we'll both be working late tonight." Mac thanked the trooper and turned back to Shaw.

TWENTY-EIGHT

MAC CUT THE PLASTIC FLEX CUFFS off Shaw's wrists when they arrived at the jail, throwing the temporary restraints used by the SWAT team in the garbage can next to the booking counter. Mac pulled his own metal set from his shoulder holster.

"Is this really necessary?" Shaw rubbed his wrists for a moment then placed them back behind his back for Mac to cuff.

Dana was filling out the booking slip while Shaw and Mac waited in awkward silence in the waiting area.

"Sure you have nothing to say?" Even though Shaw had invoked his right to remain silent after the arrest, Mac tried again.

Shaw shook his head and muttered something inaudible.

Apparently, the answer was still no. The lawyer was experienced enough not to make any initial statements until he had a chance to review the evidence against him in a preliminary hearing. Shaw had a look of defeat on his face though, obviously anxious about his future—or lack of one.

Mac could almost empathize. Almost.

Dana completed the paperwork and the jail deputy accepted the prisoner, giving Shaw a second search and asking the standard list of very personal questions. The deputy pulled out Shaw's pockets and examined them after all the contents were placed in a large plastic bag, along with his belt and shoelaces.

"Do you have any questions for me before we go?" Mac took his cuffs back from the deputy as Shaw was secured in a temporary holding cell behind a heavy steel door with a dense wire screen.

Shaw surveyed his new residence before answering. "May I have the disposition of my vehicle?"

"It's being towed to our office in Portland where we can store it indoors for processing. I'm sure you understand we've applied for a warrant for a forensic search of the vehicle."

"I assumed as much. You do not have my consent to search or seize any items in the vehicle. I'd like you to make note of my assertion in your police report."

Mac pursed his lips. "I hadn't planned on asking, but I'll make note of your request."

"Can someone tell me what the bail is set at?"

"No bail for aggravated murder, Shaw; you should know that. The judge may set a bail at the arraignment, but I imagine it'll be steep when combined with first-degree arson."

"We'll see about that." That smug look returned to Shaw's face. "I hope you realize that Cohen boy is lying. You people are going to pay dearly."

Mac didn't challenge him. He'd let the evidence speak for itself.

Several minutes later, he and Dana walked out to the car, sharing a satisfied silence. Mac loosened his tie, then yawned and stretched before unlocking the door. "I'm beat."

"You and me both." Dana slumped into the seat. "Want to grab a bite?"

"As long as it is something we can eat on the way back to the office. I don't want to delay my date with the sandman any longer than I have to." Mac started the car and started toward their office. "Drive-thru okay with you?"

"You can head straight in if you want."

"Actually that sounds better than food at the moment. I'm badly in need of a shower."

"So what's next?" Dana dropped the visor and winced as she glanced at her image in the small mirror. "I suppose you want to check on Shaw's car."

"Right. Let's make sure the Lexus is all locked up. I'm sure Philly and Russ have the vehicle secured in the evidence bay, but we'll have to swear to it in the affidavit so we better have a look-see. Then," he glanced over at her and smiled, "I'm going home. I want to get a good night's sleep before finishing up the warrant in the morning." They would need to type the information about the meeting and arrest.

Dana flipped back the visor. "That Shaw character is something else. Murder and arson. I have a hunch it all started with Clay Mullins's will." She frowned. "I have to say, though, I'm having a little trouble with motive."

"It does seem strange, doesn't it? What difference would it make to him if the property was turned over to the railroad and the city? His fee would have been the same."

"Unless he made a deal with someone. Maybe Jacob. Like, 'Keep the new will under wraps and I'll cut you in on the profits.' But then why kill the guy?"

"We'll know soon enough," Mac said. "Kevin is working on subpoenas for Jacob's financial records. I wouldn't be surprised if he was in on his father's death. Someone had to plant the ricin in the insulin, and only a few people had access to Clay's home and medical supplies."

"Right. What about Kelly? Think she might have been in on it? I'm thinking if Shaw told Jacob, he may have told Kelly too."

"The thought has crossed my mind. She's almost too clean in this whole mess. We'll have to take another run at her tomorrow. We need to expand our window of opportunity to a week prior to Clay's eventual death in the rail yard. I want the results from our warrant first, then we can see what the lab found out on the ricin supplies in the Northwest. My money's on Shaw or Jacob for Clay's death, but we better not rule out the daughter."

"Hard to believe a woman would be capable of such acts, don't you think?" Dana said.

"Please," Mac replied in a sarcastic tone. "Let's not forget the case of the woman who hired a hit on her husband a few months back."

"Maybe if he'd treated her better, he wouldn't have had anything to worry about." Dana gave Mac a crooked smile.

"You scare me sometimes."

She chuckled. "You know I'm kidding."

"Do I?"

"MORNING, MAC." Kevin grinned and lifted his coffee cup in salute. His forehead wrinkled as he sipped at the hot drink.

"Morning, partner, how you doing?"

"I'm doing great, although it looks like you could use some more shuteye. What time did you and Dana get in?"

He yawned. It was barely after seven, and Mac definitely could have used a couple more hours of sleep. "A little after two this morning. Ever have those nights where you're so tired you can't sleep?"

"Oh yeah, more than my share. I hate those nights, mulling over leads and the next day's work instead of catching Z's." Kevin paused. "Is Dana doing okay?"

"Oh yeah, great. If there's ever any shortfall in her training, it will be the trainer. I just hope I'm setting a good example for her. She's a quick learner. I'm really impressed."

"She'll do great. Dana reminds me of you. Except that she's much smarter and better looking." The grin came back. "Seriously, Mac, you're a quick learner yourself. You have that natural instinct. Just don't forget to keep yourself grounded and don't lose sight of what's important."

"You mean, like God?"

Kevin studied Mac's face, probably looking for any hints of sarcasm. He didn't find any. "God is important to me. But only you can make that call. My faith in God is the reason I'm so at peace with this illness. Don't get me wrong; I'm working like heck to get a handle on the cancer. But ultimately it's out of my hands, and I'll accept the outcome—whatever that is. In the meantime, there's prayer."

Mac nodded. A lump in his throat prevented a response. Even though he wanted more than anything for his partner to get well and get back to work, he hadn't spent much time praying about it. Maybe he should. "Seen anyone else yet this morning?"

Kevin gave him a knowing smile. "Philly was in early. He's helping out a patrol troop with a sex abuse case down in the rest area on I-5. Haven't seen Dana yet, Russ has the day off, and Frank's down at the Public Employee Retirement Systems office on a retirement meeting."

"So Sergeant Evans is serious about retirement?"

"I think his hand may be forced, Mac. The changes in the PERS actuary tables this summer may have a big impact on his retirement if he doesn't go before June 30. He's getting his monthly estimate this morning, should have a pretty good feel for his decision this afternoon. Frank has nearly thirty years in and could have retired two years ago. I know his wife wants him to. You know how this job can wear on a relationship."

"Tell me about it. Still, I can't imagine the back room without Frank Evans."

"Me either. Frank's a legend. Been a supervisor here since I transferred to the back room."

"Who do you think will put in for the job?" Mac asked.

"We'll have to wait and see. Let's not put the cart in front of the horse." Kevin looked past Mac. "Good morning, sunshine."

"Good morning yourself," Dana greeted. "You too, Mac."

He turned around to face her. "You're far too chipper in the morning."

"Had a good run this morning, wakes you right up."

"Right, like I'm falling for that again."

"No, really." Her dimples deepened. "I did run this morning."

Her cheeks did look rosier than usual. Mac thought about his three or four taps on the snooze button this morning, and considering coming in late if not for the important tasks that the day held.

"Where do you get your energy?" Mac asked.

She chuckled. "From the triple-shot latte I drank on my way in."

"So you really didn't run?"

"No." She sighed. "Wishful thinking. But I'm getting there. I jogged in place for about five minutes trying to decide what to wear."

She'd made a good choice. It looked like a new outfit—a burgundy and gray pantsuit with a classic pink shirt. Mac thought about complimenting her but thought it better to keep his mouth shut around others in the department.

"Great job yesterday, you two." Kevin moved into his office and gestured to Mac and Dana to sit down. "The lieutenant was bragging about both of you last night before I went home."

"Really?" Dana beamed. "What did he say?"

Kevin chuckled. "Well, not too much actually. You know the lieutenant. He's not much of a conversationalist, but he was definitely impressed. I understand you two are pecking out a warrant and hitting the car on a search?"

"Yeah," Mac answered. "We should be searching the car by noon. Hopefully we'll get some prints from Jacob Mullins to corroborate the story Tyler Cohen gave us. I'd really like to find some hard evidence. Shaw is already spouting off about Tyler lying. A kid strung out on dope isn't going to stand much chance against a seasoned lawyer. Still, he'll have a hard time worming his way out of last night's scam."

"We'll get him," Kevin said. "I'll get to work on those financial records for Jacob Mullins today, see if we can dig up a paper trail on him. I told you about Carl finding that deleted will for Clay Mullins, didn't I?"

"You sure did. I bet it will match the hard copy we got out of the safe-deposit box."

"Strange, though," Kevin mused. "The only reason I can see Shaw deleting that file is if he'd make more money by reverting back to the will that left everything to Clay's kids."

"We were talking about that last night." Dana folded her arms and leaned back. "There had to be something in it for Shaw. We're talking big bucks. A guy like that wouldn't commit murder and arson for peanuts."

"Which means Jacob and/or Kelly were probably in on it," Mac commented.

"Well," Kevin said, "there's your motive for the murder of Clay Mullins. Now all you need to prove is opportunity and intent."

"That's the real challenge." Dana sighed. "Shaw's not talking, and we have to somehow find out how he or his accomplice accessed refined ricin and had the opportunity to get the poison into Clay's insulin."

"And figure out why they'd use ricin," Mac added. "It's not exactly a household item."

"Looks like you two have your work cut out for you." Kevin took another sip of his coffee. "It's almost fun watching this one from the sidelines. Do I look as bad as you two when I've been up all night?"

"Worse," Mac said as he stood up slowly and rubbed his lower back. "And you never complain, which is even more unattractive." He glanced at Dana. "You feel like doing some typing, partner?"

"You buying my coffee?"

"Yeah."

"Then I'm typing." Dana pulled on Mac's shoulder-holster strap as he walked past her. "Wake up, you old grump—no sleeping on the job."

"Right. Like this job allows sleep."

"Better get me another triple. And a scone to go with it," Dana called after him.

"You got it." Mac chuckled as he headed out the door. Working with Dana was getting easier by the minute.

TWENTY-NINE

Dana typed an addendum to the original search warrant affidavit in less than an hour, adding the information Tyler had provided and the observations they had made the previous night with Addison Shaw. A Columbia County judge signed the second warrant, authorizing the search and forensic analysis of Shaw's Lexus.

Dana phoned Allison at the Portland crime lab, requesting a scientist assist with the search of the car. Allison agreed to render the forensics aid personally, meeting the detectives at the Portland office around 12:30 p.m.

The Lexus was secured within an indoor garage with yellow crime-scene tape wrapped around the vehicle to keep out the curious types who might wander inside the bay. This included the uniformed patrol troopers who would naturally want to take a look inside a homicide suspect's car. Mac didn't want any extra fingerprints or nose smudges on the windows for elimination.

Mac and Dana were photographing the car when Allison arrived at the bay, backing her blue Ford F-250 up to the suspect's car. "Hey gang, how goes it?"

"Good. We're making a little headway. Thanks for coming out." Mac shook the criminalist's hand.

"Glad you could make it." Dana waved from the front of the car, snapping a few more photos.

"This guy in custody for our ricin victim?"

"Not yet." Mac answered. "We think he's the one who whacked Clay's son and set the house on fire. Our bad guy is Clay Mullins's attorney, by the way. We set up a meet last night after an eyewitness to the arson made a pretext phone call. Our guy shows up with a gun in his waistband instead of the hush money. The SWAT team nails the bad guy's car as he's making a run for it."

"Ah, that would explain the flat tires and the gunshot holes in the hood. SWAT must have livened things up a bit."

Mac whistled. "You aren't kidding."

"You should have seen the look on Shaw's face," Dana added. "He was freaked out."

Allison walked around the car, taking a look at her project before selecting a starting point. "You have the signed warrant?"

"Right here." Mac reached into his inner jacket pocket and held it up for her to see.

"Good. I think we'll do some vacuuming first. I assume you want prints?"

"You bet. We're hoping to place Jacob Mullins in the passenger area of the car to corroborate our informant's story."

"After I vacuum I'll see if I can lift some latents with powder, then we'll fume the car if that doesn't work. Hope this guy doesn't mind having his car super-glued for prints."

"If our case works out," Mac told her, "he'll never be behind the wheel of this car again." He took off his sports coat and laid it on the backseat.

After applying latex gloves, Mac retrieved Shaw's briefcase from the passenger seat of the car. The case was empty, indicating that Shaw had planned to kill Tyler, not pay him off. No surprise there.

While Mac bagged and tagged Shaw's briefcase for later examination, Allison pulled the large rolling tray from the back of her truck bed, grabbing a bin with the words FABRIC VAC stenciled on the side in black paint. She lifted out a small vacuum that looked like the type used to clean stairs or other small spaces. This particular vacuum was specialized for forensic examination, equipped with a plastic cartridge to catch any hairs or fibers removed by the vacuum. Allison placed a new cartridge on the vacuum and went to work on the car's fabric seats and floorboards.

Fifteen minutes later, Allison removed the cartridge and secured it in an evidence bag. "You guys have hair samples from the victim, or was it consumed in the fire?"

"We have them at the medical examiner's office," Dana answered. "Jacob was partially protected by a piece of the ceiling that fell on him; some old asbestos insulation served as a fire barrier."

"Good. I'll send for the sample so we can compare the head hairs to my sweepings. Without follicle samples I won't be able to trace DNA, but I can match hairs with a reasonable certainty. I just won't be able to match the conclusive one in five billion number we like."

"Hair fibers would be great, but a latent would make my day." Mac looked at the evidence cartridge through the clear plastic bag.

"I'll do my best, guys. We're thinking right front passenger seat, correct?"

"That's right, at least that's where our witnesses put him the night of the fire."

Allison produced some print powder and went to work on the car's outer door assembly, then worked her way around the car from one quarter panel to the next. Printing the outside of the car yielded fourteen clean latents, each collected on plastic fingerprint tape before securing the evidence on a white print card.

"I want to remove the door handles on the passenger side, both inside and out so I can dust the inner handle."

This was no easy task. Removing a door handle from a modern car was next to impossible without touching the handle itself. It took several calls to the local Lexus dealership to complete the task without damaging possible evidence.

"Did you get my voicemail on the ricin, Mac?" Allison asked as he was removing one of the final components in the door assembly.

"No, no I didn't. I checked my messages around 7:30 this morning but haven't since. What did you learn?"

"With the help of a tech at the Center for Disease Control I was able to say beyond a doubt those skin samples you provided had concentrated amounts of ricin near the injection point. The ricin was examined by the CDC tech, and we have an expert opinion that the poison in Clay's system was of an extremely high quality. The tech was of the opinion the ricin in the insulin vile, although cloudy and dull in appearance, was of medical or military grade."

"So we could be looking for someone in the military too?" Dana asked.

"Not necessarily, but we are looking for a lab that's well financed or for an expert who would know how to mill the refined product in his own garage. This wasn't your home-brew Internet-instructed poison. This is high quality stuff."

"Any ideas on where we should start?" Mac removed the outer handle with a tug then placed it on top of the car.

"I have a list of three labs right here in the Northwest," Allison said. "They are independent of the United States military and have permits to possess and administer the ricin. One is here in Portland, a place called the Avalon Research Institute. A second one is in Seattle and the other in Boise. All three are experimental cancer research centers. On the military note, I can't help you there. The CDC tech was pretty reluctant to talk about those centers."

"At least we have a place to start," Dana said. "Do you have that in report form?"

"I would if you didn't keep calling me out." Allison's smile softened the retort. "You should have it this afternoon. I dictated it right after I left you the message this morning."

"You want to give these door handles a once-over?" Mac wiped the sweat off his brow with his shirt-sleeve.

"You bet I do." Allison moved in to examine the items. "You want me to tell you if I don't find anything after all that work?"

"No, lie to me, please." Mac walked to the driver's side and pulled the trunk release lever. "I want to take a look in that trunk while you're messing around with those."

"And I'll go through the jockey box and take a look under the seats," Dana offered. "Although it looks like it's pretty well cleaned out."

Mac lifted up the trunk lid after borrowing Dana's camera. He snapped a couple of photos before rooting around in the trunk. The trunk itself was fairly clean and empty except for a roadside hazard kit and an umbrella. Mac pulled out the umbrella, depressing the button on the wood handle to release it. Finding nothing in it, he set it aside.

Next Mac grabbed the small black nylon bag and unzipped the upper compartment, removing a set of jumper cables that appeared to be unused and a clean pair of white cotton gloves. The cables had their original plastic twist tie that secured the instructions for their use. Mac flipped the commercially packed emergency bag over to the other side and opened the bottom compartment. Inside he found a new flashlight, still wrapped in the black cloth loop that secured the light, and a row of three waxy red flares.

Whoa. What do we have here? There was an empty slot where the fourth roadside flare should have been. He grabbed the packing slip to the kit, reading the contents to himself, confirming the kit was originally equipped with four roadside flares.

Removing the kit, Mac placed the items on the floor of the shop and photographed the contents. He then removed the mini mag flashlight from his belt holder and more closely scrutinized the trunk's interior.

"Well, I'll be," Mac said aloud as he reached for a small plastic cap.

"What is it?" Allison asked, looking up from her work.

Dana came around to the back of the car to look at the object in Mac's hand. "That's the striker cap off a road flare." Like any patrol officer, she had handled hundreds of them at crash scenes and road closures.

"Exactly." Mac beamed. "And one of the four flares from the road-side hazard kit is missing. I bet this is the cap to the flare Shaw lit to torch Clay's house. This is great circumstantial evidence to corroborate Cohen's story. Shaw's going to have to explain this one away; he can't just sit by and have this evidence presented before a jury."

Dana handed Mac a small plastic evidence bag for the item. He placed the cap in the bag after photographing it, then sealed the bag and initialed the closure.

"Well, don't get your hopes up," Allison said, "but I got lucky on the door handle."

"What's that?" Mac asked, coming to stand beside the forensics specialist.

"I lifted two latents on the outer handle and a partial on the inner plastic handle. It'll take me about an hour, but I'll have this inside processed also. I'll go ahead and fume the inside unless you have any objections."

"Go for it. Would you mind wrapping up while Dana and I do a little legwork?"

"Not at all. I think I know where you're heading. Avalon, right?"

"Yep." Mac saluted. "I want to talk to someone at the research center, then pay a visit to Clay's daughter. I'd like to see how she handles Shaw's arrest and question her about her involvement in her father's and brother's deaths."

Dana hurried to catch up, not quite matching Mac's long strides. "I want to see Kelly's face when we ask her how the ricin got into her father's insulin. Especially since she brings him his medications."

"Right." Mac slowed a bit. "I could be wrong, but I think we're getting real close."

"Just one question, Mac. Where would she get the ricin?"

"Well, we know her husband is a doctor. She'd have access to all kinds of medical books. And ricin has been in the news." Mac shrugged. "Maybe Dr. Cassidy was in on it too."

THIRTY

MAC AND DANA ARRIVED at the Portland laboratories of Avalon Research Institute at 3:45 p.m.

"Looks like a pretty slick outfit," Mac commented as he approached the front security door and picked up the stainless steel phone receiver. He noticed the security camera inside the foyer that was aimed at him while the automated phone rang the attendant.

"ARI," the male voice answered. "What can I do for you?"

"Detectives McAllister and Bennett with the State Police." Mac held up his credentials to the camera. "We are on a follow-up and have a few questions we'd like to run by a lab supervisor."

After a brief hesitation he answered back. "Someone will be down to greet you momentarily."

"Thanks." Mac set the phone back on the hook. "They're sending someone down to meet us."

"Good, then I guess we won't have to break down the door." She grinned at his raised eyebrow.

"Getting an itchy trigger finger?"

"Not really." She folded her arms and rocked back and forth on her sturdy shoes. "I just don't like waiting."

Moments later a short, heavy-set man in a white lab coat came to the door and held up a security card to a sensor to release the door lock. "You are with the police?" Wariness was evident in his dark eyes. With his dark skin and slight accent, Mac guessed him to be of Indian or Arab decent.

Mac nodded, once again displaying his badge and photo identification. "The Oregon State Police. I'm Detective McAllister, and this is my partner, Detective Bennett."

The man eyed Mac's credentials as they shook hands. "I'm Dr. Kennerman, a research specialist here at Avalon. What can I do for you?" Dr. Kennerman, who appeared to be in his mid-forties, remained in the doorway showing no intent of inviting them in.

"My partner and I are assigned to a homicide investigation in Columbia County," Mac said. "We were hoping someone from your facility could assist us with some specialized information."

"I'm not sure I can help you. Any inquiries involving our personnel must go through our—"

"It involves ricin," Mac interrupted. "And we don't have any reason to believe any of your employees are culpable in this investigation." *Not yet anyway.* Mac stepped forward, hoping the doctor would invite him in.

"I see." Kennerman's Adam's apple slipped up and down as he swallowed. "Let me see if I understand you correctly. You came to this facility because our research involves the experimental use of ricin?"

"Bingo." Mac was getting annoyed with the game.

"May I also assume that you have a ricin victim as part of your investigation?"

"I'd rather have a conversation than share assumptions, Doctor. Do you have somewhere we could talk about this in private?"

Reluctantly, he stepped aside. "Come with me." Dr. Kennerman led Mac and Dana to an office near the front reception area. His name and title were engraved on a plaque on the wall at eye level. The office was a cluttered mess, stacks of documents and miscellaneous data sheets covering the large metal desk. He motioned to two chairs that leaned against the wall nearest the door. "Please, have a seat." Kennerman moved a stack of papers from one of the chairs to his already overburdened desk.

"Thanks." Dana took the farther seat near the window and prepared her notepad.

"Would you two like some coffee or a soft drink?"

They both declined. Mac glanced at the degrees on the wall behind the doctor's chair and was impressed with Kennerman's education.

"So then, how can I be of assistance to you?" The doctor sat up straight and leaned over his desk.

"I'll be frank with you, Dr. Kennerman," Mac began. "As I've already indicated, my partner and I are working a death in Columbia County. An elderly man was hit and killed by a train at the Terminal 9 facility near St. Helens."

He frowned. "Oh, yes. I heard about that on the news. Poor man was in a wheelchair or something, wasn't he?"

Mac nodded. "We believe the man was trying to get help when he was struck by the train. We initially thought the incident was an accident but have subsequently learned the victim had ricin in his system. We believe the ricin was placed in the victim's insulin bottle and that he unknowingly administered the poison to himself."

Kennerman gasped. "My word. And you are sure it was ricin? The signs and symptoms support this assertion?"

"Quite certain. The medical examiner was able to supply the tissue from the injection sites to accompany blood samples to the OSP crime lab. The presence of ricin was confirmed with the assistance of the CDC. We also have the actual vial of the toxin secured for testing. Again a positive."

"I can't believe it." He leaned back in his chair. "This must be the first incident on the West Coast involving ricin. To my knowledge, anyway."

"That's what brings us to your door. We haven't had much experience with ricin. Truth be told, this is the first real experience any of us have had with it. The CDC advised us of several legitimate labs here in the Northwest, independent of the military, that have the lawful authority to process and evaluate the medical uses of ricin. We were told Avalon, your center, was the only lab in the Portland-Metro area, so naturally we started with you. We were hoping you might have some leads for us. Of course, we'll also have to investigate the possibility that our killer may have an association with your center."

The doctor rubbed at the wrinkles on his wide forehead. "I can assure you that none of our researchers would have a connection to your investigation. What kind of quality are we talking about here? Do you know the grade of the ricin?"

"We were told it's a pure grade."

"I see. Well, I can assure you that the ricin didn't come from our facility." Kennerman sounded a little condescending. "We have quality-control tests daily, and you can see what type of security our building has. Our facility researches several progressive cancer treatments, ricin being only one of the experimental substances we have on site. We are currently studying the viability of ricin as it relates to uses in bone marrow transplants and the assault of cancer cells in a clinical setting. We are finding the ricin has substantial medicinal value, exceeding the poison's potential as a lethal mechanism."

"Could you supply me a list of your employees, anyone who would have access to the ricin?" Mac asked. "You understand that we'll have to draw our own conclusions as to who may or may not have anything to do with our investigation."

Dr. Kennerman sighed. "I don't see a problem with that, but I'll have to get an opinion from our legal counsel before I supply a list. There are only a handful of employees allowed access into the secure areas of our facility."

"That's reasonable. You mentioned daily checks. Can we assume you document these daily quality checks and you would know if some of your ricin was missing?"

"Even the smallest quantity would not go unnoticed. We have the strictest of quality controls in place. I'll speak with legal about your request and supply all the records I can. You must understand, however, that this research center is under extremely high security, not only to protect the substances we store, but to secure the release of information and trade secrets we develop from within these walls."

"I totally understand, Doctor," Mac said. "I think that about covers it for now. Do you have anything, Dana?"

"Just one thing. Do the names Clay Mullins, Jacob Mullins, or Addison Shaw ring a bell to you?"

"No, they don't sound familiar and I'm sure we have no one working here with those names. Though you'd have to check with personnel." He smiled. "I don't know everyone on our payroll. Why are you asking?"

"Two of them are dead, and one is in custody for murder." Dana frowned. "How about the last names Mason or Cassidy? Do you recognize either of those names?"

He frowned. "Nothing rings a bell."

"How many employees do you have at Avalon?"

"Several hundred with private contractors included. I'm afraid my position in administration limits my access to outside contractors, or those employees who deal with funding and personnel issues. Like I said, the ricin experimental operations are only a small fraction of our mission at this campus, which includes seven buildings above ground."

"Those were some names of people we've encountered during our investigation. Just checking to see if they sounded familiar to you."

"Sorry. I'll do my best to get you a complete employee list. We receive a substantial amount of grant funds from the state, so I would like it to go on the record that we cooperated with your investigation as much as we are legally able."

"Definitely." Mac stood up and handed him a business card. "If you think of anything that might help in our investigation, I'd appreciate a call."

Dr. Kennerman led Mac and Dana back to the front door and promised to call them once his legal department advised him on the employee list and ricin logs.

While on the way to the car, Mac pulled his cell phone from his pocket and dialed the office. "Kevin paged me during the interview," he said to Dana as the phone rang. After a short conversation, Mac slapped the phone shut.

"What was it?" she asked.

"The lab got a quick hit on those prints in the car. Allison was able to put Jacob Mullins in the car with a partial latent on the inside of the car and a full print on the outside. We'll have to wait for the positive ID, but it looks like our case against Shaw is getting stronger. Kevin also had some initial return on Jacob's bank accounts. The guy didn't have two pennies to rub together. If he was in on his father's death, he hadn't received any monetary compensation yet—that's assuming he would put the money in the bank."

"What now?"

"Now we pay a visit to Clay's daughter and see what she has to say for herself."

THIRTY-ONE

Dana DECIDED TO CHECK IN with Allison at the lab while Mac drove toward Copper Mountain and the Cassidy residence. After a brief conversation, Dana ended her cell phone call and turned to Mac. "Peter verified the call Allison made to Kevin. He says based on his visual comparison of the evidence, there was at least one latent recovered in the car that belonged to Jacob Mullins. He identified ten points on one of the latents with his microscope. I'd say that's a match. He's submitted the latents through the AFIS computer as well, but the conclusive results aren't in yet."

"Has Allison had a chance to review the contents of the vacuum evidence?" Mac asked.

"No, but he promised to leave her a message that I called." She slipped the cell into her pocket.

"The other evidence isn't so important now that we have that print. Two eyewitnesses coupled with that flare cap and the latent print just put a few more nails in Shaw's coffin. Unfortunately, Shaw probably won't roll over. We're going to have to build a strong case in court to prove his guilt. We still have a ways to go to tie him to Jacob's murder."

"And nothing concrete so far to charge him with Clay's." Dana sighed.

"What we're lacking," Mac said, "is the intent proof on Shaw."

Dana nodded. "We know he had access to the home, but proving he planted the ricin and figuring out when he would have done so is a reach. We know he had something to do with Clay's death, but proving it is another thing."

"I still think Kelly is involved. Her medical ties sure put her out front." Mac flipped down the sun visor and turned on the air conditioner. The day had turned into a nice one, for March, anyway, and he wished he could get to a beach somewhere to take advantage of it. "Another thought. Her husband is a doctor at the university hospital. They do all kinds of research up there."

"True, but Kelly seemed genuinely saddened by her father's death. I'm having trouble seeing her as a cold-blooded killer. And to suggest a doctor might be involved in poisoning someone . . . I don't know. Besides, it isn't like Kelly and her husband need the money."

"Nothing surprises me anymore, Dana. People have killed over a great deal less."

"How do you want to work the interview?" she asked.

"We need to lock Kelly and her husband into a timeline if they are willing. Dr. Cassidy had an alibi for the night of Clay's death, being out of town on that conference, but now our window of opportunity has expanded. The only problem with that is we never have him going to Clay's house, at least not according to any of our witnesses. I think we ought to focus on Kelly for right now. She's a family member and could very well hold the key. Of course, Jacob and Shaw could have been the only players. Unfortunately, if that's the case, Jacob paid the price for his greed big-time."

"Should we split Kelly and her hubby up?" Dana asked.

"Splitting them up would be ideal, but I don't think they'll stand for that. Not with her being an attorney. We still need to keep them on our side if possible, try not to offend them by pushing Kelly too far. I think we better lay our cards on the table, play up Shaw's involvement with her brother's death. We won't go into too much detail, but we'll give her enough to know we've been making progress. We'll have to gauge her emotional state. Hopefully they're home and willing to talk to us."

They arrived at the Cassidy's luxurious home shortly before 5:00. A lawn and garden service was dumping grass trimmings in the back of an old Chevy truck as the detectives pulled into the driveway and exited the car. The workers went about their business, loading up their equipment and moving on to their next client's home in the posh neighborhood.

"I still can't believe how amazing this house is," Dana said as they walked up the steps. "I can definitely see myself living in a place like this." She switched her briefcase's shoulder strap from her right arm to her left, instinctively leaving her gun hand free.

"You better get another job then, or marry someone with money. This place must be worth over a million bucks. Not something I could afford on my salary."

Dana rang the doorbell then turned to Mac. "I'd never marry a cop. All of you guys are way too cocky and self-involved."

Self-involved! Mac was just about to object when someone came to the door. He had a feeling Dana had planned the hit-and-run comment, not wanting to give him an opportunity for a rebuttal.

"You think we should have called first?" Dana whispered as the deadbolt clicked.

"We'll find out soon enough."

"Well, hello." Kelly smiled as she answered the door. She'd apparently been working today as she was wearing a power suit: a black skirt and jacket with a crisp white blouse. The image was toned down a bit with an expensive-looking scarf. She looked tired, Mac noted, and there was wariness behind her smile.

"Good evening, Mrs. Cassidy. Sorry to drop by without calling." Dana took a step forward. "We were hoping to have a word with you and your husband about the investigation."

"No problem, I was just fixing some dinner for myself. Unfortunately, Ray is at the hospital all night. We thought his promotion years back to an administrative position would lessen his workload, but he's working more than ever. He has to deliver some evaluations to interns tonight. Please come in."

Dana made brief eye contact with Mac as they followed Kelly into her living room.

Mac was glad they would have the opportunity to interview Kelly alone. But not having her husband here meant another trip. They might have to make a trip up to pill hill and seek him out.

"I can't get over how beautiful your home is. This is truly one of the most amazing homes I've ever seen." Dana looked around the room at the lavish furniture and decorations.

"Thank you. It's been a labor of love. I've been involved in almost every aspect of the building and design. Please, have a seat. May I offer you something to drink?"

"I'm good; thank you, though." Dana stepped into the great room and glanced around, finally choosing a mauve chair.

Mac also declined the offer.

"Please have a seat then. I'll just turn off the stove and get my drink."

Since Dana had established a rapport with Kelly, even if her interest in the home was genuine, she'd be the best bet for the interview. Mac made mental note of Kelly's willingness to talk about her home for an extended period of time. So far, she'd given no indication that she planned to ask them why they were there.

Kevin had taught him to view this avoidance—a person's not wanting to get down to business when confronted by law enforcement—as a possible sign of guilt. In this case, however, he needed to consider the source. With an elegant host like Kelly, the delay might just be good manners or an outgoing personality. After what Mac felt was endless small talk, Dana asked, "How are you coping with your losses, Kelly?"

She took a sip of the dark red wine in her glass. "All right, I guess. It's not easy."

"We've made some significant steps in the investigation during the past couple of days and wanted to bring you up to speed."

"Really?" Kelly sat up in her chair, placing her wineglass on the coffee table.

"We've made an arrest in the murder of your brother. Last night we charged your father's attorney, Addison Shaw, for the murder of Jacob and the arson of your father's home."

Her jaw dropped. "No kidding. I can't believe it. Shaw? I mean . . . I knew he was a sleazeball, but murder?"

"That's right." Dana nodded.

Kelly picked up her drink again. "I never did like him." Taking a sip, she said, "I didn't know if it was a personality clash or professional differences, but I always had a bad feeling about him. How did you come to make the arrest? Did he confess?"

"Not exactly." Dana glanced at Mac. "We can't disclose the details or items of evidence in the case—being an attorney, I'm sure you understand. But we are confident we'll be able to prove his involvement in your brother's death. He's being held without bail at the Columbia County jail. I can tell you that we have an eyewitness and forensic evidence that puts him at the scene of your father's home the evening it burned. We also have information that he and Jacob arrived at the home together, though only Mr. Shaw left the home."

Tears gathered in her eyes. "Poor Jacob." She closed her eyes, dabbing at the tears with a forefinger.

Dana looked over at Mac for an indication of how far she should take this.

Mac answered for her. "When we spoke before, we told you your brother had been murdered. We believe Jacob was dead before the fire was set. We intend to prove that Mr. Shaw killed or incapacitated Jacob prior to setting the home on fire."

"I'm confused. Why would Jacob be with Shaw?"

"We don't know the specifics." Mac rubbed at the beginnings of stubble on his chin. "The case is complicated even for us. Since we now have a suspect in the arson case and your brother's death, we're focusing our attention back on your father's case. We know now that your father was murdered; his death was not accidental or related to natural medical complications."

"Dad murdered? But he was hit by a train." She frowned. "So—so what are you saying? Did Shaw kill my father too? Was my brother in on this?"

"That's what we're trying to find out, Kelly. We don't have the evidence to charge Shaw with your father's death just yet. I'm afraid that proving or disproving your brother's involvement will take some time, if we ever are able to make that determination."

"How did my father die then, if it wasn't the train?"

"We believe your father was poisoned some time before the train accident and that he was heading for the terminal to get help. The poison was well on its way toward killing him. If he hadn't been hit by the train, he would have been dead within a few hours."

"What kind of poison? Did he eat something?"

"We're keeping our cards pretty close to the chest on this one," Mac said. "I hope you understand, the fewer people who know the better it is for your father's case."

She took another drink and eyed the empty glass. "I see. Have you talked to Mrs. Gonzales?"

"Yes, and we have reason to believe she was not involved in your father's death or any of the other crimes involved."

Kelly got to her feet and began to pace. "This is crazy. You tell me my father was murdered and my brother's killer was arrested last night, but you can't give me any details. I don't know how to react to this."

Mac could see he was losing the interview and sat back in his chair. Dana picked up the subtle clue and went on with the interview. Mac was impressed; this was almost as good as working with Kevin.

"Kelly," Dana soothed. "Please understand that we have to treat this like we're starting all over. We owe it to your father not to compromise the investigation. The information about the poison has expanded our timeline prior to your father's death, and we have to look at all the possibilities."

"Like what?" Kelly sat back down, elbows resting on her thighs. Dana was silent for a moment and Kelly heaved an exasperated sigh. "Oh, no. You think I had something to do with this, don't you?" She pinched her lips together as though reining in her frayed emotions. "Do you really believe I would kill my own father? I loved him."

"I believe you did love him," Dana said. "I'd bet a month's pay Addison Shaw is the culprit here, but we have to look at all the angles if we're going to put him away. That's why we need to ask you a few questions. Naturally, our duties require your statement to eliminate you from our investigation."

Kelly ran a hand through her now disheveled hair. "Go ahead."

"The poison used by your father prior to his death is rather rare, and we believe it may have been delivered to him by someone he trusted. This still fits the bill for Addison Shaw, but we have to ask you about your visits to his home. As you indicated earlier, you pick up and deliver your father's medications to him."

"Yes." Kelly stood up again and walked to the sliding-glass door leading to the deck. Arms folded, she stared out at the waterfall. "You're saying the poison was in his medication?" She thought for a moment. "Not the blood pressure capsules. It's possible, but it would be too difficult and time consuming to open them. The insulin vials were in a box. I'd have noticed if they were tampered with . . ." She hesitated. "I don't remember checking. I picked them up from the pharmacy, and they were in a paper bag. The insulin. I'm right, aren't I? Someone put poison in his insulin."

She stared out the window for some time before turning back to them. "This interview is over. I need to consult with independent counsel on this matter. I can assure you I had nothing to do with my father's death, but I'm going to ask you both to leave."

Mac and Dana stood up simultaneously and began walking to the door. As his hand closed around the knob, Mac decided to go for broke. They might never have a chance to confront Kelly again. "Have you ever heard of the drug ricin, Kelly?"

"Ricin?" She stared at them, her face draining of color. ". . . Oh, my word. That's what killed my . . ." She stopped and in a chilling tone said, "Please leave."

The detectives complied, and Kelly slammed the door behind them.

"That was intense," Dana said as they walked to the car.

"And just when I was starting to believe she was innocent." Mac opened the door and slid behind the wheel.

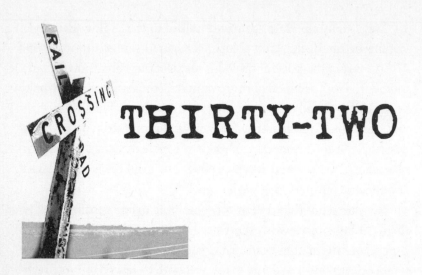

THIRTY-TWO

YOU GOING IN?" Dana asked as they pulled into the back lot of the office.

"No way; I don't even want to be tempted to check my e-mail. There must be hundreds of department updates and statewide transfer notices sitting there. Why do they forward that stuff to everyone in the outfit?"

"So we know what's going on with the rest of the department. I like the updates. It's nice to know who is promoting or transferring around. That's about the only way I keep up with some of my academy classmates."

Figures she'd like that kind of thing. Mac didn't really mind, just didn't know how she found the time to pore through them. "Anyone else in your class made detective yet, besides you?" he asked as Dana collected her gear.

"Nope, I'm the first. How about you?"

"Several have now. A few are even testing for sergeant already."

"So, are you thinking about doing that?"

"Not right away. I feel like I need more time here. Besides, I like what I'm doing."

"Me too." She nodded. "Well, I'll see you in the morning."

"Hey, Dana." Mac waved at her. "You want to catch some dinner or something?"

"Can't." Dana flashed him a sly grin. "I have a date."

"Oh yeah? Who with?"

"Brian Henderson. You wouldn't know him. He's not in the department."

Mac wasn't as affected by her comment as he thought he should be. "Where did you meet him?"

"We met while I was still on patrol. I stopped him and gave him a speeding ticket—well, a warning anyway. I ended up running into him at my gym, and we've worked out a few times."

"And you're seeing him socially?"

"Yeah, well, it's been a while. He called the other day and wanted to see me." She shrugged. "Seems like a nice guy—I checked him out."

"Have fun. And be careful." Mac didn't think much of the idea of Dana meeting someone she'd had enforcement contact with. The thought initially bothered him as a bit of a moral issue, knowing male officers had gone by the wayside in years past by dating women they had professional contact with. Mac dismissed the thought, though, remembering Dana had worked out with the guy at the gym. Truth was, you really couldn't trust anybody these days, and he was being a bit of a mother hen—or maybe it was a boyfriend scorned.

"I plan to," Dana said. "Say, why don't you give Kristen a call? Bet she'd love to get together with you."

Mac grinned. "Maybe I will."

He watched Dana get into her car and back out while he dialed the medical examiner's number.

She answered on the fourth ring. "Hey, Mac. I just got home. What's up?"

"I'm getting off at a decent time and wondered if you wanted to do something."

She hesitated. "What kind of something did you have in mind?"

Mac hadn't thought that far ahead. "Have you eaten?"

"Yeah, about ten hours ago."

"How about I pick you and Andrew up and we go out for a pizza?" The suggestion came easily.

"Really? I love pizza and so does Andrew. That is so nice of you."

"All right. I'll pick you up in, say, fifteen minutes—or however long it takes me to drive there from the office."

"We'll be ready."

Mac felt good about his decision. Funny how his inhibitions about Kristen had diminished. Was that a good sign? He wasn't sure. The more time he spent with the woman, the more he liked her, and the less he worried over his relationship with Dana. Still, pulling up in front of Kristen's house twenty minutes later, he felt a wild fluttering in his stomach. *You're just hungry,* he told himself.

As he started up the walk, Andrew burst through the door and raced toward him. Kristen came out moments later, carrying a car seat. He almost panicked at the sight of it. He'd never had a car seat in his vehicle—hadn't even considered it. Not that he ever would. It was against company policy to let civilians ride in official cars.

The car seat was a wise move on Kristen's part, though. Andrew was small for his age, and the seatbelt wouldn't be safe. His gaze met Kristen's and she laughed. "Relax Mac, it's just a car seat. And I'm just putting it back in my car. My mom was using it today while she watched Andrew. Here, you can drive." Kristen tossed Mac a set of keys.

"I know, I just . . ."

"A little too domestic for you?"

She'd nailed it. "Not at all," he countered, smiling at Andrew while he walked him to the car and opened the back door. "Since you didn't bring an operating manual, I'll let you put it in—that is if you don't mind."

"Be happy to." She leaned against him and stretched up to kiss his cheek.

Once his passengers had been seated, Mac got behind the wheel of Kristen's Volvo. A cute kid in the backseat and an attractive, sensual woman beside him set his radar into full swing. *This is a bad idea*, part of him insisted.

Another part of him thought it felt right and maybe he should think about settling down. Yet another part of him was just plain terrified.

We're just going for pizza, he reminded himself. Strange that such an ordinary action could feel so extraordinarily intimate.

"How was your day?" Mac asked Kristen, hoping to cover his confusion.

"Busy. I cannot believe the number of bodies we have coming in every day. And we have to do autopsies on every one of them. Then we get the criminal cases from all the law enforcement agencies that take priority." She tipped her head back and closed her eyes. "Some days I wish the world would stand still so we could catch up." She lifted her head and turned to look at Mac. "How about you?"

"Still working on the Clay Mullins case."

"Any closer to finding the bad guy?"

He told her about Shaw's arrest and the maze they'd wandered into. "We don't know who Shaw's accomplice is. May have just been Jacob Mullins—of course, with him dead, we may never know his role in all of it. Now we're looking at Clay's daughter. She's the one who delivers his medication."

"Wow. Betrayed by his own kids. Makes you wonder, doesn't it?"

"It does."

Kristen gazed out the window and sighed. "Mac." She flipped down the visor against the setting sun. "Not that talking about work isn't interesting, but since Andrew is with us, let's leave our jobs behind for a few hours and be normal people."

"Oh, yeah. Sure." He had forgotten about the little boy in the backseat. He moved his rearview mirror so he could see him. He looked back and Andrew gave Mac a wide, delighted grin.

"So where do you want to go?"

Kristen named a place and gave him directions. Five minutes later he pulled into the parking lot of The Pizza Palace. Mac ordered a large chicken and veggie pizza—Kristen's choice—and placed their order. Andrew insisted on sitting next to Mac. He felt a bit uncomfortable with the child's obvious attachment to him but ignored his feelings. "So, what do you want to talk about?" he asked.

"You, for starters." Kristen rested her arms on the table. "There's a lot about you I don't know. And I'd really like to."

Mac deliberated on what to tell her. He hated talking about his family. "Why don't you go first? Tell me about your family."

She gave him a look that said he wouldn't be getting out of it that easily. Then she said, "Not much to tell, really. Though you probably can't tell from looking at me, I had a normal childhood. My dad is an oncologist and my mother is a homemaker." Her soft smile spoke volumes about the relationship they must have shared. Mac envied her.

"You love them."

"Yeah." Tears glistened in her eyes. "Dad is my hero. I've always wanted to be just like him. Turns out he takes care of the dying, and I take care of the dead."

"Did you always want to be a pathologist?"

She chuckled. "Yeah. I was reading medical journals and doing autopsies on my dolls when I was ten. I cut open a snake once to see what it looked like inside."

"Normal childhood, huh?"

"Well, in most ways." She locked gazes with him. "Your turn."

Their pizza arrived, and Mac diverted their conversation to food. He placed a slice of pizza on a plate in front of Andrew then took his own. Once they'd started eating, Kristen pressed him again.

He gave up and set down his pizza. "My mother died when I was a kid. My dad was an alcoholic and a dirty cop. Once he was out of my life, my grandmothers took over, and then my childhood was great." He left out the part about his grandfather's life of crime.

She raised an eyebrow. "No wonder you don't like to talk about it. I'm sorry I insisted. I should have been more intuitive."

He shook his head. "No, I shouldn't be so sensitive. It's just that . . . once people find out about my past, I'm afraid they'll have less respect for me."

"Not true, Mac. In fact, given your background, I'm totally impressed."

"I had wonderful grandmothers." He talked a bit about them, but the conversation pretty much ended when Andrew announced he was done and was ready to go home.

They placed the leftover pizza in a to-go box and headed out.

Minutes later, Mac pulled up in front of Kristen's home. Without hesitation he went around to the passenger side and opened the door for Kristen. Then he reached into the backseat and lifted the sleeping child out of the carrier. Kristen shut the car door then went in front of him to take her keys and open the door. Once inside, she turned to take Andrew.

"I'll carry him in," Mac offered.

"Thanks." Kristen led the way into Andrew's bedroom and moved the covers aside, then watched while Mac carefully laid the sleeping child on the bed. Mac kissed Andrew's forehead and moved back so Kristen could take off the child's jacket, shoes, and socks.

After tucking him in, Kristen joined Mac at the door. "He looks so peaceful when he's asleep."

"He was great tonight."

"That's because you were here and he'd had a full day. Nine hours of sleep and he's recharged and ready to roar. You should see him in the morning."

Maybe someday I will. The thought jarred him. Mac slipped an arm around Kristen's shoulders, and they walked out to the living room.

"Can I get you something to drink?" Kristen asked.

"No. I should go. I'd really like to get more than three hours of sleep for a change."

"Tell me about it." She took hold of his hand as they headed for the door. "I'm glad you called. Thanks."

"I enjoyed it." They were facing each other now, and he leaned down to kiss her. A jumble of feelings whirled around his head as she melted against him. He wanted to hold her, protect her.

The kiss deepened, and Kristen pressed her hands against his chest. "Whoa, cowboy." She leaned back, as breathless as he was.

"I'm sorry." He wasn't.

"Hey, don't apologize. You're one heck of a kisser. As much as I'd love kissing you all night, I have to tell you something."

"Sure, what?" Mac lifted her chin so he could look into her eyes.

"This is going to sound so lame." She sighed. "Mac, I really like you. Andrew adores you. I need to know how . . . I mean . . ."

He'd rarely seen the doctor at a loss for words. Mac smiled. "You want to know what my intentions are?"

"I know that sounds crazy, but if this is just a game—I mean if I'm one of a string of women . . ."

"Hey. Why would you say that?" Her comment hurt. He wasn't the kind of guy to play around.

"I've seen the way you look at Dana. It's obvious that you care about her as more than a partner."

He sighed and ran a hand through his hair, stopping to rub the back of his neck. What was it about him? Was he really that transparent? "I did. But we're partners. I'm not dating her."

"But would you? If she gave you the green light, would you date her?"

"I don't know," Mac answered honestly. "All I know is that I like you more than I probably should. And I think your little boy is adorable. Thing is, I'm not ready to be a dad or a husband at this point." He frowned. "I have to admit, though, I thought about it once or twice tonight."

"I don't want Andrew to be hurt." Kristen wrapped her arms around Mac's waist. "Part of me wants to keep going—to see where we end up. I don't expect a commitment." She hugged him. "This isn't being fair to you, but I need some time to think."

"You're as terrified as I am, aren't you?" Mac wasn't certain where the thought had come from, but it seemed right.

She laughed, breaking the tense moment. "Why, Mac, how astute. Yes, that's it exactly. I haven't felt this way about a guy in a long time. And maybe I'm using Andrew's feelings as an excuse for my own fear of rejection." She stretched up to place her arms around his neck and kissed him gently on the lips. "I think we'd better cool it for a while. See if what we're feeling hangs around. Maybe I'm being selfish, but I hope you'll really examine your relationship with Dana. She likes you too, you know. I don't want to be the girl who helps you get over someone else."

"So you don't want to see me outside of work?" Mac asked, trying to clarify her statements.

She closed her eyes. "I do, but I think it's best if we don't. At least not for a while."

Mac frowned, not knowing what to say. His heart actually hurt. He'd miss not seeing her and Andrew. He'd already fallen for the kid and was well on his way to falling for Kristen. On the other hand, maybe she was right. She was probably having second thoughts about him. She was, after all, a doctor and he a detective. Maybe he wasn't smart enough for her. And his history had more than its share of snags. "If that's what you want." His tone was cool and clipped.

"Mac . . ."

He stepped outside and walked to the car, not trusting himself to respond. He couldn't remember a time when his emotions had been so close to the surface.

KRISTEN CLOSED THE DOOR and headed for the sofa. Collapsing onto it, she leaned forward, dropping her head into her hands. "Idiot." She hadn't meant to hurt Mac. She needed her head examined for sending him away. *Terror.* That's exactly what she had felt watching him act so naturally toward Andrew. He'd overcome his inhibitions about dating her and she'd . . .

"What have I done? It would serve me right if he never spoke to me again."

Kristen Thorpe, you may be a whiz at pathology, but you're a dunce when it comes to matters of the heart.

THIRTY-THREE

AT 10:15 THE NEXT MORNING, Mac and Dana started for the Columbia County D.A.'s office with their return of search warrant paperwork. Allison at the lab had informed them earlier that she had suspended the time-consuming search through the hairs and fibers recovered from Shaw's car after the partial print, and the one full latent was conclusively identified as belonging to Jacob Mullins. The evidence would be retained if needed for trial. Those prints and the plastic flare cap would be golden in corroborating Tyler and Mandy's witness account.

Shaw's goose was cooked on Jacob's death, but Mac and Dana were still searching for the evidence to break open Clay's case and determine where Jacob fit and if anyone else was involved.

Kevin had been working with Dr. Kennerman at the Avalon Research Institute, who was still cooperating but who now required a subpoena from the district attorney for the employee roster he had promised the previous day. They weren't surprised at the request, as most corporations wanted to protect themselves from civil liability. Kennerman was probably receiving legal advice by this time. Mac appreciated Kevin's seasoned help on the case. It was comforting to have Kevin's input, even if he wasn't riding with him.

Mac glanced over at Dana, who was staring out the window. They hadn't talked much during the drive to St. Helens, which was not a bad thing. They had known each other long enough now that the silence wasn't uncomfortable, just an outward sign of their mental and physical exhaustion from working such a tangled web of an investigation.

"How was your date last night?" Mac asked, breaking the silence.

She turned toward him. "Terrific. How about you?"

The lack of a smile made him wonder about the authenticity of her words. "Okay. I took Kristen and her son out for pizza, then went home." He wasn't up to talking about her.

"Who am I kidding?" Dana sighed. "It was a bust. The guy was a loser, and I ended up having to fight him off. Honestly, Mac, do I look like a woman who'd jump into bed with a guy on a first date?"

"Not to me." But with Dana's looks, he could see how a guy could get fixated.

"Humph." Dana folded her arms. "Well, no big deal. I fixed him. Called my friend Karon on patrol, and she'll put the word out to keep an eye on him."

"By that you mean your pals will make his life miserable?"

"I hope so. He drinks, Mac, and I have no doubt he drives while under the influence. Just because he hasn't gotten caught . . . I'm not making this personal. Just posted the car info in the briefing folder with the DUII likelihood. Anyway, he'll get his comeuppance."

"I almost feel sorry for the guy."

"Don't. He's not worth it."

Mac pulled up in front of the courthouse. "You okay?"

"Yeah. He wasn't anything more than I could handle." She

pinched her lips together for a moment then added, "Guess I'm just concerned about what he does to women who don't have police training."

Mac nodded. "The guy sounds like a real jerk. You don't think he's a rapist, do you?"

"I've thought about following up on the idea after we wrap up our investigation."

"Speaking of which, do you have the evidence list?" Dana had secured a list of the evidence seized during the search of Shaw's car to the return of warrant form. Oregon law required the police officer applying for a warrant to return a list of evidence seized during the search to the issuing judge for review. The procedure was the formal notification to the judge that the warrant had been served in good faith and there was actually evidence located at the residence or vehicle.

"If you don't mind, I'll wait in the car while you run up." Mac yawned the latter part of the statement.

"Sure, anything else for Darren except the subpoena issuance on the Avalon records?"

"No, I think that's it. On second thought, ask about Shaw's bail and see if he's retained counsel yet. While you're returning the warrant, I'll get us a to-go cup. What will you have?"

"Bless you, Mac. Straight coffee—black."

"Yeah, me too. I don't think my stomach could take anything sweet."

She tossed him a smile and patted the car top, then turned to jog up the courthouse steps while Mac took a moment to update his police notebook. *Good month for overtime,* Mac thought as he recapped his hours this past week. *Too bad I never get the chance to spend any of the extra money.* He thought briefly about Kristen and Andrew as he tucked the notebook in the glove box and stepped out of the car. Kristen had wanted to cool it, but he wondered if that meant he couldn't see her at all. Maybe he'd take her and Andrew somewhere special—like the mountains or the beach. Andrew would love a ride on a carousel. Or they could go to a game or a movie.

Mac stretched, glanced at his watch, then headed for the coffee shop on the corner, two doors down from Addison Shaw's law office. A "Closed" sign was affixed to the front door. Mac felt bad for Shaw's secretary, who was probably out of a job by now.

As Mac started across the street, he spotted a familiar face—the acting police chief, Harry Spalding. He hadn't seen Spalding since he'd let him have it over releasing the engine that killed Clay Mullins. The guy had been way out of line letting the train go without checking with Mac. The emotions Mac felt when he'd learned a key piece of evidence was being steam cleaned returned as he quickened his pace toward the man. He took a deep breath to settle his angst.

Spalding was standing in front of the coffee shop smoking a cigarette.

He took a long draw then tossed the butt into the street. The fact that a police officer would litter said it all in Mac's book. Spalding oozed of entitlement and dishonesty. Mac thought about his own father and felt his disgust grow even more.

In light of his actions regarding the release of the rail car and his drive for expediency, Mac wondered if Spalding's dishonesty included making some kind of deal with Shaw. Maybe Tyler's 9-1-1 call had been the reason for the guard leaving the scene, but Mac couldn't help but wonder if Spalding hadn't also made certain there'd be no officer at the house.

"Well, well, look who's here." Spalding took out a pack of cigarettes for another fix. "You still milking that train accident? You trying to get your picture in the paper or something?"

Mac stepped up onto the sidewalk and closed in, letting his

height advantage intimidate without words. Looking down at the weasel, Mac would have taken great pleasure in telling him that Clay Mullins had been murdered. He wouldn't mention it—at least not at this point. Mac wasn't about to share crucial information with a big mouth like Spalding.

The gold stars, formerly displayed on Spalding's collar, had been replaced by sergeant chevrons. "You been demoted since the last time we spoke." Mac made a point to stare at the collar brass longer than necessary.

With a dour look, he said, "The chief returned from the FBI Academy and decided to make a change in the agency, thanks to a certain lieutenant in your department who pitched a gripe about that train engine. Guess I owe you."

"Glad I could help. You could reward me by buying my partner and me some coffee. I was just about to get us some." Mac felt a modicum of pleasure in upping him in the sarcasm department.

Spalding took a long draw from the cigarette, never taking his eyes off Mac. "You be careful while you're in town, Detective. Try not to mess up too many lives in your hunt for fame and fortune." Spalding blew the smoke in Mac's direction.

"Thanks for the advice. If your police career doesn't work out, you can always get a job at the rail terminal. I'm betting you're already on the payroll," Mac said, amused at how he'd managed to handle this situation compared to what he might have done or said in years past.

Spalding's face contorted in rage. A group of elderly women exiting the coffee shop kept him from releasing a string of vulgar expletives. Instead, he forced a smile and said, "It's been great working with you. Be sure to stop by if I can do anything to help your case, Detective McAllister." He tossed another cigarette butt on the sidewalk next to Mac's feet.

"Count on it." Mac brushed by him and stepped into the coffee shop.

That went well. Mac could almost hear Kevin's voice. Actually, the meeting had gone extremely well. Before his days with the department, a physical challenge like that might have been rewarded with a fistfight. But Mac had matured to the point where he could brush more things off. Too bad Kevin hadn't been there to witness the encounter.

Mac purchased two sixteen-ounce cups of coffee and a giant cinnamon roll, for he and Dana to split. He had the gal behind the register cut it and place it into two boxes and put them in a bag so he could carry them.

Mac waited in the car for nearly twenty minutes for Dana to return. He'd consumed his half of the roll and was about to start in on hers when his partner pushed open the giant front doors.

"I was just coming in to get you; what took so long? Your coffee's getting cold."

Dana's cheeks were flushed, her dimples deepening as she grinned. "Better head for the office, Mac." She paused to take a sip of coffee.

"Why, what's up?"

"I got a page from Kelly Cassidy while I was waiting on the subpoena." Dana held up the paperwork. "I called her back and had quite an interesting conversation."

"Well?"

"Kelly apologized about yesterday and said she wanted to talk to us right away. I told her we could swing by her house, but she wanted to come to our office." Dana paused to take another drink.

"No way. When?"

"As soon as you stop gabbing and start driving."

"Better call the office and let Kevin know so they can be on the lookout for her."

"Already done." She opened her bag and sniffed appreciatively. "Thanks, Mac, but I thought you didn't want anything sweet."

"Changed my mind." Mac pulled out into the street and went on to tell her about his run-in with the ex-acting chief of police.

"He threatened you?" Dana seemed much more concerned about Spalding's confrontation than Mac was.

"I doubt he'll try anything. He was just blowing smoke." Mac chuckled. "Literally as well as figuratively."

"Maybe so, but I think he might be someone to keep an eye on."

"I agree with you there. I'm wondering if he figures into any of this. Spalding's been playing games with us from the beginning. Releasing the engine that killed Clay, not taking the watch on the house seriously . . ."

Dana frowned. "You think he had something to do with the lousy watch?"

"Think about it. There's a burglary and a fire. Who's to say he wasn't in cahoots with Shaw in getting the officer guarding the house to turn his back? Even with Tyler's 9-1-1 call, the officer would have had time to get back to the house before Shaw got there to do his dirty work."

THIRTY-FOUR

As they pulled into the back lot, they both caught a glimpse of Kelly's white BMW in the visitor parking area.

"Good, she's here." Dana released her seat belt and reached for the door.

"You ready to take the lead on this interview?" Mac asked as they hurried to the door.

Dana stopped in her tracks. "Sure, if you think I'm up to it."

"I don't want there to be any surprises when we sit down with her. This may be our last chance with her. She obviously trusts you enough to engage in a conversation; it was you she paged, after all. She had my number too."

"Okay, let's see what she has to say first. Who knows where she's headed with this."

When they entered the detectives' office, Kevin was entertaining Kelly in their small reception area. Mac was glad Dana had called.

"And here they are now," Kevin said with his business smile that Mac had grown to recognize, the one where he kept his mouth closed.

"Hello, Kelly." Dana offered her hand. "We came as quickly as we could. We had some traffic delays through that construction zone in the industrial area."

"No problem. I just arrived myself." Kelly stood up and adjusted the visitor badge that was clipped to the front pocket of her jeans. "Detective Bledsoe made sure I was comfortable, although he could use a little help with his coffee." She motioned toward the Styrofoam cup on the table next to her, three-quarters full of inky black brew.

"Sorry. I guess we like it a little too dark around here." Kevin gave her an authentic smile.

"It was a thoughtful gesture just the same."

Kevin nodded. "I need to get back to work. It was nice meeting you." Turning to Mac and Dana, he said, "I need to speak to you two when you get a chance. Unrelated."

Kevin winked at Kelly. "You let me know if these two give you any trouble."

When Kevin had gone, Dana offered Kelly a warm smile. "We don't drink his coffee either, so don't feel bad." She pointed in the direction of their "soft" interview room. "Please join us in here, where we can talk in private."

The room was equipped with a comfortable cushioned couch and two cushioned chairs with floral patterns. It was even supplied with a stock of coloring books and crayons and a couple of teddy bears for juvenile crime victims.

"Can I get you some water or anything else to drink, so you can wash away that coffee?" Dana offered as they entered the interview room.

"No thanks; I'm fine. I'd like to get this over with if that's okay with you." Kelly took a seat on the couch. Dana and Mac both sat in the high-back chairs after Mac shut the single door to the room.

Dana made sure she positioned herself in the seat closest to Kelly, so Kelly's attention would be focused on her.

"All right, go ahead."

Kelly took a deep breath, her broken exhale giving evidence to her anxiety. "First, you should know this is very difficult for me. I am coming here against the advice of my personal attorney, which I know is foolish, but I need to have this conversation with you alone."

"All right, but you understand you don't have to give a statement." Dana hesitated, looking for the right words to give the legal admonishment without scaring Kelly away. "I mean, you are free to walk out of here anytime you wish, but if you give a statement it may be used in court at a later date."

"Believe me, I understand all of that." Kelly raked a hand through her tousled hair. "If this wasn't concerning my own father and brother, we wouldn't be having this conversation. I have some information, and as painful as it is, I need to tell you."

"And that is?"

"I couldn't say anything last night." Kelly glanced at Mac then turned back to Dana. "I was pretty upset, as you can imagine, but when you mentioned the ricin, I couldn't believe what I was hearing. My husband is involved in some experimental research projects involving ricin. I heard him mention it once during a keynote address at a conference back east and in discussions with colleagues. Experimental research is one of many arms in his department."

Mac scribbled down the information, wishing they had discovered this sooner. Eventually they would have. "Go on."

"I'd never heard of the stuff before Ray introduced the topic some time ago with regard to medical use. Now, since the terrorist scares, it's been all over the news as a deadly poison and a possible weapon of mass destruction. Until recently, I always associated it with medical treatment, not as a method of terror or death."

"By telling us this," Dana said, "do you think your husband may have some involvement in your father's death?"

Tears gathered in Kelly's eyes, and Dana pulled some tissues from the box on the end table. "I was hoping I wouldn't have to answer that. Before this morning, I would never have believed him capable of such a thing. Now, I . . ." She covered her mouth and took a moment to compose herself. "I'm not sure."

"How so?" Dana pressed.

"I was still awake when Raymond returned from the hospital. It was nearly 3:00 a.m. I turned on the bedside lamp and, while he was undressing for bed, I told him about your visit and the details of Shaw's arrest and the circumstances around my brother's death.

"He stopped undressing and just looked at me like I'd done something wrong."

"Did he say anything to you?" Dana asked.

"Not really. He just fumbled with his wallet like he was looking for something and walked back and forth from the bedroom to the bathroom. He looked, well, nervous. That's when I told him about ricin being used to poison my father."

Kelly paused, looking up at the ceiling. Dana moved a box of tissues closer to her, Kelly took one to dab her eyes. "That's when I knew. I took one look at Raymond's face and I knew he was somehow involved in my father's death. Even in the low light of the room, I could see his face go pale. I thought he was going to be sick."

"Then what happened?" Dana asked.

"He wanted to know what I had told you. I said, 'Nothing.' Then he lit into me about how the research was top-secret and that I needed to keep my mouth shut. You need to understand that Ray is the most easygoing man I've ever known. I kept assuring him I hadn't said anything and he finally calmed down—only he didn't come to bed. He went downstairs and poured himself a drink."

"Where is he now?"

"I don't know. About an hour later, he came upstairs and told me he had to go back to the hospital. That he'd accidentally left his computer on and there were sensitive documents he needed to close out."

"Did he come back?"

Kelly sucked in a sharp breath. "No. After he left, I laid there thinking about what you'd said. You were right; I did bring my father his medication. As horrific as it sounds, I think my husband may have used me as a pawn to kill my own father."

"You think he substituted ricin for insulin?"

Kelly paused. "Are you married, Detective Bennett?"

The question caught Dana off-guard. "No, I'm not."

"Then you wouldn't understand what I'm going to say. My husband's betrayal hit me harder than my father's death. Harder even than his involvement. That betrayal is the reason I came here to talk to you directly and against the advice of my attorney. I had nothing to do with my father's or my brother's death, and I'm willing to cooperate fully with the investigation."

"You said your husband didn't come back after he left for the hospital?"

"No. Normally I wouldn't worry. He has a room with a bed there. I haven't seen or heard from him and I don't know where to turn. That's why I paged you, Dana."

"You did the right thing."

She nodded. "There's something else you need to know."

"What is it?"

"After I spoke with my attorney this morning, I went back to the house to get some of my things. I planned to stay at a motel for a few nights. I kept my attorney on the phone while I went inside in case Ray was there. To be honest, I'd hoped he would be so I could confront him about my suspicions."

"It's just as well he wasn't," Dana assured her. "If he is involved in this, he's a murderer."

"That sounds so harsh. I . . ." She shook her head as if to clear it. "You're right. At any rate, I noticed Raymond's Jag wasn't in the garage, so I knew he wasn't there. We have a safe in our bedroom for my expensive jewelry and important paperwork, along with a little cash in case of emergency."

"How much is a little?" Mac asked.

"Around ten thousand. Ever since 9-11 we've kept some cash on hand, in case we don't have access to our accounts in the event of an emergency."

"Let me guess, the safe was cleaned out?" Mac tapped his pen against the pad.

"The cash was gone, but the jewelry and paperwork are still there. I wasn't too worried about the money, but . . ." She frowned. "The thing that concerns me most is his passport. Ray's passport is missing."

THIRTY-FIVE

I NEED TO STEP OUT FOR A MOMENT." Mac stood and inched his way to the door. Glancing at Dana, he said, "I'll be right back."

Dana nodded, seeming to understand the urgency. The realization that Dr. Raymond Cassidy might be their murder suspect and that he might be on his way out of the country hit home. "We'll wait here."

Mac burst into Kevin's office, not noticing at first that he was on the phone. "Is Sergeant Evans back to work today?"

"I'll get back to you." Kevin said into the mouthpiece, then hung up. "No, that's what I was going to talk to you about. He's making plans."

At the moment Mac couldn't have cared less about Frank's plans. "We've finally got a break in our case, and I think our suspect's making a run for it. We need your help. I need everyone's help." Mac gulped in a much-needed breath.

Kevin pulled himself up to his desk, instinctively taking his pen from his pocket and grabbing a notepad. "Tell me what you have,

Mac, and take your time. We always have time."

"Not in this case. The woman we were interviewing is Kelly Mullins-Cassidy. She's Clay Mullins's daughter."

"I know, Mac. I talked with her, remember."

"Right." Mac could barely contain his excitement as he relayed Kelly's statement implicating her husband.

"Is that right?"

"Cassidy took ten grand in cash and his passport out of their safe. Sounds like he's heading out of the country."

"Do you have enough for a probable cause arrest?" Kevin picked up the phone.

"It's slim right now, all circumstantial. I don't know; all we have is his tie to the ricin and his wife's report. For all I know she could be setting him up. But we can't let this guy get away."

"He definitely had motive," Kevin mused. "He stood to gain a lot of money if that property went to him via his wife. We have enough for a material witness warrant. Guess we can at least bring him in to reduce the flight risk. That'll buy you and Dana about twenty-four hours to charge him or let him go."

"If he's still in the country. We're looking at about ten hours since his wife last saw him."

"Has she called him, any attempt at contact?"

Mac sat back in his chair. "Sorry, I didn't ask. But we could try a pretext phone call—have her call him and record it."

"Right, you get going on that. I need a DMV photo and physical on Dr. Cassidy ASAP." Kevin began to dial then set the phone back down. "Phil, Russ!" Kevin yelled. "Get in here."

Mac turned to walk out.

"Mac, get her story on tape. Like you said, she may be dirty too. We can't assume anything. I'll get uniforms at the airport, train station, and bus depot. I'll get an all-vehicles registered bulletin on their cars; you work with the wife. See if you can make contact with him."

"Dr. Cassidy is driving their Jaguar."

"Good, I'm on it."

Mac's adrenaline soared. He passed Philly on his way to his cubicle; the no-nonsense look Mac gave him was enough to ward off any jokes.

"Got a suspect?"

"Yeah, Phil, maybe a runner. Kevin will fill you in." Mac rummaged through his desk, pulling a tape recorder and a recording rig that was similar to the one Tyler Cohen had worn to set up Shaw. This one, however, was just an earpiece that recorded the phone call and would not afford Mac and Dana the opportunity to listen in on the conversation.

Mac ran back into the interview room, startling Kelly and Dana as he slammed the door. "Sorry it took so long, I had to get the ball rolling to locate your husband."

"I understand. Is there anything I can do to help?" Kelly had regained her usual composure.

"Have you had any contact with Dr. Cassidy since this morning?"

"No, but I just checked my cell phone." She bit her lower lip. "I had it turned off. He's been trying to call me."

"When was the last time?"

"A few minutes ago."

"Good. I need you to call him for us," said Mac. "We'll record your conversation."

"I don't think I can do that, Detective. I'm not sure I can talk to him."

"If you don't we may not have enough to hold him, and there is the distinct possibility he's on a flight that will take him to a country that doesn't extradite prisoners to the U.S."

She swallowed hard. "All right." She cleared her throat. "How do I do this?"

"Take this earpiece and place it in either ear." Mac handed her the padded earpiece. He plugged the earpiece cord into his mini cassette recorder.

"What do I say if he answers?"

"Ask him what he wants, then confront him."

She began to shake her head.

"You have to confront him with your suspicions and observations. Don't tell him he's being recorded."

Kelly placed the earpiece into her left ear and pulled her cell phone from her purse. "Here goes." Her hand shook as she scrolled through the speed dial. She held the phone up to her ear, while Mac and Dana sat in anticipated silence as the phone rang.

"It's me," Kelly said as the barely audible voice answered at the other end. She gave Mac a nod, and he finally allowed himself the luxury of breathing.

"I've been out," Kelly said. "In fact, I'm just coming from Walter's office."

Dr. Cassidy spoke for some time before Kelly began talking again. "Because I needed some advice, Raymond. Raymond, let me talk please. I need to know. Did you plant ricin in my father's insulin bottle?"

After a long silence, Kelly snapped the phone shut. Without speaking, she grabbed for a tissue and buried her face in her hands.

Mac played back the tape recording to the part where Kelly asked the big question.

Dr. Cassidy's voice was soft but clear. "I never meant to hurt you."

THIRTY-SIX

Mac BURST OUT OF THE INTERVIEW ROOM DOOR, nearly running into Kevin.

"We have enough to make an arrest. No confession, but no denial either."

"I got a locate on the Jaguar. Port of Portland Police found it at PDX long-term parking less than ten minutes after we put out the attempt to locate." Mac had to remind himself to breathe. This was it.

"Do they have Cassidy?"

"Not yet. Philly and Russ are heading over there right now. You two ready?"

"Sure. Hang on while I get someone to stay with Mrs. Cassidy." Mac found Detective Jan Adams in her office and brought her up to date, then ushered her into the interview room.

Dana was telling Kelly that they'd found her husband's Jaguar. Mac introduced Jan to Kelly then said, "We're heading over to the airport to pick him up. Hopefully we won't be too late. I'd like you to wait here for us, Kelly, and you could help us out a lot by giving Jan your statement again so we can get it on tape."

"Sure."

Mac dove into the driver's seat. Dana and Kevin reached for the front passenger door handle at the same time. "Oh sorry, Kevin." Dana moved to the rear door.

"No, I'm sorry. You ride shotgun. It's your spot, and you earned it." Kevin gave her a pat on the shoulder.

"Thanks." Dana jumped into the front as Kevin squeezed into the backseat, shoving over a pile of briefcases, coats, and evidence collection equipment.

"Still the slob, hey, Mac?" Kevin mumbled. "I thought Dana might have you organized by now." Mac caught his ex-partner's teasing wink in the rearview mirror. Dana laughed. "I'm working on him."

"Hey, before I was so rudely interrupted by your eagerness, here," Kevin nodded in Mac's direction, "I was coming to tell you my news. While you were getting Cassidy on tape, I got a print out from the Avalon Research Institute. Doc Cassidy was one of their outside researchers. That doesn't tie him to the ricin, but it puts him in the ballpark."

"Great!" Mac flashed him a grin. "Things are finally coming together."

"Just like I always said they would," Kevin said. "Prayer works."

"Maybe you'd better keep those prayers coming," Dana said. "We still have to round this guy up in an airport full of people."

Just as they were entering I-205 northbound, Philly and Russ checked out at PDX over the police radio, which meant they were already there. Dana activated the car's strobe lights and siren as Mac crushed the gas pedal.

They arrived in the drop-off zone in less than five minutes and abandoned the car at the terminal entrance behind Russ's brown Crown Victoria.

The threesome started for the Port of Portland terminal head-quarters, which was the police agency tasked with policing the airport. Several uniformed officers were waiting with Russ near the entry to the cramped office, while Philly was on the phone yelling into the mouthpiece. Mac looked for an update from Russ, who motioned toward Philly.

"You turn that plane around," Philly ordered, "or I'll make sure you never fly again."

"What's that all about?" Kevin asked Russ.

"We found Cassidy on the flight list in about ten seconds; the dope actually used his own name. He bought a ticket to Denmark a couple of hours ago."

"Denmark?" Mac had figured Mexico.

"It was the first flight he could get out of the country," Russ told him. "The plane departed five minutes ago. It's still over Oregon. Philly has the tower convinced he's with the FBI. He just threatened the pilot with bodily harm."

"Oh my word." Kevin groaned. "Please tell me he's not doing that."

"The pilot's giving the air-traffic controller some guff, so Philly's pulling out all the stops, telling them he has executive authority, whatever that means."

Kevin winced. "Philly's been watching too much television. We are all in trouble big-time when this is over."

Philly turned toward them, shrugged, and winked. "My name? Special Agent Frank Evans, FBI."

Kevin groaned. "I can't believe it."

Philly hung up and joined the other detectives at the room's entrance. "You don't think Frank will mind, do you?" Philly chuckled.

Keeping his voice low so passengers couldn't hear, Kevin said, "I think at the very least, you might be looking at a few days off without pay."

"They'll be docking at gate B-4 in ten minutes. Better hurry if you want to tell on me." Philly started for the gate. "Besides, Frank is retiring. What does he care?"

"Sarge is retiring, for sure?" Mac asked Kevin as the five detectives jogged through the terminal. Four uniformed officers from the Port of Portland Police joined them, putting plenty of muscle behind them as they made a mad dash through the security gates.

"That's what I was going to tell you before all the excitement. Frank announced that he was retiring at the end of the month."

"Who do you think we'll get as the new boss?" Mac asked, thinking that this was an odd conversation to have on the way to arresting a murder suspect. He also noted the look of fatigue on Kevin's face. In his current condition, Kevin had no business coming with them to make the arrest.

"You're talking to him," Kevin panted. "I'm taking the job."

"Really?" Mac couldn't hide his pleasure.

"Really." The conversation ended as they watched the giant 757 jet maneuver into the gate port.

The uniformed officers opened the door to the jet after it was docked, clearing the way for Mac and Dana to enter the plane's body. "He's all yours," one of them said. "Seat 6A."

"You get the honors, Dana." Mac stepped aside, allowing his partner to go in front of him.

They didn't need the seat number—Raymond Cassidy's fearful expression gave him away. Dana walked directly up to his seat. "Dr. Cassidy, come with us, please."

Mac stood by, ready to assist if Cassidy tried anything.

"What's this all about?" The doctor seemed to have regained his composure. He started to rise, then sat back down.

"Please, Doctor," Dana urged. "I need you to exit the plane with us, and I'd rather not have things get ugly."

"I'm not leaving until I know what this is all about," Cassidy insisted, his momentary appearance of cooperation fading.

"I was hoping we could do this without making a scene, but you are leaving me little choice." Dana pulled her handcuffs from her belt.

"Raymond Cassidy, you are under arrest for the murder of Clayton Mullins. Either you walk off this plane with me right now, or we're dragging you off."

Cassidy glanced around as if looking for an escape route. "You'll hear about this from my lawyer."

"Would that be Addison Shaw?" Dana smiled. "I don't think he'll be defending anyone anytime soon."

His Adam's apple rose and fell as he swallowed, giving away his alarm. Stepping into the aisle, Dr. Cassidy stumbled and fell to one knee. Dana grabbed an arm to help him up. "Place your hands behind your back and turn around." When he complied, Dana slapped on the cuffs. Mac followed as she escorted him off the plane.

As they headed up the enclosed ramp, Dana read the doctor his Miranda rights. Dr. Cassidy had nothing to say, which was fine. They'd have plenty of questions to ask him once they got to the office. Entering the terminal, Mac was surprised to find a media crew already set up. "Those guys work fast," he said to one of the uniformed officers.

"They were already here doing a story on terrorist screening. Guess your collar is more interesting."

A media crew snapped photos and stuck microphones in their faces.

"Get these people back," Kevin ordered, leading the way through the crowd, who were no doubt attracted by the camera crew and their handcuffed companion. The bevy of officers cleared a path for Kevin, Mac, Dana, and their suspect.

Once they returned to the office, Mac and Dana led Dr. Cassidy through the detectives' office, pausing momentarily as Kelly exited the interview room with Detective Adams.

She glared at her husband, tears gathering in her eyes. "How could you? How could you use me like that to kill my own father?"

"I didn't do anything."

"And for what, Ray? Money? You don't have enough?" Kelly turned away from him and went back into the room where she'd been waiting.

"I don't know what you're talking about," he called after her.

"We'll see about that." Dana prodded him to move ahead.

With Dana on his right and Mac on his left, they guided him into the "hard" interview room.

"Why am I here? I haven't done anything," Dr. Cassidy insisted. "What did my wife tell you?"

Mac sighed and hitched his hip on the table a couple of feet away from their detainee. "With all due respect, Dr. Cassidy, you may be a brilliant surgeon and researcher, but you make a terrible liar." Turning to Dana, he said, "Would you like to play the tape, or should I?"

Dana grinned. "Oh, let me do the honors."

While he listened, several emotions flitted across his face. After hearing his so-called apology, he asked, "What does that prove? You have nothing. I meant I was sorry for leaving."

"And why did you feel the need to get out of town, Doc?" Mac asked.

"I had a conference—"

"Save it, buddy," Mac interrupted, leaning into the doctor's face. "We know about your access to the Avalon Research Institute. You and Shaw planned this whole thing. Shaw called you when he found out about the new will, and the two of you devised a plan. You couldn't stand the thought of all that money going to a railroad museum. Isn't that right?"

"It might have worked too," Dana said, "if Clay hadn't been so determined to live. Your plan was to give him enough ricin to kill him. He'd be found dead in his house and there'd be no autopsy. Everyone would figure he died of old age." She shook her head. "Do you have any idea how much pain that poor man was in?" Dana gripped the back of an empty chair, her knuckles white. "What am I saying? Of course you do. You work with the stuff. What happened to your Hippocratic oath, Doctor, to do no harm?"

He broke down then, putting his arms on the table and resting his forehead on his fists. "I never wanted him to suffer. It was supposed to happen faster than it did. I can't explain why it took so long."

Mac glanced over at Dana and nodded. She turned on the tape recorder and sat down next to Dr. Cassidy, telling him they wanted to get his statement on tape. During the next few minutes, he told them about his plot to secure Clay's land and holdings for himself and Kelly. Shaw had called them when he found out about the will change, and he saw a way to make a few extra bucks. "I was going to pay him thirty percent."

"Did Kelly know about your deal?" Mac asked.

"No. I knew she'd never go for it. The old man was a drain on her, always needing this and that."

"Whose idea was it to kill Mr. Mullins?"

Dr. Cassidy ran a hand down his face. "Shaw told me something had to be done before Clay got the second will notarized. He told me he could still make the new will disappear. The plan would have worked if you guys had just left it alone."

"Was anyone else in on this plan of yours and Shaw's?" Mac thought about Spalding and his hurry to whitewash the investigation.

"I'm not sure. After the accident, I knew there'd be an autopsy, and I was afraid the insulin vials would be found. Shaw said he'd make sure there was no evidence in the house and told me not to worry about it."

"What about Jacob, Kelly's brother? Was he involved?"

"No. Shaw told me he'd come down after Clay's death and demanded to see the will. Maybe he wanted in on the deal, I don't know. All I know is that Shaw said he'd take care of it, and the next thing I know Jacob is dead too. I had nothing to do with that."

"Too bad the State Police had to get involved, huh." Mac glanced at Dana, wondering if they could pin anything on the ex-chief of police. He'd like to, but chances are the guy wasn't involved in Shaw's little scheme. After thinking about it, Mac doubted that Spalding would do anything to take funds away from the railroad. "I think it's time to pay Shaw a visit."

The investigation wrapped up quickly after that. Mac and Dana returned to Avalon Research Institute, where Dr. Kennerman confirmed that there were no missing vials of ricin, but one of the vials had come back from testing with a 50 percent dilution. Half the ricin had been replaced with water.

With Dr. Cassidy's confession and the evidence they now had, both men would face charges of aggravated murder and for Shaw the added charge of arson. Learning of the evidence the state had against him, the attorney finally ended up taking a plea deal and rolled on Ray. He pled to Manslaughter for Jacob and Conspiracy to Commit Murder for Clay—accepting twenty years in prison in exchange for the confession implicating Dr. Cassidy. The state would go for life in prison or the death penalty for Dr. Cassidy.

A WEEK AFTER CASSIDY'S ARREST, Mac handed in his final bit of paperwork.

"Hey, partner." Kevin looked up from his own stack of paperwork. "You all set to head out?"

"Yeah. Sometimes I think these reports take longer than solving the crime."

"True, but knowing you got your man—or in this case, men— makes it all worthwhile." Kevin had moved into Sarge's office earlier in the week.

"How's the view from the top?" Mac asked.

"I think I'm going to like this." Kevin leaned back in his chair and propped his feet on the desk.

"So you're feeling okay? I mean with the chemo and everything."

"Doing much better than I thought I would. Had my last treatment yesterday." He grinned. "I'm going to make it."

"Great."

"Speaking of which . . . has that old partner of mine gotten hold of you yet?"

"You mean Eric?" Eric O'Rourke had been Kevin's partner before Mac and was Mac's cousin on the McAllister side. He'd been working in the Salem office for several weeks. "He called?"

"Actually, he's in town. Probably up with the brass as we speak."

"You mean he's back from Salem?"

Kevin grinned. "I should probably let him tell you, but . . ."

"You sure should, baldy." Eric entered the room. "What Kevin was about to tell you is that I'm his new boss—and yours. I just got promoted to lieutenant."

"We're in trouble now," Mac said, then added his congratulations.

"Right. The first order of business is the stunt Philly pulled out at the airport."

"You're not thinking about suspending him, are you?" Kevin asked.

"He'll be off a week without pay, but I doubt that'll deter him. He's a loose cannon, but he's far too valuable a detective to lose for much longer than that. My first order of business was to suspend him; my second will be to pass the hat to make up his pay for the week."

"I know someone who made a lot of overtime this month." Kevin nodded in Mac's direction.

"I'm glad you're here, Mac. It's been a while." Eric's thin face lit up with a smile as he shook his cousin's hand.

"Yeah—this case really had us going." Mac smiled. "Do you take checks?"

"Good job on that case." Eric gripped Mac's shoulder. "I was just reading through some of the reports. Anyway, I wanted to invite you to the big shindig out at my place on Sunday. Bring Nana. We're celebrating Kevin's promotion and the end of his chemo."

"And Eric's promotion," Kevin added.

"And Dana's official promotion to detective." Eric leaned his thin frame against the wall. "So are you coming?"

"I wouldn't miss it." Mac thought about bringing Kristen and Andrew but didn't ask. He didn't know where he stood with her and wasn't sure he wanted to find out.

"And yes, I will take your check for Phil." Eric smiled back.

THIRTY-SEVEN

THE NEXT WEEKEND, Mac was stretched out on his couch, hoping to watch a game during a well-deserved Saturday off. Lucy was snuggled down on the floor beside him. The doorbell sent Lucy to barking as she bounced to her feet and rushed over to the window.

Mac ran a hand through his uncombed hair and went to answer the door, thinking it would be his partner. She was early. They'd agreed to meet and talk over the case—wanting to wrap up any loose ends. She'd been the one to suggest meeting at his place. Moving from probationary detective and filling in for Kevin and given a full time position with their team must have softened her up a little as far as being seen together outside the workplace. Dana wanted to be pals, and he was okay with that. He pulled open the door.

"Hey, Mac." Kristen stood on the porch, holding a bouquet of roses. She handed him the flowers and grinned. "I know guys usually bring the flowers, but I wasn't sure what else to bring. I know you don't drink beer."

"Thanks." He rubbed the back of his neck. "I'd ask you in, but the apartment . . ."

Kristen groaned and pushed past him. "I don't care about your apartment."

Mac followed her into the kitchen. "You got a vase or something?" she asked.

"Ah . . . There's a quart jar on the counter. I just used the last of the peaches."

She sighed. "Guess I should have brought one."

"Kristen, why are you here? Why the flowers? The last time we—"

"Shut up, cowboy." Kristen set the flowers on the counter, wrapped her arms around his neck, and gave him a long, searing kiss. Mac forgot about the game and everything else. His hands slipped to her waist, and he pulled her closer. "Does this mean we can keep seeing each other?"

"Yeah, I guess it does."

"Um—I was just about to watch the Spurs game."

"Cool. Got anything good to eat?" She turned back to the sink and rinsed out the jar.

"Microwave popcorn?"

"Bring it on. How about drinks?"

"You okay with Coke?"

"Sure."

While they were waiting for the popcorn, Mac asked, "Why the change of heart?"

"There was no change of heart, Mac. I still have a thing for you. I'm just coming to my senses. We have something going, and I don't want to throw it away. But I meant what I said about taking things a little slower."

Mac nodded, a silly grin plastered on his face. "I can live with that."

"What about Dana?"

"Dana!" He glanced at the door and, as if on cue, heard a knock. "Um—that's her. We were going to watch the game and debrief."

Disappointment flitted across Kristen's features, but only for a moment. "Well, don't just stand there. Open the door and let's get this awkward moment over with."

"She's not my girlfriend," Mac protested.

"Hmm." Kristen walked past him. "If you aren't going to let her in, I am." And she did.

Kristen greeted Dana, and Dana acted as though Kristen's being there was the most natural thing in the world. Dana set a platter of raw veggies and dip on the coffee table. "Thought we might want some real food." Giving Mac a wink, she added, "Gotta watch these waistlines, you know."

Mac wasn't sure how he felt about entertaining both women, but he needn't have worried. They settled in as though they were close friends. Mac popped an extra package of popcorn, set out bowls, and offered the women cans of soda. The three of them watched the game and talked about the investigation.

"I heard how you rounded up the bad guys." Kristen sighed. "Who would have thought the ricin guy would be a doctor? Guess I like to think of us medical people as more ethical than that."

"You never know." Dana nabbed some popcorn. "Mac, I went to see Kelly yesterday."

"Oh yeah?"

"Yep. Wanted to check up on her and ended up getting more ammo for our case against the good doctor."

She had his interest for sure. "What did you find out?"

"Well, it seems money wasn't all that plentiful in the Cassidy household. The good doctor was into gambling big-time. He frequented the casinos a little more than was healthy. Kelly is devastated. She knew he did some gambling but had no idea how much he'd lost. Turns out some of those out-of-town trips he was taking were to the various casinos here in Oregon."

"That ups our motive quotient for sure. Good job."

"Poor Kelly. She could really use the money, but you know what? She'll be handling the estate. Even though the second will was never notarized, she's following her dad's wishes. Most of the land is going to the railroad museum and park."

"Wow. That's great news," Mac said. "Somehow, I didn't think she would."

"She wants to honor her father." Dana smiled. "She's keeping a strip of the land for herself along the river and plans to build a small house there. She'll sell the one on Copper Mountain. I love that house." Turning to Kristen she said, "It's phenomenal. If you want, we can go up and take a look. Maybe you'd be interested in buying it, and I could come visit you."

"How much is it going for?"

"That's the zinger," Mac said. "She'll probably be able to get a million for it."

"More, I think." Dana popped a few kernels into her mouth.

"Gee, maybe I'll dip into my savings." Kristen laughed. "With nothing down and a hundred-year mortgage, I might be able to swing it."

"Hmm." Dana took a sip of Coke. "Do you know any guys rich enough to afford it, who are single, well-bred, and honest? Oh, and cute?"

"You know . . ." Kristen tipped her head and winked at Mac. "I just might."

While Dana and Kristen talked about eligible bachelors, Mac focused back on the game. This was one discussion he wanted nothing to do with. He reached down to pet Lucy, but she wasn't there. The dog had inched over between the women, who were both petting her and sending her into ecstasy.

Traitor, Mac thought. Three women and one man. The odds were definitely not in his favor. To make matters worse, the Blazers were getting trashed.

He leaned back in his recliner and watched the Spurs score another point.

Open up the first of
The McAllister Files

With his newly minted detective badge firmly in place, "Mac" McAllister reports for his first assignment with the Oregon State Police Department: a particularly gruesome homicide. It's a headline case, as the victim—Megan Tyson—was brutally murdered mere weeks before her wedding.

The investigation and autopsy turn up far too many suspects, and too little hard evidence. Why would the beautiful Megan, engaged to a wealthy businessman, be involved with the seedy lineup of characters who seem connected to her? With more questions than answers, Mac and his partner try to uncover the secrets Megan took to her grave and sort through the lies and alibis before Megan's murderer strikes again.

Not sure that he can trust his instincts, Mac depends heavily on the advice of his partner—a seasoned detective with a strong faith in God. A faith Mac has no use for until he must come to terms with his own past and the secrets that haunt him.

Fiction that reflects the grittiness of real life . . . and the reality of faith.

Mac Is Back!

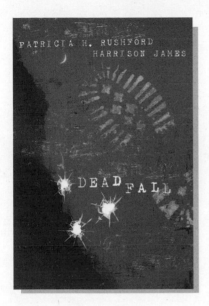

It's been just three months since Detective "Mac" McAllister solved his first homicide case with the Oregon State Police. Now he's working the search for a ski instructor who has mysteriously disappeared. The man's parents claim their son wouldn't have committed suicide, but they suspect his girlfriend of something sinister.

The case gets more complicated when Mac and his partner, Kevin, are called to investigate a gruesome homicide nearby that may or may not be related. A few days later a body turns up in the Columbia River, and the autopsy reveals surprising information about the victim's suspicious death.

When their investigation seems at a dead end, Mac is determined not to let the crimes go unsolved—even if it means putting his life on the line to catch the killer.

Fiction that reflects the grittiness of real life . . . and the reality of faith.